MW00896251

THE SYNDICATER

DARK VERSE BOOK 6

RUNYX

THE SYNDICATER

Dark Verse Book 6

RUNYX

THE SYNDICATER (Dark Verse Book 6)

First Edition

Copyright © 2024 by RuNyx

All rights reserved.

No part of this publication may be reproduced, distributed, or transmitted in any form or by any means, including photocopying, recording, or other electronic or mechanical methods, without the prior written permission of the author/publisher except for quotes for the sole purpose of review.

The story, all names, characters, and incidents portrayed in this production are fictitious. No identification with actual persons (living or deceased), places, buildings, and products is intended or should be inferred.

No generative artificial intelligence has been used to create, edit, or design any part of this book.

Book Cover by Nelly R.

CONTENTS

PLAYLIST

The Syndicater playlist is too long to list here.
Scan the code below with your camera app:

Listen on Spoitfy

Listen on YouTube

Author's Note

Dear reader,

If you're here, I hope it's after being on the ride with these characters for so many books.

Please note that this is the sixth book in a continuous series and absolutely ***cannot be read as a standalone.*** There are characters and couples who already have entire stories and arcs, so their construction isn't the focus of this book; it's their conclusion. For the best reading experience, I suggest starting the series with *The Predator* and continuing through the next five books before picking up *The Syndicater.* Without context and preestablished foundations, many characters, couples, interpersonal dynamics, and plotlines will not make sense. This is only intended for readers who have read *all* five books.

This is the last and final book of the *Dark Verse* series and is the darkest of them all thematically. Morality is void, and humanity is vile. As such, there are dark themes in the content, and I'm listing them in detail below so you can decide if you're comfortable continuing:

18+ explicit scenes, graphic sexual content, graphic violence, blood, death, grief, murder, torture, mentions of suicide, mentions of suicidal ideation, human trafficking, sexual slavery, mentions of sexual assault, pregnancy complications, postpartum, mentions of the loss of a child/miscarriage, mentions of the loss of a parent, mentions of loss of a sibling, amnesia, consensual non-consent, consensual somnophilia, consensual choking, mentions of breeding and breast-feeding, arson, post-traumatic stress disorder, depression, anxiety, mentions of panic attacks.

Your mental health matters <3
If you choose to read, I hope you enjoy this last journey through the *Dark Verse* with me.
Love,
RuNyx

To the readers who have been with me—
Through the ups and downs, the thicks and thins, the beginnings and
the ends.
I wouldn't be here without you. Thank you for an extraordinary
journey.

*

*

*

For my mom.
The best mother I could've dreamed of, the best friend I could've
had, and the best woman I knew.
You were there when I started this journey but not when I completed
it.
Not a day goes by that I don't miss you, mama.

"No tree, it is said, can grow to heaven unless its roots reach down to hell."

— *Carl Jung*

And So It Begins

Unknown, Tenebrae City, 1985

O

N A COLD, DARK night in winter, with the wind howling and the skies crying in sleet, two men from the Tenebrae Outfit met the two men from Shadow Port in the middle of nowhere.

He stood there too, a fifth man, a negotiator, unsmiling, unpleasant, unhappy—a representative of an organization most didn't know about. It hadn't been on his list of priorities to attend this meeting, especially when his bones were freezing, but becoming a god had its price. He was rising in the ranks and almost at the top, climbing on the backs of greedy, hungry bastards like the ones he was meeting with. Such smart businessmen who became bumbling idiots at the first glimpse of true power. They had tasted but a drop and already acted drunk. *Fools.*

He scoffed internally, feeling an odd kind of detachment settling in. He couldn't figure out what more he was supposed to achieve in life as he waited for the cars to reach him. He had it all—money, power, influence. He had a family where he was devoted and a place where he was deviant. He was both men—the faithful husband and the uncontrolled fiend, the doting father and the inhuman demon. But it all got old too fast. Lately, there had been a lull, a lethargy of sorts settling inside him, as though no matter what he did, what he partook, it would leave him incomplete. He fed and fed and fed and yet stayed hungry, and as of late, he wondered what would be the thing to break it.

Ennui was the end for everyone.

That would have scared anyone else, but not him. He thought differently. The lethargy with life was an opportunity for something new, a chance to shake things up and show their world something never seen before.

Leaning against his car, as a cold wind jostled him, he watched the two cars come to a stop.

The men who thought of themselves as the organization's allies got out. *Idiots.* They should know there were no allies in this trade.

Lately, there were no enemies either. It was all too easy.

Maybe that was the reason for his boredom. He needed a worthy adversary. But there were none.

Maybe, he could create one.

As the thought took root in his mind, rolling around, growing into an ugly, twisted idea.

He greeted them with a smile.

The ennui cracked.

PART I:
FOUNTAINHEAD

"This thing of darkness,
I *acknowledge mine.*"

—WILLIAM SHAKESPEARE

DAINN

CHAPTER 1

DAINN, GLADESTONE

DARKNESS FELT LIKE HOME.

No, he corrected himself. Darkness felt like a house he had lived in for many years, the rooms and nooks and crannies of which he was utterly familiar with, so much so that he could navigate it with his eyes closed. Home, home was *her*—a small, petite woman with flame hair and rare laughs and moonlit soul that made him believe in things he had only known about conceptually, things he knew but did not understand, not until her.

"That's cheating!" she exclaimed, giving him a glare that had killed lesser men, her verdant gaze glimmering with the life he felt proud to have resuscitated in her. He wondered when he would see it shining the same again, something in his chest tightening with each passing second that he knew their time was limited. He wondered, as he watched the tiny furrow of concentration between her brows, her lips turned down in the corners as she focused on her cards, how things were going to change. Because change they would. The moment he told her what was to come, the moment her world expanded to include other people who were going to become important to her, and in extension to him, things would change.

Dainn didn't like changes where it concerned her, especially the ones beyond his control.

Yet, for her, he had to sacrifice something without sacrificing her. That was her definition of love, wasn't it?

He had to tell her. But knowing her, how her mind worked, how her anxieties ate her from the insides, he knew he had to wait until the last moment or she would spend the entire time overthinking to the point of getting dysfunctional, possibly sick. His little *flamma* had strength even she couldn't see, but she was fragile right now. Her heart—the tiny organ under her delectable breasts—was too large, felt too much, and beat too fast, and yet, if it ceased to do any of those things exactly as it did, he didn't know who he would become. She was his north star, the only thing constant, bright in his tenebrous world.

"Not cheating," he told her, quietly etching this moment into his memory to relive during the time he wouldn't have her. "You have to learn how to bluff better."

Her lips moved into a pout, pillowing in a way that reminded him of small, harmless creatures the world called cute.

Fuck, she was cute when she was like this. Not a word he ever thought he'd think about anyone. Babies and puppies and kittens were cute enough, but they didn't make him warm on the inside as she did, as though the cold could never touch his bones again as long as she flickered within him.

She threw the cards down on the table, sighing loudly with exaggerated exasperation that amused him. She was a grump when she didn't get her way. *Adorable.*

A light wind caressed her open locks, moving them lazily like flames in a hearth as they sat outside on the balcony of their hotel suite high up. It was late, and if it were up to him, he would have simply kept her in bed the whole time, devouring her, defiling her, destroying her in ways he would be etched into her bones, so nothing and no one could take him out of her being. But she, unaware of what was about to happen and to distract herself from the revelations thrust upon her in the last twenty-four hours, had wanted to do something normal, something benign, something ridiculously regular. And so, he was teaching her how to play cards, which, much to his amusement, she was failing at miserably. His *flamma* was many things, but a mathematical card-counting bluff master, she was absolutely not.

She stared out at the darkness of Gladestone. The view was nothing noteworthy. The city wasn't either. It was a dark concrete jungle of shiny veneer polished with desperation and destitution. Building after building, street after street, alley after alley—corporate and manufacturing hubs that hid hideous horrors underneath. But it was the fact that the view was now laid out for her, right at her feet, ready for her to stomp and smash it. It seemed almost poetic in a way, the things she was going to do by his side, watching over everything that had used and abused her, deliberately and unknowingly. And she was sitting at the top with him, looking down at the very city that had chewed and spit her out, one amongst the many faceless humans. But the faceless weren't his. *She* was.

The soft, pondering energy engulfed her frame as she pulled her feet up on the chair and wrapped her arms around her knees, resting her head on them, gazing out. He marveled for a moment at her ability to do that—fold herself and make herself so small she could hide on the furniture. He wondered if it had been something she had learned over the years and did so unconsciously now when she felt anxious. He placed his cards down on the table and gazed at her, taking in his fill. She looked ethereal, unreal, almost like a magical little waif who would disappear if he blinked.

She would.

It was almost twenty-four hours since he had sent his text to Morana. The clock was ticking. His time with her like this, when their world was just the two of them, existing purely with the other, was coming to an end soon. She was going to have others who would love her, want her, protect her, and he would be alone again, existing in the shadows while she did in the light.

Something tight sat in his chest.

"Dainn?"

Her voice brought his focus singularly back to her, the sound of his name making a familiar rush of sweetness explode on his tongue. Fuck, he would miss the physical sensation of hearing her talk, of feeling her close, of her just being. It was incredible how she could make him the calmest he had ever been yet the craziest, how she could inspire both his chaos and his cool to the same degree.

He reached out, tugging a strand of her hair, feeling the softness on his fingers. "Hmm?"

"What do we do now?" she asked him finally. He knew it had taken her a while to process everything, and he had been giving her time. With Lyla, he had learned patience was the key. She was like the black roses he liked to grow for gifting to her. She needed the right soil, the right amount of sun and water and nourishment, the right amount of care and patience to blossom. Most importantly, just like the rose, she needed someone willing to take the thorns, someone willing to bleed for her bloom.

"What do you want to do?" he asked. Though he had sent the message out, knowing instinctively it was what she needed. But if she said the word, he would disappear with her in a heartbeat until she felt ready. Deep down, the selfish part of him hoped she wasn't ready. But the part that remembered her definition of love, of what she needed, and that part knew that she needed nourishment outside of what he could provide. And though sacrificing his selfish desires was never something he had thought to do, was never something he would do, she was the only exception.

For her, he would do anything.

But he would hate every second of it.

Lyla turned her neck and brought her eyes to him, her gaze knocking something within his ribs, the life, the vulnerability, the *trust* shining in her eyes shooting straight up his veins.

"I don't know," she whispered, the words almost tentative, afraid. She had nothing to be afraid of, not as long as he lived, and he planned to live a long life with her.

"Trust me still?" he asked, the hunger in his heart for her trust never satiated. He didn't understand what it was about it—the way she trusted—that had become both the elixir and the kryptonite of his entire being.

She nodded.

A wild rush of energy burst inside him with that one simple nod. His earlier despondency about their separation disappeared. It was temporary, anyway. As long as he had her trust, he could do everything.

He pushed the table to the side with one hand, grabbing her waist with the other and pulling her close. Her breathing escalated as he brought her over him, her weight more than what it had been when he'd found her, her curves filled out over the months under his care and her cooking but still slight. Her hands went to his bare shoulders as she straddled him, settling over his lap; his t-shirt—one of the many she had stolen from his side of the closet—ruched up around her hips, giving him an unrestricted view of her bare pussy over his groin, separated only by the fabric of his sweatpants.

Her small, soft hands moved over his shoulders, the side of his neck, her touch sure, almost proprietary, and he reveled in it—in both her possession and her quiet confidence in him.

"I don't know why you get so turned on every time," she huffed quietly, a soft smile on her face, shaking her head as if he were being ridiculous.

He tugged her closer, his hands spanning her small waist, locking their gazes. "I told you. Your trust is my high."

She just shook her head again as if the concept felt too foreign to grasp. Maybe it was. His brain was different, his thought process different, so maybe his attachment to it felt different to her too. She may not grasp it, but she accepted it, accepted him, just as he was. *Now that was a foreign concept.*

"Your brother and his friends are going find you," he told her, simply laying out the truth for her. Though he had no principles, no morality, no conscience as much, he didn't lie to her. It was simply a way to make her feel like the exception she was, so she would know that while he was a liar to the rest of the world, she was the only exception, the only special clause, the only one he was *real* with.

Home. That was why she felt like the home he had never had.

The tightening of her grip on his shoulders was the first sign of her rising panic. Her face—her beautiful face that hid nothing from anyone willing to look, an open book in all languages known to humankind—fell. "What do you mean? Find me how?"

He kept his hold on her hips firm, staying steady as he revealed the facts. "Morana, your brother's girl, is a hacker. She's smart and she has been scouring the online spaces for any traces of you for a while now. I just sent her a big crumb last night."

He watched as her eyes widened, her nails digging into his muscles in a way that reminded him of sex, especially when he pushed his cock into her, that first sensation of his piercings in her pussy making her clench around him.

"Dainn." Her whisper of his name was pure panic, her emotion leaving a sour taste in his mouth. As much as he liked her tinge of fear, especially in their sexual situations, he didn't really like the taste it left him with when it was emotional terror. There was only one effective way he knew how to change her fear into something more palatable, a way that had worked in calming her every time.

He moved his neck and sucked her nipple into his mouth over the t-shirt, dampening the fabric as the bud hardened, relishing her gasp as her hands tightened on him in that familiar way.

"We need to discuss this," she stated, pushing him back. Or rather trying to.

"We are discussing it," he spoke against her breast, biting

the side. Her hips tried to move, but he held it still, feeling moisture over his sweatpants where she was spread open. He moved his fingers down, feeling her juices on his skin, her essence the only one he enjoyed on himself. His digits pried her flesh open, teasing her edges but never touching her throbbing clit, never sinking inside her. A sound akin to a mewl left her throat, and he felt his lips twitch against her breast. He loved that sound, the one she made in desire and frustration when he teased her. It was a demand and a complaint mixed with lust so potent he felt high when he heard it. But this was a distraction from her fear; the conversation was something they still needed to have.

He teased the edges of her clit some more, enjoying her noises but keeping his mind on track. "The message I sent will be tracked by tomorrow," he told her, moving to her neck, knowing that the spot right under her ear sent arousal flooding in her body when stimulated. He had learned her body like his personal sacred text, worshipping at her altar every day, reciting her verses every chance he could. He knew exactly where to kiss gently to make her melt and where to bite hard to make her wet; he knew where to push, to pull, to pillage on his knees, waiting for her to bless his existence.

"Why did you do that?" she managed to get out right before a moan, drenching his fingers as he licked the spot under her ear, the scent of her skin of flowers and fire filling him.

"Because," he nuzzled her, "you want it."

"And you give me what I want? As long as it's with you?"

She knew the depths of his possessiveness well. "Yes."

She moved her hands away from his shoulders and down to his sweatpants, pushing them down and pulling his cock out. He moved his hand back to her hips as she settled herself on him, flesh to flesh, grinding over him, leaving the metal on him glistening, taking the pleasure she wanted from him as her right. With arousal, something like affection, adoration—he didn't know what it was, to be honest—but something softer, less harsh than his usual darkness, filled him as he watched her *take*, watched her own both him and her own sexuality so openly, knowing the depth of trauma it held for her, marveling at her resilience, letting her have it for a moment, basking in the glory of witnessing her trust take over said trauma.

"What happens after they find me?" Her question was breathless, her hips moving sinuously with an innate fluidity that was an inherent part of her.

"They will take you back with them, I believe," he stated.

His words suddenly made her stop, the glaze of desire in her eyes dimming, replaced with moisture that felt like a knife to his ribs.

"You're letting me go?" Her lips trembled. "You'll just… leave me? You said you *wouldn't.*"

Suddenly, she was scrambling away from him, trying to get away from him with a frantic energy he knew he needed to quell immediately. He tightened his grip on her waist with one hand, gripping her jaw with the other so she quietened and steadied, keeping his eyes fixated on hers. A tear escaped her right eye, trailing down her cheek and disappearing into his bare palm as he held her face.

"Do you really think—" he asked her quietly, his voice coming out cold at her immediately jumping to the conclusion even after all this time "—I would? That you would ever be rid of me?"

Her eyes glistened, but she bit her lip. "No. But that's what you're telling me." It came out as a soft accusation.

He kissed her hard, pouring his determination into her, infecting her with the same obsession—or whatever the fuck it was; he didn't even recognize it anymore—that had him in its grip.

She let him, opening, unfurling, accepting it.

"We will become ashes before we are apart," he murmured against her mouth. Her breath hitched. He knew she liked his words, that she cherished them and held them close to her heart. "I will *never* let you go."

He pulled back, brushing the back of his fingers, darkened with burns and scars, over her unblemished, pale cheek. "Think of this as a temporary adventure."

Her throat worked as she swallowed. "Why?" she questioned, innocent and accusatory at the same time.

"Because you're on a journey of self-discovery, of healing and rising from your own ashes," he reminded her. "You're finding who you are, and your mind is finally ready to face your past. You are an emotional creature, *flamma*. You need all these pieces to feel whole and happy. And I happen to like it when you're happy."

Her fingers brushed over his hair idly. "But what if I'm never whole? What if, after all of it, I'm left... empty?"

Dainn lifted her hips and slid inside her slowly, watching her eyes roll back and feeling her nails dig into his muscles, her walls weeping around him. Even after all this time, it took her a bit to adjust to his presence inside her, his piercings and his length and his girth, filling her to the brim in a way he knew she had become addicted to.

"Do you feel empty?" he asked her, watching her face closely for her reactions.

Her mouth trembled, her eyes half-lidded. "Not with you."

"Never with me. No matter what happens, you'll never be empty with me."

It was she who kissed him this time, knowing his words meant more than just the physical, leaning forward and capturing his lips with hers.

"I love you," she told him, and the words, her voice, her presence, became another core memory that etched itself deep in his brain, firing his synapses, flooding his neurons with chemicals that made him feel invincible, forcing the organ in his ribs to beat extra hard with the closest thing to the emotion she called love he could feel, love like she had described it to him.

"I know," he told her as he always did, holding her close, and knowing she understood his flawed being, understood that it was who he was, and yet she loved him anyway.

Then he began to move in her, deepening their kiss, savoring both her taste and her memory, knowing their time together was dwindling down.

AMARA

CHAPTER 2

AMARA, TENEBRAE CITY

BEING A MOTHER WAS exhausting. Being a mother while being a mob wife was extra *exhausting.*

Tempest, the light of her life, the joy of her heart, the strength of her soul, had the lungs of a beast. Amara loved her, but good god, Tempest was living up to her name, and she was only just about a year old. Lord save them when she was older. She and Dante were both tired for reasons beyond their first child's teething and keeping them up at all hours.

Amara cracked her neck as she walked into the new rehabilitation center, thanking her common sense that morning for having worn flats instead of heels. Honestly, she didn't have the strength to even get out of bed these days. Thanks to her husband, her wonderful, thoughtful husband, who let her sleep for a few extra precious minutes while taking care of their baby, and thanks to her mother, who was truly an expert when it came to managing her grandchild, Amara felt a bit relaxed leaving the house for the first time in a week.

The weather had slowly started to change in the city, the lush green hills turning more rust and orange as the cooler season breezed in. Wrapping her chic blazer around her—one of the new ones that fit her more voluptuous, post-pregnancy body better than her older clothes—Amara entered the large new compound of the rehabilitation center a few miles out of the city, not too far from the Maroni compound that she called home.

The new center—that she'd been calling New Haven in her head—had just opened a few weeks ago, just a year after starting. It was built on a large property that the Maroni family had owned—*now her family name,* she had to remind herself at times—that Dante had signed off for this project. It was a decent start to what she hoped would be something much larger one day. For now, there were three buildings manned by proper security in the compound. Two were residential for housing the children who were rescued from the clutches of the trafficking ring, most probably operated by The Syndicate. One building was for classes, food, and staff offices that included psychologists, teachers, and managers. It was comparatively a much smaller operation, but the need had been for speed, not scale, and thanks to being the wife of the Outfit boss, getting shit done on a faster timeline had been a perk.

She had personally overseen all the designs and worked with the crew that had built it from the ground up, a passion project close to her heart and the hearts of everyone she loved.

"Good morning, Dr. Maroni."

Amara paused in the lobby to see Nellie, the middle-aged woman she had personally hired as the manager of the compound, to take care of things on a day-to-day basis. Nellie, a Tenebrae native, had previously worked in the same position in an all-boys boarding school. Though she had a strict, disciplined air about her, Amara sensed her inner kindness immediately and realized she would be the perfect fit to foster the children who would be there, hopefully temporarily.

"Good morning, Nellie," Amara greeted her with a warm smile. "Sorry, I was away for a week. Tempest has been teething and her first birthday is coming up soon. It's been hectic, to say the least. What did I miss? Give me a run down, please."

Nellie pressed her hands over her grey shirt, something Amara had noticed she did out of habit before speaking at length. They had kept the attire for all staff casual, mainly so the children would feel more at home.

"Counting the last batch, we have a total of thirty-six boys right now, ages four to fourteen," Nellie began to talk as they walked down the lobby. "They're all meeting the three in-house therapists once a week, and all are attending different classes in groups of three to five times a week. They've been particularly happy about the movie weekends. Some of them have taken to the outdoors. The game room is also ready. We're just waiting for you to look it over once before we open it."

Amara took in all the information and walked into the large open area that led to all three buildings, looking around. Children, boys mainly, were running around playing catch. Sadly, in the year they had been looking, they hadn't found any batches of girls so far, just the boys they had rescued. Some were sitting on the grass, enjoying the sun. Some caretakers, all of whom Amara had personally hired and Dante had vetted, kept an eye out to make sure everyone stayed safe. It was a weekend, and on the weekends, there were no classes and no sessions. Just movies and letting kids be themselves. The sight warmed her heart in a way she'd never have thought of, not without the experience of being a mother herself. Loving a child and losing a child, both experiences had changed her from the inside.

Amara breathed in the crisp air and anchored herself in the moment.

"The detective called," Nellie continued as they stood looking at the kids. Two young boys, barely five, wrestled in the grass while laughing, their sounds tinkling in the wind like beautiful chimes.

"Any updates?" Amara asked, waving at a young boy who grinned at her. The children all knew her. She was the one who talked to them first before introducing the other doctors to them. Some days, she got them sweets, and she knew that was why most of them liked her more. But she didn't care. She liked being their favorite, liked the way their eyes lit up when they saw her. It was so pure, so precious, and she couldn't wrap her head around the fact that there were monsters who had tried to tarnish and ruin that light from their eyes.

"They've tracked three of the boys' family," Nellie told her. "Two of them had filed missing reports, but one of them hadn't. The detective is investigating that one, but for now, as soon as the families are here, they will come to get the boys. Most probably tomorrow."

Amara nodded. It made her heart happy to think of the families who had lost loved ones reuniting with them. She knew firsthand how it felt to be separated from the people you loved. But worse, she knew, having witnessed it in Tristan, what it did to someone who lost their loved ones without any answers. And every time a family came to pick their baby up, it restored the faith in her heart for all of them that one day, sooner or later, they would all be reunited and restored with love, healed from the wounds inflicted by time and distance.

"Please make sure it goes smoothly," Amara replied. It was unnecessary, though. Nellie wasn't just good at her job; she was passionate and protective of these children. That was something Amara respected a lot about her. In the beginning, every time a family had come, Amara had wanted to be there. But between being a new mother and wife and getting the center up and running, it had begun to take a toll on her, and Nellie had stepped up. Amara knew that if Nellie felt something was off, even when the families came, she wouldn't let the child leave without calling Amara or Dante. She knew what was at stake here, and that was why Amara felt like she could trust her to run things.

"Dr. Amara!" a young boy shouted from the lawn, running towards her so fast down the slight slope of the hill that he came barreling into her with his excitement. Amara felt a breath whoosh and steadied herself, holding the seven-year-old upright before he fell down on his little butt.

"Easy, Lex," she chided him before softening. She had a soft spot for him. He was one of the first boys she had bonded with here, the only boy left there from the first batch they had found. He had been in the group with Xander, and though Xander had become more family than anything and all the other boys had eventually gone home, Lex was the only one left behind with no family. He was an orphan, his family having died in an accident. He had been raised by his grandmother, who had passed away last year, leaving him vulnerable. His story, the fact that he was the only one remaining from that very first group, and the fact that he'd seen all those other kids be picked up and left had softened Amara to him more than others. Lex was a precious child with a special heart. He knew his family was dead, that there wasn't anyone for him out there. He had suffered horrors she knew about from his sessions, and yet, the boy had the most infectious smile and the most iridescent heart on him. Amara loved him like she loved Xander.

Speaking of...

"Can I talk to Xander, please?" Lex asked right on cue, his dark eyes and dark hair shining with good health as he looked up at her in an endearing, beseeching way. This was something he did every time she came to visit. The kids weren't allowed to use phones, so he sought her out. Knowing Xander was with her friends, he asked her to call him so he could talk to his friend. It was kind of adorable.

"Since you asked so nicely," Amara smiled at him, taking out her phone and dialing a number that was on her most frequently called list thanks to this young boy.

The phone rang twice before being picked up.

"Hello," the young, quiet voice spoke. Xander was a conundrum, which wasn't something she thought she'd have said about a child. Amara had seen his psych evaluations, thanks to Tristan and Morana permitting her access to his files, and it stumped her. His past was an utter mystery, with no records of his birth or his life before he was found. They had estimated his age by guessing because they didn't know how old he was, and he never said. His intelligence was off the charts, making it more difficult to guess his age correctly, and his personality was darker, more somber than any young boy's should be. He was always quiet, always respectful, but always observant. And it wasn't just him being on the spectrum. Amara knew, her psychologist intuition telling her, that there was more to it than any of them knew. She just hoped, for all of their sakes, that it wasn't something that could bring danger to their doors.

"Hi, Xander. Amara here."

"I know," the boy said in the same monotone. "I have your contact saved."

Of course, he did. She called him thrice a week. Morana had given him a phone of his own so he could call any of them at any time. While Morana was also apprehensive about his past, she had a deep respect for his intelligence and refused to coddle him because of it. Tristan was... well, *Tristan* about it.

"Lex would like to speak with you," Amara started, and Lex raised his hand for the phone. Amara chuckled, handing it over to the boy and watching as he took a few steps away to the side to talk to his friend privately. "Hi, Xan! How are you? Did you miss me? I gotta tell you about this new..." his voice trailed off as he walked to the end of the clearing and sat down on the grass. This was something he did every few days, and knowing what she knew about him, Amara let him. There was something beautiful about the bond the two boys had forged in their circumstances at such a young age, and Amara wanted to foster it and hoped it grew into an organic, powerful friendship, much like Dante's and Tristan's, as time passed. Having a true friend in one's corner could make so much difference, especially during a difficult time. She knew from experience, and that was why she wished the boys could nurture it.

Her heart gave a pang at the thought of friends. Vin, one of her closest, oldest friends, had been deep undercover into The Syndicate for almost a year now. He had sent Dante updates occasionally when he could, but Amara missed him a lot, especially since he'd been quieter for a while. She just hoped he would come out of it unscathed and undamaged, but even if he did, she would help heal him as he had helped her a long time ago. The scars on her wrists, hidden underneath her bracelets, tingled with the ugly memory of her past.

Shaking it off, she watched Lex talk on the phone as he picked at the grass and asked Nellie about him. "How is he doing?"

"Surprisingly well," Nellie answered. "He's well-behaved and makes sure others around him behave too. He's become a sort of peacekeeper. He breaks up fights and keeps all the spirits high. Kids go to him when they need something."

"He's a leader," Amara mused, watching the boy talk intently.

Nellie nodded. "Dr. Armstrong thinks he's either putting up a facade or repressing, but it's too early to tell. He needs more time to give any conclusive evaluation."

Amara understood that. It could be tricky even in general, but especially with children. It was important to take time and be sure before any kind of diagnosis or the stakes were too great and could impact the child's whole life, or worse, add to their trauma. From her experience, she knew for a fact that any child with the experiences Lex had carried baggage in their brain, consciously or subconsciously, and without proper care, it could manifest in a multitude of ways, some extremely dangerous.

"Keep a close eye on him please," she instructed Nellie. "I want to know if there are any behavioral changes with him at all."

She hoped there wouldn't be, at least not negative. She was rooting for the little boy to do well, rooting for him to have a fabulous life filled with love and joy, and she would do everything in her power to ensure he could live it.

A few other kids greeted or waved at her too, and Amara looked at the little compound, at the little lives impacted by one singular evil entity.

They didn't know much about The Syndicate. In fact, none of them had even known about the organization until Morana had become a part of their lives. It was like a pandora's box opened up when Tristan and Morana got together, aided by The Reaper and the Shadow Man, exposing them to The Syndicate. Even though the organization had been active for decades, her own trauma incited by them and executed by her biological father who worked for them, it was only recently that they all got to know about them.

There were too many unknowns in the foray, things they didn't know anything about.

And Morana's airport guy, who they were sure was the Shadow Man, seemed to know a lot but not share a lot. Amara did wonder what his endgame was. Was he a narcissist playing with them or a vigilante working in the dark? Was it a power-hungry game or fueled by something else? Was he an enemy or an ally? What was he that an evil organization that everyone feared was terrified of him? Was he a bigger evil or lesser? How could he be lesser if he terrorized the monsters so? Though he was an unknown too, she had a gut feeling about him. He had aided them so far, even saved Morana's and Zephyr's life, and led them to their first group of kids. But Alpha, the only one in their group who had talked to him at length, didn't have an iota of an inkling of who he was or what he wanted. '

'Cryptic motherfucker' were the exact words her one-eyed brother-in-law had used. Amara wasn't sure what to make of him, but the more she learned, the more certain she was that he was goal-oriented. From a psychological point of view, he seemed like a fascinating study, and in a very academic way, she wished she could talk to him just to get a better understanding of his motivations and his psyche.

Lex ran back to her with her phone, breaking her thoughts.

"You have a good chat?" she asked him, taking the phone, clicking on a random email notification and realizing it was a spam link before deleting it.

"Yes," the young boy enthused. "He thinks he's getting

adopted."

Amara felt her eyebrows go up. The boy was all but adopted. She knew Morana was looking into the legal paperwork, which was tricky without Xander's records. She knew it because Morana had told her about it on their group video call the other night with Zephyr. Though it was a little tense between the two women—Morana juggling through her identity and feeling guilty about Zenith's death, and Zephyr juggling through the darkness in their world and grieving the loss of her sister—Amara had begun doing the group calls every other night. Both the women needed to heal, and it wouldn't happen in isolation. They all needed each other, especially if things were going to get worse, as had been forewarned by the Shadow Man. Amara was willing to take his word for it—much to the consternation of others who were more emotional about it than logical. But he knew shit none of them did, and so far, he hadn't guided them wrong. So, she had made it her mission to keep the girls together. The tension would ease, but they all needed to stand up and get through it together.

But that brought her to the point, how did Xander know about the adoption thing? Because she knew Morana hadn't discussed it with him yet.

"Why does he think that?" Amara voiced the question.

Lex shrugged. "He didn't say. He's just happy about it."

Very interesting.

Another boy called for Lex, and he ran off with a "Thank

you, Dr. Maroni!" thrown her way.

Amara watched him go, her mind trying to figure things out but hitting a wall every time. She wished she had all the answers. She wished she could interrogate the Shadow Man just to put an end to all the questions. She wished she could talk to Vin to understand what was going on.

Amara walked around the kids, checking up on them, and wished that one day, they could all heal. A darker part of her wished that one day, in the future, the culprits would die deserving, painful deaths.

She could only hope.

ALPHA

Chapter 3

Alpha, Los Fortis

"Hector is dead," Victor, his second-in-command, stated without an iota of remorse in his voice.

Alpha examined him from his chair in his office, looking for any cracks. His trust had been broken too deeply for him not to be wary anymore. Hector, a man he'd once thought of as a best friend and right hand, had betrayed him in the worst ways a man could be betrayed. And all for power. He knew better than most that power made monsters of men, but he'd never expected his friend to be one. Not only had he blinded and tortured him, making him lose his memory and his sense of self, but he had taken advantage of his vulnerable state and injected himself by his side for so many years. Alpha truly was partially blind because how the fuck had he never seen his true colors? Hector had not only assaulted and murdered women, the same women Alpha had dedicated his life to protect, the same kind as his mother had been, but he had also become a pawn for The Syndicate. The one fucking organization Alpha had heard of in passing but never wanted anything to do with, which he now had to deal with because of his little rainbow.

His little rainbow, who had lost her colors when her sister had died in her arms.

Zenith, though Zephyr's sister, had been a runaway from The Syndicate, hiding and getting adopted by the De La Vega's when she'd been younger. Having met her a few times even before finding Zephyr, thanks to her dedicated work in one of his non-profit organizations, Alpha knew she'd been an extraordinary, bright, and beautiful woman. The world was a worse place without her, and the injustice of it all chafed over him every day.

Fucking Hector.

"How?" he asked Victor, Hector's brother and possibly the only one feeling more betrayed by him than Alpha was. Both brothers had been with him for so long, and Alpha didn't want to believe Victor could be a traitor either, especially not after the way he'd seen the other man go on a hunt to find his brother. Moreover, Alpha couldn't afford to lose him too, not after culling Hector's supporters and allies within his people, down now just to a handful. He needed Victor to be true so they could rebuild and restructure the Los Fortis empire into an impenetrable fortress. He didn't have the luxury of a generational legacy like his half-brother Dante did with the Tenebrae Outfit. He had built everything that he had from the ground up, right from the soil to the sky, rising from a pauper in poverty to a potentate in power.

"Burned. Arson," Victor supplied, standing with his hands behind his back, his demeanor somber. The muted daylight coming through the glass windows showed his rigid form. Nothing, aside from the clenching of his jaw, belayed his displeasure.

"When?" Alpha leaned back on the chair, folding his arms across his chest.

"Hard to say," Victor replied. "I'm waiting for the coroner's report. But they estimate it to be sometime in the last twenty-four hours."

"Are we sure it's him?" Alpha knew how crafty Hector could be. Now, with the connections that he had acquired in The Syndicate, faking a death would be child's play for him. Hell, Dante had faked death twice, and Hector was a lot more cunning.

Victor hesitated. "The body was completely burned. So was the warehouse he was found in. But the dental records are a match. I verified it myself."

Alpha considered him, pondering over it for a moment. "You okay with that?"

Just a clench of the jaw.

Alpha sighed. "Sit," he indicated the chair opposite him. "Talk to me."

Victor relaxed his arms, letting them come to his sides, before taking a seat. The table between them felt big, bigger than before, and Alpha truly hoped they could breach the distance one day again. The other man had always been quieter next to his brother, but now, Alpha needed to hear him and trust his mettle, not wonder about what the hell was happening in his head.

Victor was on the same page apparently, because he began to talk. "I'm pissed, to be honest. I wanted to find him myself. I wanted to question him and then kill him myself. I'm pissed someone else got to him faster. The only good thing is he was tortured for some time." He paused, letting Alpha take it all in. "Someone had kept him captive in the warehouse in Gladestone for a while, can't say exactly how long. He was tortured and was alive when the fire started. That tells me someone else wanted him more than we did. Could it be someone from The Syndicate?"

"Maybe," Alpha mused, keeping his hunch to himself for the moment. If his gut was right, he knew it had to be the Shadow Man. He had told Alpha clearly that he'd been following and hunting Hector for a while, and though the mysterious man didn't have any particular modus operandi, he had executed arson successfully before. In fact, from the little Alpha had been able to find about him, his only known point in the past was a massive fire he had started in some kind of an orphanage. There wasn't any information about the details, the information non-existent anywhere, but he had a source coming to meet him soon. Though he was indebted to the man for saving his wife, he was going to find his agenda if it was the last thing he did.

Victor stood up again, resting his arms on the desk, his dark eyes intent. "I know what my brother did will always be a scar between us. It is my burden to bear. But I promise you, Alpha," the conviction in his voice was deep, "I will die before I betray your trust. I have his debt to clear now, his name to taint my own. I will spend my life clearing it with you."

Before he could respond, a little hiccup made him look to the door blocked behind Victor's frame.

His beautiful wife stood there, dressed in dark jeans and a beige top that were *not* her, her hair the same sad blue that she never got the chance to recolor, her eyes misted, locked on Victor. Zephyr had always been a crier, tearing up at the drop of a hat, but somehow, in the last few weeks, it had gotten worse because she didn't cry much anymore. It was like something inside her had frozen the tears, making them more infrequent, and as much as he'd hated her crying, he hated her not crying even more. At least when she tore up, he knew that all was alright in the world. Nothing seemed to be okay in their world right now.

Seeing her eyes misted after so long made something in his chest lighter, his heart thumping and that was the only reason he didn't interrupt her.

"Oh, Victor," she whispered, walking into his office and going straight to the other man. As much as Alpha hated the bond she had with him, he couldn't deny a part of him was glad she was coming out of her shell. Victor had always been the closest to Zephyr out of all his men, directly responsible for her security, and the fact that she had been harmed and hurt under his watch, weighed heavily on him. He had been knocked out cold because he had let his guard down around his own brother.

Alpha watched Zephyr stop beside Victor, putting a hand on his arm and squeezing it. "You're not responsible for what happened, Victor. Don't take someone else's blame on your shoulders. You have enough to carry."

Alpha saw Victor's throat bob as he swallowed, possibly emotional at her forgiveness. Alpha could relate. She had forgiven him too, so easily, like lingering on mistakes wasn't something possible for her. This tiny, curvy ball of life had so much forgiveness and love in her heart that he was amazed that she didn't burst from it. Even in her grief, she knew grace. Alpha didn't think he could fall more in love with her, but she proved him wrong every day, pulling him deeper into the depths without even knowing she did.

She gave his friend another squeeze on his arm, and Alpha watched the large, lethal man soften to a degree he had not seen before.

Fuck, she was magical.

And *his.*

"Come here, rainbow," he spoke, his voice coming out

huskier than intended.

Zephyr turned to him, walking around the table to plop down on his lap as had become normal for them. None of his men even bat an eyelash at it anymore. In fact, after the funeral, they had closed ranks around her even more protectively, somehow adopting her into their odd family. Zephyr had quit her job and stayed home, locked in with the dogs, for a few days. Her mother had wanted her to divorce him, and she had refused, causing a rift that took more toll on her. Everyone had seen her sink slowly into a depression. Alpha had tried to get her out of it, but it hadn't worked. And somehow, to his surprise, his men had stepped up. They had visited her just to check up on her and sneakily dropped the info about struggling with paperwork at the office. Hector and his allies being out had left the company in a lurch, that was true, but they could hire whatever help they needed. However, just to get her out and about, they had pretended to be helpless.

Knowing his struggle with reading, Zephyr hadn't even hesitated and began coming into the office daily.

And it had helped.

Working, getting out, interacting with others, it all had helped a little. She had taken over his entire paperwork, working with a few of his men to ensure everything ran smoothly, contacting clients and women alike, writing emails, and becoming the one all came to for trouble. He knew she was trying to distract herself with the new work, leaving her old life behind, and he didn't blame her for it. His men had moved a separate smaller desk and chair for her in the office, facing the windows and the endless vista outside. They brought her lunch from her favorite place down the street. They made sure her tumbler was always full of whatever beverage she wanted. If she wanted something, she just had to say the word, and she had it. His men, all the ones remaining out of loyalty to him, adored her. They had all suffered and seen the worst in life, and somehow, they'd collectively made it their mission to get her bright and happy again.

Alpha loved and hated it in equal measure. He loved that she was so loved and adored as she should be, but he hated all the male attention on her, even though they all treated her like a little sister more than anything. So, her sitting on his lap made his breathing easier.

He put a hand on her hip, caressing her softly in a way he knew she liked, feeling her relax into his body as he gentled her.

"Hector is dead," Alpha told her, feeling her stiffen. The man she had once considered a friend too had scarred her so deeply. He had made her lose the man she loved for ten years and then made her lose the sister she loved forever.

Her hazel eyes turned to him, a hardness in them he hadn't seen before. "Did he suffer?"

Alpha nodded, and she exhaled against him. "Good. Thank god for whoever killed him painfully."

The fact that she had wished a brutal death for him spoke volumes. He let her be and looked at Victor again. "Keep me updated with any new findings. I want to know everything."

Victor gave a crisp nod before spinning around and leaving the office.

Alpha relaxed slightly, focusing on the woman in his arms. "How you doing, rainbow?"

Zephyr shrugged.

"Talk to me, baby," he urged her softly, wanting her, needing her to communicate with him, to tell him what was happening because fuck, he wasn't a mind-reader, and he couldn't help her if he didn't know what was going on in her brain.

She looked down at the ring on her finger, a ring he had gotten her without much thought but had somehow been perfect for her. He looked at it as well, wondering if there were days she regretted marrying him. Though she had told him that her sister's death wasn't his fault, he knew her parents, her mother in particular, blamed him and his involvement in their lives. Zephyr had made it clear that she knew her past would have caught up to her sister regardless of whether Alpha was in their lives or not. And she had made it clear that she would've become involved in this dark world regardless because of her sister.

Alpha knew all that, but a part of him wondered if there was a part of her that had regrets. His presence in her life had brought her nothing but pain, not now, not ten years ago. She had mourned him first, though through no fault of his, and now she mourned a sister she had loved with all her heart. Alpha couldn't even imagine how that felt, never having had a sibling of his own. His relationship with Dante was good now, albeit a little complicated, and had happened too late for him to understand the depth of that bond growing up. But beyond that, his wife now mourned the loss of her old life and, possibly, her relationship with her parents because of her choice to be with him.

"I'll be okay," she spoke to their hands, holding his tightly, hers round, soft and small, his muscular, rough and large. Yet, she held his, squeezed it, reassuring him in a way the doubts cleared from his mind.

He watched her spin the ring idly, the different jewels casting colorful reflections on the wall with the sunlight hitting them.

She'd told him one night about how he'd promised it to her as a young man, and somehow, even without his memories, he had delivered it. Some days, he wished he could remember the large gap of nothingness. He had bits and pieces up until he was twenty-ish, but things were so fuzzy after that. What he wouldn't give to remember her, just *her*, if nothing else. He wanted to remember who he had been, what his dreams, his goals, his desires had been. He wanted to remember who he had been to her, how he had felt for her, if it had been pure with the innocence of youth or dark with the turbulence of circumstances. He wanted to remember her, how she had been, pages of their story together wiped from existence for him but not for her, a burden she bore alone without being able to share, and it made him feel helpless. He wanted to share with her, to remember, reminisce, recreate.

He wondered some days. Were memories something he had or something he lost?

He touched her ring, bringing her hand up and pressing a kiss to it.

Zephyr needed physical validation. He didn't know why, but touch grounded her for some reason. He didn't question it; he just gave her free use of his body. Though, understandably, she'd not used it for weeks. While he had given her kisses and cuddles, and she had accepted them, she hadn't initiated any touching on her side for a while, let alone sex. Sex had always been incredible between them; it had helped them connect before anything, and they had been insatiable together. He knew if he initiated it, she would accept. But he didn't want her to accept; he wanted her to participate.

But he understood her hesitance, her reluctance, and he gave her the space she needed.

But his dick didn't understand. After being sated for months, it had become addicted to her. For his dick, her curves pressing against him meant a good time. Alpha would be as patient as needed, but he wished his dick could get with the program.

Fuck his dick.

Not literally.

Shit, he needed to stop thinking about it.

"Hubby?" Zephyr called softly, and he focused on her voice, trying to keep the blood from going south. Fuck, he loved it when she called him the silly names. He had missed that inherent playfulness she had.

"Yes, wifey?" He played along, hoping to cheer her up.

"I can feel your little monster poking my ass."

"Little?" The disbelief in his voice triggered the most beautiful sound, one that was a rarity these days—her giggle. A soft, feminine giggle that made his chest feel ten times lighter.

She looked up at him, locking their gazes together, the dimples that had been hiding for days making an appearance as she smiled at him. "Gigantic, ginormous, gargantuan?" she rolled her eyes. "That better?"

He gripped her tighter, wanting to lock this moment and keep her happy like this forever. "I think you might be the one with amnesia if you're calling it *little*."

A laugh burst out of her, shaking her body and not helping his situation at all, but he wouldn't have traded it for the whole world. He growled softly, and another fit overcame her, the sound loud and open, so contagious he felt his own leave his chest. They both sat there, her laughing and him grinning—about what, for what, because of what, he didn't know. He didn't care. She laughed and laughed and laughed, like a dam had burst, and suddenly, tears escaped her eyes. With the same vigor, she started to sob.

"I don't know—" she hiccuped into his neck "—what's happening to me."

Alpha held her tightly, wishing he had answers for her, trying to understand what had happened and why her switch had flipped so suddenly, but drawing a complete blank. Not to sound like a typical man, but the behavior was completely bizarre to him. He stayed silent, though, and let her bawl her eyes out, letting her get out whatever had been bubbling inside her for weeks, and just held her through it all.

She would be okay again.

She would laugh without crying again.

Alpha had to believe it. There was no other option for them.

She would be okay.

They would be okay.

There would be a rainbow beyond this, or the world would become too dark.

MORANA

CHAPTER 4

MORANA, SHADOW PORT

I T WAS THE DOUBLE beep of her phone that made her eyes open wide.

The moon cast long shadows in the bedroom, the darkness beyond the full windows a clear indication it was still the middle of the night.

Morana blinked, orienting her mind to understand why she had come awake. Her phone was silenced for all notifications while she slept—something she'd started doing after her shooting to get proper rest—all messages but one.

Mind racing, she turned on her side, aware of the heavy, muscular arm wrapped around her waist as Tristan slept deeply beside her, snoring quietly. It was a testament to how exhausted he was and how low his guards were that he'd slept through the beeping. In the beginning, when they had just started sharing a bed, he had gotten up at the slightest of sounds and the lightest of movements from her. His life had trained him to be alert, and it had followed him even in slumber—she would tug the blanket, and he would wake up;

she would get up to pee, and he would wake up; she would turn in his arms, and he would wake up. It took him just a few minutes to fall asleep again, but he woke up nonetheless.

But he was tired even though he didn't say it. She knew. She could see it in his eyes. Every day that they spent without new information chipped little pieces of him away, and seeing a part of him wither like that terrified her, though she never told him. He had enough on his plate, and out of the two of them, she knew she was more well-equipped to handle emotional freak-outs than he was. If he even got the slightest inclination that this all was scaring her, she didn't know how he would react. Though they were together and had been together for a while, they were still new to each other, still learning each other and themselves. Honestly, one day, she just wished they would achieve the level of understanding Dante and Amara shared. A part of her slightly envied the couple when she saw them together, envied the many years they'd had with each other, envied the easy way they could communicate without any holds barred.

Yet, she wouldn't change a thing. Tristan, as broken and brutal and beautiful as he was, was hers. Their story, while bloodier and messier than any other, was theirs. And just as they had gone through all the tides, they would go through it all together.

Carefully moving in order to not disturb him, she got out of bed and went to her phone on the dresser. Why was her phone on the dresser? Because Tristan had broken her bedside table. Well, that wasn't entirely true. She had helped. It had happened on a particularly enthusiastic night when they had been going hard against the door, his jeans had been around his ankles, and her leg had cramped. So he had started toward the bed with her, tripped because his jeans had been around his ankles (*and who could even walk like that with a wriggling horny woman in their arms?*), and they'd both gone down, taking the poor table with them. It had cracked, and she had cracked up right there on the floor at the look on his face, her stomach hurting, but because she was still horny, she had straddled him. That was the first time she'd laughed while having sex, the first time his dimple had been permanently on his cheek while he'd been inside her.

Smiling at the memory, she put the code on her screen and opened the notification, her eyes scanning the message. Her smile dimmed, her heartbeat picking up pace.

'You have 48 hours, Miss Vitalio. Do your thing or I'll change my mind. (File attached).'

The Shadow Man.

As fascinated as Morana was with the mystery of him, he was really annoying for the same at times. What the fuck was he playing at this time? Forty-eight hours for what? To track him? What was the point even? She'd traced all his previous messages, originating from different IP addresses all over the world, sometimes bouncing even as she was tracking. He was smart, but moreover, he was too involved in the depths of this dark world for anyone to find him if he didn't want to be found. She knew because she had tried, and he had irritatingly evaded her with ease that wasn't regular, not for someone of her caliber.

But the message, this one, it felt a little different than the ones he'd sent before. They had been a lot more vague, a lot more cryptic. This one was direct, too direct. She would've suspected someone else pretending to be him but in the time she'd been a reluctant acquaintance of his, he didn't seem like the type to let someone pretend to be him. So, what was with the message? Did he want her to find him? Morana stared at the screen, looking through their previous chats, and realized most of it had been him leading all of them chasing leads. Whatever the others thought of him, Morana was shrewd enough to not disregard him and his information.

'I'll change my mind.'

That was what was different. Whenever he'd sent her any message in the past, it had been coordinates or just a few words of information—plain, simple, direct. That last line in this message was putting her mental antennas on high alert. That last line? It was personal, more human than she'd seen him be in their textual exchanges before. He was personally invested in whatever he'd sent her, but what exactly?

She clicked on the file and saw the error displayed. She needed her laptop to access the attachment.

The last vestiges of sleep disappeared as the wheels in her mind began to turn; she put on her glasses and quickly padded out of the bedroom and down the stairs as quietly as possible. It was deep in the night, and aside from the low humming of appliances, everything in the penthouse was silent. The vast array of windows showed a view of the city and the sea that never failed to take her breath away, making her pause for a second on the stairs to just admire the vista. She was honest enough to admit that she'd fallen in love with the property much before its owner, mainly because of those windows.

Shaking her head at herself, she descended again and stopped at what had once been the guest room she had stayed in, peeking in quickly. Xander, the boy who had become such a part of her heart, was asleep, his mouth slightly open, his blanket thrown to one side, a pillow hugged to the other. He had claimed this room and space as his own, his quiet presence one she loved having in the house and their lives. Morana had never really thought of herself as a maternal figure—she'd never really had any example to understand what that felt like, to be honest—but she felt something very strongly for Xander. Her first example of a good mother was Amara's mother, who oozed maternal love not just for her own daughter but for anyone she took under her care, including Dante and Tristan, and now Morana and Xander. She had seen it better firsthand with Amara since Tempest had been born, but more than that, with all the boys she was helping in the rehabilitation center, especially Xander's little friend Lex. Morana loved knowing that her baby had a friend like that, having never had one in childhood and knowing the kind of isolation it fostered in one's soul. She was glad because it meant Xander not only had love from adults around him but also a companion his own age who already knew of his past, not like the new kids trying to befriend him at school and leaving him alone once they realized he was different from them.

Morana stared at the boy, as she did many times, trying to understand why she couldn't find a thing about him. She had used all her resources and scoured the depths of the dark web, combing through countless records, but there was nothing about him. It was like he hadn't existed before they had found him, and he didn't talk about his past much, at least not with them. She didn't really know if he told his psychologist about it either, but she'd never pried, wanting him to have full confidence to confide in the doctor if he needed it without feeling like someone was looking over his shoulder. She might not have had any maternal examples, but she'd be damned if she didn't learn on the job.

Once assured that he was okay, she padded to the smaller second room behind the stairs, which had become her workspace. In the beginning when she'd been at the penthouse, she hadn't really explored the entire vastness of it, limiting her time as a guest to the front areas and the guest room. Now that it was her home, she could appreciate the space in its entirety, and it was *massive*. Five bedrooms—one master on the upper level, one behind the kitchen that was now Xander's, and three down the corridor that ran from there to the back of the building. There was also a home gym, an office space, a balcony in the back, and a cozy room with a lot of natural light and a direct view of the port in the distance. That room had been unfurnished and empty before she had fully moved in, and now was a playroom for Xander, filled with gadgets and toys and books he liked. She wouldn't have thought the penthouse was conducive for a child, but Xander somehow fit in seamlessly into the space, making it more of a home than she would've thought possible.

Her workspace, tucked in a small room behind the stairs, was exactly her vibe—darkened, glowing with digital lights, and just monitors and devices mounted on a large desk and the wall and an ergonomic chair for her. There wasn't any space for anyone else to sit in there, though Tristan did stand leaning against the doorway sometimes, just watching her work, which always made her feel a little self-conscious. It was hard to explain why. It wasn't like he could understand whether what she was doing was correct or not, but she just felt a little fumbly in his presence in her domain. Xander sometimes liked to sit on the floor, tinkering with an old laptop she had given him. His natural inclination toward digital things was the way they connected. He liked learning from her, and she liked teaching him, his mind one that fascinated her. The boy was smart, so much smarter than she'd been around his age, and she couldn't imagine the limits of his potential with how he could use that intelligence.

Entering the room, she powered on her systems and sat in her comfy chair—one of the first things she had ordered online for their new place right after moving in. It had shown up, and much to Tristan's amusement, she hadn't been able to get it out of the private elevator, much less roll it into the room. Much to her arousal, he had done one of those manly *I got this* moves, rolled up his sleeves, and just picked it up and moved it in like it hadn't been taking the full force of her body. The thing had been *heavy*, and he had plucked it up like a feather. To say she'd been turned on had been an understatement. And as a thank you, she had jumped him on the chair as soon as he'd put it down. He hadn't complained at all.

Chuckling to herself, she pushed her glasses up and opened the chat screen on her main monitor.

'You have 48 hours, Miss Vitalio. Do your thing or I'll change my mind. (File attached).'

An hour had already passed. She had forty-seven left.

Morana set up a timer on the monitor so she could keep track of the hours visibly. She hovered over the file attached, looking at its heavy size, wondering what he'd sent her, and did her pre-download scans for any viruses. Once it came back clean, she clicked on it.

It downloaded in a few seconds, and a folder titled *'Fountainhead'* appeared on her screen. Fountainhead? A quick search told her the meaning: the original source of something.

What the hell?

She opened it and saw what was inside. Photographs. Not many, only a few photographs.

She tapped the first, and it opened up. Her screen was filled with the image of the ghost of her past—Zenith. Morana felt her stomach tightening, confronted with the fact yet again that her life wasn't her own. She wasn't the real Morana, Zenith was, or had been. Staring at the photograph of the young girl whose life had been snatched away too soon, she remembered—the unanswered questions, the unexpected death, the unstoppable bullet tearing through her body, all of it coming back to her. Heaviness sat in her gut, as it did whenever she was assaulted with the memories. She remembered lying on that concrete, wondering if she was finally going to die. She had almost believed she would, and it had terrified her. She hadn't wanted to go, not like that, not leaving behind life when she'd just begun to live it, with a man she loved and a boy who had her heart and friends who had become family. For the first time in her life, she had people, and so much love and it had all been threatened by a shard of metal lodged in her body.

She remembered Tristan, frantic, furious, frozen in fear of losing her. She remembered Xander hugging her with tight affection that clogged her throat when she saw him again.

She rubbed her left shoulder, feeling the raised flesh and the scar of the gunshot, feeling the pain that had been peaking a lot more frequently than she wanted to admit. Though she had been through physical therapy and everything possible to restore herself to her former physical self, the fact was that she wasn't the same. There were repercussions of her injury, as much as she didn't want to accept it, and they seemed to be more permanent than temporary. The bullet that had hit her shoulder, thankfully missing her heart, had still done some severe nerve damage. It had injured one of the main nerves that went down to her hand, and though the doctors had repaired it well enough that her hand was still functional, it had become quite useless. She couldn't do anything with it for more than ten minutes without it going numb and losing all sensation. It was jarring, trying to use it and suddenly realizing she couldn't. It probably wasn't a big deal to most people. In fact, everyone told her she was lucky to be alive and in good health, and she agreed. But a part of her mourned herself because they didn't understand what her hands had been. They had always been the extensions of her brain to her, keeping up as she typed away without a second thought or drove into the night without worry. And though she still had her right hand, she was scared that her left was done. She couldn't type with it the way she had before, she couldn't lift anything heavy the way she had before, she couldn't drive the way she had before. She couldn't be the way she'd been before.

Morana hadn't really said much about it to anyone. She knew she should. But everyone had so much on their plate already, and it didn't seem like a big deal right then. She was taking medication—Tristan was so disciplined with making sure she did it on time. She was taking physical therapy, and Xander always accompanied her to her sessions. And except Amara, because her friend was too astute when it came to people's brains, no one really suspected much. And to be honest, she didn't want to say it out loud. She was scared that if she did, it would become more real, and she wasn't ready to accept that yet.

Shaking herself out of the thoughts to focus on the task at hand, she moved on to the second picture, one she had already seen before. The old picture of the three toddlers—herself, Zenith, and Luna—before they were gone.

She clicked the next picture. It was an old, scanned digital copy of a physical photograph of two young girls, one brunette and one redhead. The brunette she recognized as a younger version of the Zenith she had met. But the redhead? Her heart began to pound as she analyzed the image for any special details. The background of the photo was simple, just a generic wall that could be anywhere. The girls were young, not older than eight, from her guess, and both looked scared.

Slightly shaky, she went to the next photograph, her heart skipping a beat as she took in the sight. A lone girl this time. A red-haired teen, the same girl in the previous photo but older, against another wall, this one more beige, contrasting with the long red hair.

The frantic beats of her heart drummed in her ears, terrified of what she was going to discover, knowing this was going to change everything forever whichever way it went.

There was just one more photograph, and taking a deep breath in for courage, Morana clicked on it.

It was the photograph of the same redhead, now a grown-up, mature adult with much shorter hair. The same girl without the baby fat in her cheeks, a slender curve to her features, now a fully grown woman, looking off in the distance, holding a mug in her hands, her face in profile.

There was no way...

It couldn't be.

It had to be!

He couldn't just be sending the photos and dropping this on them so casually, could he?

Yeah, he could.

Fuck.

Fuck.

It was her.

She was alive.

Luna was alive.

Tears welled in her eyes. Tristan's baby sister was alive.

Fuck.

Pausing, Morana caught herself before getting swept up in the emotion. She needed to stay on track. There was a reason she had been sent this file, sent it now, and a timer she could feel ticking with each second passing.

Focus.

Morana inhaled, and squinted at the image, scanning the most recent picture carefully, trying to find some clues in the background. It looked like a balcony or deck of some kind; it was hard to tell precisely. The light was gray, as though it was cloudy or early morning somewhere with fog and mountains silhouetted in a sliver of a view before going out of frame. A dark gray wall behind the girl was rough, clearly a stone of some kind, bringing her short, jagged red hair in stark contrast. The hair was clearly chopped by someone who didn't know how to cut it. The mug in her hands was plain black, nothing remarkable about it. What was remarkable, however, was what she was wearing—a man's t-shirt too big for her. Just the t-shirt, nothing else from the way her breasts were silhouetted against the fabric, and her thighs were visible, going out of the frame.

It was an intimate picture, the kind one would take after

spending a night together. A lover's picture.

'I'll change my mind'.

Morana felt her jaw drop, her brain computing. The personal tone hit her all of a sudden, the picture becoming clear for what it was.

It wasn't just an image. It was a statement.

The Shadow Man.

Luna.

Lovers.

He was her lover.

Holy shit.

The longer Morana stared at the photograph, the more she hoped he'd acquired it from somewhere, that he wasn't the photographer. Because if he was... she didn't know what to think of it. But the more she thought of it, the more things became clearer in her head, and yet more questions arose in her mind.

Fuck.

Morana sat stumped, trying to process, just hoping he wasn't the photographer.

Taking a deep breath, calming her mind to focus on the matter at hand while her thoughts ran chaos, Morana began to do her thing. She had forty-six hours and thirty-two minutes left.

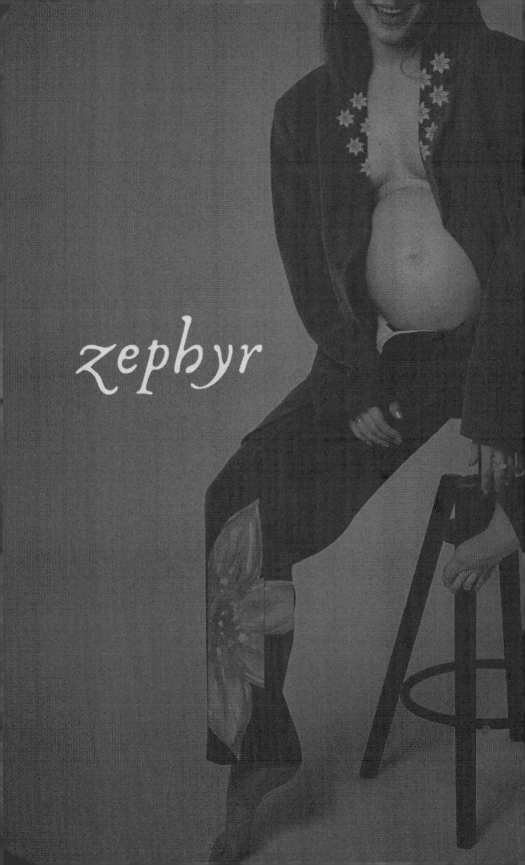

zephyr

CHAPTER 5

ZEPHYR, LOS FORTIS

S OMETHING WAS WRONG WITH her.

Zephyr didn't think it was just grief anymore. She was sick, sicker than she'd ever been, and somehow, it had gotten worse in the last week. It was times like this that she would have picked up the phone and called her sister. Zenith, level-headed and relaxed as she'd been, would have calmed her down. Zen had always been able to do that.

Zephyr rubbed Bear's soft fur as the canine lay by her side, his head on her stomach, rumbling like a motor in a way that felt soothing. Ever since the funeral, Bear had almost been inseparable from her. He had always loved her, but her sadness had just made him want to heal her. It wasn't just him either. The other two dogs had also begun lingering around her, though Baron still didn't care much for her; at least he sat close to where she was whenever she was in the house. Even the men at AV had somehow taken it upon themselves to help her. She knew of their bullshit excuse of needing paperwork done to get her out and about, and in a way, it was endearing that they cared so much.

The fact was, Zephyr didn't want to wallow in her grief either. She didn't want to spend her life being sad, especially when she knew the kind of toll it was taking on her husband and their relationship, too. Alpha, the love of her life, the giant, growly beast of a man, had been nothing but so gentle, so caring with her. It had reminded her of how he'd been a decade ago, with a gentleness inside him he rarely let anyone see. But he'd always had it even without his memories, and one of the biggest proofs of that were the three dogs around her, who had been abandoned, discarded in the trash as puppies, and he'd just picked them up and brought them home and raised them himself.

He was showing her that gentleness now, and she loved him all the more for it, but she knew she needed to snap out of this. Zen would have hated her like this. Her sister would have wanted her to move on with joy and not live in grief. But that was the thing about grief. It wasn't really in her control. As someone who'd always had a predisposition to depression, she couldn't decide how to control the grief. Some days, she woke up feeling like it was a better day, that she would be okay, that things were looking up. She would build sandcastles of hope and optimism, and out of nowhere, like an unpredicted wave, the grief would come and crumble it back to nothing but sand, leaving her to rebuild it all over again. Those were the good days. On the bad days, she woke up but wished she didn't. She loved her life, but she didn't want to move from the bed.

And that was exactly why, when the men had come up with the idea to get her out, she had let them.

She couldn't go back to her old life, her old way of being with the way she was anymore. Everything would remind her of things she needed to take some space from to heal. But the AV offices felt like home. There were no bad memories for her there, just a man who had loved her as a girl and loved her again as a woman, and a dysfunctional set of older brothers who had all adopted her into their foray.

Getting ready every day, going to the office to actually do something productive, it helped. And knowing that her help was needed, that added to it. Her husband couldn't do paperwork and was too mistrustful to ask anyone else to do it after Hector, so it felt completely natural for her to step in and take that part over. No one outside of her knew that he had issues reading, and she would keep it that way as long as he wanted.

Her phone vibrated beside her, and she looked at it to see it was her father.

Zephyr closed her eyes for a second before answering. "Papa?"

"Have you talked to your mother yet?"

Zephyr wished she could say she was surprised at the question, but she wasn't. She wanted nothing more than to pick up her phone and call her mother, but it was clear why she wouldn't. Every time she had, her mother had accused Alpha of Zenith's death, a blame that was never his, but he let her parents blame him because he didn't want to ruin their memory of who Zenith had actually been. Zephyr had never given thought to her sister's past before she had come into the family, the issue non-existent for her because, as far as she'd been concerned, she'd gotten a best friend, and that was that. But Zen had never told her, and that hurt Zephyr more than she was willing to admit. Zen had never confided in her about where she had run from, who she had left behind, why she was so passionate about working with survivors. Nothing. A part of her was so pissed at her for not telling. Zephyr would never have judged her. But she also understood why she hadn't. She'd been trying to forget it.

"Zephyr?" her father's prompt broke through her thoughts.

"I will when she can accept that my husband is not responsible for what happened," Zephyr stated clearly, making her stance clear for the hundredth time. Her father was the only one who called her and talked to her anymore. Since the funeral, her mother had done so a few times, but given up after believing that Zephyr was too blinded or brainwashed by Alpha to see the truth—that he was a monster and he had destroyed their family. A part of Zephyr was itching to tell her the truth, but that would just drag them into this dark world that she herself didn't understand fully yet. She couldn't do that to her parents.

Fact was, with or without Alpha, The Syndicate would have

caught up to Zenith. They had been searching for her for years. And the outcome would probably have been the same when they found her. Alpha being in their lives had nothing to do with that. In fact, she was alive because of his involvement, because someone called the Shadow Man had known that she was Alpha's wife and had gotten her to the hospital in time. She didn't want to think about what could've happened if she had been left alone with Zen in the isolated area that night. Hector might have killed her too. She would've been nothing but collateral damage. It was a sobering realization.

Her father sighed, the sound weary. "You're our only child left, Zephyr. Your mother might be harsh right now, but she's grieving. She loves you. You know that."

Zephyr felt a ball of lump in her throat, one that seemed to be perpetually lodged there these days. "So am I, papa. I'm grieving too. Mama needs to let go of her imagined vendetta and accept that whatever happened happened. I was there. She wasn't."

"I know," he spoke softly, the pain evident in his voice. "Well, I just wanted to check in on you and make sure you were fine." She loved her father. He had always been such a gentle, wonderful father to both his daughters, loving them and helping them grow into independent, strong women they had become. She couldn't remember a time she'd ever questioned his love, and even the fact that he still talked to her every other day while her mother was in a standoff with her spoke volumes. She knew that her mother loved her too, but her way of loving was much different, and sometimes, it hurt her.

"Are you fine, papa?" she asked, rubbing Bear's head as he made a sound at her side.

"As fine as I can be given things," her told her. "Just taking it one day at a time."

That was the way to go forward. One day at a time.

She bid him goodbye and looked out at the lush green view in the setting sun, relaxing into the lounge chair by the pool, the details of that last day playing in her mind as they always did.

In her head, she saw Morana getting shot, a spray of red seeping into her white top as she fell to the ground with a scream, urging her to run and get help. She felt the hands grabbing her and dragging her into a van, seeing her sister there. She saw the chairs, felt the ties binding them, heard the words leave Hector's lips. She saw her sister struggle, get free, run. And then the gunshot and her life leaving her body.

It was a fuzz after that. She remembered the Shadow Man there, checking Zen's pulse and saying sorry, picking her up and carrying her to some kind of vehicle. She'd thought she'd blacked out, but as the days went by, memories came in. She hadn't blacked out, not entirely, but she'd mentally checked out. But she'd been conscious for a bit.

The ceiling was moving with lights. No, that couldn't be.

"You have to stay awake. You might have a concussion."

The man driving was telling her, his voice sounding far off, but it couldn't be. She recognized his voice from before, but she didn't know him. He was right in front of her. How was he in front? She was lying in the back. That made sense.

Concussion? Why would she have a concussion? Did she?

"Stay awake."

But her eyelids were heavy.

"Tell me about your sister."

A broken noise filled the car, and she realized it had come from her.

"Why?" she sobbed, wanting to understand.

"So you stay awake." His voice was almost clinical in the command. "Did she ever tell you about her past?"

"No. I didn't... know."

"Did she ever mention any friend?"

Zephyr blinked sluggishly, her mind breaking but not processing. "No."

There was silence for a beat. "Did she ever mention any man?"

Her head hurt. She raised her hand to touch it, but it was moving too slowly. "Stop."

She heard a breath. "Of course. I'm sorry for your loss."

Tears leaked down the side of her face, and suddenly, she realized she was alone in the backseat. Her heart began to beat frantically. "Where is she? Did you just leave her?"

"No," he said. "She's being transferred. You'll see her soon."

How? Who was doing it? The questions were making a sharp pain shoot inside her skull. She wanted to close her eyes and sleep.

"Why me?" she muttered softly. "Why did I... and she didn't?"

"She was a part of something much bigger," he told her. "It caught up to her. You're powerful now, Mrs. Villanova. If you want to use that power one day, I'll give you her file."

She didn't feel powerful. She felt helpless. "How will I find you?"

A beat of silence. "You won't have to."

And that was all she remembered from that night before she had given in and fallen asleep.

Zephyr knew, thanks to her calls with the girls, everything that had happened in the meantime. It was odd being in the group with them, but Amara, the goddess that she was inside and out, insisted that the only way forward was for them to be together. Zephyr didn't disagree but her feelings for Morana were complicated, and she knew it was the same for the other woman. The ghost of her sister stood between them, impact-ing them both in a different way. It might have taken time for them to come to terms with everything, but Amara was hopeful, and her hope was contagious.

Her favorite person through it all, though, outside of her husband, was Dante. If Zephyr hadn't been in love and happily married, she would have gotten an insane crush on the man just for who he was. Not only had he constantly checked in on her and made sure she was okay, but he had stepped up and helped Alpha restructure and reorganize his empire after the hit of removing Hector and his stooges. Dante had gone as far as to send a bunch of his own trusted men to Los Fortis for a month to help train and hire new recruits, helping sustain the organization without feeling it too much. Zephyr couldn't imagine how much more stressful everything would have been for Alpha without his brother. And thankfully, that gesture had brought the two men closer. Though her husband still didn't trust people, especially now, Dante had made it on his list of people to call when needed.

And because of all that, she knew everyone was wary of the Shadow Man. And maybe she was being naive since she hadn't been a part of their dark world and maybe wasn't a good judge of character. But the two times she had met him, he had been kind to her, especially that night. That was etched in her memory, and she wanted to one day see him when she was conscious and thank him for saving her, possibly from being murdered that night, and ask why he couldn't have saved her sister sooner if he'd known so much about it.

"You have to move on, Zee." Zephyr could hear her sister speak as if she was right next to her. *"This isn't good for you. You know that."*

"I know," Zephyr said out loud. "But it's rough."

Zen chuckled in her mind. *"You like it rough, Zee."*

Zephyr felt a laugh bubble out of her before she blinked, seeing the blood all over her hands in her head, feeling the wet warmth, and knowing it was her sister's life seeping out; suddenly, she felt sick.

Jumping down from the lounge chair, she rushed to the side of the terrace, dry heaving over the railing, nothing coming out. She could hear the dogs scampering, their nails clicking on the wooden floorboards, barking around her in concern. Her jaw began to tremble, and her arms shook as she gripped the railing and dropped down to the floor. The dogs nudged at her, surrounding her, looking around as if to protect her from whatever had made her scatter.

She breathed deeply, trying to calm her racing heart, tasting the acid in the back of her throat even though nothing had come out. She didn't understand what was happening to her. It could be her hormones but they'd never made her so sick before. She'd come back from the hospital—she mentally calculated—almost eight weeks ago, and everything had been physically alright with her. She had some medication she had taken for a month, but she'd been off those for a while now. And these bouts of sickness or dizziness came out of nowhere, all of a sudden.

"Oh my goodness," she heard Leah, their housekeeper, exclaim as she came out on the terrace, led by Bandit. Zephyr hadn't even noticed the dog slipping away to bring help, and she gave him a head rub in thanks for his thoughtfulness, and he returned the gesture by licking her hand with a soft whine.

Leah waded through the canines and helped her stand up. Zephyr held her hand and gripped the railing with the other, waiting for the world to stop spinning.

"I'm calling Dr. Nei," Leah told her, speaking of their on-call medical professional. Yes, Alpha had a doctor on speed dial for his men and the women under his security. Zephyr learned that after she came back home and found that her husband had asked Dr. Nei to check on her every other day, to make sure she was fine. She was physically okay. She always had been. Aside from some superficial injuries and a concussion, they hadn't had to fix anything at all, not like Morana who had to be admitted into intensive care and had to undergo surgery to come out alive. Out of the three women that day, she was the one who got away scot-free. Maybe that was why she couldn't shake this sense of guilt that dodged her. She knew logically, it was stupid to think like that. But illogically, a part of her wondered if she wouldn't feel so guilty if she'd sustained more injuries.

Shit, what was *wrong* with her? She shouldn't even be thinking that.

Zephyr let Leah guide her inside the house, straight to the living area with the view, and sank into the couch. The older woman rushed to the kitchen, dialing on her phone and pouring a glass of water, mixing a sachet of electrolytes into them. Zephyr wasn't dehydrated but she accepted the drink gratefully and took small sips, scared of triggering her gag reflex again.

"Please come to the house, Dr. Nei." She heard Leah talk on the phone. "Yes. Okay."

The older woman turned to her, her face creased with concern. "She will be here in ten minutes. I need to inform Alpha."

Zephyr shook her head. "No, he has an important meeting." That was all she knew. He was meeting some kind of a source who had some big information about something. "Just leave him a text."

Leah hesitated, but then she nodded, typing on her device. The dogs settled around her once again, this time both Bear and Bandit putting their heads on her stomach and Baron curling up at her feet, and the sight made her lips curl up in a smile, reminding her of this video she'd seen once while scrolling through puppy videos. It had been a video of a woman with a baby and her two dogs sitting next to her, because she had been expecting another.

Zephyr brushed their fur with her fingers when, suddenly,

she stilled.

Memories flashed through her mind from a little before the funeral—of Bear, suddenly putting his head on her stomach and sticking to her side, of Bandit, always being two steps behind her, and of Baron, aloof and detached, suddenly being close to her. Zephyr had chalked all their behaviors to them missing her or being close to her during her grief. But what if it wasn't just that? What if...

She looked down at her stomach in disbelief.

Her curvy, soft stomach with love handles, that had become a bit curvier, and she hadn't even noticed.

More memories flashed—Alpha pushing her into the bed, his cock deep inside her, coming inside her body. They had never used protection, and she hadn't wanted to.

But now that the possibility was staring her in the face, she could feel vestiges of panic begin to bloom within her.

Could she be...?

"Hello, Zephyr," Dr. Nei's voice brought her head up, her mind in a daze, muddled by the fact that she'd been in a hospital and getting checked by doctors, but no one had noticed. Maybe no one had specifically looked for it, given her superficial injuries and her stress and hormonal history.

Dr. Nei, a gorgeous dark-skinned woman in her fifties, came into the living room. She was dressed in a sharp suit and carried a small suitcase Zephyr had never seen her without. She took a seat on the couch adjacent to her. "What's going on?" she asked.

Zephyr stared at her, processing, wondering how this would change everything, and spoke, hearing the tremor in her voice. "I need you to test me."

"For what?" the doctor asked, setting her suitcase to the side.

"Pregnancy."

DANTE

CHAPTER 6

DANTE, TENEBRAE CITY

T HE LOUD, HAPPY BABY giggle was the only light in their lives these days.

Dante blew a raspberry on the soft tummy of his little princess, and Tempest rewarded him with a giggle worthy enough to befall kingdoms. If happiness could be weaponized, this precious bundle of joy in their lives would have conquered everything and ruled with a toothless smile and a grubby fist.

"There hasn't been any news, boss."

The words coming from the phone speaker pulled him back out of the happy space and into the fucked up reality they were living in, where countless babies like his own were shoved into a life of pain every single day, and he couldn't do a damn thing about it, not with limited capacity and limited information. And the main source of his information was nowhere to be found for the last five weeks. That was the longest Vin had ever gone without contact, and he had to believe that was because he was deep undercover and not deep under the ground.

"That'll be all," he dismissed his man, his mind spinning in circles. So far, they'd not been able to uncover anything substantial enough for them to do any damage to the organization.

The fucking Syndicate.

Hell, they didn't even know enough about its operations to find a grip to uproot anything. Dante had been in this shady underbelly of the world long enough to contemplate that maybe, as much as he'd hate it, they might not be able to uproot a system like that. The more they discovered about The Syndicate, the more he realized that it was a lot more complex than they'd ever thought, like the underground root network of a giant tree, spread far and wide and deep under the surface, hidden from the world, mingled so tightly that uprooting the entire system seemed impossible, the roots strong enough and symbiotic enough that even if someone cut the tree down, a new one would grow in its place over time.

The others, in their optimism, somehow believed that they would be able to chop it off, even a logical bastard like Tristan. But he was more emotional than he let on, and when it came to the organization responsible for his sister's disappearance, he operated on pure emotion. Dante had been with the man long enough to witness that. But Dante, as emotional as he was, operated on pure logic when it came to The Syndicate. He didn't have the emotional baggage, even though the organization had been indirectly responsible for many things in his life. No, he thought as a businessman, as a mafia kingpin, and from his contemplation, it looked grim. It wasn't a thought he necessarily shared with the others; there was no need at the moment. It was better to have optimism and hope. He knew the ways it could motivate a man to wait patiently for things to unfold. The living proof of that patience kicked her chubby feet in the air, grinning up at him.

Dante grinned back, wondering how she would grow up in this ugly, ugly world. Though he would protect her as much as he could, so would the others she would call family; it worried him. When the air itself became poisoned, no barrier could prevent it from seeping under the cracks, toxic fumes making their way into the very lungs that needed it to breathe. He could only keep her in a vacuum for so long before she rebelled, and knowing the kind of father he had had, he never, never wanted to be like that to her. He wanted to be a good father and a good friend to her, a guide she could turn to and the ground she could grow on. He didn't know how she would do it, but as Amara liked to remind him, with all the love she got from everyone around her, she would figure it out.

The ringing of the phone broke through his worrisome thoughts of the future.

He pressed the speaker again as Tempest turned on her stomach and began to crawl away from him. Since she'd come into their lives, his office had started looking more like a daycare and less like a lion's den.

"Dante." He heard Morana's voice over the speakers, and a genuine smile came over his face. He'd never thought Morana would ever integrate into his life and become such an intrinsic part of his family. Even knowing Tristan's obsession with her through the years had never led him to imagine she'd fill up his heart like a sibling. Seeing Morana shot and heal from it had just made him realize even more how important she was to his family.

"How's my favorite hacker doing?" Dante asked, watching as Tempest crawled over to where Lulu was peacefully napping. The fucking cat had a bed and still chose to sleep anywhere but on it. With Amara away to check on the kids at the rehabilitation center they'd been working on for over a year, both their daughter and their cat were left under his care. Not that he minded the company.

"Such a charmer." He could hear Morana's eyes rolling in her tone before she got quiet

It was the silence that made Dante focus. Morana talked, and she was comfortable enough in his company to talk quite a bit. So the silence was... unusual. Anything unusual had his attention these days.

"What's going on?" he asked quietly, keeping his eyes on his crawling baby girl but his attention on the call.

Morana hesitated. "I... there's something I wanted to talk to you about, something I don't know how to say."

His heart suddenly dropped. "Is it about Amara?"

"No, no, no!" Morana rushed to reassure him. "Nothing about her. She's great, fantastic even. I spoke to her yesterday, and she's excited about planning my goddaughter's first birthday."

He relaxed, his muscles easing. As long as his wife was good, he'd be good. His *wife*. It felt so good to him to call her that, even in his head, after waiting so long for it.

"I can't believe it's already been a year." A year of the happiest he'd been, marred with scars of their world and their loss. Every time he remembered his precious angel, the one who didn't make it, it made his heart ache. Amara had planted a magnolia tree in her name next to the gazebo out back, and though it was just a small plant at the moment, the idea of nurturing it did feel good to him. That tree was Serenity, his angel baby, and she would grow roots in their home, just in a different way.

He shook off the thoughts and focused on Morana. "So, what is this about?" He watched as Tempest crawled over the sleeping feline. Lulu, used to the antics now, simply raised her head and went back to napping, unperturbed by the tiny human, the same size as she, grabbing her ears. It was amusing, to say the least.

He heard Morana take a deep breath, and his shoulders tensed as she inhaled. She uttered the one name that had been a mystery around them since they had learned of The Syndicate.

"The Shadow Man."

Of course, it was him. Mysterious fucker. They had discussed the enigma many times, so Dante didn't understand why Morana was suddenly so anxious about him. "What about him?"

"He sent me a message last night," she started. "A message with location details that I'm tracking as we speak. He's never sent them so easily, and I'm convinced he wants me to trace it."

That piqued his curiosity. What kind of game was the bastard playing? From the little they knew about the Shadow Man, his motives for doing anything were as mysterious as he was. Why he'd helped Morana, led them to the house where they found Xander, why he'd been there hunting the man who had kidnapped Zephyr and murdered his sister—only he knew his reasons. The closest anyone had come to finding anything had been his half-brother Alpha since he had met the infamous man, but only because the Shadow Man had wanted to talk. There was nothing substantial though they had an inkling it was something to do with The Syndicate, Dante hated not knowing more. It was like playing blind chess, unable to see all the pieces on the board except his own, with no idea of his opponent's next moves. It was *frustrating.*

"There were also some images attached to the message."

Morana's words made him blink, watching as his daughter's eyelids began to droop. "Images? Of what?"

He heard her swallow. Whatever she was going to say had her bracing herself, which in turn had him bracing himself.

"I think it's her... Luna."

His breath whooshed out of him. Dante stared at the screen of his phone, unable to believe what he was hearing, feeling the impact of the syllables in his chest.

Luna.

At this point, she almost seemed like a myth, an elusive legend they had been chasing for decades.

Luna.

They had never seen her, didn't know what she looked like. Her images? The Shadow Man sent her images? Dante wouldn't be surprised if the man knew they had been looking for her, but the fact that he'd just sent the images was odd. *What the hell?*

Even though she wasn't his younger sister by blood, searching for her for so many years with Tristan, someone he thought of as a brother, she felt like his own. She felt like a little sister he never knew about until too late, a sister he had never seen or met but needed to.

The blood rushed through his body, his pulse getting warmer as the words seeped into his senses.

"Are you sure?" he asked, even knowing the answer. Morana would never say something of this severity unless she was certain of it. She knew the stakes, probably better than anyone else.

"Pretty much," she answered. Dante let it sink in for a minute before something else caught his attention.

Morana had been the one to call him with this news, not Tristan. He could not imagine Tristan, the man who had relentlessly searched for his sister, sometimes chasing leads with Dante himself, not calling Dante with this update the moment he had it. For all his external disdain, he knew Tristan thought of him as family too.

That only meant one thing.

"Tristan doesn't know," Dante stated, the words leaving a sour taste in his mouth. It didn't feel right that he didn't. He should be the first to know. But knowing Morana, he knew there had to be a reason.

"Not yet," Morana sighed. "A, I want to be one hundred percent sure before I get his hopes up, which I will be in a few hours. Tonight at the latest, hopefully."

That made sense.

"And B, and this is what I wanted to talk to you about..." she trailed off.

Dante waited, letting her assemble her thoughts while his mind wrapped around the idea that they might actually find Luna, the reality of it hitting him right in the solar plexus.

Morana inhaled deeply. "One of the photos is... intimate."

Dante felt himself frown. "Intimate, how?"

"Like... like a photo you would take of Amara if she was wearing your shirt the morning after being with her, satisfied, disheveled but glowing."

"Okay." He watched Tempest distractedly as she fell asleep

94

on Lulu, contemplating what Morana meant.

"It's a lover's gaze, Dante," Morana clarified for him. "And I think the Shadow Man took that photo. There is a reason that he attached that photo with the others, why his text to me was more personal than direct. If my hunch is right, which I have to admit is more often than not, he is her lover, and he wants us to know that."

This was the second time in as many minutes that words sunk into him with impact. He picked the phone up from the rug where he sat, turned it off the speaker, and pressed it to his ear as if the action could somehow send the words deeper inside his brain.

"You're saying *the Shadow Man*," he started, his tone disbelieving, "the fucking *myth* in the underworld we didn't even know about until a while ago, that man... *is with Luna?* Isn't it possible that he simply got the photo from somewhere else like he did the rest?"

It sounded wild, even as he voiced it out. The Shadow Man was a faceless, nameless rogue with some mysterious reason for popping in and out of their lives.

"He could have acquired it from elsewhere," Morana admitted. "But he *wanted* us to see that image. It kind of makes sense the more I think about it. That's the only thing that can explain why he's been involved in our lives or why he contacted me. He wanted information about a particular shipment, and he was looking into the time we were all taken. She is the only link to all of it."

The more Morana spoke, the more the puzzle pieces fit. Not all of them, but some of them. He had to admit she could be right about this.

"So you think he was searching for her too?" Dante asked.

"Or for her past," Morana put in. "It's possible that looking for her origin is what led him to us."

Fuck.

It did sound plausible.

"I don't know how to tell any of this to Tristan." Dante heard the clacking of a keyboard in the background as she spoke. "The last time the Shadow Man sent us a location, I told Tristan immediately, and it ended up being a wild goose chase. We found Xander, and I'm so grateful for that, don't get me wrong. But I know how much it deflated Tristan that it wasn't his sister. I saw how his hope got crushed." Morana's voice cracked. "I don't want to do that to him again. You know he's not good at processing emotions, and he's already been more intense since the shooting, and I just..."

Dante sighed. He could understand where she was coming from. The need to emotionally protect the ones they loved was strong in all of them. But Dante also knew what keeping things from a partner could do to a relationship, no matter how strong. He still remembered how he had almost broken a decade-long relationship by keeping something from Amara, how he had lost her while she'd been pregnant. He remembered because they had both paid a price for it, and he felt it every day that his little princess breathed, and his little angel who never made it watched over her sister. It was a wound that would probably never heal fully, and a wound they could have maybe avoided if his decision to keep something from Amara hadn't led her to run away from him, making them both more vulnerable.

And even though he never meddled into Tristan and Morana's relationship, he needed to now. So, with the experience of his past mistake, watching his baby girl sleep peacefully, Dante gave Morana the most sincere advice he could give someone. "Take it from someone who has fucked up before, don't ever keep something from your partner. It doesn't matter how good your intentions are or that they come from a protective place; it will hurt them regardless when they find out. In fact, it hurts them more. Amara is forgiving by nature, and I'm a lucky bastard because of it. But Tristan..."

He let it trail off, hearing Morana's quick intake of breath. She knew the man better than anyone in the world, she knew his hatred and she knew his love, and she was smart enough to figure out what Dante meant. Tristan might love her enough to forgive her, but there would be a dent in his trust that might take a long time to repair.

"Love sometimes blinds us, Morana," Dante said, almost soothing her because she needed the balm occasionally when dealing with a man like Tristan. "Don't let it blind you to the fact that he's an adult. I don't see him struggling after the last wild goose chase, as you say. He might have been disappointed, but he's not broken, and that's because he has you by his side as he processes and deals with things. He trusts you, so don't break that."

He knew his words had hit the mark when the line stayed silent for a while. Morana was probably calculating all the pros and cons, weighing the different ways it could go wrong, strategizing how to break the news with the least damage.

A deep sigh echoed in his ear. "You're right. I need to tell him. I will tell him tonight when he gets back."

Dante nodded, relief flooding his chest. He was glad not to be put in the position of knowing something but keeping it from his brother, one of his heart rather than blood. He was also glad not to witness their relationship in turmoil due to lack of communication. He was extra glad because he wanted them to be godparents in his baby's life for a long time. As long as they were all on the same page, they could figure stuff out.

"Where has he gone?" he asked, getting up to scoop his little princess so she would stop suffocating the poor cat. She was so tiny half her body fit into the palm of his hand, the weight a reminder of the miracle Dante and Amara had experienced. She was small, but she possessed the soul of a warrior like her mama. When thoughts about how she would grow up in this cruel world worried him, he reminded himself of that, of the fact that she had fought her way into this world through the worst of times and shined like gold. Not the liquid gold that filled up their cracks and solidified, but the solid gold that could not be broken without immense heat. And it was his job to ensure she never felt that heat.

"He has a meeting with one of the Duncet family insiders after he drops Xander off for his session."

Dante's thoughts shifted from Tempest to the young boy who had somehow integrated into their odd family. A boy, Tristan had confided in him, was like Damian, his actual brother he protected by keeping him away from this world. Dante was glad Tristan and Morana were accepting and loving, unlike his father, who had only alienated Damian by making him feel like a burden. As a high-functioning autistic boy, it hadn't been easy for his brother within the compound. He was thriving in the outside world, and Dante would make sure he always did. Xander, as they'd recently found out, was high-functioning autistic as well. Tristan and Morana, being the incredible guardians they already were, were doing everything they possibly could to give the boy all the tools he needed to grow up into a good adult.

It was his past that made Dante a little apprehensive. The fact that they couldn't find anything on him, the fact that the Shadow Man had led them to him, the fact that he didn't trust the Shadow Man an iota—it was all too weird. They didn't know his history, and without knowing what the boy had endured, they couldn't help his future. They could just wait and watch, he supposed.

"How are they both doing?"

Morana snorted. "They have both bonded more over the fact that they don't like me getting shot."

Dante felt his lips curl in a smile even though his thoughts were going a hundred miles a minute. He placed his little princess in the little crib she had in his office, tucking the soft blanket around her as her lips settled in a cute pout. Settling her, he walked to the window, watching the hills he called home, the clouds rolling along the horizon, his mind somber.

"If you are right and the Shadow Man is her lover," he mused out loud, "Tristan won't be happy. I'd suggest keeping that little theory to us until we have confirmation. He's waited a long time for this. No point ruining that with speculation at this point. Let's just focus on her."

"You're right." Morana sighed. "I know. I don't understand any of it or what to make of it. Maybe I am wrong, and he's not involved with her. Or if yes, maybe he was and isn't anymore. Or maybe if he still is, he won't care since he's inviting us to find her. But if he is involved with her and he cares, we don't know anything about him to predict how any of it will go. The only thing I can find about him is what he wants found. We need information we don't have."

That was the issue. They were all playing chess in the dark, with a myth who was synonymous with it.

He would tell Amara tonight, and Morana would tell Tristan tonight. If she decoded the lead over the night, the game would change when the sun came up.

The clouds rumbled.

A storm was coming.

Chapter 7

Unknown

THINGS WERE FALLING APART, exactly as he intended.

The Syndicate had been alive for many, many decades, forty years of which he had spent at the helm. He had been one of the few responsible for their restructuring and organization into one of the strongest silent forces in the world. He had rebranded, rebuilt, and remodeled their organization from the top down in a way that ensured everyone at each level stayed protected. If someone did get compromised, they were disposed of and replaced. The others had called him one of the snakeheads for a reason—he led the entire body through the seedy underbelly of their world, making sure everything stayed hidden in the tall grass, out of sight, naming him after the snake ring he always wore on his middle finger, a symbol that had been adapted into the entire organization at every level, a symbol, the true purpose of which, only he and a few others knew, and most of them were dead.

He sat on a yacht, swaying with the waves, and read the report one of the junior-level associates had sent him on the phone while debauchery happened all around him. It didn't faze him anymore. In the beginning, he had partook in his own enjoyment, but over time, it all began to blend together. Pussy was pussy and cock was cock. Nudity became stale when it was the norm. It was the personality that attracted him, the spirits that he liked to break and bend and birth. The headiness of knowing he could shatter a soul without laying a finger on it is what made him feel like a true god.

And none had been sweeter to break than his little red. Such a sweet, soft delight, so malleable. He hadn't understood her malleability meant she bent before she could break. It had been a shame when he'd had to let her go because of the others in the organization.

Well, now there weren't any others. And he could have her again one last time, perhaps.

The body of the last of his associates was somewhere deep in the sea, being fed on by the sharks, not dissimilar to how they'd been.

"Sir, would you like a glass of something?" a sweet little thing asked him, and he shook his head. Usually, he would have dragged her on his lap, but he was more distracted these days.

A business party was on board for a new public leader in some corner of the world. He scoffed. Who the world thought was a good man was buried in underage pussy and snorting a line of illegal substances from another's tits. The Syndicate was the prime supplier of both for such events, hiding behind multiple layers of smaller companies. There was not a trade the organization didn't have its hands in—sex, drugs, weapons, *more*. If there was a buyer for it, The Syndicate would be involved in the supply, but never with their name. Most didn't even know about its existence.

And even though everything had a place, nothing, absolutely nothing, sold like power in the world. Human beings, at their core, were perverted beasts cloaking their true nature with civilization. Give humans a chance to let out their perversions and feel powerful, even momentarily, and they would do anything to do it again, and again, and again, just to experience the high. Some even had the thrill of pretending to be upstanding, upright humans while unleashing their inner selves in secret, another twisted manifestation of power.

He had a hoard of evidence against the most powerful kings and kingmakers of the world. If he wanted, he could release just a sliver and crumble entire systems. And that was the real rush of it all for him too—the power, but of a different kind. He truly didn't care about the systems or the sins, it was making sure he was still a god amongst men, that he was still an adversary no one would dare to cross, that drove him now.

He hadn't made many mistakes in his time except one, one crack that had split over time and became a gorge so deep everything was falling into it.

His one small mistake had come to bite him back in the

head. But it was a rush too, a challenge after a very long time, a test to prove his mettle and defeat a worthy opponent.

It was survival of the fittest in their world, and he had been and would continue to be the fittest of them all.

CHAPTER 8

LYLA, GLADESTONE

L YLA LAY IN BED, sated, sore, and still famished for him. She was panting, her heart running a million miles a minute, the momentum making her languid and lethargic, but her heart still hungered, even though they had spent the last hour so vigorously it was a miracle the bed hadn't broken, and neither had her pussy.

Turning her head on the pillow, she looked at Dainn, seeing his muscular chest rise and fall rapidly as he caught his own breath, his eyes closed, and his head turned to the ceiling. They had spent the entire day in the suite, ordering room service, eating, showering, and just making love against every flat surface they could find. They had always come together explosively, but now there was desperation there, of watching each other and etching it all to memory, of spending every second they had together pressed into each other so their flesh could remember, their bones could recall, their blood could carry the moments through their bodies in the absence. They started on the balcony, came inside to the couch, then the shower, the tub, the countertop, and finally the bed. If she hadn't been with him for as long as she had, she would've been amazed at his stamina. To be honest, she was amazed at her own. It was impressive that she'd somehow survived their fucking marathon, though her ability to move a muscle in the foreseeable future was debatable.

But knowing that she would be leaving tomorrow, that she had a new world and new people she knew nothing about and who knew nothing about who she was, and yet were a part of her past, made her want to drown herself in the pleasure of the moment and delay the inevitable as long as possible. And she knew he understood that, knowing her as well as he did. She just asked, and he delivered.

She extended her hand, running her fingers through his dark strands that were messed up after hours of his workout, her pale skin contrasting against his dark, a fitting visual for their insides too. But she wondered as she drifted her digits lazily through his hair about what was to come. She would meet her family, one she hadn't known about, and she would see her son, see how he had grown up into the boy he was. It was terrifying, but she couldn't deny it; she was thrilled not to make the choice. Had it been up to her, she didn't know if she would've been ready for years to meet them. Maybe see them from a distance to assuage her own curiosity, but her self-worth still didn't let her believe she would make any positive additions to their lives. In fact, her biggest fear was disrupting it. She didn't want that, not for a brother who had been looking for her for so long and a son she had sacrificed with such love.

"Stop overthinking." The words, low but precise, filled the room.

Her hand paused for a second before she continued petting him, marveling at the fact that he knew her thought patterns so well. But then, that was what he did. He studied, learned, and used patterns against people. Not her, she knew that. For some insane reason, she still didn't understand, she was the only exception to his entire personality, immune to his lies and manipulations, to his pretenses and deceit, to his power moves and his corruption. The only one under his protection and his care, the one he showed his true self to without any holds barred. She loved that about him, that he was real with her.

And who would've thought the man the whole underworld feared, the man with more blood on his burned hands than she would ever even know, the man who existed in the shadows, would like being petted post-coitus by a small woman with not a lot to offer? It was such a conundrum.

"Why me?" she uttered the question that had been inside her for six years. Why her? Why did he pick her of all the other girls in her exact position? She knew now that it wasn't because of her brother or his power, because Dainn had made his choice much before he traced her past and her birth identity. He had been coming to her, protecting her, long before he knew she was related to a powerful circle.

He turned his neck, his mismatched, hypnotic eyes coming to her, alert despite the exhaustion he had to be feeling, giving her the full extent of that focus that knocked her breath out of her lungs every time.

"You already know, *flamma*," he spoke in a low tone, his words direct. He didn't think of himself as a poetic man, but the words he gave her bloomed in her heart like poetry in a land of misery.

"Because I trusted you?" she implored, knowing he was addicted to her trust, something he had told her often.

He sighed, turning fully to face her and dragging her body closer, pressing his knee between her legs where she was already sore enough she knew she had to walk consciously tomorrow. But she liked that. She wanted to feel him inside her, leave with her flesh remembering the touch of his flesh, the kiss of his metal adornments deep within her. She wanted to savor it, her heart afraid, not knowing when she would be with him again like this.

He played with a strand of her hair, his gaze steady on her face. "Where is this coming from?"

She shrugged. She didn't know. She just wanted to stay there, in that moment, locked with him and away from the world, hiding in the suite high above the ground where nothing and no one could touch them. Because tomorrow would change things, and she didn't know what the fallout of that would be. She didn't want to believe that it would impact their relationship; she didn't think it would, but the part of her that had found a home with him, in him, was scared of losing it. She didn't want to be lost again, adrift out in a world full of people but alone. She felt seen with him, felt understood with him, and she didn't want to lose that.

And she knew she would, even if temporarily. He couldn't come with her.

She swallowed. "I'm scared." The words came out as a whisper, a soft confession between their faces, a safe secret she entrusted in the dark with him. As long as she was with him, her vulnerability was alright. The dark couldn't hurt her, and neither could the light. He owned both with different faces and different names, but the same man and the man was hers. For some reason, he was hers.

But he wasn't normal either. When another would have maybe gentled at her confession, he got a glint in his eyes, as if hunting the things that scared her were his favorite hobby. Maybe a part of him liked her scared, as long as she was with him.

"Scared of what?" he asked, his fingers stroking her cheek.

Lyla settled deeper into her pillow, turning her gaze lower and staring at his neck. He had a very attractive neck, muscular but not bulky, with veins vining up a side and an Adam's apple that stayed steady in the face of everything. She couldn't remember him swallowing nervously as she tended to.

"Everything," she admitted.

"Eyes, *flamma*," he demanded. She turned her gaze up and locked eyes with him.

"Tell me what scares you."

A breath left her. "I don't know. The unknown. The change. I don't know what's going to happen. I want to go back, back where I can see the mountains and the sea, where I can cook. Back where Dr. Manson sees me, Bessie helps me pick books to read, and Roy teaches me about gardening. Back with *you*. You and your extravagant helicopters and beautiful green-house and tight security where I feel safe. I want to go *home* but a part of me knows I have to see this through. And it all scares me."

"*Flamma*," Dainn spoke softly, his mismatched eyes staring deep into hers, his term of endearment for her always soften-ing her inside. "It will always be yours. I will always be yours. No matter what happens, you can come home whenever you want. All of it is yours. You know this."

He must have seen the doubt in her look because he pressed a kiss to her nose. "I'm not going with you for a reason."

She knew. She understood. But her brain still didn't accept. "Tell me again," she urged him. She needed to understand why he would choose to leave her alone now after all his actions and promises.

He exhaled. "Because if I did, it would make it about me.

About the Shadow Man. They would get distracted by that, and you deserve better. It's about *you.* As much as I don't like it for selfish reasons, it's your past and possibly your future if you choose it that way."

"And if I choose it?"

"Then you will have it."

Just like that. She asked and he delivered.

Her eyes began to burn as his words penetrated. He was doing it for her, letting her have her moment with her past. And knowing him, it couldn't be easy. He was as territorial of her, if not more, as she was of him. He could've easily stood by her side, and she would've wanted him to, but his words made sense. Shadow Man was a much bigger entity and even without wanting it, it would've attracted their attention. He was giving up a lot for her.

"There's also an added element to it," he continued, his thigh comfortable just between her legs, muscular and strong and more than double the size of hers. While sex was nothing new to her, intimacy was. Holding another body close, looking into someone's eyes after letting them into her body with desire and consent, was a heady feeling, a different feeling, one that almost made her feel a little shy sometimes. He had seen the ugliest parts of her, and yet, it was in these moments that she felt the most vulnerable. And he fed off of it. She knew her emotions, her ability to feel so much, the entire range of it, was something he was hooked to, and she didn't mind one bit. Because she was hooked to his cool, calculated outlook on things, his lack of consciousness yet his ability to do the right thing, his ability to remain calm in crisis and control every conundrum. They were so different, she and him, and yet so complimentary.

"What?" she asked a little breathlessly, her nipples tightening with the stimulation. It was crazy how her body had trained itself to respond to the littlest stimuli for him, flooding itself with arousal and pooling with wetness to prepare to accommodate him, even if they weren't being sexual and just snuggling like they were right then.

"Some of them know the Blackthorne name or recognize me as the reclusive CEO of the Blackthorne Group."

His ability to remove himself from a part of his identity was impressive. The words hung between them, and Lyla blinked as she processed them.

"Who could?" She knew all about the group from the photos he had shown and explained to her. Tristan, her brother, and Morana, his girlfriend. Dante, their friend, and Amara, his wife. Alpha, Dante's half-brother, and Zephyr, his wife who was also the sister of Zenith, the real Morana, who had been Lyla's friend and was now dead. And Xander, who was almost adopted by Tristan and Morana.

It was complicated, understanding so many interpersonal dynamics and how they all operated. To someone who'd always been alone and hadn't had any friends, she didn't know how they all managed so many relationships with ease, but it wasn't something she was opposed to learning if need be.

"Who knows? Dante possibly," he told her. "I've seen him socially a few times during his father's reign. Maybe Amara. I attended a conference she'd been speaking at once a few years ago."

This was fascinating, this facade of his life she wanted to see more of too. It made her feel powerful seeing him fool everyone while being in on the truth with him.

"Did you know who she was or was it a coincidence?" Lyla asked, curious and invested in this side of his past that she didn't know about.

He played with her breast, almost mindlessly, as though it was a stress ball. "I knew who she was."

Lyla waited in silence, letting him decide if he wanted to share more. Thankfully, he did. His eyes sharpened on hers, and he began speaking again. "The conference had been about topics related to children. Special children, child behavior. Her presentation had been about child loss and coping mechanisms, especially for mothers. We spoke for a few minutes afterward. I was interested in the topic."

He didn't have to specify why. Lyla knew. Still, she asked. "When was this?"

"Six years ago."

Of course, it was. She wasn't even surprised. They had met six years ago and he had taken Xander under his care, and next thing, he had gone to attend a conference about children and child loss coping. Her stomach felt heavy as she realized the extent of things he'd silently done for her over the years, never once letting on what he'd been doing. Back then, she remembered so vividly, she'd just been wanting to see him again and have him bid on her so he could take her out of that hellhole. But in retrospect, she realized how shortsighted she had been, though she didn't blame herself. He had been playing the long game, keeping her safe, building her a home, raising her child and getting him to family, all the while working to take down the biggest, most dangerous organization in the world that had been in existence for longer than she knew. Just the extent of everything hit her all at once, making her heart race.

Before he could move, she tackled him, pressing a hard kiss to his lips, pouring the intensity of everything she was feeling, everything happening inside her into his lips, speaking to him in the oldest language that communicated everything words could say, and he reciprocated. His hand tightened possessively over her breast, the other on her jaw, guiding her mouth and giving her more intensity in return.

After a few minutes of just making out naked, he pulled away a few inches, his gaze searching hers, possibly for why she'd suddenly attacked him. He likely found whatever answer he was looking for, and an air of satisfaction enveloped them, buzzing around him, frolicking around her.

She returned back to their conversation, her curiosity still alight. "So, they've all met you?"

"Not all of them. Some as Blackthorne, some as Shadow Man," he replied, answering her question but not elaborating more on that.

The more Lyla learned about him, the more enamored she became with both sides of him. She'd seen him be the businessman, a sharp, dominant force of a man who cut deals and charmed people in a blink, a mask he wore with such ease she would never have suspected anything otherwise if she didn't know the man underneath. And she'd seen him be the Shadow Man, a lethal, dangerous, quiet personality that liked hiding more than being seen, that only saw people before killing them. And then she had seen him real, as he was right then.

"But only I have met Dainn." She loved that.

"And only you will, *flamma*," he promised. "I will become whatever I have to for everyone else. Not for you. For you, I am as I am, every damaged, deranged part of me."

She leaned forward and kissed him softly this time, both their lips sensitive from all the kisses they had shared but not caring. He plunged his hand into her hair, holding her still as he ravaged her mouth, a sound leaving him as their tongues danced that filled her with awe. They had learned this art together, kissing with this mix of sensuality and softness, of passion and possession, of deviance and devotion. Lyla had never known kisses could mean so many things, that mouths could move so beautifully in a dance against each other.

They broke free, and she brushed his hair back from his forehead, bringing her hand lower to his jaw where the shadow had darkened. The marks of them were tingling around her mouth, her breasts, her inner thighs, everywhere he had feasted on her.

"Will you miss me?"

He plucked at one of her nipples almost lazily, the action full of propriety, one she knew was mirrored in herself.

"No."

Her heart sank at the one word before she could stop it. He chuckled, pinching the nipple hard as though punishing her for the thought, making her gasp.

"I might not be going with you, but I spent six years being your shadow. I will not miss you because I will be watching you."

The thought put her mind at ease. She knew from the books she had been reading that it was probably not the normal response to what he said, but Dr. Manson always reminded her, other people's normal could never be hers, that she was completely valid in feeling however she felt. And all she felt hearing him say that he'd not be letting her out of his sight was a relief. Because if he was watching her, nothing could get to her again. And all she felt was cherished, protected, adored by his entire attention, his own affection, for her.

He would be there, even if no one could see. Even if she couldn't see, he would be there, and everything would be okay.

"Promise?"

He just kissed her in reply. He was as addicted to their kisses as she was. There was something about them that just felt... *right*. So right.

She pulled back and stared at him, giving him another one of her fears. "I... I have always been Lyla. I don't know Luna. I don't feel like her. But what if I can't be either of them? What if they want me to be Luna and I can't be? Or what if I want to be her and lose Lyla? Who will I even be if that happens?"

His thumb brushed over her cheek. "You will always be mine, *flamma. My flamma.* Names don't matter. They're clothes you can choose to wear one day and discard the next. You could be Lilith or Lily or Lina, Luna or Lyla, or completely nameless. It doesn't matter. What matters is who you are in your skin and bones. And all I see—" he held her hand, bringing it up to his lips "—is a woman who owns the world in her small, soft, sexy little hands and doesn't even know it." Another kiss to her fingers.

"You asked me why you?" The intense look in his eyes, combined with his words, was undoing her. "Because you're my flame, a little source of light and warmth in a void full of darkness and death, small but capable of becoming an inferno with the right fuel. And though I was always full of dark and death, for you, I have embraced it, become it, so you can keep flickering without fear. I am the void all monsters fear so *you* never have to be scared of anything. Not with me."

Words locked in her throat in a ball of fire that made her eyes burn. He called her his flame but the truth was that he was hers, warming her in places she had always been cold, sustaining her in places she had been shivering, illuminating her life in places that had never seen the light.

"I love you," she told him for the millionth time, meaning it more and more each time.

"I know," he replied for the millionth time, everything in his gaze saying what his lips never did as always.

"I think you might love me too, Dainn," she whispered in the space between their mouths.

His eyes darkened. "If there was ever any love in this world of mine," he began, then stopped, his words tattooed in her bones.

"It would be me," she completed, still marveling, wondering, at how this was her life. The things he said to her, the most beautiful words in that cool, direct way of his, made everything inside her melt like the wax on a candle. When she had been a little girl, alone in the dark, she had dreamed of someone saving her from the demons that fed off of her. As she'd grown up, the dreams had died. And then, she'd bumped into a man on a stormy night, and everything had changed.

Some days, she still couldn't believe it was all real and not a dream, that she was lucky enough to have found herself, to have had the chance to heal, to be so deeply loved by a man who had and would continue to burn the world for her.

But she wasn't going to complain.

No, she was going to spend the last night with her man and love him with all her heart, etching it into their memories until they could be together again.

MORANA

CHAPTER 9

MORANA, SHADOW PORT

X ANDER WAS UP TO something.

Morana didn't know why exactly, but she was sitting on one of the kitchen island stools with her laptop on the countertop, keeping an eye on her programs running the trace, watching the little timer in the corner ticking down with each second. She was getting closer to the twenty-four-hour mark, and her anxiety was peaking with each declining number, both because it was her responsibility and her forte to crack this thing open and because Tristan was going to come back any second, and she couldn't hide it from him.

Talking to Dante a few hours ago had given her the perspective she'd needed. Tristan was an adult, and though every instinct inside her wanted to protect him from any disappointment, and though it came from a place of love, she had to quell it down and let him make his own informed decisions. She could only stand and support him regardless of how things panned out.

Even though she was very sure Dante had been with Tempest—there was a certain softness in his voice whenever he was around her goddaughter—he had given her solid advice. Morana couldn't believe some days that she had a life now where she not only had family and friends but a generation of kids she was now responsible for as well. Speaking of, she looked at Xander making a cucumber, tomato and cheese sandwich, one of his favorites for some reason, and narrowed her eyes.

He'd been making that sandwich for fifteen minutes. It usually only took him five.

He was hovering for some reason.

Morana rested her arms on the countertop, feeling the cool stone on her skin, and watched the boy. "What's going on with you?"

Xander stopped in the process of slicing bread, the knife midway between the loaf, his head bent in concentration. "What's going on with you?"

Morana blinked, surprised at the question. "What do you mean?"

The boy pulled the knife out from the loaf, wiped it once, twice, and then started slicing again. Surprisingly, Tristan hadn't been the one to teach him how to do that. The sandwich had been one of the first things he'd shared was his favorite, and he didn't let anyone else make it for him. The cucumber and tomato had to be cut in a certain way, and the bread had to be sliced precisely in a certain thickness, and no one got

RUNYX

it right but him. Tristan had made him the sandwich once and Xander had politely said, "You are a great cook but a bad sandwich maker."

It had been one of the funniest things to see the look on Tristan's face.

But it was just one of those very *Xander* things. That was exactly why Morana knew how long it took him to make.

Xander finished slicing his bread *just right* and Morana didn't interrupt him, knowing he would start all over again if disturbed. Once he was done, he neatly put away all the ingredients and plated two sandwiches, bringing one to her.

Surprised, Morana looked down at the offering.

"You haven't eaten anything all day."

She shouldn't have been surprised he had noticed. The boy was more observant than people gave him credit for. Just because he was different, people didn't care to notice him. Morana had seen that happen in the school he was in, with his peers and even some teachers, and it made her blood boil. She had almost decided to pull him out and homeschool him, get him the best teachers who could appreciate and encourage his keen mind and hunger for learning new things, but his psychologist had suggested otherwise for the time being. Dr. Kol, one of Amara's trusted colleagues, had been fabulous with Xander. He believed that Xander would do better if, at least for a few years, he was a part of social settings and learned different social environments, good and bad. That would help

126

him adapt and operate better as an adult in the future. That didn't mean she couldn't leak certain *secrets* of people who were mean to him. He'd also suggested getting him a dog, which they would soon do since Xander had shown a preference for canines.

"Thanks." Morana felt her stomach rumbling at the sight of the food. She picked it up with her right hand, her left feeling numb after the grueling typing she'd been doing throughout the day, and took a huge bite of it. The fresh flavors burst on her tongue, making her groan. "This is amazing," she mumbled through a full mouth, chewing slowly.

"You should eat on time. You have medicines to take," Of course, Tristan would train his miniature medical disciplinary to monitor her in his absence.

Morana rolled her eyes. "Yes, sir. I'll keep that in mind."

"You should also get your left shoulder checked. You haven't moved it in three hours." Xander dropped his observation, his tone without inflection, his eyes on the counter as he picked up the sandwich with both his hands and took a neat bite, chewing slowly. His mouth moved in counts of three, paused, started again, paused, started again, and then he swallowed. Morana knew the patterns, having seen them daily. Patterns made him feel good, and they were used to him now.

Fuck, even she hadn't given him as much credit. He had noticed. Of course, he had. Ever since she got shot, he had been keeping an eye on her like a hawk. The first time he had initiated a hug had been when she'd come out from the hospital, and he'd put his arms around her waist for exactly thirty-three seconds—he had counted—and told her never to get hurt again. It would be just her luck to be stuck with two quiet men—one grown-up and one miniature—who had difficulty expressing emotions, though for entirely different reasons. Tristan's issue was more because of nurture; the traumas he had sustained that had made him build a wall around himself so impenetrable he didn't know how to break it himself. Xander's was nature, as Dr. Kol had told them. He was born different, and there was absolutely nothing trauma-related about it, thank goodness. It would've broken her heart to even think of him going through anything traumatic. That was why maternal instincts inside her didn't understand how Tristan's mother could have just left him to be tortured by monsters all his life. Morana would have killed them or died trying if any of them even looked at the boy she thought of as her son now.

"Are you okay?" Xander's question broke through her musings.

She took another bite of the sandwich. "Yes, why?"

"You're not behaving normally."

She wondered what her normal behavior was to him. "I just have a project I'm working on," she told him the easiest truth. "It's time-dependent, so I'm a little distracted."

"What's the project?" He took another precise bite and

chewed in his pattern of threes.

From any other child, the question would have been odd. Not from Xander. He was naturally interested in the digital space, spending time with her as she taught him some stuff. Surprisingly, he already knew a little. When Morana had asked where he'd learned, he'd just shrugged, remaining quiet about his past.

That was the only thing Morana was yet to understand about him to fill all the spaces. His missing past and his resistance to talking about it intensified the itch in her brain.

"Just tracing a location using a message IP." She simplified it.

A little frown burrowed between his brows as he ate. "That doesn't take you so long."

She chuckled, amazed that he caught that. "No, it doesn't. But this is a little tricky."

He nodded as if he understood. "Don't worry. You got this."

Morana was touched by his implacable faith in her abilities. "Thanks, little man."

"I'll be taller than you in a few years," he pointed out the obvious. He was already tall-ish for his age group, or at least what they estimated his age group was.

"You'll always be *little man* to me," she stated. "No matter how tall you get."

He shook his head three times, like she was ridiculous, but she knew he liked it. He liked that she was ridiculous and affectionate with him. They both finished their sandwiches in silence, and then Morana took the plates and picked them up in her right hand, walking around the counter. She went to the sink to rinse them, forgetting that her left arm was numb, and halted, taking a deep breath in as the realization that she couldn't do something basic as rinsing the plates dawned upon her.

"I got it." Xander butted her away with his hips, his height letting him stand at the sink and wash the plates before popping them in the dishwasher. Morana stood frozen to the side, not knowing what to do, watching the younger boy take over, his observations having made him realize that she couldn't do it.

"Thanks," she uttered quietly, leaning against the counter, grappling with the new reality. Was this how she was going to live now? One-handed? Not able to do the most basic tasks for more than a few minutes?

She felt a little hand slip into her left, and looked down at Xander, giving her hand a squeeze. "Don't worry," he told her for the second time in as many minutes. "You got this."

Morana felt her lips tremble and she pulled him into a hug. He let her, standing there patting her back in threes, counting in his head while she held him. He had become so precious to her, she didn't know how her life would be like without him anymore if they couldn't adopt him. She didn't even want to imagine it.

The sound of the private elevator opening had them pulling away and turning to face the doors.

And *he* walked out. Once her enemy, now her lover.

Tristan.

And fuck if her heart didn't pound the way it had back when she'd hated him.

It all had the same effect—the closely cut hair was a little longer than the first time she'd seen him at the Maroni party but still short enough to look sharp, the thick neck with that delicious vein she had licked more times than she could count, the muscular body hidden behind a white shirt and dark pants.

And those eyes. Those magnificent, electric blue eyes that still zapped her the moment they landed on her.

He did a full-body perusal of her like he always did, checking to see if anything had changed in his absence, before doing the same with the boy next to her. And then he walked toward them, and her heart thumped in her ribs like it was the first time, like he was going to press her into the counter and whisper murder across her skin, like they were locked in a bubble with the world pounding on the door outside.

Her ovaries began singing opera every time he was in the vicinity.

"Why did you not eat the whole day?" were the first words out of his mouth, in that whiskey and sin voice, effectively bursting her bubble of orgasms through eye contact.

She turned to Xander, her mouth pursing. "Traitor. You

didn't have to snitch to him."

The boy just shrugged and high-fived Tristan before throwing a 'good night' at them both and walking to his room.

A hand settled on her neck, bringing her face back to him, blue eyes looking deep into hers. "Why didn't you eat?"

It wouldn't have been a big deal, but since the shooting, everything she didn't do to take care of herself was a big deal. The fact that he'd asked her twice meant he was concerned and that he knew her well enough to know she wouldn't have concerned him without reason.

Fuck.

She had to tell him.

She bit her lower lip, swallowing, turning her eyes down to his collar, where his tie hung.

He had never worn a proper tie before because he had never known how to make a knot. It was something she had learned when they got together. Growing up in the Maroni compound, people had thought that it had just been his way of rebelling, of not abiding by how Lorenzo had wanted the people dressed. He had leaned into the narrative because it had hidden a vulnerability—he was never taught how to knot a simple tie, and he never trusted anyone enough to ask. Though he did begin to trust Dante later, it was too late by then, and he didn't know how to be emotionally vulnerable and open himself up to anything. Even Morana had had to force him, bit by bit, to allow himself to be with her.

So, when she'd found a pair of pre-knotted ties with hooks in his closet, she had asked him about it. He still didn't admit anything, but the next morning, she had gone shopping for gorgeous silk ties in different shades of blue that matched the shades in his eyes. The morning after, after he had dressed up for the day, she'd shown him the new collection in his closet and asked him to select one for the day. He'd stood there, taking it all in, and pressed her against the closet wall for a brutal kiss that still made her toes curl just thinking about it.

And then, she had knotted his tie for him.

She had been doing it for almost two years.

Morana looked at the knot in the rich blue silk, her eyes misting because she didn't want to admit how much harder it had become for her to just tie the fabric. She did it perfectly in the moment, but her shoulder and arm felt it afterward, even the minimal action leaving behind an aftermath of pain.

She touched the silk with her right hand, her mouth trembling because she didn't want to lose that. It was stupid. It was just a tie. But it was *theirs*. It was a part of their morning routine, something they both shared in the quiet moments before their world expanded to let all the shit in. But if she couldn't rinse a fucking plate, for how long could she knot his tie? Would she lose this too?

Summoning strength, she raised her left hand, feeling a sharp pain shoot through her shoulder at the movement. She ignored it, and placed her hand over his wrist, feeling his pulse under her fingers as he felt hers against his palm.

And then she looked back up at him, only to find him staring intently at her. He knew something wasn't right, but he was waiting for her to tell him about it. Over the years, the more she had opened up and let herself be, the more talkative she had become with him in their home. She knew this was sending alarms ringing inside him as he waited.

Taking a deep breath in, ignoring the matter of her arm for now and focusing on the more important thing, she spoke.

"I received a text from the Shadow Man last night."

He stilled, his fingers flexing around her neck, his eyes darkening. She knew he didn't like the Shadow Man; he hadn't since the beginning because the man had been contacting her, and she had been talking to him whenever he did. Tristan was territorial about her, and the idea of a strange man finding ways to talk to her and meet her secretly fired up all his synapses, turning him into the caveman she called him. Tristan didn't like him more because he had been the one to lead them down paths and disclose information they should have found themselves. That was why she knew he wasn't going to like what she had to tell him.

"He sent me a folder and asked me to track him."

Tristan stayed still, waiting, watching, like the predator they called him.

"I am tracking the message as we speak. But the folder, well, it was titled *Fountainhead*, which is an odd name I know. But it means the original source of something. I couldn't open the folder on my phone since it was heavy, so I came down and opened it on my system. It—"

"What was in the folder?" His voice cut through her nervous rambling, getting straight to the meat of the matter, and Morana swallowed.

"Photos. Five photos. One was Zenith." She couldn't help but slightly flinch at the mention of the girl. "One was the photo I showed you before, the three of us girls after being taken. And the others. Well."

Morana didn't know what to say, so she stepped back. He let his hand drop from her neck but followed her as she moved to her laptop.

The numbers were ticking and the trace was almost complete. She was confident she could get it done in time. Or maybe, the Shadow Man had been confident that the time would be enough for her skills.

Shaking off that thought, she minimized the software and opened the folder she'd saved right at the front. She turned her neck to see him watching her, and with a deep breath, she clicked on the folder.

Tristan crossed his arms over his chest, his gaze now on the screen, waiting for her to show him whatever she had.

She opened the third photograph.

She heard him inhale sharply as the image filled the screen, the younger version of his sister in high definition, much older than his memory of her or the last time he had seen her. This was years after she had disappeared, years after he had become a tortured young boy, wanting to die but not dying because he thought of his sister, alive somewhere. His faith in that belief for over twenty years was the true definition of love. That was the kind of love this man possessed, the kind that believed across time and distance without evidence, with just sheer force of will. Morana didn't really believe in manifestations, but if she could, this would be all the proof she needed.

She watched his arms flex, his fingers gripping his biceps, as if holding himself together, his eyes moving across the screen feverishly to take in each and every detail, committing it to memory.

Morana let him take all the time he needed, just standing by his side in silence, her heart in her throat watching the man she loved so much finally find the answer he had been looking for, the answer he had spent his whole life searching but never finding until now.

He didn't wait for her to scroll to the next picture, leaning forward and pressing the side key himself.

The next photo filled the screen. The teenage version of his sister. He did the same thing as with the first. Stared and committed every detail to memory, looking for long minutes at the image, before hitting the side key again.

Morana held her breath, keeping her eye on him. "That's the last photo."

She watched him closely, unsure how to react to how he would react to this one. It looked intimate to her, but maybe he wouldn't notice. Maybe, in his emotional state, he wouldn't suspect what she did. She hoped he didn't, not at this time. This moment was pure; it was just for him. He deserved this. As Dante had said, they could talk about suspicions and speculations later.

There was nothing on his face for a few seconds, no twitch, no microexpression, nothing she could read, which was saying something because she had become an expert at reading him.

He just stared at the screen, still like a statue, and Morana couldn't even imagine how his brain was processing things, how his emotions were storming inside his body. She just stayed by his side as he took his fill of the adult version of his sister, his eyes moving over the hair, the face, the being.

There was silence in the penthouse for long, long minutes, before a loud clap of thunder suddenly shook the sky.

Morana glanced out at the windows, seeing a splattering of raindrops assault the glass, the lights of the city twinkling in the distance against the backdrop of the night. It reminded her of the first time they had talked about his sister against those very windows, on a night similar to this. It felt fitting somehow, as though the universe was coming full circle at that moment too.

"When was this photo taken?" His roughened voice, fueled by his emotions, brought her eyes back to him.

"Three weeks ago."

Her words hit him. She could see that in the slight tremor of his jaw, yet he stood unmoving.

"It's her, Tristan," she said as softly as possible. "She is alive. She is real. She is found."

Both his arms dropped to his sides at her words. His eyes stared at the screen, unseeing and unfocused, the pupils down to little points, swallowed by the blue. She didn't know what to do or how to help him process this, so she just stood next to him, hoping for a signal that she could do *something*.

And then, his hands began to shake.

Morana rushed to hold his hands in hers, ignoring the pain in her shoulder and numbness in her left arm at the sudden movement.

"Tristan?"

He looked right at the screen, lost deep in his head.

"Tristan?"

She shook his hand, but it just intensified his trembling.

"Tristan."

His lips parted as if to say something, but no words came out.

"Tristan!"

Tristan finally turned to face her, coming out of his stupor, his jaw clenching, his eyes misted, his hands shaking in her grip.

She held them tighter, hoping it would subside, and when it

didn't, she stepped into him and wrapped her arms around his body, wincing at the stabbing pain in her shoulder but keeping it at bay through sheer stubbornness. It took a split second, but his arms came around her, crushing her to himself, and Morana bit her tongue, swallowing her noise of pain down.

Her physical pain could wait. His emotional pain was more important right then.

He needed to take this from her right then, and that was what she needed to do. She needed to let him *take*.

And with that thought, she let herself be crushed into his embrace and be what he needed in that moment.

TRISTAN

CHAPTER 10

TRISTAN, SHADOW PORT

R ED HAIR. GREEN EYES. Pale skin.
Burned on his retinas.

She is alive.
She is real.
She is found.

The words sank in.

She is alive.
She is real.
She is found.

He couldn't hear anything else.

She is alive.
She is real.
She is found.

There was a buzz in his brain...

She is alive.
She is real.
She is found.

... like he was underwater...

She is alive.
She is real.
She is found.

... but not sinking...

She is alive.
She is real.
She is found.

... just being.
His limbs were slowly numbing...

She is alive.
She is real.
She is found.

... heart erratically thumping...

She is alive.
She is real.
She is found.

... something lodged in his throat...

She is alive.
She is real.
She is found.

... tight, hot, almost choking him, yet...

She is alive.
She is real.
She is found.

... he felt like he was drawing his first breath.
Nine words.

She is alive.
She is real.
She is found.

... repeating, over and over...

She is alive.
She is real.
She is found.

...bouncing around his brain, off the walls of his skull...

She is alive.
She is real.
She is found.

For more than twenty years, he'd dreamed the words.

She is alive.
She is real.
She is found.

For more than twenty years, he'd thought the words.

She is alive.
She is real.
She is found.

For more than twenty years, he'd lived the words.

She is alive.

She is real.
She is found.

Yet, he'd never heard their sound.

They had a sound. A melody of a lifetime spent sustaining a hope, spoken through lips he had kissed countless times.

"Tristan!" the voice, the melody, the sound, shook him from a trance-like state. His gaze focused. Morana was looking at him, waiting for his response. He realized that he'd been standing like stone for a few minutes, long enough to prompt her to physically shake him.

He still stood mute, slightly numb, unable to understand what was happening to him. The words rebounded in his brain, injecting *something* into his blood, sending it rushing to the organ underneath his ribs, making it pump extra hard, doubling the *something* back into his veins.

She is alive.
She is real.
She is found.

Someone was shaking his hands.
He looked down.
Nothing was shaking his hands.
They were just shaking in the air.
Why were they shaking?

What was happening to him?

Smaller hands gripped his, stilling the tremors. He raised his eyes up to lock gazes with hazel eyes he had learned like a litany. The look in them was heavy but happy, emotional, a sheen of tears filmed over them, making them appear glossy like the stuff she put over her lips sometimes.

"Tristan."

Just one word. His name. Her eyes. Her hands.

And it crashed into him.

A noise escaped his chest, one he had never heard before, something raw but confused, and Morana stepped up like she always did, wrapping him in his arms like she always did.

He stood motionless, trying to find the words and compute as she hugged him, his own eyes beginning to burn.

She was alive.
She was real.
They had found her.

He crushed her to himself, trying to still his trembling with her body, but it just got worse and worse.

She was alive.
She was real.
They had found her.

Tears escaped his eyes, for the first time in a long time, and her arms tightened around him.

His baby sister.
Finally.

PART II:
METAMORPHOSIS

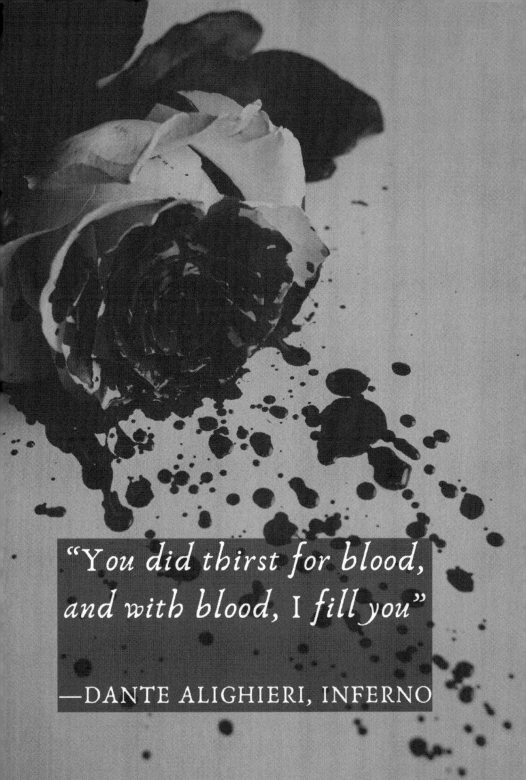

"*You did thirst for blood,
and with blood, I fill you*"

—DANTE ALIGHIERI, INFERNO

TRISTAN

CHAPTER 11

TRISTAN, GLADESTONE

H E WAS GOING TO buy a fucking jet.

No one knew this but Tristan was and had always been scared of heights. Given his choice of residence, one wouldn't have thought so, but that was the truth. Flying had always been something that put him off-kilter, which was why he had always tried to sleep through the journey whenever he'd traveled via the Maroni jet, which he most often had. Though he preferred being on the ground, using a car, or even better, his bike to go places, time was often of the essence in their line of work, and he'd needed to simply travel as soon as possible. The idea of being thousands of feet above sea level, hanging in the air in a metal can, made his stomach queasy, yet, no one could have suspected that from looking at him.

The penthouse had been the first real purchase he'd ever made for himself and also the costliest. Though he'd been investing in property for a while—thanks to the pain in the ass Dante—he'd been piss poor growing up with nothing to his name. It hadn't really mattered since he'd been living at the Maroni compound, getting all his physical needs met, and he hadn't really cared at the time. It had been Dante who had guided him into growing his wealth. Dante had the kind of generational wealth Tristan had never seen anyone else have, with a lineage of net worth more than he even knew about. Tristan hadn't had a thing to his name; it was just a bank account with a 'salary' that was getting deposited and going untouched. Dante had had access to his information and had obviously looked him up, so he knew exactly how much Tristan was worth.

And because he was a good man—Tristan could admit that in the recesses of his mind but probably never out loud, or the man would get more on his nerves—Dante had advised Tristan to buy some property in the city, small stuff, so he could begin growing his portfolio. Money was power, and Dante had wanted him to have his own outside of his role in the Outfit. So, as annoying as Dante had been, Tristan had taken his advice because if there was one guy who knew how to make and keep money, it had to be the Maroni prince. He had bought small commercial property in the city and grew his investments until, one day, he decided to get a base in Shadow Port.

If someone asked him why he'd made a home for himself there instead of any other city in the world, he wouldn't be able to give a reason. Maybe it had been to be closer to Morana, whom he had planned on killing eventually. Maybe, it had been to just get away from Tenebrae and all the shitty memories the city held for him. Or maybe it had been because Amara had already moved to Shadow Port, and he hadn't wanted to leave her completely alone in a strange city. He had, and still did, feel protective of her ever since the day he'd found her broken after being missing for three days.

Tristan remembered the moment, something he doubted he would ever forget. He doubted she remembered, though. She'd been in and out of it, but the relief in her body when she'd seen him still hit him in the gut. It had been the first time in a long time Tristan remembered feeling something so visceral. The emotion had surprised him, making him realize he still felt things beyond rage and revenge and agony. Amara didn't know, but she had given him a purpose, especially during her years of recovery. Somehow, making sure she was going to be okay had become an added goal in his life. So, moving to Shadow Port had been a multi-factor decision.

He had bought the entire lot before construction had even begun, the area a little out of the main city but still close enough to be immediately accessible. He had liked the idea of being on top with the entire view of the city and the sea laid out before him, the idea of conquering his one fear of heights and staring it down. He had worked with the project architect and had the penthouse made for himself. And he still remembered the first time he'd entered it. It had taken a few weeks of standing at the windows to convince his mind that the glass wasn't going to break and the building wasn't going to fall. Now, it was one of the only spaces in the world he felt good in, regardless of the height.

But he still fucking hated flying.

Sitting in Alpha's private jet—because Dante had taken his and rushed to get to Gladestone—Tristan was feeling off-kilter again. He hadn't slept in the last twenty-four hours, ever since Morana had shown him the photos, images that had been burned onto his retinas, appearing in high definition every time he closed his eyes. Hair that had gotten even redder over the years, vivid green eyes that had looked like precious jewels, pale skin that he wondered about turning red when she laughed. It had taken him a few minutes to process and accept the fact that she was alive and looked well.

And then it hit him.

He had missed so much of her life, so many moments and milestones where he should have been there as a big brother. Though it wasn't through any fault of his own, it didn't stop the guilt from weighing him down. Since the day she had disappeared from her room to the day he was flying to get to her, there hadn't been one where the guilt of not being able to protect her hadn't eaten him alive. He didn't know what she'd been through, how she'd survived, but the fact that she looked healthy and content in the latest photo from three weeks ago eased something in his chest.

She was okay, and she was only going to get better.

He gripped the armrest, which was not something he would have usually done, but he didn't have it in himself to care for it at the moment.

"You alright?"

Tristan turned to look at the one-eyed man opposite him. He had to give it to Alpha—the man had dropped everything and gotten on his jet within an hour of Morana calling Zephyr. Tristan knew there was some awkwardness between the two women, but that didn't stop them from being there for each other. About twelve hours ago, when the trace had been almost completed, the general vicinity of the location becoming clearer, Morana had called Dante first, alerting him. Since the direction was east and a straight route for Dante, he had gotten his jet prepared and had already gotten ready to get in the air at her word.

Then, surprisingly, Morana had called Zephyr.

"How are you guys getting there?" Zephyr, Alpha's wife, asked, her voice on the speakerphone as Morana sat in front of the laptop and Tristan paced.

"I don't know," Morana said. I'm figuring it out, but there are not any private services available at such short notice."

There was a pause. "Will you take Xander with you too?"

Morana exchanged a look with him. In between all the chaos, they hadn't even thought about it. Fuck. He had a routine, and though they often traveled with him to Tenebrae, it was a different thing to take him on a whim like that during an operation without knowing what was going to happen. They couldn't do that. He was a kid.

The silence was answer enough because Zephyr's voice came again. "How much time do we have?"

"Six hours, maybe less," Morana answered.

"How about we come there?" Zephyr suggested. "You can fly on our jet, and my hubby can go with you. I'll come to your place and keep an eye on Xander in the meantime."

Tristan stared at the speaker, surprised by the kindness. The few times he'd seen Zephyr, she'd seemed sweet enough but he hadn't really given her much thought, but her offer, especially at a time like this, wasn't something he would forget.

Morana pressed the mute button, looking at him for the final say. "It's a good idea. I'd trust her with Xander."

He knew the three girls had become a group of sorts. He'd found them on the phone—and listened in on some of their conversations—more often than he cared to admit. Knowing how serious his wildcat was about the boy's safety and how protective she got about the tiniest things, her saying she trusted Zephyr to look after him in her absence was good enough for him.

He gave a nod and Morana unmuted the call. "How soon can you get here, Zee?"

Zephyr muttered something, possibly to Alpha, and then her voice became clear again. "The jet is getting ready as we speak. You guys get to the private strip."

Morana nodded, even though the woman couldn't see. It was cute how she sometimes gestured and mumbled just to herself without an audience.

"One of our guys will pick you up and bring you here."

"Perfect! We'll be there soon!" The sound was sweet, and this moment alone put Zephyr under the oddly expanding list of people he would protect.

"Tristan?"

Morana's voice brought him back to the present.

He realized Alpha had asked him a question about how he was holding up and nodded. He was as alright as he could be.

Morana put her hand over his, seated right beside him, and turned to look at the other man. "Thanks for this," she said.

He should be the one saying thanks. Alpha didn't owe him shit, and it wasn't like he was doing a favor for Dante. This was just because that man's wife asked him and he did it. As a man who would do whatever Morana asked, he could understand the sentiment. And seeing Zephyr through a new lens, he could understand why, too. The moment she had landed, she had hugged Morana and turned to him, giving him an *"I hope everything goes okay"*. He wouldn't have cared for the words had she not immediately told them not to worry about Xander, that the boy already had a vibe with her from Dante and Amara's wedding and their recent trip to Los Fortis, and that they would be perfectly fine.

With that alone, she became one of the few people he would not only tolerate but, if need be, protect. He still didn't care much about Alpha, though, not forgetting that Morana had gotten shot in his territory by his man. While Alpha didn't pull the trigger, and he was as much a victim of Hector as anyone else, Tristan wasn't rational. He never had been where she was concerned. Morana had always elicited emotion in him—bad and good. Logic didn't exist in the same space as her in his brain.

His logical little wildcat kept her grip on his hand and kept her phone screen lit up on her lap, the timer and location visible on there for him to see.

"Could this be a trap?" Alpha asked them, his one eye taking them both in. It was a question Tristan himself had wondered and thought about, but it was too big of a stake not to see through.

Morana pursed her lips, thinking it over. "I doubt it," she began. "I know you guys don't like him, but the Shadow Man hasn't given me any direct leads that never panned out into something. His info has been pretty solid."

Just hearing her speak for the fucker got on his nerves. He hadn't liked the man ever since he'd found out he had been interacting and meeting Morana in secret. At first, it had been raging jealousy because they had been very new together and figuring their way out around each other, and Tristan didn't like any man, especially one he didn't know shit about, near her. Over time, though, the jealousy had changed into mild jealousy and sheer annoyance. Mild jealousy because the man was obviously smart and connected with Morana on an intelligent level that Tristan did not, and sheer annoyance because he was playing them around like puppets on invisible strings, and Tristan wasn't into that shit. The idea of being puppeteered by someone else made his blood boil, and for that alone, he was pissed at the asshole who thought he could lead them around. But he couldn't deny they wouldn't be where they were without his leads, with no idea about the existence of The Syndicate and now, his sister. And that pissed him off even more because he felt indebted to him too. If the lead panned out and was real, which he hoped with everything that he was that it was, he would have to come to terms with his annoyance of the man.

"Hate to admit," Alpha said, his tone grudging, "but he saved my wife's life. I spoke to him after, outside the hospital. But I still have no clue what to make of him."

"I get what you mean," Morana nodded. "He's been confusing. While he's been the best source of whatever information we've had, I wouldn't be surprised if he's been lulling us into a false sense of security only to ambush us, so I suggest we keep our eyes open."

Alpha agreed. "Question is, why send you this lead now?"

Morana was silent for a bit, thoughtful. He saw her glance at him from the corner of her eye and felt his own narrow. She wasn't sharing something, some theory cooked up in that smart brain of hers. Was it because they were in company or was she not sharing with *him*?

"I want to hear this," Tristan spoke, for the first time in hours.

Morana swallowed. That old fire from when he'd wanted to both throttle her and fuck her, one that only simmered now because of their relationship settling into something so beautiful, became a blaze inside him. She was hiding something from him.

He turned his wrist, palm facing upward and captured her own, squeezing it, his eyes glaring into her profile. She looked at him, blinked innocently, like she hadn't just given him the biggest tell with that fucking swallow and that corner of her eye look.

"Maybe," she began, focusing back on the other man who had asked the question. "He just found the relevant information now. Or maybe, he wants us to owe him so he's using this as leverage."

Yeah, she was fucking smart, but she was sneaky. No one knew Morana Vitalio like he did, and the little tremor in her mouth distracted him long enough from what was coming to focus on what was going on.

"Yeah, possibly," Alpha mused out loud. "From the word on the ground, he's been going up against The Syndicate for many years now. That alone is a point in his favor in my book."

Tristan wondered about that. How was it possible that they had never even heard of The Syndicate if it had been in the operation for so many years? Unless...

"Any news about The Alliance?" he asked.

Morana immediately turned to face him, eager to share what she had, a clear contrast to her previous response. Fuck, she was so obvious it would've been pathetic had it been anyone but her. No, for this, he was grateful because it kept him in the loop of everything going on in her head. It was her body's and face's inability to keep things from him that had made him realize how much he aroused her in the beginning, how he'd known to follow her into that bathroom, knowing she wouldn't reject him. It was this inability that had told him how much she craved being free while still belonging, how much she hurt, how she still went on. It was this inability that had told him how much she had struggled with the revelations about her real identity, how much she had struggled after getting shot, how many demons still haunted her about Zenith's death.

But that was the thing about her demons. They had always looked out from her eyes, baring their soul for him to see, and called his own to the fore.

That was what she'd told Dante once on a plane ride like this. His demons danced with hers. Well, at least they were graceful enough to because he couldn't dance for shit, even though he'd tried that one time at Maroni's party because she'd been confusing the hell out of him.

Something clicked in his brain suddenly. "Can you get a guest list for a party?"

Morana blinked, her eyes looking like an owl's behind those oversized glasses she hadn't taken off since yesterday. Her look of confusion was cute, and so was the wild look she shot Alpha's way before focusing on him. "What party?"

"The one Lorenzo had given," he reminded her. "Right after we went to Tenebrae."

A smile turned her lips up as she remembered. "That was years ago, Tristan."

"The Shadow Man had been at the party," he reminded her. "He'd warned you that night."

Her smile fell as the memories of that night came back to her. That night had shifted so many things for them, changed the course of their entire relationship. And begrudgingly, he had to admit the Shadow Man's warning for her life had kept him alerted, more than he would've been otherwise.

"So?" she asked.

"So, no one crashed a Maroni party."

"I did," she gave him a smug grin, reminding him of the first time they'd met as adults.

Tristan felt his lips twitch. "Did you?"

The way her grin fell was amusing. Her eyes narrowed, the hazel in them shining with murder he had seen so often reflected. "You didn't!"

He didn't confirm or deny her allegation, just stayed silent.

"You mean he must have had an invitation?" Alpha's voice made him turn and consider the other man.

Tristan nodded. "Lorenzo used to amp up security even more than normal at his parties. The guest list demanded it. He didn't want anyone trying to kill him or anyone dying if he wasn't killing them."

The other man leaned forward, elbows on knees and hands hanging. Tristan glanced at his scars covered with tattoos visible under his shirt. He was possibly one of the most physically damaged men he'd seen. Tristan had enough scars of his own, and he knew the kind of torture that left them. He might not be particularly fond of Alpha but he could respect the strength in him to survive whatever he had gone through and still come out on top of his game.

"You're saying if we can get the guest list," Morana deduced, all excited, "we can get a pool of names, one of whom could possibly be the Shadow Man?"

Tristan gave a nod.

"That means that father dearest—" the sarcasm in Alpha's tone was obvious "—knew him in real."

"You think he knew who the Shadow Man is? In real?" Morana asked with shock, which was evident in her tone. Lorenzo Maroni knowing someone didn't bode well. If true evil had a face, it would have been Lorenzo's.

Alpha shook his head. "I doubt anyone does. I literally tracked a man down who I thought might give us a clue."

"Who?"

"One of the earliest rumored kills by him," the scarred man explained. "It's a rumor on the ground. An orphanage that burned down about twenty-five years ago. Oddly, no kids were there, just a bunch of adults. There were some whispers that it was his doing. The man had been a caretaker of the place and escaped."

Morana gasped. "Let's say he did it. If we assume he did it in his twenties, that puts him in his mid-forties."

"You don't have to be an adult to kill, wildcat," Tristan pointed out, knowing from experience that children could be murderers.

Morana sobered at his reminder. "True. Even then. Even if he was young and he's the one who did that, he'd be at least in his thirties right now. That does narrow the pool down." She turned to Alpha. "What did the man say?"

Alpha considered them both. "He was senile. I mentioned the incident, and he lost it, muttering just one phrase over and over in fear."

"What phrase?" Morana leaned forward.

"Demon eyes."

Silence settled as his words resounded in the space.

"Fuck," Morana shivered. "I just got a chill. Is he the good guy or the bad guy? Someone please tell me."

That was the fucking question.

As far as Tristan was concerned, the Shadow Man could go to hell.

He just gripped Morana's hand and waited for the damn flight to be over, swearing to buy a jet if he landed and actually found his sister this time.

Only a few hours left.

CHAPTER 12

LYLA, GLADESTONE

GLADESTONE HAD TOO MANY abandoned warehouses. Lyla stood in front of one of the smaller ones in the industrial district. There were blocks and blocks of abandoned areas like this in the city going to complete and utter ruins, factories and companies either shutting down after the turn of the century or moving to greener pastures. There was nothing green about the city. It was a concrete jungle cloaked with corporate greed while hiding crime underneath. Lyla had never really been in the city much, but whatever little she had seen from the windows of cars she had traveled in, it had left her feeling numb.

She looked up at the sky, seeing nothing but gray, not a star visible in sight, and sighed. She missed the skies in Bayfjord. Lyla hadn't known skies like that could exist in real until she'd seen them herself—skies so vast and endless and open she felt like she could fly just looking at them; skies the grayest when roiling with clouds and the bluest when clear and the orangest when burnished at sunset; skies the blackest canvas at night with the brightest stars splattered across it like the most surreal painting. The view of the mountains and the sea from the deck outside the bedroom, the freedom to roam the property knowing the best security was working around the clock at the border, the people she had made connections with, she missed all of it. She missed *home*.

But she had to do this.

"This is for meetings." The voice made her turn her neck to look at the man at her side, the one holding her hand in his gloved one. He stood next to her in a black hoodie and jeans, the casual attire not hiding the sheer danger he wore around him, holding an overnight bag in his free hand. He led her into what looked like a dilapidated little warehouse from the outside, punching in a code and opening the rickety-looking door that appeared like it was going to fall any second.

A gasp left her as she stepped in, the inside not matching the outside at all. It was like an office but cozier and smaller. High ceilings were covered with beams that gave the building more structure than it looked like. A pair of armchairs sat on a rug on the left. A coffee machine, mugs, and snacks occupied the far left corner of the space. The major portion was taken up by a long table she'd seen in the offices in movies, mostly in boardrooms, with ten chairs around them. A projector was fixed on one of the beams, pointing to the back wall that was painted white.

"What kind of meetings is this for?" Lyla asked, taking it all in.

Dainn walked to one of the armchairs, dropping the bag down on it. "The clandestine kind. Some people like to have meetings completely off the radar, with no paper trail, and places like this are for such."

Lyla followed him in, going to the middle of the space and looking around. "Really?"

He chuckled, the tone dry. "You'd be surprised. Humans are pretty predictable in some ways." He moved to her. "The more power they get, the more important one thing becomes."

"What's that?" she asked, fascinated by how he thought.

He bent, his face close to hers. "Secrets," he said, like sharing a secret between them. "People will do anything to keep secrets."

She swallowed, realizing the truth in his words. "And you?"

"I hoard them," he told her, his hands coming to her waist. "Use them. Manipulate them."

It shouldn't have turned her on, the way he spoke about manipulating and playing people, but it did. Knowing him as she did, seeing how he was with her in contrast to the persona he shared with the world, made her feel in on the secret. It gave her something she'd never had before—power. She realized that while he hoarded and used others' secrets, he had given her all of his. And it was a rush knowing that and keeping it close to her chest, just something between the two of them, no one in the world privy to their bubble.

And what a bubble it had been, especially the last twenty-four hours.

Lyla was so sore, more happily sore than she'd ever been in her life. She could feel him in every step she took, her pussy battered and her thighs still shaking in the aftermath of what had been the most intense, insane sexual marathon of her life. He had bent and twisted and turned her every which way, and she had pushed and bounced and moved back, their touches tinged not just with desire but with desperation, memorizing each other, gorging on each other to keep themselves satiated for longer during the separation.

She placed her hands on his chest, feeling the solid beat of his heart underneath a hand, as if she could soak his innate confidence. "What should I tell them?"

He nuzzled her nose, the gesture so soft it made her heart clench. "Anything you want."

Her eyes widened. "Anything?"

He shrugged his broad, muscular shoulders she'd witnessed hold his weight so many times it had become a constant core memory. "Tell them whatever you want. It's your truth and your choice. *Yours.* You decide how much to share, when to share, who to share it with."

"Except with you," she clarified. "You get all my truths."

"And all your lies. And everything in between." He looked pleased. "Just don't mention Blackthorne yet."

It fascinated her every time he mentioned his different personalities like that, like they weren't the same man wearing different masks. "What about the Shadow Man?"

A twitch near the corner of his lips. "If Morana is as smart as I believe, she already suspects who you are to the Shadow Man."

She felt her eyes narrow at him. "What did you do?"

His grooves in the corner of his mouth deepened but he stayed silent, his hands firm on her waist. She basked in the presence, his warmth and his scent, for a few moments before laying another one of her fears out in the open for him. She was scared of everything—meeting all the new people she had never heard of until a bit ago but who had known of her for years. She was also scared of being... less. From what she'd found, Morana was a tech genius, Amara was a renowned psychologist, and Zephyr had been a hairstylist but was now working with her husband. Even Zenith, her old friend, had been working with people and helping them. Lyla was none of those things. Through no fault of hers and because of her circumstances, she hadn't had the opportunity to be something, her focus always on survival when it hadn't been on death. Even now, she was barely learning herself, her own likes and dislikes, little things about her that she'd never known before.

"What if... they are disappointed? I don't know how to... be. Who to be."

He pressed a hard kiss to her lips. "You're perfect. You burn so bright you could blind a man, *flamma*."

"What if others don't see it?"

"I don't want anyone to see it," he stated plainly. "Man has tried to steal fire from the sun since before the dawn of time."

She took that in for a few seconds.

"I just want you to promise me one thing," he told her, his tone serious. "Promise me to take care of yourself. Eat and sleep. Drink your tea. Talk to Dr. Manson at least once every two days. And," he slid a phone into her hand, one similar to one that he kept in his office drawer. "Keep your phone with you all the time. There's a tracker inside. I will watch it."

Oddly enough, that calmed her down. "Okay."

"Oh, little red," he kissed her nose, something warm in his mismatched eyes. "Look at you feeling relieved that the big bad wolf to watch you."

Lyla gazed up at him. "*My* big bad wolf."

Gripping her jaw with one hand, he pressed a hard kiss to her mouth. "Trust me still?"

She nodded.

"Then close your eyes and count to ten."

Lyla complied, her heart in her throat as he kissed her again, as if he couldn't help himself, and she clung to him, opening her mouth, letting him in and tasting him, that lava that lived in him melting, pouring, solidifying into her. They kissed, tongues dancing, sensitive lips becoming more so, but she didn't care.

It was over before she knew it, his mouth leaving her, his

hands leaving her, his presence leaving her.

Lyla counted to ten, her heart thudding and sinking, and then opened her eyes.

She was alone.

He had gone back to the shadows.

Lyla spent an hour alone. An hour pacing, going to the coffee station, and making herself a cup before putting it down, her nerves too taut, too high-strung to let her stay still. She sank into one of the armchairs, bringing the bag closer. He'd packed and stashed it in his helicopter before they'd left Bayfjord, which told her that he'd been planning to tell her the truth and expected her to leave even before they had started their journey here. He was always going to let her go and meet her past.

She kept a hold of the bag, not opening it, not wanting to, not yet. She would look into it and see what he had packed for her when she was in a new space and needed to feel a sense of belonging.

Quietly, she set the bag to the side and sat on the edge of the plush chair, her legs nervously fumbling and her limbs jittery with anxiety and with anticipation.

The sound of a vehicle coming closer and closer to her location sent her heartrate spiraling, her mind blanking to thought as a flush of adrenaline filled her. It could be a stranger, it could be someone just passing by, or maybe something more dangerous. She immediately discarded the thought. He wouldn't have left her here alone if he wasn't sure of her safety. That only meant it had to be someone purposely heading her way.

She sat with baited breath, her heart pounding in her entire body with one thump after the other, as footsteps approached. Seconds later, the door rattled, someone trying to break in. It got harder and harder for her to try and move, her body freezing in her spot as she watched the door with wide eyes.

The wood splintered and someone shouldered it, and then there was a tall man silhouetted against the frame, a gun in his hand as he entered the space, his face coming into the light.

From the photographs she had seen, she recognized him as Dante Maroni, her brother's friend. Lyla felt a drop of sweat roll down the back of her neck under the collar of the blazer she was wearing—an attire she had put a lot of thought in to try and make the best first impression and appear less like the damaged goods that she was compared to the rest of them.

She watched from the left side of the entrance as Dante Maroni scanned the space, photographs not doing justice to how handsome he was in real. His eyes went over everything with quick precision before finally moving to the side, to her.

She saw his mouth part as shock flitted across his face, his hand with the gun going lax and falling to his side, his dark eyes taking her in. He pressed something in his ear. "Got her."

Lyla gripped the seat on her sides, her arms trembling, coming to terms with the fact that this was a man, right there, who had looked for her and helped her brother for so many years. She tried opening her mouth to say something, greet him and be less odd, but words strangled in her throat, her eyes blurring as she blinked rapidly to clear the mist, not knowing what to say.

He didn't either, but he was more in control of his faculties because his face gentled, and he gave her a smile—a big, warm smile that reached his eyes.

She began to tremble, realizing that it was the first real smile she had received from someone who had known her. It was a good sign, one that made her hope that she might receive some more. She would hoard them and keep them close to her heart, not having been gifted such expressions of joy, not even having witnessed it often. Smiles in her dark world had been cruel. And her lover, he didn't really smile with purity, his own soul as darkened as hers, more tarnished. The smiles he gave to the world were fake, and the ones he gave her were twitches of his lips tinged with warmth in his eyes. Dante Maroni's smile was megawatt, radiant, having to adjust her eyes to it.

He made no move to get to her but stood at the door like a sentry in a protective stance.

Before she could think more about it, a screech of tires

came from outside, followed by the rapid footsteps of someone running. A second later, a silhouette came barrelling at the doorway, stopping at the last second. Dante moved to the side, giving whoever it was at the door a silent nod.

The silhouette took a deep breath in, before walking into the space, his eyes searching it.

She saw him before he saw her. Short dark blonde hair, light eyes that she knew were the most vibrant blue, a tall muscular frame that held itself ready to move at a moment's notice.

Tristan Caine.

Her big brother.

His eyes finally came to the side where she sat, and he *stilled.*

She saw his chest move rapidly, and her own matched it, her heart galloping like a wild horse freed from the cage of her ribs, her arms shaking with the tight grip she had on the cushioned seat next to her, their eyes locked.

His eyes traveled all over her, detailing every little thing about her that he could see, and hers did the same, taking in every little thing—from the shirt that was wrinkled to the scruff on his jaw that looked like he hadn't touched it for days to the shadows under his eyes that looked like he hadn't slept for days either. She took all of it in as did he, their eyes moving over each other, coming back and locking, and moving again, and coming back again.

Then, after seconds, minutes, hours of just taking in the other, he took a deep breath in, and took a step forward.

Her knuckles began to hurt with her grip.

He took another slow, measured step, watching her closely, as if she were a spooked animal that he didn't want to scare away.

She stayed frozen, unable to form words, unable to process feelings, unable to do anything but just sit and watch.

Another step, and her nose began to tingle.

One last step and he was before her, so close she could touch him. She wanted to touch him. But her arms didn't move, locked by her side, bound by chains she couldn't see but feel tying them up.

He looked down at her as she looked up, their stare never breaking, the weight of the emotions in his eyes heavy but not something she could read. All she felt was its intensity and it made her own come to the fore, burning her eyes and condensing the vapors of her feelings into the tears that flooded them.

And then, without a word, seeing the moisture in her gaze, he went down on his knees before her. Suddenly, she was looking down at him while he was looking up at her.

They just looked, breathed in the presence of the other for the first time in decades, memories hanging between them, the ones she didn't know and he couldn't forget. He brought his hands up, roughened palms facing upwards, leaving it between them, just watching, waiting, his own eyes red and misted as hers.

She could see his hands shaking in her periphery.

Somehow, seeing that sent the epiphany crashing into her—this was her *brother*.

Her big brother.

The man who had looked for her since she had been missing.

The man who didn't give up on finding her for over twenty years.

The only blood family she had left, the roots to the tree she had never been able to see.

Lyla didn't even look at his hands, nothing in her letting her remove her eyes from his, but somehow, seeing his hands there broke the chains on hers.

She brought her trembling hands up, and slowly, placed them in his.

A breath shuddered out of him, his eyes closing for a second, tears that had been hanging in them falling down his cheeks and over his jaw.

Lyla felt her own fall, hiccups wracking her body as she tried hard not to make a sound, not to break this moment, her breaths short and tight.

He looked at her again, something so *soft,* so *beautiful* in his eyes it made a sob crawl out of her throat.

It was as if her sound triggered him. Before she could blink, he pulled her down on the rug and into his arms, drawing her smaller body into the large warmth of his, his big arms curling around her protectively, and the feeling of them broke her.

She had almost died believing she would never have this.

She had lived her whole life believing she didn't deserve this. Every time someone had broken her as a child, as a teen, as a young adult, before Dainn had found her, she had craved the arms of a brother that would protect her, dying on the inside when they didn't come. The way he held her, crushing her to himself, broke her all over again, reminding her of every single time she had wished for this, begged for this, prayed for this, and never got.

Sobs wracked her body, her wails loud in the space, echoing, but she didn't care, crying her heart, her body, her soul out, and she wasn't alone. He was crying with her, not as loud but just as heavy, his body shaking with hers, his arms locked around her like he would never let her leave.

She was mildly aware of people coming to the door, but she didn't even look, and neither did he. They didn't care, a broken brother and a shattered sister.

The world could have ended, and they would have stayed locked there, both of them holding each other, crumbled on the ground, reuniting and restoring and repairing over twenty years of open wounds that had never stopped bleeding.

DANTE

CHAPTER 13

DANTE, GLADESTONE

S HE WAS REAL.

After searching for her for so long, she had almost become a legend to him. Though he'd never doubted they would find the truth of what happened to her one day, for the sake of Tristan, he'd hoped they would find her, but he'd never expected it to actually happen out of the blue. As grateful as he was, there was a suddenness to it all that raised his hackles. Why now? Why not earlier or later? There had to be a reason for it because if there was one thing he knew about the Shadow Man, it was that he didn't do things without his own agenda, whatever it may be.

He took her in, only having seen her photos as a baby. She had grown up into a beautiful woman. Petite, with an air so fragile about her she looked like she would splinter any second, but he doubted that was true. Appearances could be deceptive, and anyone who survived whatever the hell she had had to have an inner strength bigger than any of them could imagine. And anyone who was with the Shadow Man, if what

Morana suspected was true, had to have balls to steel or the feminine equivalent, he didn't know.

Dante remembered getting the call in the middle of a very hot makeout session with his wife. He had told her everything Morana had shared with him, and Amara had been stunned, to say the least. But when the call had come that the trace had been complete, triangulating the location to a warehouse in Gladestone, a city closer to Tenebrae than it was to Shadow Port, Dante had immediately called for the jet to be ready and been in the air within fifteen minutes.

That was the reason he had arrived before the others. Two of his men were scouting the area outside, though he doubted they would find anything unsecured. The Shadow Man wouldn't have left her alone unless she was a pawn in his plan or a trap for The Syndicate.

The girl—Tristan's baby sister, he had to remind himself—looked terrified, and he felt something tug at his chest at the look on her face. He gave her a smile, one that he knew had a soothing effect on other people, and thankfully, her body relaxed a fraction.

But Dante noticed something else. Along with the deer-in-the-headlights expression, as she kept her eyes on him, there was a flare of recognition on her face.

That surprised him.

She knew who he was.

How? Was it The Syndicate or the Shadow Man? What the

hell were they playing at?

Maybe it was nothing noteworthy at all. Maybe it wasn't recognition at all, and he'd misread her. That was possible.

He looked her over again.

Damn. He couldn't believe it was her.

Dante was happy, fucking ecstatic for his brother. He was moved for himself too, having witnessed firsthand and even initiated ways to find her over the years. He'd always thought that if and when they found her, everything would just fit in perfectly. But back then, he'd been more naive. He hadn't known about the depths of degradation in their world, the levels of hell going much deeper than any of them had known. She had been in those depths, and somehow, she was spit back out. And Dante couldn't afford to be as naive now.

Back then, he hadn't had a wife, a child, a family to protect, and a city to lead. Now, as he had taken up the mantle, the rational part of him, the one that had led his father to his own execution, was a little skeptical. He didn't take things at face value, and as much as he wanted to open his arms and accept her completely and let her into his family, the fact was that he didn't know who she was as a person yet. She had lived her entire life under or with The Syndicate, was somehow involved in some capacity with the Shadow Man, and had suddenly been dropped into their laps out of nowhere. He had seen the kind of ways trauma changed people. Amara had barely escaped with her life and their daughter's after her half-sister who had betrayed them. And more recently, he had seen firsthand the kind of scars it had left on Alpha and his family when his long-time friend and right-hand man had betrayed him.

Dante Maroni, over the last year after becoming a father and seeing the shitshow happening around them, was comparatively lower on trust than he had been. Until she proved that she wasn't a pawn or, worse, a perpetrator coming for them, Dante was going to keep a very keen eye on her. But he was going to welcome her, comfort her, and be family to her just in case she was innocent and just a victim of her life. If she was, he would lay his life for her if need be.

But until he knew either way for sure, he was also going to keep his logical reasonings to himself, only sharing them with Amara. In fact, he was eager to listen to what she had to say, her intuition and experience being something he trusted with closed eyes. There was not a soul more astute about people's personalities than his queen. She had known and trusted Morana way before he or Tristan had. She had told him to trust Alpha and it wasn't a decision he regretted, his relationship with his half-brother getting better with time, filling the void that Damian's absence had left in his life. And despite all indications to the contrary, she was telling him to keep trusting Vin, and he was going to until he saw proof otherwise.

Fuck, he missed Damian, and he knew exactly how he was

doing. Dante respected his decision to stay completely out of the world that had never accepted him. His brother had made a beautiful life for himself, with a woman who loved him, and Dante did have the occasional security checking in to make sure everything was okay; he had accepted that Damian would never return home, that their relationship was going to be limited to phone calls through burner phones. Though it wasn't the same, he knew the pain of losing a beloved sibling, feeling like he'd failed to protect him as an older brother, and there, he could understand Tristan's pain, though it was much more intense and deeper for the other man.

Dante kept the reassuring smile on his face, taking in her beautiful form, but beyond that, taking in other things. She was well-groomed and looked polished in a brown oversized blazer, dark jeans, and leather boots, all simple but all expensive. Dante knew good clothes, and he could tell by looking they were a top-of-the-line luxury. There was minimal jewelry on her—just dainty hoops in her ears, a ring on her index finger. The main eye-catcher was the gold necklace close to her skin, a choker-type with a swirly pattern that immediately gave away the fact that it was custom-made.

And it reminded him of some of the things he'd seen in his time going undercover—one of them being owned sex slaves who had worn collars around their necks at some of the parties. They had been forced to wear them, to chain themselves to their perverted, vile masters. Dante had sat at such a party, around naked boys and girls who were collared and leashed like animals, the people controlling them the monsters of the worst kind.

At the memory, Dante looked closely at the gold on her long neck. It didn't look like any of the collars he had seen, and the fact that she was wearing it comfortably while sitting free indicated that perhaps it was not. He hoped it wasn't. Because if it was a custom-made expensive collar on an invisible leash? That could be a problem for all of them.

His mind swirled with questions as he waited for Tristan to arrive. Dante had arrived earlier, both to secure the location and to get to her as soon as possible to verify that it wasn't a false lead. Tristan and Morana, not having a private jet, had waited for one of Alpha's planes to pick them up and bring them over. Dante had called the man and let him know the update, asking about Gladestone since it wasn't a city they had much idea about, but Alpha had connections here. His brother's contacts had been ready to receive him at the airport and take him straight to the location.

The last time they had been in Gladstone had been for a lead, too. It had been months ago and the last time he'd heard from Vin before he had gone deep underground, and they'd all ended up at one of the nightclubs. The tip had been about the number, a number they had tried to track but hadn't been able to. The last time Vin had tipped them off about a number, Zenith had ended up dying. This time, they had been on top of the game, heading together to the new city to get a change of scenery—though there wasn't much scenery there anyway—and find out what the fuck was up with the numbers 5 and 7. They had seen it a few times now for it to be a mere coincidence.

Morana had uncovered a file in the dark web after months of looking, and during recovery, the numbers 5057 and 5507 had popped up again, a number they had thought belonged to Zenith and another girl they had never found. But Dante didn't think it did, or if it did, he didn't believe that was all there was to it. There was more, a lot more they hadn't discovered, and hopefully, today would be a good step to unraveling things a lot more.

Dante didn't want their world to be as ugly as it was when Tempest grew up. He wanted to leave it even a little better for her, and for that, they needed answers that could give them leverage over The Syndicate.

The screeching of tires had him turning his neck and the gun in his hand going up immediately.

He let it fall as he saw Tristan jump out of a limo while it wasn't even fully stopped, jogging over to where Dante stood, looking like he hadn't shaved or changed clothes in a day, his eyes wilder than Dante had ever seen them, asking him a silent question, begging for an answer Dante was so fucking happy to finally give him.

Dante gave him a nod, and Tristan stopped, as though that

one nod had rendered him immobile, knocking the breath out of him for a split second.

Seeing the vivid reaction on the face of the boy he had befriended, the man he considered a brother, moved Dante. Tristan had always been a blank slate, one of the reasons Dante truly enjoyed provoking a reaction out of him. But the Tristan who stood before him then wasn't the man who didn't give a fuck about the world; it was the boy who had made a mistake and paid the unreasonable price for it. And seeing him like that made Dante's own eyes burn.

There was no one in the world who deserved this more than Tristan.

Fuck, pawn or not, the fact that she'd come back and filled the huge, gaping hole that had always been in his friend's life alone had his gratitude.

He watched as Tristan stepped inside, scanning the room and Dante almost told him to look left, but stopped. This was *his* moment. Nothing else needed to exist.

He saw the exact moment Tristan's eyes landed on her. To anyone else, it would look like he froze out of shock, but to Dante, who had worked and learned his body language for years, it wasn't freezing. Tristan was moving on the inside, his body locked into place so his emotions didn't scatter everywhere all around him.

Dante almost stepped outside, wanting to give them both privacy in the moment, but his protectiveness of the younger man didn't let him move. He didn't think she would harm Tristan—he had seen assassins, and she was the farthest thing from one he could find—and he didn't want to *not* trust her, but until he knew her better, it was better to be safe than sorry.

Tristan walked to her and sank down on his knees.

"Is she...?" Morana's words drowned out as she came to stand next to Dante, a phone in her hand with the navigation screen still lit, her eyes immediately finding Tristan and his sister on the side.

A gasp left Morana as she looked at the scene, her eyes tearing up and her hand coming up to her mouth. Dante pulled her into his side, rubbing her shoulder.

Alpha came to stand with them silently, exchanging a nod with Dante, taking in the scene.

No words were spoken by any of them.

They stood there like that, siblings of the heart, watching siblings of the blood be reunited after twenty years.

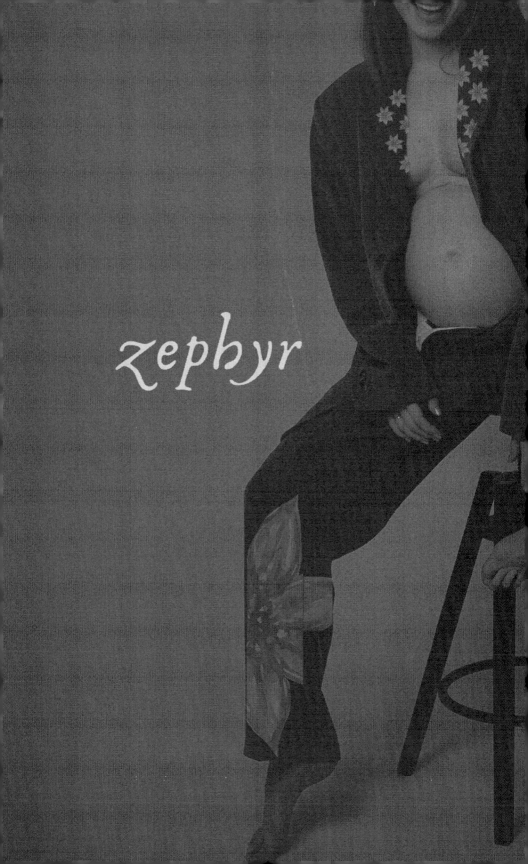

zephyr

CHAPTER 14

ZEPHYR, SHADOW PORT

S HE'D THOUGHT THEIR HOME in Los Fortis had a view but *damn*.

Zephyr stood near the windows, having just entered the penthouse, being delivered by a very quiet man to the building. She had used the code Morana had given her and rode up the elevator. It was already morning, sunlight filling in the entire space from behind the clouds, leaving a clear view of the new city before her. Zephyr had never seen the sea like this, and imagining seeing the view every day was incredible. She took her phone out and opened the camera, holding it up to take a photo.

"You should lower the exposure," the voice came from behind her, and she yelped, dropping her phone to the floor. It clattered, the screen cracking, and she groaned, bending to pick it up while looking up at the boy who had padded into the kitchen at the same time. The sudden movement sent a wave of dizziness crashing over her. She extended her arm to hold onto something but, with nothing but air, fell to her knees on the hard floor.

Ouch.

She sat her ass down, trying to let the wave pass, breathing in carefully with her eyes closed as the good doctor had told her.

"Count to three," the voice came again, and she opened her eyes, seeing Xander watching her curiously from the kitchen. He had grown up since the last time she'd seen him. His hair was a little longer with boyish waves, his frame a little taller. The most notable physical difference were the frameless glasses perched on his nose that hadn't been there before.

"Three what?" she panted, catching her breath and holding her heart.

"Three. Like one, two, three. Breathe. One, two, three. Breathe," the boy instructed, going so far as to demonstrate.

Since she had nothing better to do, Zephyr followed his tutorial, breathed in, counted to three, exhaled, and repeated—once, twice, thrice. By the fifth set, her heart was beating normally again, and her dizziness was a distant memory.

She gave the boy a grin. "Thanks, Xander."

"You're welcome," the boy said, opening the fridge. She watched as he took out a glass bottle of orange juice. "Have you had breakfast?"

Was this boy, who couldn't be more than eight, offering to make her breakfast? What was Morana feeding him?

"Not yet," she replied, getting back to her feet and heading into the kitchen. It was a dream kitchen with so much open space and top-of-the-line appliances that it made her want to cook. "What are we making?"

He paused, looking her up and down but never quite in the eyes. Zephyr knew he was high-functioning autistic, and she had done her research on how she could make sure he had a good time with her on the flight over. The two times she'd interacted with him, he'd always been such a cool kid. She liked his company.

"Can you cook breakfast?" he asked her, his tone slightly disbelieving.

Zephyr blinked with exaggerated drama. "Excuse me? Of course, I can."

"I had to ask. Morana burns water. Tristan and I have agreed to never let her in the kitchen. It's a hazard."

A laugh bubbled out of her. "That's kind of cute."

"It's a safety precaution," he said so seriously that it cracked her up even more.

"If I promise not to burn your house, can I cook? I make killer pancakes!" Zephyr offered, her own stomach grumbling in response to the thought of food.

He nodded, pointing to what she assumed was the pantry. "The Ingredients are there. Please make sure they are buttery."

Zephyr saluted him. "Yes, sir." She opened the pantry and took out the ingredients. Xander poured her a glass of orange juice and then got her the mixing bowls and pans.

"So, I'll be here for a bit." She informed him while making the batter, hoping he didn't have an issue with that. From the little she had seen of him, he seemed pretty chill.

He validated that judgment when he said, "I know. Morana texted me."

Zephyr felt her eyebrows go up. It was definitely a little odd for a child his age to have a phone and be texting, but she didn't judge. Everyone had a different dynamic, and both he and Morana were quite unique personalities.

"What did she text you?" Zephyr asked, more curious than anything.

The boy fumbled in his pajama pockets, bringing out a small device. It wasn't as high-tech as most of the ones she saw; it was more basic than anything. He tapped on it several times and turned the screen so she could see.

Zephyr squinted at the tiny alphabets, wondering if they were the reason for his early eye prescription. The text read:

Morning Xander!

Something super urgent has come up and Tristan and I have to go take care of it. Aunt Zephyr *(please tell me you remember her or this will get awkwardddd melting face emoji)* is going to be here when you wake up and spend the time with you until we get back. Fingers crossed, we have some good news when we come home! *fingers crossed emoji*

Have a great day and lots of fun Love youuuuu *heart emoji* *kiss emoji*

Text or call if you need anything!

Cool *thumbs up emoji*

I like Aunt Zephyr. She cries a lot.

Don't say that to her face! It's impolite!! *hiding face emoji*

thumbs up emoji

He was a smart cookie because he had found a way around saying it to her face but instead showing her. But his replies threw her off, making her chuckle again. The contrast of the messages on the screen, especially the little thumbs up, was hilarious. The fact that the boy would always call her the crying lady set her off even more. Zephyr laughed again; after so long, it felt good.

Fuck, she felt good. After so long, there was something to feel good about.

And the fact that Morana had referred to her as 'Aunt Zephyr' made her soften inside. Whatever their hangups, she was relieved and glad to have a friend like Morana in her life now.

She looked back at Xander, realizing he was almost as tall as she was short, wanting to ruffle his bedhead hair but not wanting to make him uncomfortable.

"Awww you like me," she teased him.

He just pocketed his phone and drank his orange juice. Zephyr noticed he took three quick sips before pausing for a second and doing it again, his eyes on the mindless way she was mixing the batter. The sips, combined with him telling her to breathe in threes, made her take note of it. To match, she rotated the wooden spatula in her hand through the batter three times clockwise, paused, and did it again. "That better?"

He nodded. "It tastes better when you do it in threes."

"Really?" She was fascinated. "How?"

"Three is the dimension of the space we occupy physically," he told her, looking at her mixing the batter in the pattern now. "Anything physical we do, if we do it in threes, our systems align with the space we are in. Our eyes are trichromatic and can perceive only three primary colors... the rest are all added to them. Three is also the triad number and is important in geometries, which makes architecture we see all around the world. There is a progression in three and probability. The probability for any event can be concise in the rule of three. There is a primary triad in music, too, though I'm still reading about that. In mathematics, any equation will come down to three numbers, two on one side and one on the result. And the most interesting thing is computers for me. We can use three binary numbers to code anything, 01, 10, and 11. Morana told me she'll teach me when I'm older. There's rules of three in psychology too, Dr. Kol told me about that."

Zephyr was frozen, the mixing bowl forgotten. She watched in stunned shock as the boy spoke stuff most adults didn't know about, launching into more words than she'd ever heard him speak. He was not just special; he had to be *gifted.* This kind of intelligence and articulation was by no means normal in a child his age.

"Wow. Who's Dr. Kol?" she asked, genuinely not knowing but also fucking fascinated by the passion with which he was talking, his cadence quicker than usual.

Xander took some butter out of a fancy ceramic thing she needed to get. The butter was perfectly soft inside.

"He's my psychologist," Xander shared. "He talks to me and helps me." His tone let her know he didn't want to talk about that.

Breaking from her slight daze, Zephyr put on the pan, waiting for it to heat, and added the batter in. "Do you want three?"

He bit his lip, in a way that finally was like kids his age. "Can you make big ones so I'll be full?"

She grinned. "Of course." Adding more batter, she asked him. "So, have you made any friends at school?"

He shook his head. "No. I think some kids are mean. Most of what they say goes over my head. Morana gets mad though."

Shitheads. She hated how cruel kids could be, having been bullied herself, but she was glad he didn't get most of it. She pointed the spatula at him. "If anyone bothers you too much, tell someone about it. Tristan or Morana or a teacher. Anyone. Don't take shit from people, especially ones who don't know you."

"The pancake is burning," he pointed out and Zephyr immediately flipped it over, exhaling in relief when she saw it was fine.

"Are you sick?" the boy asked her out of nowhere.

Zephyr blinked at him. "What?"

He pointed to the living room. "You fell down dizzy. Are you sick?"

Zephyr stared at him for a long second, biting her lip. She hadn't had a chance to tell anyone. Dr. Nei had tested her and she'd come back positive. To say she'd been stunned would have been an understatement. Though the doctor had reassured her that it could have been missed due to her recent stress, and maybe the hospital hadn't tested her for it at all, it was completely normal and she just had to schedule an appointment with a gynac in the next week to make sure everything was as it should be.

She'd thought she would break the news to Alpha when he got back home. But before she could have, he'd been onto her, kissing the daylights out of her, just kissing because he'd been waiting patiently for her to give him a signal that she was ready in the headspace to have sex again. And then, in the middle of their makeout, Morana had called and the entire mood had shifted.

And now, standing in a strange apartment in a strange city looking at a boy who wasn't that strange to her, she realized he was about to be the first one to hear the news.

"Well," she began. "I'm pregnant."

Xander stilled, his eyes slightly widening, moving to her stomach. "There's a baby in your belly?"

Zephyr looked down at it, the curves hinted at in her loose top and smiled. "Yeah."

"How did it get there?"

Blood rushed to her cheeks at the innocent question, her gaze darting everywhere, mildly panicking because what the hell would she tell a child about how babies were made? She didn't want to be his first conversation about it, didn't want to say something that would traumatize him. She looked around the room for inspiration, before taking a deep breath in, realizing he was waiting for an answer.

"Well," she swallowed, taking one pancake off and putting it on the plate, then adding the batter for the second one. "When a man loves a woman, he gives her a special... gift that only he can. And when the woman loves him back, she accepts it. That gift becomes a baby."

There. That was very child-friendly and very simplistic.

Xander kept looking at her stomach. "That's not true. I was a baby but I don't think I came from a gift of love."

The heavy words, said with that simple, direct tone, shot through her heart. Zephyr looked at the little boy, wondering what his life had been like before, who he was born to, and knew she couldn't say anything to counter his statement because she didn't know anything.

"What do you think you came from?" she asked him casually instead, making another pancake, busying herself so it didn't seem she was too curious about his answer.

"I don't know," he simply stated. "I saw love after I was born, not before."

Zephyr bit her tongue to keep from prying. She didn't know anything about his past experiences and didn't want to tread over any trauma he may or may not have. "You're very loved now, even if people don't tell you."

He nodded. "I know. People express love differently. Some tell me, some show me, some do both."

"Good. You deserve all the love." Zephyr finally finished cooking—three with extra butter for him and one for herself—and plated up their food, placing them on the table. Xander, as well-mannered as he was, added glasses of water and more orange juice next to her plate first and then to his, and Zephyr wondered if that was something he'd learned before or after he'd come to live there.

They both hopped up on the stools, both their feet dangling in the air which made her chuckle, and dug in.

"Has Tristan given Morana his gift?" Xander asked just as Zephyr took her first bite. Her eyes widened, food going down the wrong pipe as she choked. She coughed, taking sips of water to clear her airway, her eyes tearing up both in shock and laughter. Oh, she was pretty sure Tristan had given Morana his *gift* many times. Just the way the man stared at her was enough to overheat libidos all around, but aside from that, there had been too many occasions on their video calls where Morana had had a look on her face Zephyr recognized very well—a woman well-satisfied and well-pleasured by her partner. She knew the look because she had seen it on her own face many times, though not recently. *Fuck.* She needed to get laid and needed her husband to lay her.

"You'll have to ask them that yourself," Zephyr told Xander, giggling at the thought of the boy asking Morana this and her reaction. Tristan probably wouldn't react. She'd never really seen much of any expression on his face. "It's a private thing."

Xander chewed his bite of food thoughtfully. "Tristan loves Morana, but she doesn't have a baby in her belly, but she loves him too, so he must not have given her the gift, or she would have accepted."

Oh, sweet summer child full of logic. Zephyr was absolutely not going to get into the discussion of protection against the gift with him. With his brain, he would have her talking about things a child should not be learning this early.

"How are the pancakes?" she asked, changing the topic instead.

"Good." He chewed some more. "Tristan makes better."

She'd heard he was a good cook but damn. Morana often talked about Tristan and Xander bonding over food, how it was somehow both of their love languages and how they plotted ways to keep her out of the space. She hoped someday she could taste something he made and see for herself what the reputation was about.

"Is it a boy or a girl?" Xander asked after a few minutes of companionable silence.

Zephyr shrugged. "I don't know yet. It's too early to tell."

"When will you know?"

"Maybe in a few weeks. I have a doctor's appointment soon, so they'll give me an exact time."

He cleaned off his plate, inhaling three pancakes faster than she ate her one. Damn, the boy could *eat.*

"Will you text me when you know?"

His question surprised Zephyr. "Sure." She'd take his number later. "Why do you want to know?"

"It's interesting," he told her. "Your body is like the oven. It cooks the baby, and it comes out when it's ready."

Wow. He was such an astute young man. Zephyr had zero doubts he was going to grow up into a force to be recknoned with. Good thing he was her friend now.

"I hope it's a girl."

Zephyr tilted her head at his words, her brows furrowing. "Why?"

Xander finished his juice and wiped his mouth with the back of his hand in a move that belied his age. "Aunt Amara has a tree for one of her babies that died," he told her, tapping his finger on the counter. Zephyr already knew about the tree. In fact, she'd been the one to send Amara a list of ideas when she'd talked about it.

"I know," Zephyr told him. "Why does that make you wish it's a girl?"

"So Tempest can have her sister, even if it's a cousin."

The words landed like a blow to her chest. Zephyr felt the tears fill her eyes as the thoughtfulness this child possessed, even in his logic, filled her heart. She knew he was protective of Tempest, but the fact that he wanted her to have a sister she'd lost. *Damn.*

"Are you crying again?" he asked, and Zephyr didn't know if she was projecting it but he sounded amused.

"No," she sniffled.

A noise left his mouth, and she realized he was chuckling next to her.

They wrapped up the breakfast in the next few minutes,

and she took her phone out to feed his number, forgetting that it was dead. Groaning, she let it down on the counter. Xander picked it up, turning it around and examining it with intent. She left him to it and cleared up the plates, rinsing and washing and stacking them on the side of the sink to drain. She cleaned up the cooking area and washed the bowls and pans, all the while aware of the young boy opening the back of her phone and tinkering around with something. It took her about half an hour to restore the entire space to its former glory. She returned to the counter, where Xander now sat with her phone lit up through the cracked screen.

She picked it up in amazement. "How did you fix that?"

He shrugged, like it was no big deal. "I just checked if something had come loose in the back when it fell. I've added my number to your list. You should really add a better password than 1234."

Zephyr began to laugh, a deep belly laugh, at being chided about it. Zen had told her countless times to do that, too, and she'd never done it. Shaking her head, not brought down by her sister's memory for the first time in months, Zephyr opened her texts and sent him one.

Hi!

I'm right here. Why are you texting?

204

She liked this game. Chuckling, she typed again, leaning on the counter opposite the boy.

Do you have any plans for today?

No.

"What do you say about a haircut?" she asked, brushing her fingers over the hair that had fallen on his forehead.

He pulled away. "No. I want it to grow more."

"Okay, okay. What about assisting with a makeover?" she suggested; her heart felt light, lighter than it had in weeks. "Should we do it?"

Xander looked at her stomach again. "What's a makeover?"

"It's when you change something about your appearance to feel good," she explained to him.

He gave her a once-over. "Why would you change anything?" The words seemed absurd as if she were absolutely perfect as she was.

Xander had no filter, and that just made what he said even more precious to her. "Can I hug you?" she blubbered, wondering if he knew how good he was for her soul.

He nodded, and she walked around the counter, wrapping her arms tightly around him and pressing a kiss on his head. He sat still, not moving but not resisting.

"Thank you," she whispered into his hair.

"For?"

"For being you." She stepped back, blinking at him with wet lashes. "Never change, Xander. You're perfect as you are."

A slight flush filled his cheeks at her words. "What are we doing for the overmake?"

"Makeover," she corrected and walked to the living area where her overnight bag and a kit she always had on her were. She opened the bag and took the large kit out, unzipping it and searching for the items she was looking for. Once she had them all, she turned to find him watching her hands curiously.

"Now, show me to a guest bathroom."

"Why?" he asked, looking at the items in her hand.

"Because we, my young grasshopper—" she grinned at him "—are going to color my hair."

It was time for a change.

MORANA

CHAPTER 15

MORANA, GLADESTONE

T RISTAN HADN'T STOPPED LOOKING at his sister.

Morana watched from the seat of the limo, which was taking them back to the private airstrip where they had landed not even an hour ago. She wondered what was going on in his mind and his sister's.

Morana looked at the girl, her emotions in turmoil inside her. A part of her was curious, and another was cautious. Curious because she wanted to know and understand who she was. Cautious because she wanted to know and understand who she was to the Shadow Man. Luna obviously knew who Tristan was and who all of them were.

After they had both finished crying holding each other, Luna had said a tremulous 'hi' to her brother, and Tristan had responded with his own soft 'hey', so much softer than she'd heard him be with any adult. She'd heard him speak that softly sometimes to Xander or Tempest, especially when he knew no one was around to see that side of him. Now, sitting in the back opposite her with Luna, his arm around her, holding her

208

close like he was never letting her go, emotion choked Morana. There was something so deeply moving about seeing him like that. He looked lighter than she'd ever seen him, as if a dark cloud that had always lived within him had dissipated, leaving room for some light to peek through, as if the rock that he had been rolling up the hill over and over had finally been put to rest.

His eyes locked with Morana as he tucked his sister close. He said so much to her, conveying so much with one look that she didn't have enough words to express it even to herself.

"Are you okay coming back with us?" Dante's gentle voice came from the side, speaking to Luna.

The young girl close to Morana's age opened her eyes that she'd closed resting against her brother, almost like she'd been napping. The brilliant green in them shimmered as she looked around the back of the limo, where Dante and Morana sat on one side, she and Tristan on the other, Alpha sitting at the front with one of his contacts who was driving.

Luna's eyes darted for a second before she gave a nod. She'd barely said any words, but then neither had Tristan. They'd both just been taking in the moment, basking in their new bond, what had been lost in their childhood refound in adult life. Morana could understand the sentiment, but her brain was also firing up with questions she wanted to ask the other girl. Where had she been all these years? What had she been doing? Who had she been with? What was her connection to the Shadow Man, and more importantly, did she know who he was? What was her connection with The Syndicate, and did she know about their operations? Who were the key players? There was so much she could know, so much Morana wanted to ask, but she kept quiet out of respect for this moment. They had all waited for so long for all the answers; a few more days while she adapted wouldn't kill them. Or at least she hoped it didn't.

Her phone vibrated in her hand with a notification, and she opened the private encrypted thread.

Get your codes ready again.

Fuck.

She hadn't even thought of the codes in over a year with everything that had been going on. The codes, she assumed, were the same ones she'd written as a bet that her ex-boyfriend Jackson had stolen from her, all on the command of her real father, whom she didn't know as anything but The Reaper. He had not only blocked her attempts to create another set of codes that would undo her first, just in case, as a failsafe. He had framed Tristan for it so she could go after him.

Morana watched the man she loved, thankful for the fact that her father had seen something she hadn't been able to in the beginning, enough to drive her to the point where they clashed over and over again. If he hadn't, Tristan would probably just have killed her, and she never even would have known why, and they never would have found a love so fulfilling it made everything that came before it disappear.

But why did the Shadow Man want her to work on the codes again? The man really just needed to meet her once so she could ask him the ten million questions she had.

She quickly typed in the encrypted text.

> Why would I do that?

For answers.

> Can we meet?

Tristan would go apeshit. He'd never liked her meeting the Shadow Man, but it wasn't like Morana had much of an option, not when she had been the one he'd contacted multiple times. She had to make do with the little leverage she had.

She waited for a text, but it didn't come. She typed again.

Thanks for the file. Can I ask why?

No response.

Sighing, she put the phone down, looking at her side to Dante, who was typing a text to Amara.

> We got her. All of us will be at the compound in a

> few hours.

Morana watched Amara's reply come immediately.

> I'll get things ready. How is she?

Dante hesitated, and Morana frowned, side-eyeing his screen as discreetly as possible, curious to learn about his thoughts.

> Will talk later.

> Ok. Love you

> Love you, my queen

Cute. But also interesting.

Dante clearly had some thoughts he wasn't comfortable sharing over text. Was it because of the suspicion she'd shared with him about Luna's possible, rather probable, connection to the Shadow Man?

She texted Dante, not wanting to break the silence and disturb the siblings, even though they weren't saying a word, just sitting together, occasionally looking at each other and holding each other. It was a sight that filled Morana's heart.

Any update on Vin?

Dante read her text and slid her a glance. He just shook his head once.

That was very off. Unless the man was genuinely doing some solid work undercover, in which case she would have heard something, he was either dead or he had never been who they'd thought. With the way betrayals were playing musical chairs, she wouldn't be surprised if someone unexpectedly took a seat next.

Since they had a few minutes before they got to the plane, and there wasn't anything else for her to do, Morana opened her encrypted texts with the Shadow Man again, ready to weasel out whatever she could unless he blocked the thread like he had many times before.

Do you know anything about Vin?

A few minutes went by, and nothing came.

Ugh.

The frustration mounted in her, and she put her phone down and got her tablet out from her tote bag, a tablet she used solely for her programs and nothing else. She logged into the special browser she had customized for herself, scrolling through any public and private databases. She added a filter of the age and set the program running to grab her a list. Parallelly, she pulled up one of Vin's photos she'd taken from Amara and ran the program to run facial recognition in the background, cross-referencing with the age-filtered database. If Vin had appeared in any camera in any part of the world, her programs would find him. She just hoped it was sooner rather than later.

That done, she went into the dark web. Rotating the cuff of her shoulders, she pulled out the data she had found for one of the many questions they'd had—how had Alpha's real name been on the lease of the property near Tenebrae that Tristan and Dante had found an initiation for The Syndicate in? Alpha had told them that his real name was known to his closest circle, but with the new knowledge that one of his closest people had been a henchman for the organization, sure enough, Hector had been the one to lease the property under Alessandro Villanova. Idiot had written it in his handwriting, that Morana had matched to his other work.

She checked everything to make sure she didn't miss anything. Morana had started trying to find tracks of his activity, retracing Hector's steps. Hector, who, as Alpha had told them, died brutally right here in Gladestone.

Morana pulled the coroner's report his brother, Victor, had shared with her—long-term torture and burned alive. It had either been an interrogation or been personal. And the thought of the burning, she looked up fire reports in orphanages. Even though she was certain there would be many, she added a filter for '20-30' years and hit search. A few results came up, and she began to scroll through them.

Wiring malfunction.

Next.

Gas tank explosion.

Next.

Forest fire.

Next.

Suspected arson.

She paused and clicked on the link. An old, black-and-white photo of a dilapidated, blackened building loaded with a headline under it.

Suspected arson at the Morning Star Home for Lost Boys

She looked under the headline, but the page didn't load, nothing but whiteness under the main text. She frowned, refreshing the page a few times and getting the same result over and over. Leaving the page, she typed the keywords *'arson'* + *'morning star home for lost boys'* and hit search.

Only three results popped up. One the page that was broken. One a small fire fifteen years ago at a completely different location—it seemed the orphanage had multiple homes. And a last one, again a broken link.

And it only gave her a hunch—it had been deliberately wiped clean. Someone hadn't wanted anyone to find anything about that fire, and the lack of information with the broken links only convinced her that it was about the Shadow Man.

Demon eyes.

She shuddered again.

"You okay?" Dante whispered from her side, looking at her with mild concern. She nodded.

There were still so many questions she had, and the deeper she dug, the more intense they became. And the one man she knew in her gut could answer all of them had refused to give them anything straight until two days ago. She glanced up, looking at the girl with such a pretty face and soft countenance, who was leaning on Tristan with her eyes closed.

Morana had a feeling they had opened a pandora's box, something that was old and powerful, and the demons were now out, hunting to get them all.

She just hoped they all made it out to the other side unscathed.

AMARA

CHAPTER 16

AMARA, TENEBRAE CITY

CLOUDS ROLLED ON THE horizon of the hills.

Amara sat in the gazebo, looking at the darkening sky, her phone in her hands, her heart full.

They had found her.

After decades, years and years of searching, Tristan had finally found a glimpse of peace. Amara felt like her heart would burst for the man she considered a brother, a man who had been her silent, vigilant protector as a boy, her only companion in a strange city when she'd been exiled, her closest confidant of one of her secrets for such a long time. If there was one man she knew who deserved peace and happiness, it was Tristan. Morana and her love had brought some semblance of both into his life, but now, with his sister found, he could finally feel the completion he had been chasing all his life.

The wind picked up, rustling the leaves in the garden, and her eyes landed on the tree she had planted just a few months ago. A magnolia so small it looked like a stronger gust of wind would blow it away. But it had taken roots, gripped into the soil, and was growing, little by little, every single day. Her little Serenity.

"When are they getting back, Mumu?" Her mother sat with her, rocking a sleeping Tempest side to side. Amara didn't know what she would have done without her mother, not just in life and her own healing but now, as a new mother. On days when she got overwhelmed, her mother just knew and stepped in, easily plucking her granddaughter and taking her care over for the day, giving Amara a moment to just *breathe.*

And as of late, the moments of being overwhelmed had been more than not. Juggling her roles of mother and wife, mafia queen, psychologist, rehabilitation center owner, friend, and everything in between, she felt like she was drowning some days. While Dante and her mother did so much, she didn't know if it was enough.

As if sensing her anxiety, Lulu climbed on her lap, put her front paws on her chest, and began to *purr.*

The rumbly motor-like noise relaxed her immediately, and she gave the feline head scratches just as she liked, intensifying the purring. The little feline, who had been with her for so many years, knew when her mama needed her love. Taking a deep breath in, cuddling the cat who was still so small though she was old now, she answered her mother. "They just got on the jet. They'll be coming here."

Tempest began to fuss slightly, and her mother patted her back, naturally quieting her down. "Not Shadow Port?" she asked in a low voice, trying not to wake up the sleeping child. "I would have thought Tristan would take her there immediately."

She had thought the same, but Dante had been the one to suggest bringing Luna here first. Though Tristan had a massive penthouse he called home, it could be too overwhelming for the girl to suddenly be there. They had no idea if she was afraid of heights or claustrophobia that apartments could give some people. The compound, in contrast, was more open and less suffocating, just in case. There was also incredible security here, as well as Amara, who was an expert at assessing trauma and just seeing how she would be. Tristan hadn't protested to that, a mark of how much he trusted her and Dante to take care of them.

"Dante thought she might be more comfortable here at first," Amara explained. "It's a neutral territory in a way and a good place for transitions for both Tristan and Luna."

Her mother nodded, her age now more evident on her face with the crow's feet and mouth lines that were embedded deeper into her skin. Her heart gave a pang at seeing her beloved mother get older, but she acknowledged what a privilege it was. Her friends didn't have mothers they could spend time with and see grow into their older ages, no one except Zephyr, and she was currently in a conflict with hers. It made her even more grateful for the relationship and bond she and her mother always had, one Amara hoped she and Tempest would also have one day.

Her coming into their lives had changed everything so much. It had not only changed them all as people but also their ambitions and what they wanted to do in the world. Both she and Dante were on the same page about wanting to make their dark world a better place for her to grow up in, so even if she saw all the darkness, she could see the light too. The only thing she hoped, having seen it too often with friends and clients, was not to give her any sort of parental trauma. It wasn't in their control but she could hope.

"Do you want me to have his cottage ready?" her mother asked. Amara looked in the direction of the lake, though she couldn't see it. Tristan's cottage had sat empty since she and Morana had left. They came visiting occasionally and stayed there, so she had the staff keep it clean, but for the special guest they were bringing, she didn't know.

Going with instinct, she looked at her mother and shook her head. "I got it cleaned last week, so it's ready for them. But I'm thinking of giving Luna the guest room in the west wing. That way, they could live close to each other and have enough space. In case she wanted to stay at the cottage, she would have the choice."

Her mother nodded, starting to get up but Amara stood before she did, depositing Lulu on the space she'd vacated. The cat immediately curled up, ready to nap.

"I'll check things," she reassured her mother. "You enjoy

your time with your grandbaby."

"My little Tutu," her mother kissed the baby's head, her nickname for her matching Amara's. Amara smiled and headed out of the gazebo, brushing her hand over the leaves of the magnolia and moving toward the mansion.

Over the last year, a lot had changed in their home but a lot hadn't. Structurally, it was still the same stunning marvel that it had always been, the heritage and history of the place preserved in its walls. But energetically, it felt different.

For one, she paid her staff a lot better than her mother had ever been paid. That, in turn, had not only made the staff happier but more loyal to her and Dante. And her mother, who had been well-respected by them for years, had taken over managing any issues. It had brought forth a much better work environment for them, and a much better home for her family.

The security had also been changed, men loyal to Dante promoted into better positions and those loyal to Lorenzo cut out. Though Dante was soft with his family, he was a badass with his men, something she saw every day that they looked up to him to lead them. He'd been cleaning up the businesses, getting out of all the shitty contracts and deals his father had been a part of, and though they were still mafia, it wasn't the same as Lorenzo's time.

And the extended Maroni family, the one that leeched off of them, had been kicked to the curb, including Chiara, much to Morana's delight. Adding Tempest to the mix of an already great atmosphere had just put a burst life into the place that hadn't been there before. Everyone, and she meant *everyone*, doted on the little girl. One gummy smile from her and the harshest of trained guards melted. She had literally seen a man she'd never seen smile wave at her daughter the other day when she waved at him enthusiastically from her pram.

Entering the kitchen, Amara informed the head chef about the additional guests they were expecting and to prepare a fabulous dinner for all of them. She then instructed the housekeeper to have the guest room prepared and the smaller family dining room ready for their meal together. Done with those, she looked down at her phone at a notification that had come in and frowned.

> Hi Dr. Maroni. Sorry to disturb you but you asked me to inform you in case anything odd happened with Lex. Please call me when you have time. It's not urgent – Nellie

Immediately, she dialed the number. The phone rang twice before being picked up.

"Dr. Maroni," Nellie greeted.

"What happened?" Amara demanded, walking out of the kitchen and down the corridor into the main living area.

"Lex had a session with Dr. Armstrong today," Nellie informed her. "And he said something Dr. Armstrong found very odd."

Amara knew all three in-house doctors reported anything

and everything odd to Nellie so she could report it to her. "Tell me."

Nellie hesitated. "Lex was speaking about friends before he was found, and we think he slipped up. He didn't mean to mention it because he clammed up immediately after that."

Amara waited, and after a beat, Nellie continued. "He mentioned Xander and talked a lot about him and how much he liked the boy. Went so far as to say Xander felt like a brother from another mother to him."

"Okay," Amara acknowledged, waiting for the odd part. She already knew how much Lex and Xander liked each other. It was amazing to know their friendship had somehow solidified so deeply.

"He mentioned something, Dr. Maroni," Nellie told her. "The way he was talking, Dr. Armstrong thinks he and Xander have spent much more time together than we know of."

That gave Amara pause. She looked out the window at the driveway, deep in thought. They had assumed when they found the boys that they'd all just been together temporarily, because none of the boys had shown a lot of bonding with each other. None except Lex and Xander. Could they have been together for longer? Could Lex actually know about Xander's past and history that none of them knew?

"Did he say anything else?" Amara asked, holding the ledge, eyes unfocused as her brain tried to put the missing pieces together.

"He mentioned a guardian," Nellie said, her voice perplexed.

Amara frowned. "A guardian angel?" Children had active imaginations, especially those who were alone. Maybe the boy thought of a guardian angel watching over him.

"No, an actual guardian," Nellie clarified. "He said something along the lines of how he wanted to be a cool badass when he grew up, just like their guardian was. And then he clammed up. He's never mentioned it before so Dr. Armstrong thinks it was a slip, especially since he tried to prod more. But he completely shut down."

"Did he mention the guardian in singular or plural?"

"Plural. *Their* guardian."

Their.

Lex and Xander's.

Who the hell was their guardian? The boys had been with them for a year, and they had never let anything like this slip before. Hell, she never would have suspected they grew up together if this seed of suspicion hadn't been planted in her head. Now that it was, their behavior and bond were making a lot more sense.

But who had been the guardian? Someone from The Syndicate? Or someone else? Lex thought he was a 'cool badass,' so who?

The more she mulled it over, the more her head began to hurt. Hell, she needed a little break. But there was no break to be had. She loved her life and was grateful for every blessing that she had, but lately, she was beginning to feel burnt out, and the candle from both ends almost melted completely.

"Dr. Maroni?" Nellie's voice in her ear reminded her she was still on call. *Shit.*

"Sorry, Nellie," Amara apologized. "I just got thinking. Please let me know if anything else happens. And keep an eye on him."

"Of course. Have a good night."

With that, they disconnected, and Amara looked at the hills she called home and wondered when this would all be over—all the questions, all the mysteries, all the chaos.

At least, a huge step in that direction had just been taken with the finding of Luna. Though she'd told her mother valid reasons, she sensed that Dante had another reason for wanting to bring her here first.

"We'll talk later."

The *"We'll talk later"* was their undecided code for *"there is a lot more that I can't talk about right now but will discuss when I see you."*

Amara was curious as to what it could be. Knowing they would be in the air and that she had time to kill, she pressed the video button for one of her favorite people.

The call was picked up, and a sight she was not expecting

greeted her.

Zephyr, sitting with her hair in a transparent shower cap, the disposable kind, some kind of creamy product slathered onto her head and contained in the cap. It was already dark in Shadow Port, and from the light in the penthouse, Amara could tell Zephyr was on one of the stools around the kitchen island. A glitch at the corner of the screen marred the video.

"What happened to your screen?" Amara asked, laughing.

"Long story," Zephyr sighed. "But good news is that Xander fixed it for me enough that it's functioning."

At the mention of the boy and the questions around him, Amara felt her smile dim slightly. She wished there was a way for them to just get him to talk, but he was locked down tight about anything to do with his past. "How is he?" she asked instead, focusing on her friend and sister-in-law.

"I love him," Zephyr was enthused. "We had such a good day. We cooked, colored my hair, played god-knows-how many rounds of uno, and I lost most of them. Then we watched a sci-fi movie that went completely over my head, but at least the main guy was hot."

Amara chuckled. "That's what matters, eye candy."

"I know, right?" Zephyr laughed too, and Amara was so happy to see it. It had been too long since she had seen her friend so bright, her eyes shining and lips so wide. The death of her sister had hit her *hard.* Amara couldn't even imagine the kind of pain she must have been dealing with, but the light had gone out of her eyes for so many weeks, Amara had begun to worry. And she knew she hadn't been the only one. Grief was inevitable, but they couldn't lose sight of life and the relationships they did have.

Zephyr hopped down from the stool and picked up her phone. "I have to wash this out so come with me."

"Where's Xander?" Amara asked. It was too early for his sleep time.

"He had some homework to do, so he's in his room," Zephyr told her, setting the phone down on the sink. Amara watched the ceiling as she heard the sound of the door locking and the shower turning on.

"You could have just flipped your hair down and washed it, you know," Amara told her, talking to the guest bathroom ceiling. It looked to be the same guest bathroom she'd used when visiting.

There was just the sound of running water for a few minutes before Zephyr spoke. "I would have usually. But I get dizzy if I bend too much or too quickly these days."

Amara felt a furrow come between her brows. There wasn't any connection between grief and dizziness that she knew of. Unless she wasn't eating or keeping herself hydrated enough. But she'd just mentioned cooking and eating so that was out.

"Have you seen a doctor?" Amara asked, concerned about this. Dizziness, especially persistent, wasn't a good sign.

"Yup." The sound of water shut off, and Amara could hear

the shampooing instead. "I'm pregnant."

A gasp left Amara. "No way!"

Zephyr chuckled. "Yes, way!"

Amara shrieked with happiness, a sound Zephyr matched on the other end before her face suddenly appeared on the screen, shampoo and all. "Don't tell anyone!"

She ran back to the shower, and Amara laughed. "Your secret is safe with me. Why haven't you told your husband yet?"

"I want to surprise him."

Ah. So that was what the whole makeover was for. They talked as Zephyr rinsed her hair out, telling Amara about the safety of dyeing hair during pregnancy, what to use and do, and how she'd done many dye jobs for pregnant ladies when she'd been a hairstylist. After a few minutes, she came back on the screen in a cute loungewear set and a towel wrapped around her head.

"Do you know if Alpha be staying over at the compound?" Zephyr asked her, moisturizing her face. "I haven't talked to him yet. I'm scared I'll spill the beans on the phone, and I don't want to. I need to see his face when I tell him. Possibly doing something naughty."

Amara shook her head. "I have no clue," she answered the first question. "But if he does, you need to pack up Xander and get here. Both of you!"

Zephyr nodded, her hair hidden under the towel. Amara was

curious about the color, but she wanted to let it be a surprise. It was good to see the other woman so excited about things. Amara knew firsthand how becoming a mother changed her perspective on things. Suddenly, her worldview became more focused, life shifted and realigned to make the best of things. Or at least it did for the good mothers. She had no idea how some, like her friend's mothers, let their children alone to be devoured by the demons.

"Are you doing okay?" Amara asked, genuinely hoping for a good answer.

Zephyr sighed. "I guess. It varies from day to day, you know." Amara knew exactly what she meant. "Some days, I miss Zen so much I feel like I won't be able to breathe. But some days, like today, the world feels a little brighter again. I feel like the baby," she held her stomach for a second, "is her way of looking out for me, you know? Like she saw me struggling and wanted to send me something to live for again."

"That's a beautiful way to look at this, Zee," Amara told her, touched by her perspective. It was no news how deeply the death had shaken her, and seeing her be optimistic felt like a balm to her soul.

"It's so weird." Zephyr massaged her face, her skin plump and glowing. "I've only known about the baby for less than a day, but I already love her so much!"

Amara could relate. Learning she had been pregnant had shifted everything for her. It was why she'd run away. "Her?"

Zephyr just smiled. "It's a feeling."

"Then trust it," she advised. "Take it from one mom to another. When it comes to the babies, trust your gut."

"I just hope nothing bad happens now."

Amara bit her tongue on that. She hoped too, but something inside her, something deep-rooted that was worried for her family and friends, told her it was far from over.

DAINN

CHAPTER 17

DAINN, GLADESTONE

DAINN WATCHED THE REUNION from the shadows behind the beams. There was a secret cache of space up
in the rafters, and he crouched down there, watching them.

If his *flamma* had thought he'd leave her alone, especially in
this part of the city, she still didn't know him very well. There
wouldn't be one moment that he wouldn't have his eyes on her,
not after she'd given herself to him, and definitely not after
the last time he'd left her unsupervised. His one mistake had
cost him six months of scouring the filth of this city, killing
more people in the span of weeks than he had in years, until
the black on his body had absorbed all the blood he'd spilled.
It had almost cost him her life, and that wasn't a mistake he
was going to make again.

Head tilted to the side, he silently lingered and saw the raw
emotion wash over Lyla's face as she looked at her brother, so
much so that he knew he'd made the right decision. She needed to have this in her life, needed to see where she came from
so she could understand where she was going. Lyla needed to

find her roots to bloom. Her brother would root her. And he? He would be the thorns on the stem, leaving the soft petals to spread her fragrance while spilling the blood of anyone who tried to pluck it.

Her brother, Tristan Caine, the cold predator of the mob, weeping like a boy.

Dainn didn't know what he'd expected from the man, but this display of emotions hadn't been it. It seemed like the siblings were more similar than anyone had thought, both feeling too many things, only Tristan had learned to hide his better and Lyla still wore her on her sleeves for anyone to see.

His eyes moved to Dante Maroni standing at the door like a guard, protecting the pair inside. But it was the look on his face, almost contemplative, that gave Dainn pause. Dante was looking at Lyla like he couldn't decide if he was going to trust her yet. Had he felt normal things, he would have been offended by that on behalf of his *flamma.* He almost felt pride instead, proud because a powerful man wasn't underestimating his *flamma.* That pleased him because she wasn't to be underestimated. As innocent as she was, she had a fire within her that could raze the world down, so powerful it could be a force to behold, but so hidden she didn't see it herself.

"Hi," Lyla's little whisper had his eyes going back to the siblings.

"Hey," Tristan whispered back. From the angle, it was difficult to make out the other man's face, but Dainn was sure it was a reflection of what he was seeing in Lyla's. A reunion full of emotions. It was almost like watching a movie, trying to strategize and dissect everything, except the main protagonist was his woman.

Morana stood at the door with Dante, her face unguarded, posture slightly funny. Dainn narrowed his eyes, watching the way she leaned a bit more to her right. He knew she'd been shot, but from the medical reports he had accessed, she seemed to have made a good recovery. Maybe it was the exhaustion of the last forty-eight hours since he'd sent the text out. He doubted she would've had much rest in the ensuing chaos.

But he hoped she rested a bit, that they all did because there was more chaos yet to come.

He looked down at his watch, noting the time. This should be wrapping up soon, and then he would have somewhere else to be.

Just as he thought it, Tristan stood, still holding Lyla's hand, and brought her to her feet. They stared at each other, before Lyla launched herself at him, and he caught her, hugging her tightly for long minutes. As much as he disliked the man, mainly because of the power he was now going to hold in his *flamma's* life, he couldn't deny that Tristan Caine loved her. He didn't know her, but he loved her. His ceaseless search for her for decades was admirable, especially because of how rare it was in their world. People gave up hope more quickly than they gave up their life. For Tristan, it had been the opposite and a part of Dainn, the one that wanted Lyla to be happy, was glad. Because had Tristan Caine not been the brother he had been, Lyla would have never known. Had he just been an excuse of a man like most waste-of-space men he saw, Dainn would have happily kept that information to himself if he'd had a single shred of doubt that her relationship with her brother would do her any emotional or psychological damage.

"We should go," Alpha announced from the door, and Dainn took him in as well. The man was a giant but a gentle one. His wife, a sweet little thing, was gentle too. The whole group would be good for his *flamma*. It would be good for her soul, so when he came back for her, she would be more whole, more at peace. He hoped it would make her laugh more easily too, the memory of the sound and what it did to his brain enough to make him grip the beam at his side.

Listening to Alpha's words, the group wrapped up. Tristan led Lyla to the door after she took the bag Dainn had packed for her, pausing for what looked like introductions in a voice too low for him to hear. Morana hugged her, and both the men gave her nods since Tristan refused to let her out from under his arm. And then, they all exited.

Dainn waited a beat, making sure they were gone from the immediate area, before jumping down from the rafters, landing in a crouched position for the least impact. He straightened fluidly, moving next to the door and peering out.

A limo was parked in the front. Everyone got in, and the limo rolled out.

Once the coast was clear, Dainn exhaled, the sound louder than he'd wanted it to be. He looked at the exact spot he'd stood with her for the last time with her, tasting her lips and hearing her voice, knowing that even though he would keep visual on her, her sound and touch would still leave him empty. It hadn't been five minutes and he already felt hollow.

But he had things to do and a threat to annihilate. And then, they could be together again.

He walked out into the industrial block, pulling his hood over his head and hands in his pocket, adopting a hunched gait so anyone looking would think it was a random junkie. Daylight was trickier to navigate. In daylight, he had to adapt and adopt personas to give the illusion that he wanted to any onlookers. He could be a billionaire executive as easily as he could be a homeless junkie, both personas that had a slight grain of experience lending it more credibility. As he made his way to the next block, he thought about the time he'd been on the street as a teen, wondering how things would have been if he'd had a sister or a brother to look after. Dainn didn't know if he wouldn't have cared at all, or if him caring would have culminated into more chaos. Watching Tristan with Lyla, he wondered absent-mindedly how things would have been if he'd had her much before as kids. Would it have been the same? It wouldn't have surprised him if they'd crossed each other's paths sometime before since they'd both been in the same dark circles all their lives.

A factory came into view, and this one was not abandoned. It belonged to some manufacturing company, with tall gray chimneys emanating tall gray smoke into the sky. Even daytime in Gladestone was gray. The city was a shitshow.

Dainn walked into the factory with the same hunched demeanor, inconspicuous and hiding in plain sight. Workers were focused on doing their thing. Some homeless people took up space in the side, thanks to pimping to the manager of the place. Even without The Syndicate, the whole machinery was corrupt as fuck. Humanity was corrupt. That was the only truth of life. Except for rare occasional exceptions, morality and humanity were selective facades opted by those in power to hide they were powerful. The whole system was rigged, and Dainn had zero compunction making use of it for his own benefit. If power was to be had, better *he* have it than someone else.

He slipped to the back, knowing the entire floor plan having looked it up earlier. Had to thank public databases for making it so easy.

Walking down a corridor, much less crowded than the front, he headed to the office area, where his prey was hidden.

Sounds of grunting came from behind closed doors, and Dainn wondered how humans could find pleasure in something without any connection. He couldn't imagine being inside a woman who wasn't his *flamma*, couldn't imagine his skin touching any other, couldn't even tolerate the sound of anyone else's moans in his ears. Sex without connection had zero meaning and zero purpose. The world was idiotic to engage in something so stupidly unsatisfying, creating a hole bigger and bigger each time that needed more and more stimuli to fill it, like a toxic endless loop.

Lyla would have chided him and told him not to be so judgemental of people's decisions. His lips twitched, imagining it.

With that smile, he pushed the door open. Idiot hadn't even locked it.

The round, older man looked up with anger, panting as his tiny cock flapped to find a hole, the boy he had pressed over the table looking around in desperation to escape. The boy couldn't have been older than fourteen, maybe fifteen, and Dainn grit his teeth. The dicks who preyed on children were cowards. It wasn't his morality or his own experience speaking, it was just the fact that children were helpless. There was such a power vacuum in that dynamic that it was just wrong, like pitting a puppy and a snake together. Of course, the snake was going to bite and poison the trusting, innocent creature. They ate their own eggs if need be, and the older man was exactly such a snake.

Xavier, also known as Mr. X, also the man who had knowingly sicced his dirty dogs over his own flesh-and-blood daughter, had been hiding in plain sight for a week. Mr. X had sent his men to abduct, torture and rape Amara Maroni when she had been fifteen years old. Dainn had read the reports and heard the stories during his interrogations, and the reason he'd wanted to see Amara speak at the conference years ago had been to see how she'd grown up after that. It had been a surprise to see the beautiful woman with her head as high as her empathy. She was an interesting study of how some victims took their trauma and turned it into something better. Zenith had been similar in that sense. After escaping The Syndicate, she had dedicated her life to rehabilitating victims of violent crimes.

It made him wonder how Lyla was going to be once she fully healed, because heal she would. Would she be like her old friend, or would she be something that surprised him yet again?

"Out," Dainn told the young boy. "You didn't see me. If you say a word to anyone, I will come after you."

The boy nodded and ran off. He was terrified enough that Dainn knew he wouldn't say anything. Usually, he didn't leave loose ends but he didn't touch the kids. There were a lot more ways to silence them if need be. Even better to bring them over to his side.

Dainn closed the door and strolled into the office, a tiny congested room with a tiny window, and sank down on the chair. "Tsk tsk. You've been hiding, Xavier."

The man spluttered, his dick still hanging out. "Who the

fuck are you?"

"Sit down," Dainn commanded. How this man had given Amara Maroni her genes would be one of life's greatest mysteries. Maybe she took more after her mother.

His hand inched toward the phone on the cluttered table and Dainn shook his head. "I wouldn't do that if I were you."

Xavier's hand stopped. "What do you want?"

"To talk," Dainn lied. He was going to gut him like a fish. "Sit."

He sat. Good.

"Now, tell me about dear boy Vinnie. Where do you have him?"

Xavier's eyes shifted to the side. "If you work with Maroni, I already sent a message that he was fine."

Dainn just stared at him silently. He knew with the hood and his eyes the way they were—*demon eyes* as people had called as a child—were freaky when he stared like that. He knew the exact effect his eyes had on people given how he looked at them. A hard stare to make cowards piss, a soft stare to make people comply. The only time he didn't manipulate them was when he was with *her*. He let his raw, unfiltered intensity show, and she looked him straight in the eyes, absorbing it into her, taking his harsh into her soft.

After moments of uncomfortable silence and shifting, Xavier spoke again. "Last I heard, he was using a girl to go undercover with her master."

Lyla's only other friend, Malini. The girl who, Lyla had told him, helped her during her pregnancy and delivery. The girl who had helped her escape the night she had met him. For that alone, she warranted his consideration. Had it not been for her, he would have never met his *flamma* or her boy, the only two people he cared about living.

Though he'd taken Xander as a baby, he had grown up so smart it had impressed even him. Dainn had always given him honesty—although a child-friendly version—and he had always respected him for it in return. Surprisingly, Xander and that crazy boy, Lex, had convinced him to become an unlikely duo. And for Dainn, it had been convenient because Lex liked chaos, the little shit being the one going undercover for him at the orphanage he'd led Morana to.

"That's funny," he told Xavier, coming back to the conversation. "I don't remember seeing her or him while skinning the master." The master had been one of the Syndicaters that Dainn had tracked and killed during the time Lyla had been missing. Usually, skinning wasn't his style, but he'd been slightly... *unhinged* during the time, his need to send a message to all the Syndicaters loud and clear:

He was coming for each and every one of them unless they released her.

The only reason they had suddenly let her go after six months had been because he'd gone on a rampage and tracked and killed three of the leaders and dozens of their underlings.

The Shadow Man had never been as terrorizing or as feared as he had been during and since then.

Lyla had no idea why she had been released suddenly, and he was probably never going to tell her, never remind her of the time she had been violated. He still remembered seeing it on his screen, them broadcasting it to him from the little room while he went ice cold trying to track her down. They had kept someone on their payroll dedicated to distracting him and diverting his leads, which was the only reason it had taken him so long to track her.

It had been the third leader, Malini's master coincidentally, who had squealed like a pig and told him of where they had kept her and how they'd let information about her leak out. The fact that he had squealed had gotten out and by the time Dainn had reached the warehouse, she had disappeared again, leaving behind the filthy sheets and bed they had violated her on. Dainn had taken it all in, breathed in the space, and vowed to bring the men back exactly to the same place and let her have her vengeance... after he had his fun. He'd deserved some vengeance too.

But first, he'd had to find her. From that, he had simply tapped into any leads Morana had found, finding a location Vin had texted her about, and he'd gotten there a few minutes after them.

A few minutes almost too late. He remembered. The way she'd been limp in the ugly, barren room, a bottle tipped to the floor, almost empty. Her eyes open but unseeing, the life almost out of them.

It had taken everything, *everything* inside him, to stay calm and get her out undetected. Because the way she had been, the way she had almost gone into the gorge over the brink, he knew no one could bring her back. No one except him.

He had walked the darkness she had been in, conquered it, and made it a part of himself. He was the only person she trusted, had trusted for years, even if she was wounded. And most importantly, he was the only one with the answer she had held on for, a leverage he was going to use ruthlessly if it meant bringing her back from the edge. Had her family found her then, the way she'd been, they wouldn't have been able to save her. They would have loved her but wouldn't have understood her, wouldn't have known every ugly thing that happened to her, and still looked at her the same. Even an inflection of sympathy, of pity, would have tipped her over the edge. She would have died from depression or tried to kill herself again.

And he couldn't let that happen.

The world would cease to exist if she did.

It was the way her mouth would open on a silent scream as he made her come again and again, after she had already screamed loudly for a while. It was the way he saw something vulnerable in her eyes so alive and vibrant it pulsed with life. It was the little laugh she had when he touched a ticklish spot by accident, sometimes on purpose, before a soft smile replaced it. It was how she never held back her responses from him, letting him know with everything she had how he pleased her, even as she chided him, even as she clawed him, even as she consumed him. She let him restrain her, let him keep her under him, let him do whatever the fuck he wanted to, and took everything from him in return. It was how all of those never ceased to thaw something in his chest that had been frozen for a long time.

She could never lose the life in her. He would deaden the entire world without remorse if that meant she *lived.*

But thankfully, that didn't seem necessary for now. The Syndicate had no idea their existence had been hanging by a thin thread of sanity built by the breaths of a broken girl. She was in a much better place, good enough that he didn't worry about her harming herself on her own without his supervision. Though he would keep an eye on her, he knew she was going to immerse herself in the experience in a way that was healthier for her compared to what it would have been before, something he had discussed extensively with Dr. Manson. Before, she had never seen the sky. It had taken her months of seeing it to get to a place where she now realized she had wings. Now, she was learning how to fly.

"S...shadow man?"

The stuttering words broke through his musing.

Ah, fear. Good old fear. Fuck, he reveled in seeing it in the eyes of his victims.

And Xavier's eyes were telling him he knew his time was up, that he knew from the rumors that you didn't see the Shadow Man unless you were going to die.

And Dainn was sitting there in front of him, completely casual. Xavier knew. And Dainn enjoyed seeing that look on his face.

"Please," he begged like they always did. "I'll tell you anything. I'll join forces with you. Don't kill me, please."

It was pathetic, the snot and tears as he blubbered like a baby. Babies had more dignity than this piece of shit. He knew because he'd handled one.

"Then tell me what I want to know," Dainn stated, letting him think he had a chance to be the exception and make it out alive. He should know better. There were no exceptions for the Shadow Man but one, the only one they had all messed with and were going to pay the price for.

"I'm telling the truth," the older man beseeched. "That was the last I heard from him. After you killed the master, everyone went underground. I've been hiding here since then."

That tracked with what he knew. "Tell me about the Syndicater."

Xavier swallowed noisily. "Which one?"

Dainn just leveled him with a look, one he knew was scary.

"There were four, I think."

"Wrong answer."

"I swear," Xavier rushed out. "My handler is dead, and all

he talked about were the four snakeheads. You know, like the snakes they have everyone wear in some way or the other?"

Which was genuinely stupid for a top-secret organization. Why the fuck would they want to have such a recognized mark on their members? Unless it was narcissistic and fed into their illusion of power.

"Four snakeheads," Dainn mused. Hector had told him there were five, that of the last two remaining, one had killed the other and taken control. Was there actually a fifth one, or was there more misinformation spread down the line? Had there always just been four? It was important to know because he needed to weed out and eliminate possible suspects, his own sperm donor being one. While he had been a leader back in the day when Dainn had been conceived, it was entirely possible that he was already dead and gone, power being seceded to others. Dainn hadn't been able to track some information down, since it was buried deep under the rubble of dirt and darkness, but he could feel himself getting closer to it.

"This is all I know. Please let me go. I can tell you something else," Xavier started, then hesitated. "I don't know if this will be helpful at all, but there was a rumor once."

Dainn waited him out. Patience was one of the most powerful tools and one not enough people possessed.

"A few years ago," Xavier started. "I heard rumors of some kind of experiment."

Dainn waited more, wondering where this was going.

Xavier leaned forward, his voice getting lower. "It wasn't a big rumor. I only heard it in passing at one of the parties, but there's never been any evidence of this. I never found it."

After the rambling, the older man took a shaky breath. "If I tell you, will you let me live?"

Dainn chuckled at his attempt at bargaining. He could just find out another way. "Depends on how good your information is. So far, it's looking bleak for you, Xavier."

"Okay, okay," the man hurriedly let out. "The rumor was that the Syndicate was supplying flesh to some government organization for experiments. Human experiments."

Dainn raised an eyebrow. This was the first he had heard of this. While there had always been conspiracy theories about the dealings and activities of The Syndicate, this was something he'd never even heard whispers of before.

"Alright," he conceded to the man. "I'm intrigued."

Xavier beamed as if he had granted him life and not a concession to continue. "I don't know what kind of experiment." His voice got more hushed. "I don't know when or if it happened, or what was involved."

"So, you know nothing but a vague rumor?" Dainn asked, his tone even.

Xavier pursed his mouth.

Well then. Dainn straightened, getting to his feet and coming around the table.

"Please," the other man began to beg with desperation. "I

can find out if you want. Give me a chance. I have sources and ears on the ground. I'll get you every information you want."

Dainn leaned his hip against the table, taking out a metal wire from the inside of his hoodie pocket.

"If information about it exists," he told Xavier, uncoiling it, seeing the other man shaking so much he began to piss. Dainn walked around behind him, wrapping the wire around his fat neck and pulling, leaning down to say. "I will find it. But thanks for the tip-off."

And with that, he snapped his wrists apart, a spray of blood jetting out from his severed neck as Xavier Rossi died a brutal death.

ALPHA

CHAPTER 18

ALPHA, TENEBRAE CITY

S OMETHING WAS UP WITH his wife.

He didn't know what it was, but the fact that she hadn't called him once all day had him slightly worried. They didn't message since she knew he wouldn't be able to read the message with his single eye, and knowing that, she always called him. He'd sat on Dante's jet, which was so much more opulent than his was, expecting to see a missed call from her when he landed. And there had been nothing. He wanted to think maybe she had just gone to bed early, Shadow Port a few hours ahead of them. He would call her once he got to the compound.

The phantom ache in his missing eye, one that flared up occasionally, made him sigh.

His half-brother, Alpha had learned, was a man of expensive, refined tastes, more airy and polished than Alpha's rugged, earthier preferences. His mansion and compound in Tenebrae were a gazillion times older and more opulent than his exotic, more raw one. Dante's property was polished and mowed; Al-

pha's was wild and natural. They were such drastically different people in terms of taste, and yet, Alpha had to admit they
were very similar when it came to two things—their workouts
and their women.

One of his favorite things about being in Tenebrae was the
early morning fight-offs he and his brother had. It almost felt
like playing. Both of them were almost matched in size, but
where Alpha had more strength, Dante had more speed. It
began at Dante's wedding a year ago, and they continued it
whenever they were together.

As for women, that was self-explanatory. They had both
found the love of their lives early—though Alpha had forgotten his and Dante hadn't. Where Alpha had spent years alone
believing he couldn't have love, Dante had spent his years
being in love and fighting for it. Now that Alpha had it too,
he understood.

The hills outside the city where the compound was rolled
around them as the fleet of vehicles made their way up. He
sat in a Range Rover with his brother driving, Morana and
Tristan with his sister in the one behind them, and two more
security guards behind them. It was a little extra, but Alpha
didn't blame him, not after everything Dante had to protect
on his territory.

"What do you think about Luna?" Dante asked Alpha, driving over a curve in the empty road that led only to his property.

Alpha turned his neck to look at him. "She's been through stuff." Luna Caine, if she even went by that name, which he highly doubted, was an ethereal kind of beauty with a haunted look in her eyes. Alpha had worked with and seen too many women with that kind of look. He didn't need to talk to her to understand she'd seen and survived horrors most people couldn't imagine. And seeing how tiny she was, it immediately brought forth an innate protectiveness inside him.

"I agree," Dante said. Alpha knew the man recognized that look too, probably having seen it in his wife's eyes in the past.

"I want to ask if you think she could be working for The Syndicate," Dante spelled out, much to Alpha's surprise. "I can't discuss this with Tristan or Morana, not right now. They should focus on her and their relationship."

Alpha mulled it over. "If she's working for The Syndicate, which I do doubt, then she's both highly brainwashed and a good actress because deception isn't what I smelled on her."

Dante let out an exhale, his shoulders relaxing. "I'm relieved to hear that. I want to trust her, but I'm taking her to my home to my family. My only daughter. It's—"

"—understandable," Alpha interrupted. Betrayal made people question everything. "Better safe than sorry."

Dante took another bend, expertly swerving around. The gates to the property opened, and he drove through, on and upward.

"How's Zee doing?" his brother asked, and as much as Alpha

had come to like him, he was still an annoying shithead when it came to ribbing him.

"You tell me," Alpha grumbled. "You talk to her more than her own mother these days."

Her mother was a sore topic for his wife, both stubborn women of two generations refusing to budge from their stances.

"She does like me." Dante chuckled, making Alpha want to do some damage to his pretty face. He wondered idly if Dante would look half as good with a scar and eyepatch as he did. The thought gave him some comfort.

"She likes everyone," Alpha corrected, not wanting his brother to believe he was special. If liking people and seeing the good in them was a championship, his wife would be the first in line, a quality that both enticed and exasperated him about her. But a large part of him hoped she didn't lose that, that his world didn't make her jaded enough to forget what made her *her*.

The mansion finally came into view, a grand monstrosity of construction against the backdrop of the setting sun. Amara stood at the mouth of the driveway with Tempest on her hip, his little niece who was growing up too fast. Dante stopped the vehicle and got out, heading straight for them.

Alpha watched in mild awe as Tempest, who had been looking at the cars curiously, burst out into the biggest smile, a smile bigger than her face, her gums exposed, her little mouth wet, her bright eyes lit up at her father. Something moved inside Alpha's chest at the sight, seeing the way Tempest immediately raised her chubby little arms dimpled at the elbows, a clear indication for her father to pick her up, and as soon as Dante did, she began to babble baby nonsense interspersed with the sounds of *dada ,dada, mama, dada.*

And looking at them, Alpha realized he wanted that nonsense too. He wanted to come home one day to a little part of him that would light up his life, looking at him like he was the best thing in the whole world, loving him with the wholeness of a tiny heart.

Fuck, he wanted to be a father too.

But for now, he would be the uncle.

He headed toward them as well, greeting Amara with a small smile. "Looking good as always, Amara."

"So good to see you," Amara gave him a side hug.

"Stay away from my wife," Dante said from the side, in a ridiculous sing-song voice as he talked to the babbling baby.

Alpha grunted. "You don't stay away from mine."

"Boys," Amara sighed, rolling her eyes.

Alpha ignored them and went straight to Tempest, who turned that megawatt grin at him and easily came into his arms.

"How's my favorite niece?" he asked her, and she'd seen him enough times to recognize him as a favorite person, too. She immediately lunged for his eyepatch, which she loved to put

RUNYX

into her mouth for some insane reason.

"No, baby," Amara chided. "We don't chew on people's clothes."

As if she understood, she went for his nose instead, biting the top of it. Alpha felt the unscarred side of his lips go up. There was something so simple, so pure about being in her company. Were all babies like this? Because if they were, he was going to make a fleet of them with his wife. The idea of knocking her up was immensely appealing to him.

Another car pulling into the driveaway made them all turn. The doors opened, and Morana came out first, followed by Tristan, who extended his hand and brought out his sister.

His wide-eyed sister, who was looking at the mansion with her mouth open, like she had never seen something like it before. Alpha paused with that thought. Was it possible that she hadn't? He observed her closely, seeing her eyes moving around to take the structure, the front lawns that sloped down, the entire vista of hills, before coming back to the people, all of whom she'd met except Amara. Her eyes stayed on Amara for a long second before moving and stopping on Tempest in his arms.

He watched like a hawk as her face froze, her eyes staying on the baby much longer than it had on the house or the strangers. He exchanged a look with Dante, seeing that he'd noticed it too. Of course, he had. It was his little princess. Then, as if catching herself, she immediately looked to Amara.

Interesting.

Amara took that as her cue and moved to her with a soft smile, one he'd seen her give Zephyr when she'd been grieving.

"It is so good to finally meet you," Amara greeted in her raspy voice. Luna's eyes widened slightly at hearing it, her eyes going to the scar Amara had on her neck, completely exposed. She had covered it up until recently, but he'd noticed her leaving it uncovered more often now.

"Welcome to my home." Amara took hold of both her hands, giving it a squeeze even he could see. She looked to Tristan, who stood right next to his sister, not having left her side since he'd found her. He kind of understood. Had he been in Tristan's place, he probably wouldn't have either.

"I'm so happy for you," Amara told Tristan sincerely, and he gave her a nod. Alpha didn't understand their friendship much, but he knew it was a deep one.

"You..." Luna began, her tone soft, but everyone looked at her. "You have a beautiful home."

Amara beamed at her, pulling her in and leading her toward the entrance where they stood, the perfect hostess. "You've already met my husband, Dante, and my brother-in-law, Alpha?"

Luna nodded, glancing at them both before looking at Tempest.

"This is my daughter, Tempest," Amara offered, her eyes also seeing what he was. She was a professional head doctor;

she was probably ten steps ahead of all of their observations.

Luna gave Tempest a small smile that trembled on her lips. "Hi, Tempest."

Tempest looked at the newcomer with a wide look, her big eyes on her gold necklace. She lunged for the necklace, almost grabbing it in her grubby hands, and Alpha contained her squirmy, wiggly body.

There was silence for a few minutes, slightly awkward, as they all just stood there, not knowing what to do next. He wished his wife was there. She was an expert at breaking awkward silences and putting people at ease. Fuck he missed her, even though it had just been a day.

"Okay," Morana clapped once, commanding everyone's attention. "This is awkward."

Dante huffed a laugh, Amara grinned, Tristan's lips twitched as he tugged his girl closer to himself.

But Luna looked around them all, biting her lip. "I'm sorry if I'm making things awkward."

Jesus. This girl had some solid damage done to her if her first thought was blaming herself.

Her words made Tristan place a hand on her shoulder, looking her intently in the eyes. "We are family here. There's nothing to be sorry about."

That made Morana emotional for some reason, making her sniffle. Amara looked at Tristan in mild awe. Even Alpha was slightly surprised. He'd not heard the man say an emotional word in all the time he'd known him.

His sister, maybe not knowing how rare it was for her brother to say emotional things, just took a deep breath and nodded.

Dante slapped Tristan on the back, breaking the bubble. "I knew you weren't a lost cause."

"Fuck off," Tristan shot back, and Alpha felt solidarity with him. While he wasn't close to the man, they could agree Dante was a pain in the ass.

Amara sighed, apparently having seen this side of them for too long. "Let's just go in."

After a delicious dinner, a cozy affair with just them, Alpha followed Dante into his large study. Alpha had been there a few times before, and it always reminded him of what a legacy looked like. Their father had worked in the space, and his father before him, and so on. Generations of Maronis occupied the same seat, and though Alpha had never wanted any part of Maroni, that legacy was something he felt a little envious of. It wasn't that he wanted any of it, but the idea of growing up knowing the family line and being raised to take it over, it was something he was always reminded of in the study in particular.

Amara joined them with Tempest on her hip, resting her head against her mother's neck in a lazy way.

Dante poured him some scotch and Amara a glass of wine as he sat down. A few minutes later, Morana entered. She looked exhausted, and Alpha felt a sliver of respect for her. The girl had worked herself to the bone for the last two days, tracking and tracing and traveling back and forth. Though she had recovered, it still had to take a toll on her body. So when she slumped next to him on the couch, Alpha put a hand on her right shoulder, squeezing it slightly.

"You did good."

Morana gave him a small smile, her body lax, her eyes heavy behind the glasses. "I feel like I could sleep for a week."

"You deserve it," Amara reassured her. "Tristan is with Luna, I'm assuming?"

Morana nodded. "They're talking a walk outside. I wanted to give them time alone. Let them get to know each other better."

Amara took a sip of her wine. "That's a good idea. The girl Tristan remembers isn't the same one who's come to him. He'll have to adjust to that reality. And we don't even know if she remembers anything about him at all, but I imagine it must be an adjustment for her as well."

"We don't know much about her," Morana agreed, curling her feet under her, giving Alpha a look as she rested against him since his body was taking up the majority of the space. "Do you mind?"

He shook his head, letting her rest, feeling sympathetic. Her body relaxed into the cushions and pressed to his side, and he moved his arm on the back so she could get more space without having to touch him in case she wasn't comfortable.

"We know one thing," Dante spoke for the first time, swirling his drink as he walked to where Amara sat and perched on the arm. "We know she was waiting for us there. The Shadow Man sending you her exact location and her waiting there for us, recognizing all of us means..."

"She knows him," Amara completed the thought.

"Or he knows her," Alpha pointed out, defending a girl he'd just met for some inexplicable reason. "I've talked to the bastard and trust me, he could put you in places and tell you infirmation without revealing a thing about himself. Just because she was there or she knew us doesn't mean anything. He could've given her a file for all we know."

They all went silent, conceding his point.

"Should we ask her?" Morana questioned.

Amara immediately shook her head. "I don't think so. Not yet, at least. She's just come into a strange place, surrounded by strangers. She's trying to reconnect with her long-lost brother. Interrogating her will only add unnecessary tension right now. We have to be patient. This isn't about any of us."

That was true. He didn't think Tristan would be very happy with that either.

Dante downed his drink in one go, and Alpha took a sip of

his.

"Let's just take it day by day," Dante finally said. "I just hope she becomes a part of our family."

They all did. Somehow, in the middle of a dark and cruel world, Alpha had found a group of good people he was willing to open his heart to slowly, his own extended family of sorts. Which reminded him, he had to call his wife.

Bidding others good night and taking his leave, he headed for the guest suite he always occupied when he was on the compound, the same suite he and Zephyr had slept in for the first time. Entering the rooms, he locked the door and took his phone out, pressing the call icon on his screen on the first contact. She had added herself to his favorite contact so her name would always be at the top, along with a picture of them that Leah had taken—him behind her, holding her wrapped in his arms, her laughing as the dogs went zooming and blurring around them.

Fuck, he loved that photo.

"H'llo," his wife's mumbled voice came after the first ring, drowsy with sleep.

"You didn't call me today, rainbow," he told her, almost sounding petulant.

"Didn't want to disturb you." She yawned loudly. "How did everything go?"

Alpha relayed the events of the day to her as he prepared to take a shower, telling her about everything from his thoughts to others' reactions to Luna.

"I feel protective of her," he admitted, untying his hair from the bun it had been in all day and taking his eyepatch out, placing both the hairtie and the patch on the sink. Stripping his clothes off, he turned and looked at his reflection—the ugly scars, the missing eye, mottled flesh, and tattooed skin. How his little rainbow found anything beautiful in him was a mystery. She looked at him with such love and adoration he forgot he wasn't a monster on the outside, a beast of patchworked flesh. Flesh that she kissed, skin that she licked, scars that she loved. How, he had no idea, but fuck if he wasn't grateful for it.

"Of course you do," she said softly, her voice breathy. "That's because you're a good man, Alessandro."

His eyes closed briefly. She didn't call him by his given name often, but when she did, it was in the deep moments, so he knew she was saying what she meant, so he would remember that she knew all of him and loved all of him.

"What are you doing?" she asked quietly, almost whispering.

"About to take a shower," he told her. "Why?"

"Are you naked yet?"

Blood rushed from his head right to his cock. Alpha watched as it hardened, standing to attention, his heart beating loudly. This was the first time in weeks that she'd initiated something sexual, weeks of celibacy suddenly hitting him.

"Yeah," he said, but it came out low, almost animalistic. Fuck, he wished she was there.

"Are you hard yet?" The breathy sound and rustling of fabric made him even harder.

"Yeah."

Her breath hitched, and his cock twitched in response. He gripped it in a tattooed hand, tugging it, the pleasure not half as intense as it was with her anything—her mouth, her pussy or her tits. Fuck, her *luscious tits.* Just remembering them was making him feral.

"I wish you were inside me," she breathed, and he groaned.

"Me too."

"Look at yourself in the mirror," she told him, her voice a soft command. "Look at the body I worship. Wrap your hand around your cock."

"It's already there," he informed her, holding the sink with one hand and tugging on his cock with the other, tip to root, spreading the little fluid leaking from it.

"Imagine it's my hand," she whispered into the line. "My hand wrapped around you, getting you hard and ready for me. Where would you come?"

With his eyes closed, he imagined the scene, imagining her hand, her on her knees, asking him where he wanted to spill.

Inside her.

He wanted to put his cum so deep inside her that it made a baby. He'd breed her so hard into the bed if she were there.

"Your pussy," he rasped.

"Then do it," she urged him on. "Spill inside me. Come inside me."

An orgasm wracked his spine, jets of his cum spraying and spilling into his cupped hand. He felt like a teenager and not a grown man as he came within two minutes. *Fuck.*

His heart raced as he caught his breath, realizing he'd just nutted for the first time in weeks.

"Shit, I needed that," he told her honestly and heard her light chuckle, the sound making him feel warm.

"I wish I could've joined in." Her breathing changed as her voice got lower. "But I'd feel weird accidentally squirting in someone else's home."

"You will when you get here," Alpha promised her. "I'm going lap you up, rainbow."

She giggled. "Alright, Tarzan. Send the jet over. I'll see when Xander and I can come. It depends on his school schedule."

"Fine." He washed his hands in the sink and walked to the shower, finally turning it on. "Now go sleep. It must be late there."

"You have a good night too, hubby," she chirped into the phone.

Fuck, he loved this woman.

Alpha cleaned himself up and headed to bed. The day had been eventful, but at the end of it, partially sated and partially hopeful, he had one realization. He wanted a family with her.

TRISTAN

CHAPTER 19

TRISTAN, TENEBRAE CITY

IT FELT SURREAL.

She felt surreal.

He had been touching her constantly since he'd found her, and yet it felt like she would disappear into the ether, slip through his fingers like smoke, never to be found again.

Tristan sat on the edge of the lake, in a spot he had sat in countless times alone during his teens. If someone had told him that one day, he would be sitting in the exact spot with his sister by his side, he would've done anything for them.

The night descended around them, the skies still lighter with the last rays of the sun. A gentle wind blew through the hills, causing the water on the lake to ripple on the surface. Aside from the sounds from the lawns of the mansion in the distance—where the preparations for Tempest's birthday party were going steady—it was quiet. Tristan wouldn't have noticed so many things in detail at a time like this when he felt so emotionally raw, but it was like his senses were extra sharp, extra alive.

"It's so beautiful here," her gentle voice said from his side. She had a voice he imagined windchimes would sound like in the breeze, soft, sweet, melodic.

She was sitting with her arms wrapped around her knees, her eyes looking over the lake and fleeting coming to him before gazing out again, like she was nervous.

Tristan looked at the view through her eyes and admitted that, objectively, it was beautiful if it didn't have so much of his trauma associated with it. He opened his mouth, realizing how difficult it was for him to communicate even when he had so much he wanted to tell her, so many things he wanted to ask, so many stories he wanted to share. But a lifetime spent training his brain to stop the access to his vocal chords interfered, not letting him speak.

"Do you remember me at all?" he finally gave in, asking the one question that had been on the forefront of his mind since he saw the recognition in her eyes. She had known him when he kneeled before her, and a part of him hoped that, by some miracle, she had even a single memory of him. Otherwise, it would be too cruel of fate that he'd spent twenty years thinking of her and she hadn't.

She shook her head, and something in his heart cracked. He took a breath, telling himself it was okay. She had been too young, and at least she was here now. They could make new memories together.

"Your eyes," she started, then bit her lip.

"Yes?" Tristan encouraged her, needing to know, grasping at any straws.

"I don't remember, but your eyes feel so familiar."

Emotion clogged his throat. He had already broken down once, spilling so many tears, like it had been building and storing within him all this time. Tears were never something Tristan had let escape in front of people. He had cried silently on nights alone many times. But the only time he had cried in someone's company had been Morana's and, now, his sister's.

He stared into her eyes, realizing that they had changed the shade as she'd grown up, becoming more green. There was silence for a bit, not awkward but teeming with so many unsaid words.

He heard her inhale before she started again. "I like your friends. I'm glad you had... have... people who love you."

Tristan turned his neck to look at her. "What about you? Do you have friends?"

Her body stiffened slightly, her shoulders tensing. "No."

A wave of sadness washed over him at that, at how much was left unsaid in that one word. For all the pain in his life, he'd had good people even in the periphery, a closed circle that had expanded slowly but surely.

She hadn't.

He extended his arm and wrapped it wordlessly around her shoulder, pressing his nose into her hair. She trembled slightly against his side, before heaving in a breath as if to control herself. "I'm okay."

"Yes, you are," he said, his words a promise in his heart. "You always will be."

She gave him a small smile, her eyes drifting to his hand. The smile grew bigger. "I like your tattoo."

He looked down at the tattoo on his ring finger, the dark ink swirling to spell *Morana,* and something warmed his cheeks. He'd never felt this... bashful. How strange.

"How did you get together?" she asked, curious, and Tristan blinked. How the fuck was he supposed to explain his and Morana's twisted story to her? Their enmity, their history, their relationship. How was he to tell her that she'd been the only constant in his life that he could see, how he'd vowed to kill her but it had become something else, something so permanent he didn't know how he would exist without it?

And then something else occurred to him on the heel of that thought. What was he supposed to tell her about their parents? That they didn't have a father because he had killed him? That they didn't have a mother because he had driven her away?

Fuck.

Fuck.

She looked at him hopefully, waiting for a response, and he cleared his throat, his heart racing. Something akin to panic shook his bones at the idea that she might hate him if she found out the truth.

"We met at a party," he told her their story's bare bones. It was the truth but too simplified. "Kept meeting after that. One thing led to another."

"That's nice," she rested her head on his shoulder for a second, as a gesture, as she said it. "I'm happy for you, to see her with you. She's nice."

"She's perfect," he said before he could stop himself, and his sister smiled at him.

"You love her."

He looked out at the lake, not correcting her. Love wasn't the word for what he felt for Morana. It was too simple, too basic, like the answer he had just given. His emotions when it came to her were complex, they always had been, and too intense, which they always had been too. To someone on the outside, it could look like love, but it was so much more nuanced, so much more intense, so much more. Saying that he loved her was as basic as saying that he was living because his heart beat in his chest. Living was so much more than that, life was so much more than just that, and it was something he had learned just by being with her. Waking with her every morning, sleeping with her every night, being with her every day.

It had taken almost losing her to a fucking bullet for him to understand the difference so completely. Without her, he would be a meatsuit with a beating organ.

"How did you know me?" he asked her, the question another in a line of too many that he needed her to answer.

"I saw your photos and some articles. It had your name." Her answer mirrored his, basic, simplistic. There was more to it but he didn't press her like she didn't press him, both of them too new at navigating this.

"And how did you find out? That I am your brother?"

She hesitated. "A dying man told me."

His gaze sharpened on her at her words. "Who?"

She looked straight ahead, her jaw tight. "A monster," she whispered, her voice trembling.

The word felt like a dagger to his heart. Someone had hurt her. Someone had hurt her deeply enough for that edge of pain and vengeance to come forward. His blood simmered with the need to hunt, to find who it had been and may them pay. He rubbed her shoulder, his jaw tight, and focused on what she'd said. A *dying* man. Good thing the asshole was already dead or Tristan would have made him feel what real pain was.

"When did you find out?" He moved on, changing the topic from whoever the monster had been.

"Two days ago."

Right when the Shadow Man had sent Morana the message. Could it have been because he found out somehow that Luna had learned the truth, and he'd wanted to control the narrative and the situation so they would owe him rather than her finding them on her own? To have control over them? Could the Shadow Man have been the dying man? He fucking hoped so. He couldn't stand the thought of the bastard, especially with how he interacted with Morana like it was his right. Tristan wished he knew his face so he could at least have the satisfaction of mentally beating it to a pulp. Morana *was* right. He *was* a fucking *caveman* where she was concerned.

"Do we have any family left?" Her question fell between them, silencing his thoughts of murder and bringing back his earlier panic.

He grit his teeth. "No."

Just one word, with so much history she had no idea about, no context for. She gave a nod as if she understood that it was a touchy subject and let it go for now. For now, because it was their first time talking to each other. What would happen when they were comfortable, after weeks or months or years, when she asked him where their parents were? Or worse, if someone else told her and she found out what he'd done through them? He watched her, trying to take a measure of her and gauge if it would break their bond, nascent as it was. Because he hadn't been the only one emotional in the last few hours, she had been too. She had clung to him and gripped his hand so tight he was surprised his bones weren't crushed. He wouldn't have cared if they did. For the joy, the relief, the emotion of holding her hand for the first time when he thought he never would, he would have crushed every bone in his body if that was what she'd needed.

His little Luna, all grown up.

Fuck, he had to wrap his head around that and stop seeing

the baby his parents had come home with, put into his arms, a baby who had scrunched her face and cried so loudly it had made his ears hurt. Yet, he'd loved her with all the love his little body could have felt, right from the moment he had felt her weight in his arms, feeling like the biggest brother who would protect her at all costs. And yet, he had spent more than two decades failing.

"You were born as Luna," he told her, memories washing over him. "Is that the name you have?"

She shook her head. "No." For some reason, she didn't share the new name with him. "I want to be Luna for a bit, see if I feel like her, if she's who I can be."

Tristan got it. It was a conflict Morana was going through as well, not wanting to know her birth name and not wanting to feel an imposter in hers. "This is your trial period then."

"Something like that."

"And if you decide you're not Luna? Will you go back to your other name?"

She stayed silent for a moment, contemplative. "I don't know."

He gave her shoulder another squeeze. "There's no rush."

It was the most he'd talked in a conversation in a long time. Tristan didn't like talking and didn't talk much, but he sensed she was like him in that regard. If they both stayed silent and didn't make the effort, they would rarely ever get any words out.

He tilted his head to indicate the cottage at their back. "I grew up here," he shared with her. There were days I didn't know if I could make it. But I knew you were out there somewhere, and I had to make it for you." He looked to see her watching him, her eyes misting over again. "I'm so glad I didn't give up."

"Me too." Her tear fell, and his eyes burned. She looked away. "I almost gave up too."

"What kept you going?" If she hadn't known about him, about her past, there had to have been something that had driven her to get up every morning and survive.

She swallowed and shrugged her dainty shoulders but stayed silent. Tristan didn't pry. One day, he would, but not right then.

"Are you happy?" he asked.

She looked at him, her eyes sincere. "I'm trying to be."

That was enough, more than enough.

Right then, he just reveled in the fact that he was sitting in the same spot he had all his life, with his baby sister finally by his side.

CHAPTER 20

LYLA, TENEBRAE CITY

THERE WAS TOO MUCH activity around her.

Lyla stood at the back door of the mansion, watching as teams of staff put up tents and prepared a large open lawn area for a party. As Lyla had learned over the last few days, it was one of the many lawns on the massive compound. Everything about this whole property was massive, too much, too overwhelming. She couldn't wrap her head around that, even after being here for three days. She had never seen a place like it before. Her home in Bayfyord was large and unique, but nothing like this... castle that was as old as it looked, being in the Maroni family for generations.

The Maronis were the nicest family too, though she didn't think Dante trusted her. She didn't really blame him either. She was a stranger who had come into his home and from questionable sources and could be a threat to his family. In fact, seeing a man be so expressive and emotive, so loving to his wife and baby, had been somewhat of an eye-opening experience. Her experiences with men, especially rich and powerful men—outside of Dainn—had been ugly. The men she had seen had been the ones cheating on their wives, selling their daughters, and apathetic to females outside of the sexual ways they could use them. The men she had seen in her time here were three completely contradictory examples, three completely different personalities with three very different partners, and yet Lyla didn't doubt their love for each other for a second.

Tristan, her brother, was the most silent part of the group, but he felt deeply, much like she did. He was quiet, but his energy was a forcefield, and the way he looked at Morana every time she walked into a room, tracking her with his eyes, made her so happy for him. She didn't know him very well yet, but from the little she knew, the little she could deduce, and the little she saw, he deserved it. And Morana was just incredible. Lyla could feel the intelligence in her eyes behind those glasses, always walking around with her phone in her hand and t-shirts with cool quotes on them. If she was being totally honest, Lyla was a little intimidated by her even though she had been nothing but nice, and she clearly loved her brother deeply.

If she'd had to pick a brother for herself, Tristan would have been the one. He was quiet but constant, always somewhere close to her, never prying or forcing her into conversation. They spent every evening talking, learning each other a bit more, and the more she learned, the more she liked. His protectiveness of her, as silent but strong as he was, was a balm on her soul. It healed parts of her that had been so alone and so hurt growing up, and knowing that he had been looking for her even then made her feel so many things. As an older brother, he was perfect. She only hoped she didn't disappoint him as the baby sister.

When it came to others, Dante, though mildly mistrustful, was still very kind to her. He adored the ground Amara walked upon and treated Tempest in a way that made her heart clench with joy for the little girl, who would grow up with so much love. He was good-looking, charming, and more approachable than the other men. She didn't doubt women would throw themselves at him. But his eyes never strayed from his insanely beautiful wife. Amara wasn't just beautiful, though. She was accomplished, polished, and so *nice*. She made Lyla feel both comfortable in the mansion and uncomfortable in her skin through no fault of hers.

It was maybe the fact that female companionship hadn't been a part of her life. Growing up, being made to feel worthless and then healing in isolation, her only other younger female interaction being with Nikki—she thought sourly at just the mention of the girl, the image of her naked, trying to seduce *her man* still making her so angry—that seeing these incredible, smart women who had been friends for so long made her feel a little out of place.

The one person she automatically gravitated towards,

though, was Alpha. He was the embodiment on the outside of how she felt inside. Just looking at him, all stern and scarred, yet still standing, made her feel safe. It was absurd. He was the largest man she had ever seen, bulky and huge, with arms bigger than her thighs. Out of everyone, he would have been the one she would have run away from first because he could pick and throw her so easily, kill her with a crush of his fist. Yet, he felt the safest outside of her brother, like a giant but a gentle one. He looked at her through one eye; his lip was pulled down on one side, and she could still *feel* his gentleness when he was near. She didn't know why, but it made her want to cry.

And out of all the girls, it was his wife who made her feel the most relaxed. Maybe it was because Lyla knew Zenith, her childhood friend who had escaped their hell, had been loved all her life by the woman. When they had been kids, Zenith had been a number Lyla couldn't remember anymore. But Lyla had called her Sky, for the one thing she'd wanted to see but never could. They had been taken together in a small batch, and they had slept in the same room, talking about everything they would do when they got out.

And one night, her friend had managed to get out. Lyla had seen her running toward the tree line, one of the guards running after her. Lyla had jumped on the guard and bitten him, giving her friend the freedom she could never have. Her life had become hell after.

She shook off the memories, focusing on the staff.

Somehow, knowing Zenith had been so loved by her sister made Zephyr feel like a sister to Lyla too, like her friend had bridged the space between them. If joy could be a person, it would be Zephyr. Though there was still an air of sadness around her sometimes, her soul felt happy.

Lyla remembered the moment Zephyr had come the day after they had, her heart aching because along with Zephyr, *he* had come.

Xander.

Lyla had seen him from her window in the guest room of the mansion. Her room overlooked the driveway and a horn honking had made her go to the window and look out. And there he had been, getting out of the back of the large car, wearing loose light clothes with big headphones in his ears, typing on a phone. He had taken the headphones off and hung them around his neck, waiting for the woman with the pink and blue hair.

Lyla remembered gripping the edge of her windowsill, her jaw trembling with the need to shout his name and have him look up at her. But she controlled herself. She couldn't barge into and disrupt his life like that. So, she had just watched him go into the mansion, hoping she would see him soon.

It had been two days, and he was nowhere to be found. Lyla didn't go roaming around looking for him because this was a new place and a part of her was still scared of stepping out of line when everyone was being so nice to her. But her hope and patience were slowly turning into desperation, knowing he was so close but so distant, messing with her head. It was different when she hadn't been able to see him, but now that she had, she just wanted to look into his eyes and hold him once before she let him go.

Tempest babbled to Amara as she carried her out.

Seeing her sent an occasional pang through her heart for what she'd lost and never experienced and would never experience again. It wasn't that she wanted to have a baby. She didn't think she could be a mother, and to be honest, she just didn't have it in her. It would be a miracle if she healed her trauma by the time she died, and a child deserved love and a healthy environment like she saw all around her. It made her happy to witness all of it, because that meant her son was surrounded with the same love, growing up with the same love, exactly what she had hoped and wished for him.

"Morning!" Zephyr came to stand next to her. They were almost the same height, but Zephyr had curves Lyla never had.

"Good morning," Lyla greeted her back, seeing her take a sip of some kind of juice.

"Why are you standing here all by yourself?" Zephyr asked her.

Lyla didn't know how to explain it. She felt overwhelmed but underwhelmed too, overwhelmed by all the emotions she had felt in such a short span of time, all the things she had seen, all the people she had met, but underwhelmed with the fact that she missed home, a part of her wishing for the solitude, wishing for *him.*

She touched her necklace like a talisman as if reminding herself that he was real, and so was everything they had, that she hadn't dreamed it all in a deluded state of a broken mind.

But she hadn't. In the bag he had packed for her, his t-shirts that she'd stolen to wear at home, a pack of the tea she liked until she could restock, and a puzzle box that opened every twenty-four hours and popped out a small strip of paper with a handwritten note. It had taken her a while to figure out how to open the puzzle box, and when she had succeeded that morning, she'd gotten her first note.

'My atoms miss your voice.'

Her atoms missed his too.

"Hey, you okay?" Zephyr's concerned voice brought her back to reality. She was spacing out a lot as her brain caught up with all the information thrown at it and processed everything.

"Yes," Lyla reassured her. She was okay, better than okay. Just a bit overwhelmed.

Zephyr gave her a long look that made her think nothing got past her. "You know, you have absolutely gorgeous hair?" she began, changing the topic. "That natural shade of red is so rare."

Lyla touched her strands, longer than the length she had chopped them off at, feeling a little self-conscious, a flush coming over her face at the compliment. "Thanks."

Zephyr raised her hand, her colorful wedding ring catching in the sunlight, before pausing. "May I?"

Lyla gave a nod and the other woman ran her fingers through her hair, rubbing the ends between her tips, holding them and moving them.

"You want a haircut?" Zephyr suggested, her eyes going over her face. "You have such lovely bone structure, I feel like a little cut will frame everything so nicely. What do you say?"

Lyla felt her nose tingle. She'd never had a professional haircut. Her handlers had wanted her hair long and forbidden her to cut it. It was one of the best selling points for her. All she'd been allowed was a little trim at the ends or the threat of a severe punishment. Until she had cut them off herself in a frenzy, they had remained pretty much untouched. And here was a woman who didn't really know her, who offered her kindness. She had no idea what it meant to her.

Lyla gave a tiny nod and saw a wide smile transform Zephyr's face, dimples popping in her cheeks that made her look so pretty.

Zephyr clapped her hands. "Yes! Come with me." Taking hold of her hand, she pulled her inside and down a corridor to a part of the mansion Lyla hadn't been in yet. It was slightly different than hers, with more artwork on the walls and more warmth. They went down one corridor, turned into another, and up a flight of stairs, so long Lyla forgot the direction she had come from. It would be so easy to get lost in this place.

Finally, Zephyr stopped in front of a wooden door, punched in a code to the side, and opened it. "Tada!"

Lyla entered what looked like a suite, something similar in size to the Gladestone hotel she had stayed in, but with a completely different vibe. The Gladestone suite had been very modern; this felt more antique. Antique sitting area with polished furniture, antique wooden windows right opposite the entrance, antique rugs, and drapes. Even the doorknob was antique. Lyla's suite in the other wing was smaller, more suited for one person than a couple, and less antique, more gothic. But the living and dining spaces were more opulent. She realized that each wing had a different interior theme and marveled at that for a moment. How *amazing* was that?

Zephyr opened one door and went in. Lyla glanced in and saw it was the bedroom. All she caught was a peek at the twisted sheets before her face flushed, and she immediately pulled back, not wanting to invade their privacy.

Zephyr came out with a large kit, leading her to another door. "Come on."

It was a large tiled room with a fancy sink and faucet, a huge ornate mirror, and a high stool in front of the counter.

"Hop up."

Lyla hesitated, before getting on the stool. Zephyr opened a cabinet and got a towel out, wrapping it around her shoulders.

"Won't it make a mess?" Lyla asked, not wanting to be the cause of any problems.

Zephyr shook her head. "I'll clean it up. You don't worry about a thing. Just relax and trust my expertise."

Lyla inhaled deeply, seeing in the mirror as Zephyr turned the faucet on, taking some water in her hand and wetting her hair slowly but steadily. Once that was done, she opened her kit and took out some kind of clips. a pair of scissors and a comb. She brushed her hair back, focused, and looked at the uneven lengths before sectioning it. Lyla watched in fascination as Zephyr's hands moved with surety over the strands, a confidence the likes of which Lyla had never experienced herself.

That was what she realized all the women in her brother's world had in common—confidence. They were all confident about something or the other, all of them carrying an air of certainty that came from being good at something. And even though Dr. Manson had specifically told her not to, Lyla compared and found herself coming up short.

What was she confident about in herself?

She didn't know.

She swallowed.

"You know," Zephyr began, working without stopping. "Alpha has this place that helps survivors. My sister used to work and help there."

Lyla's heart gave a thud at the mention of her old friend. She wondered what it would have been like if she'd been alive. Would she have remembered her or forgotten? Lyla didn't even know how old they had been. The concept of birthdays was foreign to her. She made a mental note to ask her brother about it when she saw him again.

"I used to volunteer there," Zephyr continued, finishing clipping her hair in the final section, all the twists making her look weird. Lyla had no idea how the hell Zephyr would figure out what to cut from where in the form that her hair was in.

"What did you do?" Lyla asked, curious.

Zephyr smiled. "Give free haircuts."

Was this a charity case for her, too? Was that what she was? She hoped not.

"We girls—" Zephyr told her, taking out her scissors and pulling one section out "—have so much importance attached to our looks, people don't realize how much difference a little change can make." She snipped and moved on. "It's like shedding your old skin, becoming something new. It's a choice you make—" she made another cut "—and you get more liberated."

Lyla mulled over her words, remembering how she'd felt different after she had cut her own hair. There was a certain truth to what she was saying.

Silence descended. Lyla sat quietly, and Zephyr worked, one

section after the other, cutting and pulling, never asking her once why her hair was cut so badly, never commenting about anything related to it.

Finally, after a few minutes, she brushed the fallen pieces off her shoulders and plugged in a hairdryer in the socket. The loud noise of the dryer made her wince, and she sat still as Zephyr ran her fingers through her hair, turning it this way and that way under the focused blast of air, drying and framing it. Lyla kept her eyes closed to avoid the air in her eyes, letting herself enjoy the sensation of fingers over her scalp and strands.

The dryer turned off, and the noise cut off suddenly.

"So, do you like it?" Zephyr's voice came from behind her, her hands on her shoulders.

Lyla held her breath, her heart beating fast with fear for some reason.

She took a deep breath and opened her eyes, facing her reflection in the mirror.

She looked... different. Her red strands fell around her shoulders in a straight line, the length a little longer than she'd been expecting, wisps of shorter strands framing her face in a way that made her cheekbones look more prominent, her eyes sharper, her chin softer. She was amazed at the difference something like a haircut could make to her appearance and, moreover, to her insides. She looked like a woman who knew what she wanted, a woman who was poised, elegant, and more fitting into the circle she had been a part of.

Her eyes moved up to Zephyr's, conveying everything she couldn't put into words—a family problem she was coming to realize, a trait she shared with her brother. "Thank you."

The other woman squeezed her shoulders, giving her a wide smile. "Anytime."

Lyla's eyes moved back to her face, a smile coming over her lips as she imagined Dainn's reaction to seeing her like this. He had taken her out with his arm around her while being Mr. Blackthorne, and she'd always felt like the shoes she was filling out in society with him might not fit her. For the first time, looking at herself and feeling the surge of surety inside her, she felt like she could be Mrs. Blackthorne. Appearances had never mattered to her, her own beauty weaponized against her all her life by others. This wasn't about external beauty, though. This was about inner confidence.

And though she wasn't fully there yet, it felt like a big step in the right direction.

CHAPTER 21

UNKNOWN

H E WAS BEING HUNTED.

There was no other word for what was happening. Like the other leaders before him, all slain one by one, a genuine threat of death loomed for him next.

It was *thrilling*.

"Backup anything you haven't." He called one of the only loyalists he had left, one that none of the other leaders had known about. "Delete everything else."

"Is everything okay?" she asked over the secure line. He would have to give her a gift to keep her loyal until his task was finished. They had been laying low for a while, restrategizing their next move. There was no dearth of patience for him where operations were concerned. The Syndicate was such a well-oiled machine that even without any evident leadership at the top, nothing would be affected at the bottom levels. For all intents and purposes, everything was as it should have been. Only the ones in the top tiers of the organizational pyramid knew about the gaping vacancies.

He was the one at the top, always had been. The few who knew how The Syndicate was structured thought there were four main leaders at the top, a council managing and running everything. There had been, except that the council had had a leader, too.

Him. The one at the tip of the pyramid. The one making sure everything worked the way he'd wanted to.

It hadn't always been that way, especially not when he'd been rising in the ranks. But over the years, he had done more for The Syndicate than any other member, negotiating deals with legal and illegal organizations, bringing in unprecedented power and making it the secretive, notorious, omnipresent snake in the grass it was.

And it was the first time in decades he actually felt threatened, like he finally had an adversary worth playing the game with.

The Shadow Man.

He was perfect in every way, except for one little thing. A weakness, a leverage so obvious that it could be used to defeat him, an Achilles heel he had exposed to all of them.

The girl.

Dangerous men with singular weaknesses only came into their full glory once that weakness was removed. The girl had to go for the Shadow Man to become a force unlike any the world had seen, a pride jewel on the bloody crown of The Syndicate, the perfect example of the level of power the organization could breed into a being—born of its womb, raised by its hands, shaped by its mind.

"Yes," he told his loyalist, a small smile on his face as he watched the mutilated body of Mr. X be carried out of the factory. "Everything is falling into place."

Everything was going to be perfect.

LYLA

CHAPTER 22

LYLA, TENEBRAE CITY

S HE MISSED *HIM.*

After a week of being at the Maroni compound, of feeling so many emotions she couldn't even explain them properly to Dr. Manson each morning that she talked to him while having her tea, Lyla missed Dainn so profoundly it left an ache in her chest. In one week, she had slowly seen everyone relax more around her, felt their trust in her climb as they got to know her better. She had meals with them all, spent time with her brother every evening after that, learning what his life had been like and sharing a bit about hers. It wasn't something she did easily, words as halting for her as they were for him, but they had begun to understand each other.

And though she could feel the biggest looming question in all their minds remained about the Shadow Man, they hadn't pushed her into giving any answers yet.

But they would. She could feel the slight impatience as their need to give her space warred with their need for answers. And she had no idea what she would tell them. While the idea of being honest and telling them the truth was appealing, after a week, she had learned one thing—they didn't like the Shadow Man. Especially her brother. The one time Morana had mentioned him in conversation, much to the increased blood rush to her brain, Tristan had made a face so hard she realized how gentle and open he had been with her in contrast.

That in particular did not encourage her to admit to the truth. The very Shadow Man they didn't like was the same man she loved, the same man who had saved her time and again, the same man who had made sure she remained alive and healed enough for them to find her.

Lyla looked around the party, her eyes seeking out every shadowed corner that he always claimed and blended with, hoping he was there but knowing he wasn't. For a week, he had been completely out of contact. All she had were seven notes, one that was dispersed each morning from the box, something she looked forward to each day.

Notes that went from the sweet *'Cook for me again soon'* to the steamy *'My cock has withdrawals from your pussy'* to reminders like *'I'll be very displeased if you're not taking care of yourself.'*

They were literally one of the high points of her day.

People were milling about, champagne glasses in hands, dressed to the nines. Waiters walked around the massive lawns of the property, circulating with different foods and beverages for the guests. The guest of honor sat on broad shoulders, wearing a fluffy pink gown with a tutu and a tiara, grinning at everyone with a smile that was so disarming Lyla could feel herself melting. Tempest Maroni had turned one and it seemed like the entire world was there to celebrate it—people she had never seen or met before, coming up to her and introducing themselves suddenly. Her heart gave a little pang looking at her, wondering at the first birthday she never witnessed for the child she'd birthed.

Speaking of, her eyes sought out Xander, finding him sitting in a corner with Tempest's grandmother, looking bored.

She had met him, actually met him, over the last week.

Lyla had come down for dinner and there he had been, sitting on a seat very far from her, reading a book on a tablet, his glasses almost falling off his nose.

"Xander, say hi to Luna," Morana had told the boy.

Lyla had sat down, gripping the edge of the table, her heart thundering out of her chest, seeing as the young boy didn't even look up from his book but just waved at her. "Hello."

Lyla had managed to croak out a 'hi', before clearing her throat and focusing on her plate, watching him from the corner of her eye throughout dinner.

And for a week, it had been the same, just watching him around the compound, near the lake, at the table, playing with Tempest, sitting with Morana or even Zephyr, walking around with Tristan, doing his homework since he was attending school virtually for a bit. Lyla had just watched him, taking in her fill, learning his personality through observation, letting it seep into her heart, coming to a realization that made everything she had done worthwhile.

Her child, her special beautiful child, was so loved, so taken care of of, had such a good life.

And that was all that mattered.

Lyla took in a deep breath, keeping a hold of her wine glass just to have something to do but didn't sip from it. She didn't drink. Trauma associated with seeing girls get trashed and used after being drugged one too many times had completely turned her off of it. Moreover, even though it was a party hosted by her brother's friends, people she knew she could trust, old habits died hard.

"Trust me still?"

The words came to her, whispered in her mind as though carried by the wind, memory of them imprinted on her being. It was there, standing at a party of people she would trust eventually maybe, that she realized her trust was important, that she didn't give it to anyone. It was rare. Maybe, that was why he valued it so much.

"Oh my god, you're *stunning!*"

Zephyr came into her frame of vision, dressed in a dark green velvety gown that fell to the ground, a raunchy split on one side letting her walk freely, her curves on display, so much curvier than Lyla's petite frame but looking tiny next to her husband, the one-eyed gentle giant. Alpha had been so kind to her, it had almost made her cry imagining how different life could have been if she'd had someone like him in her corner to scare people away during her younger years. Zephyr, with a heart that matched his, maybe even more compassionate, had styled Lyla's new hair and done her light makeup with gentle hands. Things like grooming and styling had been such terrible events for her, things that had been done to get her the highest bid, primp and prepare her to be sold for her beauty.

Zephyr hadn't done it like that. She'd done it like she'd wanted Lyla to *feel* beautiful rather than look it. And she was feeling it.

Her hair, which she had chopped off roughly and had grown out the same way, was now in a sleek mid-back length—a bob-type cut as Zephyr told her it was called—that framed her face. It made her look pretty but more importantly, it made her feel more powerful. She looked like someone who had control over her life, not someone who was lost. And her dress added to that.

For the party, Morana had barged into her room with multiple dresses, all new and still having their tags.

"Your brother wanted me to go shopping, so who was I to say no?" Morana had told her with a wink.

Lyla had picked a strapless one with a built-in bodice and an elegant, fishtail style fall, giving her legs room to move. The design was amazing but that wasn't the reason she had picked it.

She picked it because it was black.

His color.

The color of *home.*

And she didn't know if it was her longing that was making her hope he was there, making her imagine his eyes, or if it was real, but she stood straight, reveling in the idea that maybe he was watching her like he'd told her he would. How, she didn't know, since the party was exclusively invite-only and the guest list was curated, security was all around, and the grounds were being patrolled. She didn't know how, didn't question why, not this time. It felt familiar, the weight of his eyes on her, watching from a corner she could not find. She had felt this weight, craved this weight, sought this weight every day for years, her heart like an erratic bird in the cage of her ribs every time she had waited. And then, feeling it, the bird had broken free, pounding with heavy wings, escaping into her bloodstream.

Though there were many eyes on her as there had been many-a-times, the weight of his had always been different. Darker. More possessive.

She was most likely imagining it. It had been days and he hadn't contacted her.

"Thanks to you," Lyla told Zephyr sincerely. "I appreciate everything."

Zephyr waved it off. "Don't mention it." She turned to her

husband, who was standing next to her but looking around.

"Honeybuns?" Zephyr tugged his arm, and Lyla raised her eyebrow at the fact that Alpha actually responded to the ridiculous nickname. She had seen him respond to all the ridiculous nicknames.

"Yes, rainbow?"

It made her wonder if this was how couples were supposed to behave. Was this an unsaid relationship rule she hadn't known about? God, they were cute, but Lyla wondered if she needed to think of a nickname too. She already had one he called her, but she'd never given him one. Shit. Had she messed up? Had he felt neglected because of it?

He doesn't feel like everyone else does, she reminded herself. Being around other people, surrounded by couples who were clearly head over heels in love with each other, had somehow made her humanize him more in her mind. But he wasn't like everyone else. His brain didn't work like everyone else. She had to remind herself of that.

All the lovey-dovey stuff was firing her faculties.

Tristan and Morana joined them. Her brother—it was still surreal to call him that—was dressed in a navy suit with a silver tie that brought out his eyes, and his girl was dressed in a sequined short, strappy silver dress. They were matching. *Adorable.* Though, from the little she knew of her brother, he would kill anyone who called him that except maybe Morana. Her lips twitched and her eyes locked with his.

God, she still couldn't believe he was related to her, that she had actual blood, and now extended, family.

He watched her smile, something shifting over his face. His mouth relaxed, giving her a matching smile, albeit much smaller. And a hint of dimple popped out on his cheek, taking him to another level of handsome. Lyla wanted to see what it would look like when he smiled fully, how deep it would go.

It was so tentative, nothing like she could have imagined. They were both learning their way back to each other, understanding who they had become and working around it. But one thing was for certain—he loved her, no matter who she had become. She could feel it in her bones, calling to the love inside her, deepening it when she saw the way he was with her son. Her silent brother had such deep love for the people around him even though he never said it. He *showed* it. And Lyla had learned how to understand actions of love, no matter what kind it was.

"So, met anyone interesting?" Zephyr asked, and Lyla watched the smile drop off her brother's face.

Oh boy, they had no idea.

Morana gave her a long look, one she couldn't decipher. *Huh.* Maybe *she* did. Lyla remembered what Dainn had told her—that Morana would be stupid not to figure out whatever clue he'd dropped.

"A few people have introduced themselves," Lyla answered Zephyr's question instead. "Now that the lost sister has returned, people are curious." She got it. It was big news, Tristan Caine's long lost sister coming back from—what everyone had assumed to be—dead.

In the few days Lyla had spent with Zephyr, she had learned one thing about the girl—she was a hopeless romantic. It was such a luxury, a privilege that she'd led a life that had allowed her to be one. Despite her hardships, she had grown up in a loving home, loving her sister and loving her man. To someone who had spent the majority of her life wishing for death, hanging on just to get one answer that had sustained her, it was such a bizarre idea, but not an unwelcome one. It felt almost aspirational. Lyla wanted to be in a place where she would be hopelessly romantic and hopelessly optimistic about love and life.

That was the reason why Zephyr's next question didn't surprise her one bit.

"Anyone hot?"

Lyla shook her head, casting a furtive glance toward her brother who was glaring at Zephyr, in turn causing Alpha to glare at him. As patient and gentle her brother was being with her, he was a completely different person anyone someone even vaguely mentioned anything about her potential love life. Her brother was having a difficult time reconciling his baby sister to the grown adult.

To diffuse any building tension, she immediately answered and reassured everyone. "No one here interests me."

Which was the truth. She doubted anyone could, not after the man she had claimed and been claimed by.

"Let's go dance, caveman," Morana changed the topic, dragging Tristan away with her to the middle of the dance floor where couples were already swaying to the live orchestra playing by the bar. Lyla expelled a sigh of relief. She could understand why her brother, knowing how he was now, would feel protective over her potential romantic overtures so soon, but damn when he found out the truth, it would not bode well. Lyla didn't want a confrontation with him, which was why she had no idea how she was going to tell them.

But also because she was possessive, protective of *him*. She didn't want to share him with the others, because the moment they found out who her lover was, there would be questions she would have to answer.

Dante dragged Amara to the dance floor, both of them moving gracefully together as Tempest and Xander were escorted inside the mansion by her grandmother. Zephyr, though next to her, swayed pressed into Alpha.

Lyla watched all the couples dance, feeling a pang of loneliness. She stood in the middle of a grand party, the likes of which she had never seen, filled with people, some who truly cared about her, and yet, she felt lonely. She imagined what it would be like if he was there with her, standing behind her like the mountain she called home. She missed him. His voice, his body, his eyes. His *everything*.

Watching the couples, it was nothing like the dances she'd been forced to do. She had never danced before with a partner. She had never danced with *him.* Did he even dance? Did she? She didn't know if she could but with the way his body moved during his workouts, during sex, she did think he would be fluid. God, the hunger in her to find out was so acute.

A well-dressed man walked up to her, a man who had introduced himself to her before but she couldn't remember the name of, extending his hand. "Would you do me the honor?"

She didn't want to. She had already politely declined two other invitations before.

But Zephyr gave her an encouraging look, and Alpha, who apparently knew the guy, gave her a nod, letting her know he was okay. Not wanting to create a scene by refusing again, Lyla put her hand in his, immediately recoiling, her body revolting against the touch of another.

She pulled her hand back but they were too close to the dance floor. Walking away now would only cause a scene, and she didn't want anyone asking her questions, asking her if she was okay. She wasn't. There was a gaping void inside her and she could feel herself falling into it, the loneliness so much different, in some ways so much worse this time. Earlier, her loneliness had been a result of being alone. This time, she was surrounded by people, good people she was beginning to care for and who clearly cared for her, and yet, the loneliness persisted. She would need to talk to Dr. Manson about it tomorrow, find out ways to work around it.

The man stopped on the dance floor and put his hands out, intending to put them on her waist, and she stepped back, keeping a distance between them.

And just as his hands almost reached her, a voice came from behind her.

"Mind if I cut in, Rochester?"

Everything inside her froze for a split second before it came alive at that voice, the voice of death, right behind her. Her senses sizzled, every cell in her body electrified, as if touched by a live wire, responding to the sound in ways she completely recognized. heartbeat racing, nipples pebbling, walls clenching. She was so empty, had been so empty for days, and just his voice, knowing he was there, she felt whole.

"You will never be incomplete with me."

He had promised her and he was right.

She had seen enough of genuine love, deep love around her to know when it was meant to be, it was meant to be. And she and him were. She and him, they were written in the stars. Had been since the moment they had met under them.

"You can take the next one, Blackthorne." The man in front of her, Rochester, had the audacity to say. Didn't he know who he was talking to? Of course, he didn't. Blackthorne was the facade people didn't look under, something that served him just fine. Lyla held her breath, knowing the man beneath the facade, knowing his absolute possession of her, knowing he wouldn't let another man touch her as long as he lived.

Hands, familiar hands in leather gloves, slid around her waist.

Her body melted into him, thriving in the public display of his possession even though no one was looking, their corner of the dance floor a little darkened under the shadow of the trees.

Rochester glared at him when he didn't say another word. She could just imagine him giving the other man a dead stare, his face unflinching and unmoved by the vitriol coming his way.

"You don't get to steal both my deals and my dances, Black-thorne," Rochester spit out.

Ah, a business rival. Lyla pressed back into his chest unconsciously, her body simmering, vibrating with need. After getting used to taking him for so long and so many times every day, the sudden lack had been causing withdrawal in her body, all of that coming back with a vengeance in her system tenfold. If he pressed her against a tree and flipped her dress up, she wouldn't care. Her state almost reminded her of the time she'd been drugged—mindless, guileless, listless, just waiting for him to relieve the ache throbbing everywhere in her body.

"Can't steal what's already mine," he said to the other man, his tone almost lazy, deliberately provocative. But Lyla heard the sharp edge of possession to it, the underside of a blade that cut into her sternum and exposed her bloody heart.

The man finally left with an angry huff, leaving them both alone in the corner of the dance floor.

Her heart pounded in her ears, her whole body throbbing and messy and burning, sweat pooling between her breasts, moisture pooling between her thighs. She stayed the way she was, watching the couples, realizing no one was looking their way, the shadow and her dark dress hiding them in plain sight.

His hand moved from her waist, up her ribs, cupping her breasts, his large hands covering them, squeezing and temporarily relieving the ache in them.

"Dainn," she whispered, saying his name for the first time in days.

"Shh," he spoke in her ear. "You've been a bad girl, *flamma.*"
A kiss to her ear.

"You let another man touch you."

A kiss to the side of her neck.

"Tell me, what should your punishment be?"

Her brain was muddled for a moment before his words sank in. Punishment? A thrill ran down her spine, making her shiver, her nipples hard points under her dress.

"Anything you want," she told him, her voice so low she didn't know if he heard it.

"Silly little red," he chuckled darkly, "trusting the big bad wolf with the keys to your kingdom? You know what that does to me."

God, she'd missed him so much. Before he could say anything, she saw Morana looking around for her.

She felt the body behind her disappear, leaving her cold and
alone on the dance floor. Lyla took a deep breath in, not letting
desolation set in, knowing that he was at the party enough to
raise her spirits.

She walked to where Dante and Amara were now sitting,
a round table filled with the others. Morana spotted her, her
whole body relaxing, and joined her on the walk back to the
table.

"Listen," Morana began, not missing a step. "I can't keep
things from Tristan. I haven't said anything about him yet."

Lyla kept a straight face, looking straight ahead. "About
who?"

Morana stopped, taking hold of her arm, her eyes serious.
"You know who I am talking about."

Lyla stayed silent, not knowing what to say. She hadn't
decided when she would bring up her relationship, but not at
the moment. He had been right about things becoming about
him once people knew. Right now, she was focusing on her
relationships and building them with others. She wanted to
keep it that a little longer.

Morana sighed, suddenly looking too weary. "If it's not what
I think it is, great," she told Lyla, her tone empathic. "But if
it is, I get it. Trust me, I do. But sooner or later, you'll have to

make a choice."

"Thank you." Lyla extended her hand, placing it on the other girl's arm, and watched her wince slightly. She immediately pulled back, her brow furrowing. "Are you okay?"

Morana nodded. "Just pulled a muscle. Don't worry about it."

Lyla let it go, not wanting to pry. It could be a sex injury for all she knew. *Ew.* She *did not* want to think about what her brother and Morana got up to.

They reached the table and took a seat.

"Where's Tristan?" Dante asked Morana, taking a sip of his scotch. Amara sat by his side, holding a glass of wine.

"He's checking in on Xander."

Lyla's heart stopped. Tristan loved the boy and she was so grateful for it. She gripped her dress under the table, looking straight at the orchestra, trying not to let her nerves show. No one knew who he was, who she was to him. It was going to be fine. She just wanted to look at him up close and not from a distance and see how he was, maybe talk to him and see who he had become in-depth. Dainn had told her he was smart, and she had seen the same, but she wanted to know more. For now, seeing her brother and Morana loving him so deeply settled an instinct that had been turbulent inside her for years. Her baby was loved, he was safe, just as she'd wished upon him that fateful night.

Dante, standing up, broke through her thoughts.

She turned to look at what had caught his attention, and her heart stopped for the second time in as many minutes.

Dainn was heading to their table, out in the light and out in the open, dressed in an all-black suit that just added to the aura of danger he wore like a cloak around him, a tiny gold box in his hand.

Lyla drank in the sight of him after so many days, that felt more like months of separation than they did days, greedily swallowing him with her eyes, taking him into her veins and getting high off of it. There was something so ridiculously sexy about him, from the dark hair she had run her fingers through countless times to the chiseled jaw she had kissed to the tall frame she had climbed over.

"Ooh," Zephyr whistled opposite her and Alpha groaned. Lyla felt a smile come over her lips, feeling something akin to pride. Even though she wasn't on his arm in public, that man was *hers*.

"Blackthorne," Dante stepped forward, extending his hand and greeting him warmly.

"Maroni," he replied back in the same tone, so convincing even she would never have doubted how sincere it was if she didn't know him.

Both men shook hands. It was such a bizarre thing for her to witness, her worlds colliding without anyone knowing anything about it. She discretely looked around to see if anyone had noticed anything, but Morana was on her phone, Amara was smiling politely at the new guest, and Alpha and Zephyr were now whispering to each other.

Her entire world was vibrating with a force strong enough to knock the breath out of her and not one person was noticing it.

Dainn didn't look at her, didn't give any indication that he knew her at all. He gave the gift to Amara, a smile on his face that looked warm but she knew was fake. She knew his real smile, the way the corner of his mouth twitched, one higher than the other, defrosting his mismatched eyes just a bit.

He dialed up the charm to a hundred. "For the princess."

Amara's eyes widened slightly, and Lyla felt a slither of jealousy coiling in her stomach. It was completely unfounded. She knew Amara was madly in love with Dante and knew Dainn was not flirting, but just the fact that his undivided attention was on another female reared up something ugly in the lizard part of her brain. She grit her teeth, narrowing her eyes at him, wanting to stand up and bite that infuriating lip, show everyone that he was hers and hers alone, have him kiss her back so it would become clear to every single soul present at the party.

Her hands fisted on her lap with the need to restrain herself from doing just that. It was such a change too. In Bayfjord, she'd been free, free to do anything she wanted, free to be anything she wanted, free to behave in any way she wanted. But she was learning that society wasn't free. Society gave the illusion of freedom while trapping everyone with invisible strings. There was nothing free about being in a social setting, and she could see that clearly, having experienced what true freedom meant.

He had been the one to give her freedom, and then send her back to a cage. She wanted to return, but things were complicated now. She had to see it through or none of it would have been worth it.

But that didn't mean she couldn't silently seethe as he refused to look at her, but only watched Amara as she opened the gift. It was a tiny gold chain with two gold charms, a tree and a wing. The twins.

"This is beautiful," Amara exclaimed, exchanging a look with Dante. "I'm sure she will love it."

"You didn't have to," Dante told him.

Dainn turned to him. "Of course I did. I'm happy for you and everything you have done with the empire."

Dante gave a nod, putting a hand on his shoulder in thanks. Dainn did not like people touching him but the look on his face never faltered. Dante turned him to face the table, introducing everyone.

"Everyone, this is Blackthorne, CEO of the Blackthorne Group. One of my old business associates," Dante announced, finally getting everyone's attention. Lyla wanted to scream that this was her man, but she was curious too, curious to see what he was playing at. Dainn didn't do anything without planning it ten steps ahead. There was a reason he was at the party that night, a reason beyond just a social event. It could be just to see her, but he could've done that any time privately. This public presentation was for a particular reason, and she couldn't wait to ask him when she got the chance, understand the fascinating ways his mind worked.

Morana extended her hand to him first. "Morana Vitalio."

Dainn shook her hand once. "Shadow Port Vitalios, I assume?" he asked, as though he already didn't know everything about her. Lyla wondered why Morana didn't recognize his voice if she'd met him before. Even without her bias and the ways his voice affected her, she could admit he had such a distinct voice and the slight accent, it would be hard for anyone with working ears not to recognize it. Maybe he modulated his voice somehow when he met them as the Shadow Man? Knowing his ways with technology, it wouldn't surprise her to know he used some kind of a modulator, even though he'd never done so with her—not as the Shadow Man, not as Blackthorne, and not as Dainn.

Morana nodded at his question. "The very same."

Dainn kept the charming smile on his face. "You've been doing good work there. I would like to discuss some business ventures later?"

"Of course," Morana gave a polite smile back. "My partner, Tristan, and I would love to arrange a meeting later."

Lyla wanted to chuckle at the subtle way Morana told a

strange man that she was with Lyla's brother. Lyla liked that though. She liked that her brother had such a loyal, smart, beautiful girl in his life.

Alpha bent forward to shake his hand next. "Alpha Villanova. This is my wife, Zephyr."

"Nice to meet you," Dainn nodded to them both. "Quite far from Los Fortis."

"We're family," Alpha stated, and Lyla felt a smile on her lips at the gruff way he said it. Out of everyone she had met in the group—Tristan aside—it was the Villanovas and the work they did and the fact that Zenith had loved them both that drew Lyla to them.

Her smile froze on her lips when finally, *finally*, his gaze came to her.

Electricity ran up and down her skin as their eyes connected—his mismatched to her green—after so long. Fuck, she had *missed* him, missed the intensity of his gaze, missed the scent of his skin. His mask, the one he'd been wearing flawlessly since he'd come to the table, faltered, a slight crack for a second that only she saw because she knew to look for it. His eyes notched up the intensity, taking her in.

"And you are?"

Oh, fuck.

Him looking at her like that, asking her that question in his voice—when she knew what his piercings felt like pounding into her pussy and his cock knew what her walls felt like weeping around him, when they knew how the other kissed, moaned, clutched the other in the throes of passion—with no one else knowing a thing around them, it turned her *the fuck on.*

She swallowed, not knowing how to answer.

Your flamma wasn't a response she could give here. She was being called Luna yet she thought of herself as Lyla, both sides of her existing together, the girl she didn't know and the girl she'd thought she was.

"Tristan Caine's sister," she answered with the only truth she could admit to openly in front of everyone.

His eyes flared a bit, before one of his fake charming smiles took over his face. "Well, Tristan Caine's sister—" he took her hand in his, eyes on her "—it's a pleasure."

His lips touched the back of her hand on the word *'pleasure,'* firing an arrow of arousal straight into her core. She kept her breathing normal somehow, the touch of his lips burning the skin of her hand, singeing it in a way she was surprised it wasn't smoking.

He let her hand go, and she immediately tucked it in her lap, preserving the memory of his mouth on her skin, their eyes still connected.

"Why don't you join us?" Amara offered, more warm than polite now.

He broke their eye contact, turning to Amara. "Thank you."

And he sat down right next to her.

Lyla kept her heartbeat regulated, or at least tried to. Her eyes went to Zephyr who mouthed *'hot'* while fanning herself, making a chuckle burst out of her.

His hand came to rest on her thigh, his possessive grip burning through the fabric at the sound, strangling it in her throat. She wished she'd picked a dress with a slit so she could have felt the leather on her skin instead.

The catering staff came around and took their orders. Many guests took to the dance floor, the kids all having left the party.

His hand stayed still, not moving, not doing anything as he talked about anything and everything with every-one, motsly asking questions he already knew the answers to—Morana about some codes he'd heard rumors of, Alpha about the underground fighting circuit, Zephyr about her new work-life balance, Dante about Lorenzo Maroni's old busi-nesses. Through some feminine intuition, Lyla was suddenly aware of Amara watching her man with focus, a focus she didn't understand and didn't like.

"Have we met before?" Amara asked suddenly, interrupt-ing the conversation he'd been having with Dante. The table stopped, looking at Amara, then collectively at Dainn, who sat with a puzzled expression on his face. Fake puzzlement because Lyla remembered him telling her that he'd met Amara years ago once.

"Have we?" he asked, as any normal person would if they met someone once years ago. God, he was so good at how convincing he was, the reminder of how real he was with Lyla warmed her.

Amara frowned. "I don't know. I feel like we've met before."

Yes, at a conference where he'd asked about coping with child loss for his wife, who hadn't been his wife then but was now legally.

Amara shook her head, trying to place him but failing to. He played along. Everything continued.

And then her brother came back.

At first, he didn't clock the stranger sitting at the table, his focus on Morana as he took the seat next to her. But then his eyes landed on Dainn, his face tightening when he saw him.

"Blackthorne."

"Caine."

Fuck.

Did they know each other?

Lyla's eyes wandered between them, and she realized that Dante's business associate would be known to her brother. In the real world, they knew each other; in the dark world, they didn't.

And sitting next to her lover, whom no one knew, opposite her brother, whom she was just getting to know, Lyla realized that things were getting a whole lot more complicated.

MORANA

CHAPTER 23

MORANA, TENEBRAE CITY

"OH FUCK, TRISTAN!" A curse left her lips as his hips pounded into her, folding her into a pretzel, her legs over his shoulders, his hand on her neck.

Their eyes stayed connected, the contact carrying the same weight it had since the first time their gazes had locked. His cock thrust in and out of her, the power behind each making her feel like the mattress under them was going to give, the bed frame creaking, pelvis slapping, lips inches apart.

His blue eyes stared into her soul, pupils blown so wide the blue was a rim around them, and Morana panted, her body turned on to a degree it hadn't been since her recovery.

Between all the pain medication and her left shoulder, between taking care of Xander and finding Luna and being social in Tenebrae and being exhausted by the time they came to bed, finding time to fuck had been difficult. It had reminded her of the old times, of tension building between them with each glance, heating their bodies with each touch, without there being a resolution. Unresolved sexual tension had been a thing of the past since the moment they got together. Thankfully. Morana was horny enough for him to be shameless about the fact that fucking Tristan Caine was one of her favorite activities in the world, just next to kissing him, the only way of burning calories she supported wholeheartedly.

So, after days of going without getting into his pants, Morana had decided after the party that she was going to get what she wanted no matter what.

And so she'd gone all out with the strappy silver dress, the same one she'd worn in that casino years ago when he'd shot her arm and then proceeded to hate fuck her like nobody's business in the shower. Tristan's eyes had flared seeing her in it, especially because she had filled out more in the last few years of being happy, and that flare alone had been worth the effort.

"I'm not wearing anything underneath," Morana had whispered in his ear, giving him a saucy smile before leaving him standing with the others and heading to the cottage. Thankfully, Xander had fallen asleep in one of the rooms in the mansion, so they had the entire space just to themselves.

As she'd expected, Tristan had stalked after her within minutes, not even saying farewell to whoever he'd been in conversation with.

Morana had taken off her heels and run through the grass barefoot, adrenaline filling her veins as she'd almost made her way to the cottage, down the hill, and with so much buoyancy in her heart, a thrill of the chase getting her hormones high. It had been then, running and her blood rushing in her ears, that he had caught her from behind, his arm going around her waist and picking her up. He'd thrown her over his shoulder and carried her into the cottage like the caveman she called him, barely making it in before dropping her down and pushing her against the door. Their hands had grabbed at each other in desperation, hers taking his cock out and him picking her up, no foreplay, nothing, just him sliding right into her.

Morana had grabbed his shoulders, her head tilting back as a moan of deep-rooted pleasure left her, the feeling of completion that she had only ever found with him making her eyes roll back in her head.

"I'm going to fuck you like I hate you." His hands had gripped her under the ass, his words turning her on even more. She loved it when he fucked her like that, their early days of going at it some of the hottest.

"I'll hate fuck you back," she'd told him.

That was all it had taken before he had pounded her into the door, rattling it on the frame so hard she was surprised it hadn't broken like some of the other furniture that had become victims to their shenanigans over the years. They had both come within minutes, both of them too-keyed up to hold on for too long, before he had carried her up to the room, still inside her while she leaked and stained his pants. He had dropped her on the bed and stripped before ripping her dress off and leaving her in nothing but her glasses, his eyes going over every exposed inch of her skin, from her hardened nipples to her little belly to her leaking pussy.

And then, he had kneeled on the bed, pushed her legs back, and folded her in half, rendering her immobile, and thrust inside her again.

His mouth came down, close to her, so close she flicked his lips with her tongue, tasting the sweat on his upper lip, feeling dirty and messy and so fucking hot it felt like it would never be enough. It never would be. If there was one thing Morana had learned in the last two years, it was that they would never get enough of each other, that this deep, intense need would never go away. In the beginning, she'd had her occasional days where she'd wondered if it was too good to be true, but now she never did. He was more committed to her than she had even expected, his eyes, his body, his heart, everything solely on her. He had once promised her that she would never walk into a room and question his loyalty, and he'd been right. No matter where they were, every time she walked into a room, the first thing she felt were his eyes on herself, and they never strayed, not once, to any other person unless someone was directly saying something that mildly interested him.

She tried to move her hips and push back against his movement, but the position she was in didn't allow even a little bit of leverage, her effort only making him slide in deeper.

"Tristan," she begged, telling him to move more, move harder, move faster, and his hand on her neck tightened, fingers pressing into the side of her throat and keeping her useless as he used her body as he pleased, at the pace he wanted, dialing her arousal to an even higher degree.

Heat began to pool in her abdomen, getting hotter and hotter with each slide of his cock in and out of her, the walls of her pussy gripping him tight, wanting to keep him in place and weeping when they couldn't. She whimpered as he hit somewhere deep inside, almost blurring the pleasure to pain, the angle of his thrusts touching a spot inside her that made her mind almost blank every time he touched it. She gripped his wrist with her hand, holding onto his neck with the other, her mouth opening as he seated himself so deeply inside her on a downward stroke that his pelvic bone rubbed over her clit, making her almost blackout with the sharp, sudden sensation that overstimulated her. Her skin felt clammy, her breaths coming out too quick as the heat coiled and coiled and coiled and he moved and moved and moved and she tried to tell him to slow down because it was becoming too much. She was going to fall, shatter apart into smithereens, but no words came out, just sounds, sounds of her moans and his grunts and their skin and her wetness and the bed, creaking and creaking, and suddenly, he went in too deep.

She almost did black out, right before a scream left her throat and the coil snapped.

Her orgasm shook her entire body, making her eyes clench

shut as her muscles squeezed around her, her limbs jittery and her spine arched, her breasts smashed into her thighs and nipples pebbled into points that almost hurt.

Her orgasm triggered his own, making him rock his hips once, twice, before he came inside her again, flooding her for the second time that night, his body going lax on her for a second as he caught his breath, before he moved and lay down to the side. They both stared up at the ceiling in silence for a few moments, panting, letting their hearts calm down and come back down to earth.

Distant noise from the party penetrated their bubble. A clock ticked somewhere in the cottage. Her heartbeat drummed in her ears.

She turned her neck to look at him, running the back of her left hand over his scruffy jaw, catching her breath. "I love it when you hate fuck me."

At her muttered words, he turned to his side, going up on an elbow and resting his head on it, his eyes, his energy, lighter than it had been before. Finding his sister had done wonders for his demeanor. Though he was still a grouch, now he was a grouch who took a joke.

He leaned forward, running his lips along her jawline, down her neck, and over the scar left by the bullet. His lips pressed into it, kissing it softly, before finding her lips, tasting her the way he did that made her toes curl.

Morana pushed him back against the bed, their lips coming

apart, joining again, smiling and locking together. His hands wandered down her naked back, cupping her ass in a grip that always made her breath catch, his hold the only kind of possessiveness he allowed himself to express usually. His rough fingers teased the skin at the edge of her pussy, their breaths mingling harder as her blood heated, the small tracing motion making her core tighten as desire coiled low in her belly.

Tristan leaned back against the headboard, widening his stance, and Morana pulled back, breathing heavily, his hot eyes and blown pupils sending a current right to her core. He kept looking at her, his chest heaving, and Morana felt his fingers tighten over her ass, pulling her up in one motion, bringing her higher on the bed over him.

"Again?" he asked in a hoarse voice that tugged right in her groin.

"Again," she replied, her breasts heavy, nipples aching as they pressed into his chest.

Before she could blink, he picked her up in one of those crazy moves she'd fantasized about for weeks while watching him work out in their home gym, and one of those moves, a bicep curl thingy he did, always shot her libido right through the roof no matter how many times he demonstrated it. She expected him to pull her over him. She expected him to spread her while filling her with screams. She expected him to cup her ass with both hands and hold her still while he drove into her.

But Tristan did none of those things. Morana blinked in surprise as she felt his naked erection against her thigh as her legs wrapped around his waist. His big, rough hand came to grip her neck in a move that was *so Tristan*, his blue eyes blazing with that combination of lust and love that made her heart pound, that combination of wild and soft that made her throb.

"Tristan?" she murmured, not understanding what he would do.

"Patience, wildcat," he whispered softly, and Morana groaned, feeling his length rub against her small nub, sending a thrill of pleasure over her nerves.

"Screw patience," she panted, moving her hips to get more friction. "Actually, screw me. Now."

His lips quirked up even as his eyes glazed, that primal look in them making her heart batter like a ram. She felt his other hand settle on her ass, using their combined fluids to push two fingers into her rear as he lifted her a little higher, his erection pulsing right against her entrance, their eyes locked. Over the years, she had learned he was an ass man through and through. The first time he'd done that, she'd been surprised but it had rocked her world so hard she now begged him. He did take her ass some days if he was in the mood, but sometimes, when they were insatiable, he penetrated her with his fingers and his cock, filling her so completely with himself she felt like he could never get out.

That's what he did right then. With his fingers in her ass, in one smooth motion, he thrust his cock up just as he pulled her down.

Morana cried out, her head falling back as intense sensations assailed her, her walls clamping on his length and eyes closing as her fingers dug into his shoulders for support. Before she could catch her breath at the feeling of being so full, Tristan lifted her again with one hand, stuffing her in the back with his with the other, sliding his cock almost completely out of her before suddenly impaling her down on him, his hips bucking up into her, her loud cries drowned against his tongue.

Picking up the motion, he repeated it again, and again, and again, lifting her and pulling her down, pulling out and thrusting up, the angle allowing him to move so much deeper inside her, pleasuring nerves she didn't know she possessed.

Her walls clenched around him, again and again, with each motion of his hips, convulsing around his erection as it slid home again and again, her eyes closed, small bursts of pleasure assaulting her, combining into a tighter fold, making her whimper louder and louder. Morana pulled away from his mouth, openly panting, hearing his own ragged breaths matching hers, his arms never stopping, his hips never pausing in their pistoning motion.

"Oh fuck," Morana breathed out in between gasps. "Oh

god."

Tristan stared at her intensely, the way he did, leaning his head forward and biting a nipple with his teeth. Morana shuddered at the overload of sensations attacking her from everywhere, clenching him so tightly he let out a very caveman noise. Her walls clamped around him at his guttural growl, and suddenly, the sensations inside her intensified in that familiar but addicting way, the friction between their bodies making her simper in pleasure.

She bit her lip, gasping as Tristan kept hitting the small spot he had discovered inside her, a spot so sensitive to his touch it could trigger beasts of orgasms and had, much to their pleasure.

"Oh god, I'm going to come," she uttered beside his head, her hand grasping him for support as her hips started thrusting back on their own, her other more desensitized hand going between their bodies to rub on her clit, knowing he would never drop her, her finger furiously moving over the bundle of nerves.

"Then fucking come," Tristan growled against her jaw, his teeth nipping the skin and Morana felt her toes curl, the heat infusing in her blood as it started from where her finger rubbed her clit and where he moved and moved and hit her so hard with each damn thrust and her walls started quivering around his shaft but he kept pumping it in and out and in and out and up and down and up and down and never stopped and...

With a mangled scream, Morana felt wave after wave of ecstasy wash over her, an orgasm more potent than either of the others she'd had that night. She felt Tristan's fingers pull out, his arm wrapping around her back, pulling her right into his chest as he pulsed inside her, twitching, coming with a raw sound from his chest, his face buried in her neck, his cock spasming inside her trembling walls, filling her with his essence, her own hands smushed on his chest.

They breathed heavily for long seconds, staying locked together, not moving, just coming from the high they got every single time.

"I love it when you love fuck me too," she told him, dropping over his chest, content, her ear pressed over his thundering heart, hearing it slowly calm back down to its normal beat, matching it so hers did too.

She could feel his amusement at her post-coital blissful words and she relaxed into him, content as a kitten, which reminded her.

She drew loops around his muscular chest with her finger. "When are we getting a cat?"

His hand stroked the line of her spine lazily. "A cat for you. A dog for Xander. It'll be a madhouse."

The exasperation in that whiskey and sin voice made her giggle. She folded her arms on his chest, ignoring the twinge in her left after the vigorous activity she had put it through, and rested her chin on her hands, looking down at him.

His eyes were closed, a peaceful look on his face.

"You'll enjoy it," she assured him. She hoped. "Your sister will come back with us, right?"

"No idea," he told her gruffly. "I hope but I'm not pushing her for anything. It's too soon and she's...she needs time. We both do."

"That's okay," Morana pressed a kiss to his heart. "We have all the time in the world."

A small smile lifted his lips, her favorite thing in the whole world—his dimple—popping out as he kept her eyes closed, stroked her spine, and let her snuggle into his heart.

AMARA

Chapter 24

Amara, Tenebrae City

A MARA HAD READ THAT finding the time and the urge for sex was a little difficult in the first year of parenthood. Thankfully, it was not a problem she and her husband had. From the moment the doctor had given her the green light, she had been on her, in her, around her more than not.

"Lift your knee," Dante commanded her, his voice so fucking rough it sent a shiver down her spine, his dark eyes so hot on hers it was a miracle she had not combusted then and there on the study floor. The very study floor he was currently kneeling on.

The gold silk dress she'd worn to the party was next to the locked door, possibly ripped, along with his clothes, which had finally come off after teasing and testing each other throughout the party. His lips had been at her ears all night, appearing to the guests to be sweet nothings into the ears of his wife, while he'd been whispering all the dirty things he would be doing to her and forcing her to keep a straight face. It had been rough trying to be a perfect hostess with drenched panties.

Amara lifted her knee to the edge of the desk and bent down over it. It was ironic to her that Lorenzo Maroni had cursed her in this same office over the same desk that she now owned, and her husband worshipped her over it.

And looking behind her, seeing him stroking himself, large and hard, she felt another gush of wetness. Amara licked her lips, knowing it had been a very good idea to abstain from sex for a few days. She knew it had driven him mad, but boy, was she reaping the benefits now. It hadn't been intentional on their part, but it had just been an extra busy few days. Dante bent forward, covering her back, his lips at her ear again.

"My mouth or my cock?"

God, she loved how dirty he talked to her in private. The world knew Dante Maroni as a polished, perfect gentleman, and he was, but he was also a dirty, sexy man and he let the full scope of that out when he was with her.

A hard choice to make, Amara grinned. "Both."

"Dirty girl," he growled in her ear, pressing a soft kiss to it.

The next thing she knew, Dante lifted her leg higher, exposing her obscenely to the room and his gaze, and licked a stripe with his tongue over her pussy.

A small lick. Amara bit her lip. Another. She mewled. Another. Her chest heaved. Another. Her eyes closed.

His thumbs rubbed hard circles over her inner thighs, each little circle wounding her up tighter and tighter, and she barely kept her eyes open. Dante alternated, taking his time, and deliberately, slowly, took her skin between his teeth and gently bit on it. A long moan escaped her unbidden, her nerves making her entire body even more erogenous than it already was.

Slowly, planting bites and kisses over her thighs, Dante trailed his lips to her wet core, opening her lips to his hot gaze and just looking into her eyes, spiking her desire even higher.

Amara felt her eyes roll back, her juices gushing out as she gripped the edge of the desk. Dante's mouth, that mouth that should be categorized as a weapon, unleashed on her, eating her out with skill and desire that she could feel in every lick, every thrust, every roll of his tongue. He took her clit in her mouth, sucking on it and her knees buckled in response, going weak and she grabbed his hair, her own falling down her back.

The moment she grabbed his hair, Dante dived in, making her cry out, his tongue plunging inside her, tasting her, feasting on her like a man quenching his thirst, and she plunged her fingers into his hair deeper for purchase, her head tilting back and body humming loudly with the pleasure shooting out from her center, fanning out over her limbs, her arm stretched back to keep a hold.

This was one of the special times Dante was eating her out over the desk. He had a billion times in every other place she could think of, but somehow, the desk was reserved for special occasions when he liked to say a mental *'fuck you'* to his father.

"Dante," she whimpered, her body rising higher and higher,

her pussy slippery against him. His hands tightened on her hips, keeping her upright with his sheer strength that only aroused her more. Holy gods of sex, the man was hot when he did stuff like that.

The noises filling the study were acute, filling her with even more profound desire as she started shaking, almost at the edge, his tongue flicking continuously around her clit and plunging inside her and back again, the smell of her arousal stark in the space. Just as she felt her limbs turn languid and her body strain, he pulled back.

Amara waited a second to see if he would do something else, but Dante just kneeled behind her, her leg held up by one large hand. She looked back, and he smirked at her. Her frustration made her snap a sharp "What?" at him.

"It's the first birthday of the baby I told my father I was going to put inside you," he told her, grinning. Ah, that was the special desk occasion. She giggled, feeling like the young girl with a big crush.

He dove back in, this time with so much more aggression she peaked quickly.

"I won't last," she warned him, feeling the beginnings of the familiar heat in her lower abdomen, one that spread to her breasts and neck and up to her face, flushing her cheeks.

"Come on my mouth," he ordered, going at it *hard*.

And within seconds, with a tight grip of her fingers in his hair, Amara came, her body shaking with the ferocity of the fever in her blood. She went limp over the desk, breathing hard, and felt him stand up.

Before she could catch her breath properly, he was carrying her with an arm around her stomach, right over her pregnancy scars and stretch marks, across the room.

He sat down on the couch, the one they always sat on when their friends came over. He took a hold of her hips and, before she could even balance herself, impaled her on his length.

Amara screamed, her voice raspy, trying to find something to hold, but nothing came to her. Her legs dangled over his, and she leaned back, her back to his chest, trying to find purchase with one arm on the back of the couch. Dante stayed still inside her while she adjusted, his hands on her hips that had gotten wider since the pregnancy. Putting her leg down so her toes touched the floor, Amara finally felt like she could take a pounding he was in the mood to mete out.

Her breath whooshed out as he took her lobe in his mouth, tugging on it with his teeth. Her body, already on the verge of an orgasm, swung wildly out of her control, the fullness inside her gnawing, needing him to move already.

"Dante," she whimpered, tilting her head back as his lips took over her neck, nibbling and biting, brushing and tasting right under her ear, her supernova spot of sorts, and Amara felt herself tumble towards more pleasure, just to have him pull back a bit.

"Stop playing, Dante," she snapped in annoyance and frustration, turning her head to glare at him. Dante leaned back in to kiss her neck, his hands traveling to her full breasts, cupping them completely in his hands, squeezing once before pinching her already engorged nipples lightly, tugging on them. Amara cried out at the intense sensation, her ire forgotten, just on the precipice, a bead of milk coming out since she was still breastfeeding, when he stopped again.

She was getting mad now.

But before she could even say a word, Dante was lifting her right leg by the knee, high, putting it on the couch, and spreading her other one. He pulled her hips away from himself and towards him, making her lean her torso forward to move with the rhythm. He kept a hold on her leg by draping it over one strong forearm and held her hips with the other, securing her in place.

"Tonight," he spelled out for her, his cock throbbing inside her "I am going to fuck you a week's worth. I am going to make you come so many fucking times you'll forget what it's like not having me inside you."

Her muscles clenched around him at the words, her body heating up again, and she wrapped an arm around his neck, pulling him closer. "Take me however you want. I'm all yours."

With a hoarse sound from his chest, he pulled her up by the hips, pulling out completely.

"Dante," she begged, needing him, or she'd explode.

"Fuck, Amara," he ground out, before she felt him slip inside her again, slowly, inch by torturing inch.

She tried to push back, to get him to go faster, but he held her still, going excruciatingly slow. Her muscles shivered and welcomed him inside, wrapping around him like a glove, trying to urge him to go faster. But he stayed still, and he throbbed.

"Move, Dante," Amara muttered, feeling her hips strain with the need to move. But he stayed motionless, only moving her knee over his elbow and putting his finger on her clit. He pushed the tiny muscle, rubbing it while completely inside her, and Amara cried out, feeling so full and so sensitive, so on the edge that one more flick of his thumb and she lost it. Her head leaned back against him, her hands slipping for purchase and her back bowed, stars exploding behind her closed eyes in such a powerful orgasm her entire body shook, her inner walls fluttering around him, as his mouth clamped down on the side of her breast.

And mid-orgasm, he pulled out and thrust in, hard, making her scream out loud, her orgasm unable to end, his hand rubbing on her clit as he pistoned his hips roughly into her, hammering them over and over again, the angle from behind him making him go much, much deeper inside. Her chest heaved as cries and whimpers left her along with his name, moans, and breathy sighs mingling together, her fingers trying to clutch on the couch but unable to. She moved one hand down to his, where he held her hips and dug into his flesh, feeling the warm muscles contract under her touch as he increased his pace, the motion of his hips cutting her completely open, so fast and so quick that he would be in and out before she caught a breath, her body never leaving that almost orgasmic state.

And then he bit her on the side of her breast, hard, while thrusting so deep into her, his rough voice muttering a rugged, "Fuck, you are mine. All mine. My queen, my dirty girl, just mine," right over his mark and Amara panted, her legs completely giving out under her.

Dante pulled out and turned her immediately, picking her up in his arms and taking her weight, making her straddle him as he entered her again.

"Ride me, my queen. Show me what it's like to sit on this fucking throne."

That turned her on even more, She pulled on his hair, pulling his face up for a sloppy kiss as she started moving her hips sinuously against him, just as he liked, her body completely languid in his arms, his to do whatever he wanted to do with it, following his lead and building up to another peak together.

His hands cupped her breasts, teased her nipples, uncaring for the milk that ran down them. Their mouths meshed and tongues tangled, and she felt him twitch inside her one second before he spilled in jerky movements, keeping her aloft, his seed warm and triggering her own final orgasm, making her mewl against his mouth and clamp down hard on him, pulling him completely into her. He stilled, letting his own orgasm ride out, his arms wrapped completely around her, and pulled his head back, leaning their foreheads together.

They opened their eyes and looked at each other briefly before smiling simultaneously softly at each other.

"That was hot," she told him, slumped over him.

"Yeah," he agreed, breathing hard, still inside her.

"Happy first birthday to the babies we made," he said after a long second of getting his bearings.

She kissed his lips again. "You know you're the best dad in the world already?"

"Yeah?"

"Mmhmm."

He gave her a serious look. "You want more?"

"Sex? Always."

He chuckled, rubbing a thumb over her wet nipple. "I meant babies."

Her heart stopped at his question. She pulled back and looked into his eyes, looking at the sincerity on his face. "I don't know. I'm not sure but if it happens..." she shrugged. "I wouldn't mind it."

Dante whooped, crushing her to him again. "I better get to practicing then."

And then, he lay her down on the couch, making her laugh with years and years of practice and proving why physical connection would never be a problem for them.

zephyr

CHAPTER 25

ZEPHYR, TENEBRAE CITY

HER HUSBAND WAS AROUSED.

He had been since the time she had come to the compound, had been since the time she had picked up Tempest and given her kisses, had been since he'd seen the new pinks with the old blues in her hair.

He had been aroused when she'd taken his hand and taken him away from the dwindling party, down the hill to the little clearing she'd found on one of her earlier visits, knowing the place would be empty especially since the guests had left and most of the people were tired and in bed. He had followed her, of course he had, and he'd been hard, thinking she was taking him away for a little wham-bam action. She was, but she was especially taking him away because she had to tell him and she wanted to be away from people, in a place that reminded them more of home, than inside walls of another house.

But if he had been aroused before, he was *stunned* and aroused now.

Zephyr's breath stayed stuck in her throat as they stood in

the little clearing, her ears rushing with blood as she let the words out, hanging in the space between them. He stayed completely still, his singular gaze piercing hers, heavy with something she could not pin, and it was turning her on. Gulping, wetting her lips with the tip of her tongue, she muttered again. "I'm pregnant."

He blinked.

She waited.

He blinked again.

She swallowed.

She had been nervous about telling him, contemplating for a brief moment to give him one of those greeting cards. But he would have just told her to read it to him and it would have defeated the purpose.

When long minutes passed and he didn't do anything except the damn blinking, more than he usually did, she felt her stomach roil even more, and straightened her shoulders. Retreat. She should probably just step away and give him time to process this alone. Yup. Maybe he processed it with excessive blinking the way she processed it with ice cream. Not that she had ever noticed this before. Well, she had never been pregnant before too.

Nodding to herself, she took a step back, and felt his grip tighten on her arms, keeping her captive right on the spot. Okay, then. Retreat was out.

Suddenly, before she could panic some more, he lifted her

up by the arms—she always got so hot when he did that—and deposited her on a high rock a few steps behind her, making her sit on the edge as he looked down at her face, his fingers like firm vices around her arms, long and warm, his musky scent wrapping around her the sounds of the party wrapping up came through the distance in a rumble, the muted lights from there and the moon casting a soft, intimate glow all around them.

Heart pounding, she kept her eyes on him, reminding herself that he took time to process big things, and that was all this was. He was processing. And he sure needed an upgrade for the speed.

His hands slowly loosened their grip on her arms, sliding down to her elbows, going to her wrist and finally, settling on her waist as his one light brown, almost gold eye, unwavering in its intensity still knocked the breath out of her, even after all this time.

Slowly, he went down on his knees, his height putting his torso between her legs, spreading them so he could fit, resting her feet on his thighs, and settled in between, her stomach at level with his face at the height. He pushed her dress up, bunching it under her breasts, and exposed her midriff and her flowery underwear to his piercing eye.

Zephyr had absolutely no idea what he was going to do next, and the anticipation was twisting in her gut rapidly as she looked down at his face, seeing his eye riveted onto her stomach. It still felt odd to her at times to be so fully exposed when her stomach wasn't perfect and he was only looking at it, but then she reminded herself who he was.

He was her Alessandro, her Alpha, the boy and the man who had loved her ten years ago and loved her now.

He leaned forward and planted the softest of kisses right below her belly button.

Zephyr's heart stopped, her eyes closing as tenderness filled her, a smile lifting her lips.

She felt his lips brush the skin again, and she opened her eyes, looking down at his dark hair pulled back in a bun as he planted soft, soft kisses repeatedly at the same spot, slaying all the tiny doubts in her head to the ground. His lips brushing over her soft skin was all the reaction she needed.

"Hubby..."

"Shh," he shushed her as soon as she began, his mouth never leaving her stomach, his hands holding the sides of her waist almost reverently.

Leaning her head, she saw his eye closed, savoring the moment, an expression of such peace on his face. Her eyes moistened for no reason, and she slid a hand over his head, cupping the back of his skull, loving the way it felt against her small palm. She felt his soft hair brush over her fingers in a familiar way that still enthralled her.

They stayed that way for long minutes, not speaking, not moving. His head against her stomach, he laved small kisses all over her midriff as she kept her hand on his head. She looked down at him, at his acceptance, his silent joy, celebrating what they had created together without words. The sounds of their breathing were the only sounds in the area.

Finally, she didn't know after how long, Alpha looked up, tilting his head back to lock their gazes together, his eyes luminous with moisture. He pulled her face down with one hand, resting their foreheads together. Zephyr felt his warm breath over her face and tightened her grip over the back of his neck, letting him just breathe, absorb whatever he wanted to absorb from her, settle whatever thoughts were racing through the labyrinth that was his mind.

He stood up a second later, making her tilt her head way back in surprise, hiking her legs around his waist as he gripped her hair in a firm hold and slanted his mouth over hers roughly, almost bruising, their teeth gnashing as he opened her mouth with his tongue, kissing her deeply, the softness from a second ago pushed back by whatever intensity he was feeling. Zephyr gripped his shoulders in surprise at the suddenness of it, pulling him closer instinctively and hooking her legs around him, the table cool under her butt, his body warm against hers, his mouth completely untamed on hers.

And then the kiss became a paradox, like her husband.

While he plundered her mouth over and over again, feasting on her lips and meshing their tongues, the electricity between them leaving her breathless and leaving her heart hammering as usual, his other hand settled over her stomach, tenderly, his entire palm covering her flesh right above the pelvic bone, his thumb caressing her skin almost soothingly as he kept kissing her like he was at the end of a rope she was tethering, his hand on her abdomen moving in contrast like he had all the time in the world.

She was truly confounded by this man sometimes. But dang, he could kiss.

Their lips parted sloppily and he pulled back, looking down at her with that same emotion that was the theme for the night.

"Rainbow," he whispered and her breath hitched, her stomach fluttering. God, she loved the way he spoke her nickname.

"Alessandro," she replied, shaking off her thoughts, feeling the blood rush to her lips, the skin around her mouth tingling deliciously from the friction with his scruff.

"Are you okay to have sex?"

Zephyr blinked at the unexpected question, but then remembered how careful he was with making sure he never hurt her during sex.

She tightened her legs around him, raising her eyebrows because it was the end of the night, she was on a very sturdy rock, they were both hot and heavy and had kissed like foreplay, and they had to celebrate. He was not going anywhere.

Alpha gave her a stern look, not budging an inch closer.

She hated his strength sometimes. She flicked her tongue across his lips, rubbing his chest just with her hard nipples, knowing they turned him on.

With a low roar, he pulled away her legs from his waist and ripped her panties off, the cloth falling victim to his strong hands, and spread her legs wide, exposing her completely to the night and to his heated gaze. He bent down, and she hesitated, thinking he would kiss his way up to her center, but she was wrong. She had apparently unleashed the monster, and without missing a beat, his mouth covered her, his tongue already plunging inside her, tasting her. A loud moan escaped her and she wanted to let him continue, but her body, her soul probably realized how close it was, and she craved him more than anything else right now.

She gripped his hair and pulled his head up, staring deep into his singular orb, telling him wordlessly how much she needed him. He came up to her mouth, twining his tongue with hers, and she tasted herself of him, her arousal spiking to unbearable levels.

"Fuck me," she told him pulling back, giving him the free reign to go ahead. "It's been too long and my pussy needs you to f..."

The rest of her words were swallowed by his mouth as his fingers touched her nether lips, plunging one, then two inside her, testing her readiness, not wanting to hurt her.

"Fuck, you are so wet!" he muttered hoarsely against her mouth.

She smiled. "What are you going to do about it, sexy?"

Her challenge was the last straw on his back. With a deep rumble, he spread her legs farther, pulling them up and over his shoulders. She silently thanked her pilates instructor for allowing this moment to happen and placed his arms beside her head. She looked up at the stars, breathing heavily when he ground out. "Look at me."

Swinging her eyes lower to his, she let them lock as he lined himself at her entrance. Her breath hitched, and she waited with bated breath to see what he would do. She had thought he would enter her slowly. She had been wrong again. With another rumble, he thrust and buried himself to the hilt in one deep stroke, making her breath catch and a loud yell escape her lips at the sudden *massive* invasion, leaving her clinging to him.

She mewled as his cock pulsated like a live being deep inside her, surrounded by her wetness, and feeling his own arousal so much better turned her hornier than she had been, than she had ever thought possible of being. This was what being in heat felt like, multiplied by ten, probably. Apparently agreeing with her thoughts, Alpha pulled back and out of her completely before plunging down back in, hitting her right on that elusive spot in the position, making her spine arc and her breasts smush into his chest. Before she had regained her breath, he was out and going in again, hitting the spot again, and she bit her lip to keep from screaming from the intense dual feels.

His thumb caught her lip, pulling it out from her teeth, and he demanded roughly. "Scream for me, Zephyr. I want to hear you."

His words made her clamp hard on his cock, making him hiss and pump faster in and out of her, making her moans get louder and louder, and something incoherent escaped her mouth as she grabbed for purchase to keep from flying off. He pulled her dress down, and she tilted her head back, looking at the trees as he clamped onto her exposed nipple, biting and laving the area with his tongue. The only sounds in the clearing were coming from them- moans and hisses and groans and loud breaths and the sound of flesh slapping furiously against flesh. It was so fucking hot, and it was so arousing, and she could feel the pleasure her walls were giving him, feel the pleasure that zinged through him every time her nipples brushed across his flesh, feel the electricity that zinged through his spine every time he pushed in and pulled out again.

She was panting now, the mutual pleasures she could feel becoming too much for her senses, becoming too much for her body to take. She kept her eyes on the trees as he moved and moved and moved above her, in her, so so big and so so real, sweaty and musky and all hers. He pistoned his pelvis against her, one hand gripping her ass so tightly and keeping her in position, his mouth sucking and eating on her breasts, his speed increasing and his movement gaining a momentum she had not thought possible and suddenly, without warning, her flesh clamped down hard on him as a loud scream escaped her throat, seeing stars behind her closed lids, tears escaping the corners from the excessive pleasure. Her climax rocked through her body, making her walls flutter around him as he made his pace faster, chasing her orgasm with another one, banging her brains out just like she had asked him.

Another explosion rocked through her. It was too much. She couldn't take all the sensations thrust upon her, and she opened her mouth, screaming silently as Alpha thrust and thrust and thrust before exploding inside her with a loud grunt, flooding her with his cum and making her twinge again around him.

She couldn't come again. She would not survive it. She bit into his forearm beside her head and waited for the twinge and the flutter to pass, but it didn't, making her clamp and clench onto him, milking him for all he was worth. She bit into his arm, and he bit down on her breast, setting off a last, albeit small, explosion inside her. She clung to him as a lifeline, making him anchor her from floating out into the sky, and after minutes, she finally opened her eyes, looking back at the stars, feeling him pull out of her. A moan escaped her at the feeling, and she let her legs down, feeling thoroughly used and sore, and she would feel it tomorrow. She liked that.

Alpha fell on the grass, pulling her over him, laying down under him, and looking up at the sky with a hand over his head.

Zephyr turned sideways to face him, feeling the soreness in

her vagina and biting back a mewl. "Wow."

He slowly turned his head to her, smiling a little. "Just wow?"

She slapped his arm. "Well, I would say I saw stars, but that would be too literal."

He grinned, only with the unscarred side of his face, and she pushed up to press kisses to the scars.

Alpha didn't smile like she had hoped he would but just looked at her. He brushed his lips across hers once before staring at her intently. "I see you, rainbow."

"I see you too," she told him softly.

Nothing screamed 'endgame' like a man who's forgotten everything, lost in his own mind, and found himself guided back home by the sheer memories of the woman he loved. "We're endgame," she echoed her thoughts. "Who would've thought, right?"

He chuckled softly, his hands letting go of her hips, letting her touch his skin under the shirt he'd been wearing for the party. He moved his hand down her left thigh, caressing the skin under the knee and hiking it up to her chest, flipping her in a way she loved, back to the ground. His other hand held him up from crushing her as he lined up, brushing himself against her folds.

"Are you sore?"

She flushed, which was ridiculous considering how naked and intimate they already were. "A bit."

He smiled, his mouth coming down on hers in a soft, languid kiss, his stubble rasping over her skin, and she was pretty sure her entire mouth and chin and cheeks and neck and breasts would be suffering from beard burns. Oh, she wouldn't have it any other way. He entered her slowly this time, carefully, the angle of her one leg hiked up making him slide in easier that she would have thought, till he was buried completely to the hilt. She didn't think his size would ever stop surprising her.

"Gah, you feel so good," she muttered as he littered her neck with kisses and bites.

"Yeah?"

"Mm-hmm," she whispered on a ragged breath, biting her lip. He pulled out slowly before entering her again, hard, and she keened, not having realized that this angle made him hit her g-spot directly.

"You must, ah," she panted as he started moving his hips slowly, pulling back and thrusting in again, hitting her spot again, "oh my god, practice, ah yes, for this."

He bit the underside of her jaw as her fingers dug into his back. "Practice makes perfect."

His rough growl against her skin turned her on even more as she closed her eyes, letting herself feel everything happening over her, inside her, letting herself feel his tremendous arousal for her, his aching hunger for her, the need in his groin to take her.

"But we love imperfections, sexy."

He groaned, his hips speeding up slightly but still very much slow. "Perfect is overrated," he reminded her.

"Exactly," she muttered, thrusting back at him. "Give me your scars."

With a loud groan, he gave up and thrust inside her so hard he mind blanked out for a second, her walls clamping all over him, gripping him like they would never let go. He pulled out and pushed in again, his movements getting more erratic, the angle of his penetration making her cry out over and over again.

She felt his arousal reach its peak, his movements getting wilder as he thrust into her, nipping at her jaw. "Fuck, Zephyr. I'm close."

Knowing she had to come with him, she gripped his hair with one hand, pulling him up for a heated kiss, and put her other finger on her clit, rubbing it furiously, feeling him enter her again and again, feeling him get so turned on knowing what she was doing and the sensation was more than she could bear. With a cry drowned around his tongue, she felt her entire body lift up the grass as her walls quivered around him, exploding in heat, her finger on her nub stopping. His own replaced it, rubbing it continuously, prolonging her climax as she shook in his arms, clamping all around him, gripping his hair so hard and kissing him for all she was worth. Her clenching walls spurred him on and with a sound deep from his gut, he came too, thrusting just one last time inside her, before collapsing on top of her, breathing heavily.

She wrapped her arms around him, mewling in pleasure as he pulled out of her, and dropped to the side.

Catching their breaths together, she grinned up at him, feeling icky and knowing she would have to take a bath, but happy.

Zephyr was happy. He was happy.

After a long time, they were happy.

And for now, that was all that mattered.

LYLA

CHAPTER 26

LYLA, TENEBRAE CITY

S HE NEEDED SEX. NOT a thought she'd ever thought she would think, not when sex had been a weapon of trauma throughout her life.

But things had changed. Sex was pleasurable now, potent, powerful.

Her body was burning up—both literally and figuratively. It was almost as though the heated touch of his gloved hand during the party had thrown up a previously lowered switch. Hours had passed, and this hunger, this mad, raving hunger inside her, had only festered and grown like a beast. Her skin tingled from the heat she could feel pulse through her entire body, each and every pulse throbbing ardently at the juncture of her thighs. Her breasts felt uncomfortable, heavier, each rasp of the dress against her hard nipples sending a jolt of pleasure straight to her aching core, molten lava pooling low in her belly. She couldn't remember the last time she'd been so wet without Dainn doing something. She couldn't remember the last time she'd felt so empty, almost mindless, the need to be filled and taken so acute it almost hurt her.

She was in heat. There was no other way she could describe it.

Lyla closed the door to her suite and headed to the bathroom, needing to take a shower to cleanse herself and rid herself of this heat.

She closed the door behind her quietly, and switched the lights to low, casting the same warm, mellow glow around the lavish bathroom, the dark brown tiles and granite sink top gleaming in the soft light, the dark granite ledge around the tub cool against her heated palm. She stared at the tub, remembering all the times she'd tried to go under when she'd been alone, her memories of taking baths by herself not a good one, only made better with Dainn rewriting her trauma with her—bathtubs and masturbation, both things that she'd hated.

Maybe it was time to rewrite some of her own.

She filled the tub quickly, knowing if she had to do this by herself, she'd take her sweet time and not rush it. Not when she was going to masturbate for the first time in her life.

Cracking her neck, filling the water with bath salts he'd packed for her, Lyla stepped over the wide ledge and into the tub, her toes making contact with the warm water before her foot dipped in, followed by the rest of her body. She sank into the water, another gasp leaving her lips as the warmth tingled over her skin, teasing her between her legs, the water swirling

around her heaving breasts. And she reveled in it, leaning her
head back against the rim as the water rippled over her before
slowly settling down.

Everything was *sensation.* She was utter sensation.

Gripping the edges of the tub, eyes closed, she let herself
drown in them. The scent of the lime and something musky
combined in a heady sensation, reaching her as she took a
deep breath. The water lapped over her nipples, like slow, soft,
smoother caresses of his hands, pooling between her thighs
and teasing her aroused little nub with warm, warm currents
she felt through her whole body. Her toes tingled, feet arching
slightly as she let herself bask in the sensory pleasure, the
sound of her own heavy breathing mingling with the occasional sound of water at the edges of the tub, the only sounds in the
huge bathroom.

She let her hands move away from the tub and drift into the
water, the buoyancy tickling her palms as she kept her eyes
closed.

Slowly, ever so slowly, she put her hands over her aching
breasts, squeezing softly. A loud moan escaped her lips at the
sudden amalgamation of relief and pleasure that shot through
her, her nipples hard points against her palms, and she rubbed
them wantonly, her neck arching along with her spine, seeking
that relief. His hands always held her breasts firmly, sometimes with tenderness, sometimes with utter possession. Her
thoughts lingered on the possessive grip now—the way he

squeezed her breasts in his large, burned hands, tugging at the nipples with strong, sure fingers. Her actions matched her thoughts, pulling on her nipples with the same intensity, and a current of pure electricity shot straight to her core, her walls clenching madly.

Heart hammering as her breathing fastened, the sounds heavy in the room, her gasps and moans mixing together in a heady combination, she bit her lip, letting herself fantasize.

He bit too. On the tops of her breasts, he took the flesh between his teeth and just nipped, enough to send fire licking into her belly before flicking her nipple with his tongue. This way, then that. Her fingers moved in sync, playing with her sensitive breasts, her arousal a sharp ache in her core, her hunger gnawing in her belly.

Leaving one breast, she slowly trailed her hand over her wet skin; feeling the stomach, Lyla let herself linger on the soft skin. Like he lingered, with his calloused fingers catching over her skin, with his scruff rasping over it, with his teeth nipping his way down, with his tongue tasting every inch of her, god, he lingered. So much he drove her mad, left her a writhing, quivering mass of arousal, biting her hipbones and over her thighs, coming to a stop as he spread her legs.

She spread her legs, the water lapping against her heat, rising like steam inside her blood.

Lyla dipped a hand down over her inner thighs as the other tugged on her breast. He loved the softer skin of her inner thighs. He loved nipping at it, seeing it flush. He loved licking it with small strokes of his tongue, teasing her like that for minutes. And with that heat in his mismatched eyes. So much heat. In his eyes. In her blood. Everywhere.

She panted as she caressed the skin, so, so close to where she needed the relief but tormenting herself because that's how he drew it out, and he was there, right there, inside her head, tormenting her.

Her mouth opened as she breathed heavily, and slowly, finally, she touched her folds, parting them. She could see in her mind the way he watched her as he did it, see his own heavy breaths as he exposed her to his eyes, see the blaze in those before he dipped and tasted her.

Lyla moaned loudly, canting her hips up as her finger found her throbbing little nub, sending waves after waves of heat crashing through her body, her heart skittering and her pulse pounded in her ears, her body shaking, so, so sensitive she couldn't believe it.

Biting her lips, she opened her eyes.

And locked eyes with his intense ones.

She froze, her chest heaving, her finger on her clit as the other hand rested on her breast, eyes on him.

He sat there on the ledge, still dressed in his dark suit that he'd donned for the party, watching her with those intense eyes, his own breathing heavy.

How long had he been watching her? How had she not heard

him come in?

She didn't care.

His eyes traveled the length of her body under the water, resting on where her hands were, before coming back to clash with her own.

Her breath hitched, a new wave of arousal, sharper, starker, washing anew over her.

Licking her lips, never removing her eyes from his, Lyla dipped a finger inside herself, the sensation almost making her eyes flutter close. Almost. She couldn't remove her gaze from his even if she wanted to. She didn't. Because he watched her like she was the finest dessert and he was a man starved.

He *was* starved.

Another finger joined the first, pumping in and out of her, never reaching the depth he did, the skill his fingers did, the satisfaction. But he was there, and watching him watch her as she pleasured herself was heady. She would never have been able to do it a few months ago. Now, there was no cloud of hesitation anywhere.

A moan left her as she pressed the heel of her hand hard into her nub, and suddenly, Dainn removed his suit jacket. She watched with lidded eyes as he took his gloves off, taking his time, placing them on the counter, along with the jacket. Then, he did the same with his cufflinks, and then, he began rolling his sleeves up over his forearms, exposing the burns on his hands and the dark hair and the ropes of muscle. He sat back down on the ledge and leaned forward, one muscular arm over her to the opposite edge of the tub, caging her in the water.

She tilted her head back, to keep their gazes locked, the dark, musky scent of his flesh and cologne wrapping around her as he leaned closer and closer and closer.

And kissed her pulse. It fluttered.

His scruff rasped over her skin as he kissed her neck, coming up to her jaw, biting and licking and suckling on her skin, the heat an inferno inside her body as her fingers worked over it.

"You're a fever in my blood, *flamma*," he muttered against her ear, the sound of his low, deadly voice tipping her over the edge. Lyla turned her face into his shoulder, biting his hard muscle over the shirt as pleasure washed over her, her body trembling but hungering for more, more that she wasn't able to find no matter how hard she rubbed herself.

"Dainn," she whimpered against his skin, and suddenly his hand was right there, cupping her. Lyla watched his muscular forearm dip under the water, the fabric of his shirt wet and clinging to his arm, and she panted.

He swirled a finger around her opening, once, twice, teasing, tormenting her as she came down, before boldly pushing two fingers inside her. She felt her walls clench around him as he pumped his fingers skillfully, over and over and over, building her right up, her body arching into his touch as her hands came out of the water, gripping the back of his neck, wetting his shirt even more as she pulled his face down.

Their mouths clashed together in a frenzy, his fingers increasing in speed as the heel of his hand pressed into her, his tongue spearing her lips in sync with his mad, mad fingers, making her heart thunder as the heat coiled at the base of her spine, coiling tighter and tighter and tighter and he kept stroking and moving and kissing and never stopping and she couldn't breathe as her breasts heaved and water lapped over the rim and he was surrounding her, inside her, moving in her, just as he always had and he always would and suddenly, he pushed his fingers in, curling them, and she shattered with a loud scream muffled against his mouth.

He pulled back his lips as he pulled out his fingers, and Lyla opened her eyes, her body limp but not sated, watching him. His lips were wet, as was his torso, the front of his trousers tented with the evidence of his own need.

Lyla blinked up at him as he stood up, his own fevered eyes on hers, and removed his wet shirt from his body, throwing it in a corner. She watched the play of muscles over his flesh, his abs rippling with every heavy breath he took, as he undid his belt and removed his trousers, standing there without hiding his piercings.

Fuck, she'd missed them.

She watched him with unabashed hunger, feeling that warm, low coil of arousal spring forth from her core.

Before she could do a thing, he had her out of the tub and into his arms, carrying her out of the suite and to the bed.

He dropped her on it, his eyes intense. "Hands."

The words, the command, filled her with need. She extended her hands, watching as he wrapped his belt around her wrists.

He turned her to face the headboard, climbing up behind her, his face scenting her neck and his hand cupping her breast possessively. "You got one, but you're getting punished tonight, *flamma*. For touching another man."

She whimpered, needing it, needing him. She could feel his heavy erection against her back, the metal on them kissing her skin as one of his hands traveled lower, cupping her boldly again.

Fire shot through her blood.

"I'm proud of you," he whispered into her flesh. "For taking your pleasure yourself. Did you think of me?"

"Yes."

"Such a good girl for me, *flamma*."

His words inflamed her even more.

His fingers played with her, plunging and rubbing and stroking, bringing her to the edge. She began to breathe heavily, her breasts heaving, her eyes rolling back into her head.

And he stopped.

Lyla came crashing down, a cry leaving her lips.

"Shhhh," he hushed her. "You can't be loud, flamma." His fingers restarted. "Someone might come in if you make a noise." He pushed a finger inside, nipping the side of her neck. "You know what they'll see? A stranger with their precious little guest. They will see you begging for my cock, see you a needy mess for me, you don't want that, do you?" The heat in her body was going to give her a stroke as sensations assailed her. She bit her lips to wrangle her cries.

He brought her right to the edge again and stopped.

Lyla moaned, and she bit her tongue to strangle it.

He started again, and stopped again.

Again and again.

Until she was a whimpering, needy mess that he'd called her, eyes cheeks wet with tears and her mind gone from almost pleasure that he kept her coasting on, never fulfilling her.

"Please," she begged, sobbing in frustration. "Dainn, please."

"Who do you want, *flamma*?"

"You. Only you."

"And what will happen if someone else touches you?"

"You'll kill them." It turned her on even more.

"Now tell me."

"I love you," she whispered, her pussy on fire. "I love you so much. I missed you so much. Please, complete me, Dainn. Fill me. Please. Touch my soul."

Her words must have triggered something in him because the next thing she knew, she was pushed forward, her cheek against the mattress, her hands tied with the belt in her front, her legs spread apart, and he plunged into her in one stroke. Lyla muffled her scream in the mattress, coming around him immediately, his piercings rubbing against her walls in ways that felt like coming home, his cock so deep she couldn't tell where she ended and he began.

His hands gripped her waist and kept her in place as he fucked her into the bed, hard, fast, brutal, taking out days and days of distance and separation in one hard thrust after the other, and Lyla kept coming and coming and coming, until she was a mess of fluids and mindless and dazed, just letting him fuck her until, after what seemed like hours of him battering her pussy, she blacked out.

Lyla came to on her side, feeling him inside her again, wrapped around her back, not moving, just staying in her, locked in like he was finding home too.

Lyla turned her neck to look at him. "I think you missed me."

He pressed a kiss to her lips. "I did."

Her pussy and heart both clenched at that.

"How's everything been?" he asked her as if he didn't already know. Or maybe he didn't.

Lyla turned back to face forward and he spooned her, and she began telling him everything that had happened, talking more than she'd talked in days, all the while, he stayed still inside her pussy, inside her heart, inside her soul.

Things had changed. She had changed. She was still changing, transforming, and for the first time, it didn't scare her. As she lay in the arms of the man she loved, the man who never let her be lonely, a man who had always touched her soul, Lyla looked forward to seeing who she would become on the other side.

PART III:
OUROBOROS

"The snake which cannot cast its skin has to die."

— FRIEDRICH NIETZSCHE

DANTE

CHAPTER 27

DANTE, TENEBRAE CITY

V IN HAD GONE OFF the radar.

He didn't know if the man was alive or dead anymore—for the sake of his wife, he hoped it was the former—but he wouldn't bet on it.

Dante sat in his study, looking down at his phone at the last message he'd been sent by Vin. It had come from an unknown number—the same one he'd used to send the previous ones, the same one Dante had asked Morana to trace and found in the river. The text was nothing but numbers that he wouldn't have looked at twice had it not been for the two numbers he recognized—5057 and 5705. There were others there too—7505, 7055, 0755, 0557, and so on, all a combination of those digits, all confusing.

"Is that a game?"

Dante looked at Xander, who sat next to him on the couch, his eyes on the screen of Dante's phone. Dante's heart warmed at the boy. He reminded him so much of Damian in some ways, but he was much different too. Sharper than his brother had been, definitely more technologically inclined than Damian had ever been. Xander had been attached to Zephyr since he'd found out she was pregnant but had been in the study since the girls had all gone out. They had collectively decided to take Luna shopping, to spend a girl's day out bonding and give her some new experiences, with a dozen of his security gone with them.

Tristan was out doing whatever Tristan did; Alpha was taking calls in the gazebo and coordinating everything back at his base since they were staying a week before leaving.

In the beginning, everyone had decided to stay a week until his princess' first birthday party, but after Zephyr had told everyone that she was pregnant the next morning, Amara had insisted on her staying a bit longer to celebrate the good news. Morana decided it would be a good way for Tristan and Luna to spend more time together before the girl decided what she wanted to do, living situation-wise since she had begun relaxing in the space. And so, they all had one more week before they went back. Dante liked the house so much, though, realizing that he would miss having the whole family together when they left.

With everyone scattered, Xander was in his care, sitting next to him and playing with Tempest in his own way. Dante liked the fact that the boy felt comfortable enough to roam the compound as he pleased. Even though the boy was young, he had a soft way of being with Tempest that made Dante trust him with her, and his princess liked the boy too, trying to use his smaller body to stand on shaky legs. She should have already been standing alone at her age, and Dante hoped there was nothing unusual about her growth. For now, his mother-in-law reassured him that babies took their own sweet time to do things, and they needed to worry only if things were slower even then. Dante really fucking hoped it wouldn't be. Just the idea that the event which had made them lose one daughter could have impacted the other made his heart heavy.

"No idea," Dante told the boy at his, looking back at the screen. He'd have to show it to Morana and try to get her to analyze it.

"It looks like some kind of code." Xander pushed his glasses up his nose, holding Tempest with one arm as she talked to him in her baby talk. She was a yapper, as Zephyr said.

"Different sequences all summing up to the same number. Five plus five plus seven. Seventeen."

Dante blinked at the screen, realizing the kid was right as he pointed at the screen.

It was all summing up to seventeen. Why seventeen? What was the significance of the number? A date of some kind?

"You're right," he praised the boy. "Good catch."

They were silent for a while after that, with Dante perusing his other texts and catching up to things he'd missed, and Xander sitting on the rug so Tempest could climb over him better. Lulu napped in the corner as she always did, a lot more now that she was older and her energy reserves lower than they'd been before. Dante remembered picking her up as a little kitten, so tiny she fit the palm of his hand, her little meows tugging at his heartstrings, making him realize she was perfect for his queen. He had seen the same meows tug at a younger Amara's heartstrings too when she'd discovered her behind a potted plant, her whole face melting as she'd picked her up and cooed to her softly. In that moment, Dante had known she would be the mother to any children he had or he wouldn't have them at all.

Looking at their baby growing older too quickly for his liking, he hoped Amara would actually be okay—when she was sober and not high on post-coital bliss—with the idea of maybe having another sibling so Tempest could have the love growing up that neither he nor Amara did, him having been kept away from his brother and Amara never having any in a way.

His phone suddenly rang in his hand, the noise making Lulu perk up for a second before she changed position against the window and curled over again.

"Maroni," he said as he picked up.

"Mr. Maroni," Nellie, the rehabilitation center manager, greeted him from the other side. "I tried to reach Dr. Amara, but no one answered."

The girls were at the movies, their phones silenced. His security guy had updated him.

"She's occupied elsewhere," he told the woman. "Is it something urgent?"

"Not urgent," she reassured him. "Just that a woman came. Since we don't have her listed on the visitor's file, I didn't grant her access. She was mainly interested in Lex."

That was highly unusual. Dante knew all about the boy, Xander's friend, knowing what a soft spot Amara had for him. "Did she give a name?"

"That's the thing," Nellie cleared her throat. "She called herself Mrs. Maroni."

Dante frowned. "She was impersonating Amara?" That was stupid.

"No," Nellie clarified. "She said she was related to you. I didn't know what to do but since Dr. Maroni had given me clear instructions, I told her to come back later."

Dante stared at the window, thinking. The only one alive who went by Mrs. Maroni was Amara. His dead uncle's widow, Chiara, had been a Mancini. Rest of the relatives had different last names. And though Chiara was shady enough to pull shit like this, she had pretty much gone into the woodwork since his uncle died, and Dante cast out any of their loyalists. What the fuck was she playing at, if it was her at all?

He'd need to check the footage at the center just to verify it was her or see if it was someone else. Amara needed the breather and he didn't have anything better to do, so he decided to check it out himself.

"Thanks, Nellie. I'll be there in an hour and check things out."

He cut the call and picked up his little princess, Xander standing up and accompanying him as he strode out to find his Zia, his wonderful mother-in-law, without whom he had no idea how he or Amara would function as parents. She was the only one they could leave their daughter with without a shred of worry, knowing that Tempest and her grandmother had a bond, that the older woman absolutely doted upon the baby.

He found her in the gazebo talking to Alpha about kids. He was happy for his brother. Fatherhood was a joy and a blessing he wished his brothers—blood or not—could experience in their own ways so their lives could be as rich as his was. And knowing both Zephyr and Alpha, he already knew they were going to be fantastic parents.

Zia saw them coming, her face creasing with a smile, wrinkles around her eyes that had once been smooth when Dante had been younger.

She automatically took Tempest from his arms, placing her on her hip, and turning to head back into the house.

"I'm taking a trip to the rehab place," Dante told Alpha, knowing the other man hadn't seen it yet. "Wanna come?"

Alpha straightened. "Sure."

"Can I come too?" Xander asked from his side. "I'll meet Lex."

Since Lex had been the center of attention for the strange impersonator, Dante saw no problem in letting the boy accompany them. "Of course." He took the younger boy's shoulder, and they all walked to take one of his vehicles.

In a few minutes, Xander was strapped in the back and Alpha took the passenger seat. Dante drove out, down the driveway and down the hill, heading toward the city. The rehabilitation center—or New Haven as Amara wanted to call it—was half an hour away, on the edge of the city. In just a little time, Amara had somehow managed to make it stand. He didn't know how she did it, between being a new mother and taking on her role by his side and her own practice, and take care of their new undertaking. Even after so many years of knowing her, she never ceased to amaze him with the sheer strength she possessed. he couldn't have imagined a better partner than her.

"How're you holding up?" Dante asked Alpha, breaking the silence. "With the baby and everything?"

The other man relaxed in his seat, so big he occupied the entire space in the large vehicle. "Good," he said, his voice gruff. "I was ready for a family, and she needed something to keep her going. I'm glad for the baby."

Dante nodded, happy to hear that.

"How did you give her your gift?" A voice asked from the back, and Dante looked in the rearview mirror to see Xander looking out the window.

"What gift?" Alpha asked him, his face frowning permanently on one side. Hector, the sick bastard, had done a number on him. Good thing he was dead. Alpha had told him that the Shadow Man might have killed the man after brutally torturing him. For once, he was on the same page as the mysterious man. Anyone who tortured and killed a piece of shit like Hector had a point in his book. He didn't know what the Shadow Man's beef with him had been. He'd cryptically told Alpha that Hector had broken his toy, and it made Dante wonder. Had it been a thing or a person? Did he have someone he cared about that Hector had hurt? Given that asshole's tendency to hurt people, Dante wouldn't be surprised to learn it.

"The one you gave Zephyr," Xander brought him back to the present. "She told me you gave her a gift that made the baby."

Dante exchanged a look with Alpha, a grin splitting his face as he swallowed his laughter. His brother sat stumped at his side, floundering to find the appropriate words.

A streak of mischief, the one that loved pissing off Tristan, came over him. "That's a great question, Xander. But it's something I think you should ask Tristan. He can explain it to you best."

"But he's not given Morana his gift," the child retorted.

"Oh, I'm sure he has," Dante chuckled. If he were to count the number of times he had seen them before or after they did dirty things, he would need ten hands. He was happy for both of them, really. They both deserved a happy relationship and great sex. But the way they'd been at it in the beginning especially was hilarious to Dante.

"But Morana doesn't have a baby in her belly."

Tristan was going to murder him, but what the hell. "Well, when you talk to him about it, maybe you should suggest he do it correctly. He might not be delivering the gift properly."

Alpha snorted next to him, making Dante laugh again. Xander was going to grow up one day and look back on this conversation and think Dante was his funniest uncle and thus the best. It was all about future planning and investment in child favoritism.

They reached the center's gates, guards on the side opening them when they saw Dante's car pulling in. Nellie was at the entrance waiting for them.

Dante parked the car, and they all got out, walking to the main building. Alpha looked around and took the place, and Xander looked around like he was searching.

First things first. "Nellie," he greeted the efficient woman. "This is Xander, Lex's friend."

The woman smiled. "Oh, I've heard so much about you. Let me call Lex so you can meet him. He'll be so happy to see you!"

Nellie flagged one of the staff members, asking them to find Lex and bring him out. In the meantime, Dante introduced Alpha and let the two have a conversation about the place's running, how things were managed, and so on. He looked up at the camera, pointed at them, and nodded to one of the security guys.

"Get me the footage for the last twelve hours," he instructed.

"Yes, sir."

The guard left and entered the surveillance room to get the tapes just as a boy barrelled out toward them, his teeth crooked and exposed in a big smile.

"Xan!!" Lex came to a stop in front of his friend before hugging him tightly. Xander pat his back, which was the equivalent of a tight hug for him, and pulled back. Both the boys went to the side, Lex talking rapidly with loud gestures and Xander much quieter, more subdued. Nellie took Alpha on a little tour of the place, and Dante leaned against the wall outside, taking a cigarette out while waiting for the tapes. He had quit smoking, rarely doing it anymore at home, especially after Tempest was born. Sometimes, though, he liked to take a puff, especially when he was out and about.

He lit it up, taking a deep drag and letting the smoke roll out of his nose, looking around the beautiful property. The city he had called home all his life, that his daughter would call home, was becoming better since he had taken control. The violence had been curbed a lot more; his rules were strict—play dirty in his domain and die. The system might not eradicate the criminal elements, but he did, especially in his territory. There was only space for one criminal empire in Tenebrae, and that was his. The rest could stop or move.

"Have you talked to him?" Lex's voice reached Dante. Dante stayed still, realizing the boys were standing behind the wall he was leaning on, hiding him from their sight.

"Yeah," Xander said in a quieter voice. "He said everything was going as planned."

Dante's ears perked, honing in on the conversation. Who the fuck were they talking about? Could it be the guardian Amara had mentioned?

"Cool," Lex's tone was excited. "I wish he'd give me another task. I like being on cool secret missions. Since the morning he dropped us off, it's been soooo boring."

"Do you like it here?"

"Yeah," Lex nodded. "Everyone is nice. But there's no excitement. I want some more fun adventure, you know. The last time we had fun was when they all found us. That was like more than year ago!"

"You need to chill, Lex," Xander echoed Dante's thoughts. The boy had a lot more to him than met the eye. He focused on Xander talking. "Things are going as planned. It takes time for everything to happen. Don't make it difficult."

Lex laughed a little, almost like a little maniac. "I already broke a rule."

Xander's voice was serious. "What did you do?"

"I talked about him in therapy. Just a little mention. Nothing more."

Xander was quiet for a second before there was a slight thud on the wall, like he had pushed the other boy into it.

"Are you mad?" Xander hissed. "Why would you do that?"

"I was bored." Dante could hear the grin in Lex's voice. *Well hell.* The boy was a little chaotic and much more complicated than they'd suspected. More cunning than they'd given him credit for. What they'd thought was a slip of the tongue was a deliberate seed.

Who the hell were these boys?

Dante narrowed his eyes as he stared ahead, wondering why Xander had never said a word about any of it to any of them. The boy loved his new family, that was pretty evident, but his loyalty wasn't fully theirs, not yet. He was in contact with someone else, in cahoots with someone else, and the instincts inside Dante were conflicted between protecting him and protecting his family.

"Fine," Lex grumbled. "Don't get mad. I won't do it again, Xan."

Xander stayed quiet.

There was shuffling before the boys came out from behind the wall. Lex blinked up at him innocently but it didn't fool Dante, not anymore. Xander stared straight ahead, his face grim.

The guard chose that moment to come through and hand him a drive with the footage with a laptop. Dante refocused, letting the matter of the boys go for now, and skimmed through the footage.

And just as he'd suspected, it was Chiara, the older, gorgeous, reptilian woman who had been unfortunately related to him. What was she doing back in Tenebrae, and why hadn't he been told about it, especially since he had an alert out for whenever she stepped into the city? Chiara might have had the face of an angel, but Dante had seen her prey on young boys in a manner that was demonic.

He thanked the guard, and once Alpha and Nellie came out, he thanked her, making a mental note to call her and let her know to keep an eye on Lex, but in a different manner now.

As he drove them back to the compound, his eyes going to the reflection and seeing the boy in the rearview mirror, wondering how much of what they knew about him was true and how much wasn't, once again wondering who the fuck he was and where he came from, Dante felt grim.

The boy was in contact with someone else. Morana would have to break her own code and hack into his phone.

They needed some fucking answers.

DAINN

CHAPTER 28

DAINN, TENEBRAE CITY

D AINN CUT INTO THE Maroni compound from the back side of the hill through the woods.

As secure as the place was, there was a small break in the electric fence that ran around the property, a security measure that was easy for him to distort since the technology was old and the circuit easy to break in one spot. He had entered through the space but rewired the circuit to make sure no one else could. He wouldn't have cared for trespassers if his *flamma* hadn't been in the mansion.

Keeping his hood up over his face and blending in with the dark night, he walked quietly, careful not to snap a twig or make any noise to alert any of the guards patrolling the property.

What he'd found needed to be confirmed, but he didn't want to contact Morana directly anymore, not when he knew how much it angered Tristan Caine. And the only reason he was even giving a shit about it was because his little *flamma* had asked him to. In fact, with her eyes glazed with satisfaction, she had begged him not to make waves deliberately with her brother. She liked her brother.

Fuck him.

He sighed, a part of him pissed that he'd had to share her with other people, even if they were her family, another part of him pleased to see her coming into herself.

It was the middle of the night, the cloud coverage making it dark enough for him to make his way across the lawn undetected. Once he got to the wall, he slinked along it, carefully walking around the periphery to ensure no one was around. No one was. There were just the occasional patrolling guards and nocturnal creatures. Just as quietly, he reached the back door, carefully moving the knob to test if it was locked. It was. And thanks to Morana, it wasn't the kind he could pick. He'd need to crack it, and that would send a security alert out. Plan abort.

Moving onto Plan B, he walked around the edge of the wall, checking every window, and found them all locked.

There was only one option now, and not one he'd wanted to use since it risked exposure.

He made his way around the property, pausing every time the guards passed, and to the wing Lyla was in. It was the one closest to the driveway and the main gates and, hence, closest to the security station at the front. Regardless, he went under her window, taking hold of the trellis of vines that climbed up to the roof, knowing it was strong enough to hold his weight.

He'd tested it the other night when he'd been in her room, leaving her slumbering form after having the most intense little fuckfest.

Fuck, don't think about it.

He exhaled, clearing his mind of those memories because they would distract him, and he needed all his senses to be alert. Because if what he'd learned was true and verified, it would put everything in place.

Gripping the trellis with one hand, he pulled his body up with one arm, his muscles trained in bearing his weight and moving lightly, thanks to years of calisthenics and martial arts. Something he had done for function but now did for another added benefit—the way Lyla ogled him from behind the window in the kitchen. He had deliberately moved his workouts to the deck outside that window, knowing she enjoyed watching the way his body moved. For him, his body was a tool but for her, his body was liberation, a means to free herself from her sexual traumas, a tangible proof to let herself connect with him. He knew how much she appreciated it, how it meant more to her than just sex, and so he gave it to her however she wanted—visually, sexually, simply.

Taking hold of the edge of her window, he pulled himself up with the other hand, glad she was on the first level. And if he knew her, which he did, she would have left her window open. His *flamma* liked openness and hated being locked in. If she could leave anything open, she would just for her peace of mind and to remind herself that she wasn't locked in. Her claustrophobia wasn't one of tight spaces, it was of locked spaces, no matter how big or small.

Just as he'd predicted, her window opened inward when he pushed it.

He heaved himself up, jumping in on silent feet just as a pair of guards passed under the window. Close call.

Still crouched down, he shut the window slowly, and moved next to the wall so no one could see him if they looked up. He straightened, his eyes going to the bed where the reason for his existence lay slumbering. Blankets tucked around her, a pillow close to her chest as she curled around it, exactly like she curled around him, lips slightly parted, and she snored softly.

Dainn had no intention of doing anything with her tonight since he had a mission, but he couldn't resist walking to the bed and standing over it as he watched her sleep peacefully. Extending a gloved hand, he tugged the blanket down a little, exposing the side of her neck where he'd left a deep mark, then lower.

She was wearing one of his T-shirts, he noticed, very pleased.

It hadn't been his intention to come to the party the other night. He'd received the invitation and kept it just in case. But then, while eavesdropping on a conversation between Amara and Zephyr through the bugs he'd installed in their phones with a little email virus, he'd heard Zephyr say she hoped his little *flamma* found love and someone hot at the party, because she deserved someone amazing. And it had occured to him that in all their niceness and love and good intentions, they might try to set her up with someone.

And that would absolutely not happen. If she were going to even fake date anyone, it would be the man she was already married to. *Him.*

And so he'd dressed up and gone to the party, just to introduce himself and make himself known to the circle, charm the ladies enough that Mr. Blackthorne seemed like a good prospect if they were to push her into dating anyone. He'd seen the way men had already been circling around her like sharks, attracted to her ethereal beauty, mistaking her as fresh blood. They didn't know that she wasn't the red of blood but the red of fire. He had always seen the way men had looked at her, but it had never been as annoying as it had been then, possibly because these men didn't just want her beauty; they wanted her soul. A soul that already belonged to the devil in him.

Brushing his gloved finger over her cheek, wishing he could touch the softness of her skin, he memorized her face until he saw her again and then turned to leave. He had an important mission to complete.

He quickly opened her door a bit, slipping outside and sticking to the shadows. He knew the basic layout of the mansion, thanks to a little bribe to a drunk older relative of Maroni who had lived there once. Making his way down the west wing to the main area, being careful to check for cameras, he finally ended up where he'd hoped to be—the study.

Picking the lock was easy enough, since it was still the old antique type, and so was slipping inside.

Dainn stood in the dark, surrounded by the shadows, and looked around the space, first to check for cameras and then to search.

When he saw no surveillance, he relaxed and went to the desk. Now, the real search would begin. Knowing Dante Maroni had occupied this study for almost two years, he doubted what he was looking for would be anywhere easily found. If it was, then Dante would have found it already and told Morana. Dainn would have known about it. The fact that he hadn't even known of its existence made him realize that it was either a false lead or it was well-hidden.

Guess he'll find out.

He checked the furniture, the sides, the back, and the front, for hidden compartments but found none. It was just a simple but well-made old desk.

Next, he moved to the wall, lightly tapping it to check for any hollows. One wall, two, three, four. Up, down, sides, center. Minutes passed, and nothing.

Next, he crouched on the ground and looked at the flooring, under the rugs and outside of it, for any loose or uneven areas. Nothing.

Almost an hour passed, and Dainn didn't find anything at all. He was in the middle of the room, recalling what his source had said.

"The Reaper had a file," the man he was interrogating choked on the water he was holding him under. *"Maroni kept it in his office after he killed him. Please. Let me go."*

Since his conversation with Xavier, Dainn had spent his time tracking down any seeds of the rumors he had talked about. He had started with tracking Maroni's man Vin through the last contact he'd had with them, seeing all the texts going back months for clues but not finding much. Word on the ground said he'd run off with the slave he'd been using to go undercover, but Dainn was doubtful. They had run, that was true. For their sakes, he hoped they'd gotten out but if they hadn't, it was likely that Vin was already dead and buried with the girl somewhere.

And after days of weeding through nothing about the rumors, he had found a thread. A man who had worked with the Alliance—the deal between Lorenzo Maroni, Gabriel Vitalio, and The Reaper, a deal which had looked like a partnership for cooperation for business, but the first two had joined hands with The Syndicate, and things had gotten messy. This was why he preferred to operate solo. People were messy and liabilities, especially in shady business. That one little thing had spiraled out of control, destroying both the Reaper and Gabriel, to the point that no one talked about the Alliance anymore because of what an example it had been for anyone who dared to step out of line against The Syndicate. People thought it had been Lorenzo Maroni's doing since he had been the only one left unscathed, but Maroni had been a puppet, invisible hands pulling his strings behind the scenes, untouched because he had kept himself in their line.

Dainn stayed crouched on the floor in the dark, examining the entire space with clinical, methodical eyes and a cool mind. He thought to himself where he would hide things he kept as leverage that he never wanted anyone to find. His eyes stopped on a small painting of the hills, one he knew Dante Maroni hadn't moved because it had been his mother's creation.

Could Lorenzo Maroni be that predictable?

Dainn straightened and went straight to the painting, hoping he didn't have to destroy it. He might not have been emotional, but Dante Maroni was, and he'd loved his mother. In fact, Dante's blind love for his mother must have been something Lorenzo had relied on and expected that his son would never touch the painting.

Dainn tilted the small painting to the side, finding nothing but a wall at the back. He tapped it just to be sure. Stone.

He took the painting off the hook and turned it around. Sure enough, the inner lining at the back of the frame bulged. What a *foolish* place to hide shit. This just proved what he knew even more—Lorenzo had been more stupid than smart, more balls than brains.

Quickly removing a knife from his inner pocket, he made a small cut at the back and peeked inside.

Papers.

Clinically, he cut the back open, being careful not to nick the painting, and removed the singular file.

Pressing the lining back and hanging the artwork back exactly as it had been, he turned the file over, making out nothing in the dark.

Nothing but a symbol, one he'd seen many times. Two intertwined snakes eating their own tails.

He tilted the file toward the window, looking at the large print on top of it in the minimal light. Two words.

PROJECT
OUROBOROS

It was real.

Fucking hell.

He pocketed the knife and put the file inside his hoodie to keep it safe, knowing its importance. He was going to read every fucking word of it when he got to a secure location.

Returning to the desk, he left the photograph he had brought with him for Dante Maroni to find. A gift since his *flamma* had asked him to keep them in his circle of protection now.

And then the Shadow Man slipped away like he'd never been there.

AMARA

Chapter 29

Amara, Tenebrae City

Thisanation was what she'd needed. A day spent with the girls, relaxing, away from all responsibilities.

The four of them had taken one car while another with security tailed them. Morana had refused to drive for some reason, which had been odd given how much she enjoyed being behind the wheel. While she'd said she just wanted to relax, it did strike Amara as odd. However, Luna took her focus. Luna, who looked at the shopping mall like she'd never seen one, who was constantly looking around with an amazed expression on her face, who was shopping so hesitantly like she'd never done the process before. It had taken Morana urging her to pick whatever she liked, reassuring her, telling her not to worry about the cost of things at least a few times before the girl had started to relax and get in the groove of things.

Amara had kept her eye on the girl, analyzing her internally, wondering what her life had been like for her behavior to be this way. In a lot of ways, it was almost childlike, reminding her of the way her daughter looked when she discovered something new for the first time. How did she not know something as simple as buying things, choosing things, or the process of paying for stuff? Luna's sense of discovery was tinged less with joy and more with sadness, which seemed to be an inherent part of her. Over the last week, Amara realized this girl wasn't a pawn. She had secrets and certainly had a truckload of trauma, but she wasn't evil or a threat. Even Dante had softened and warmed to her within a day of watching her closely, her wide eyes constantly looking at things in wonder and caution, as though one wrong step could unravel her. Given what they knew about The Syndicate, it didn't take a genius to figure out some of what had been done to her. A part of Amara—the traumatized, scarred girl—recognized the same within her even though she didn't know the specifics.

She also recognized the healing. Like Dante had helped her heal, someone had helped this girl. That was the only reason she was functioning and enjoying the day and not dissolving into a panic at the overstimulation. That kind of healing usually came from three bonds—parental, friendly or romantic. The parental bond was out of the question, and she'd told Tristan she didn't have friends (yes, Tristan had discussed some of what they'd discussed with Amara to gauge how to talk to her). That only left one bond, romantic. This was all theoretical in Amara's mind, something she'd not told anyone but her husband, who was her best friend, but she did wonder.

The one time she'd offered Luna the space to talk to her in a professional capacity, the girl had sweetly thanked her and told her she was already seeing an older man, a Dr. Manson who was amazing.

Amara had looked up Dr. Mansons in her field, finding a few, most in her own age group, one older lady, and one retired gentleman. The only one who fit had been the retired doctor, and if that was who she was seeing, then that meant he had come out of retirement specifically for her. Why? Did he know her somehow? Or did he know someone who knew her?

Amara was still wondering when Zephyr said she had to pee for the fourth time. Morana gave her company and stuck to the rule of never letting a girl go to the bathroom alone, and Amara didn't say anything, but she was concerned. While bladder control was one of the worst things about being pregnant, it was too early for Zephyr to be feeling it so strongly. Amara had nothing but her own experience, but she had been much bigger before she'd had to pee four times in as many hours. She would keep an eye on her and if it got worse, she was going to intervene.

"Poor thing," Amara shook her head, browsing the aisle of silk scarves, saying something just to make conversation, and Luna browsed opposite her. "Peeing is the worst during this time."

"Yeah," Luna agreed. "It's so bad."

Amara's hand stopped, as did her body. She turned to look at the girl, her eyes narrowing. How did she know? Not to freak her out, Amara relaxed her body and asked casually. "You've seen pregnancies?"

The girl froze completely, her wide eyes coming to Amara. Something passed between them, and Amara understood. She'd been pregnant once. But what happened to her child? Did she lose it like Amara had lost hers? Was it taken from her? Was it still somewhere? Because if it was, Tristan would want to know.

Luna swallowed. "Something like that."

The girl couldn't lie for shit.

Before Amara could say anything else, the other two girls joined them.

"C'mon, we'll be late for the movie." Morana looked down at her phone where she had the tickets and led them all through the mall, a ring of security around them. Amara let it go and followed her friend as they made their way up the elevator and into the empty movie theater.

"I booked it all out," Morana told them sheepishly, her eyes flickering to Luna, letting Amara know that she had noticed the girl's newness to the whole experience too.

The girl in question looked at the empty seats and the wide screen where the logo was displayed. "Wow."

Worth it.

They all took seats, and after checking that they were safe, one of the guards brought them popcorn and drinks. The movie, a romantic comedy, started.

And Amara felt her heart fill with wonder at having four girls she could call friends now when once she'd had none. Morana, who sat beside her, gripped her hand, exchanging a look with her that told her she was thinking the same thing. They'd met as friendless, lonely people and found a family with each other.

Amara gripped her hand back, grateful for her life and hopeful that nothing would tarnish it.

And then, Zephyr had to pee again.

She lay in bed with Dante, drawing circles over his muscular chest, lost in thought.

"What's going on in that beautiful head of yours?" he asked her softly, his voice husky with sleep. It was early morning, the light barely filtering into their room. In a few minutes, they'd be up and running through the day, so they were taking a little moment for themselves.

"I think we need to ask Luna some questions now."

He brushed his fingers over the scars on her wrist. "What brought this on?"

She told him about her suspicion that she'd been pregnant,

about how she didn't want to tell Tristan until her doubts were confirmed. Dante listened to her theories quietly. This was something they'd done since as far back as she could remember, just laid in bed and discussed the things on their mind, sharing things with each other they would never tell anyone else. Before her husband and her lover, Dante had been her best friend, her first crush, and she was so glad that it was still just as true. Being married to the man she loved, the man who had been her friend through the worst time of her life and become more, the man who had been her first crush, her first kiss, her first love, it made her feel all gooey inside.

Tempest began to whimper from the crackle of the walkie-talkie, and Amara kissed Dante softly. "I'll feed the beast."

He grinned, nipping at her lower lip.

She walked into the adjacent room, the one they'd made into a nursery, and picked up the light of her life. Tempest stopped whining when she saw Amara, pouting instead at being kept waiting.

"Apologies, your highness," Amara cooed, picking her up and placing her on her hip, the weight super familiar now. She sat down on the rocking chair, pulling the strap of her gown down and exposing her nipple. Her daughter lurched towards it, and Amara winced as she clamped down, suckling hard and drawing out the milk as it let down for her. They were slowly weaning her and switching to the bottle during the day, but she got very fussy in the morning if she didn't get her meal straight from the source.

A movement made her look up to see her gorgeous shirtless husband leaning against the doorway, arms folded over his chest, watching both his girls with a supremely satisfied look on his face. She switched breasts expertly, moving Tempest around to the other side, leaving one wet and exposed. Dante strode in, leaned down, and slashed his mouth over hers, ravaging her lips while pinching her freed nipple, making her gasp.

He straightened, licking a drop of milk from his thumb, staring into her eyes. "Fucking sexy."

Swoon.

Turning, he left to go and get ready for the day, the massive dragon tattoo breathing fire across his back rippling with the motion of his hips, and sighed with contentment. He was the one *fucking sexy.*

When she was done feeding Tempest, she quickly got ready for the day and left out her scarf. She'd started leaving it out of her attire more and more, letting her scars out, a lot more confident in her skin than she had ever been. Maybe it was becoming a mother. Maybe it was the love of a good man. Maybe it was being Dr. Maroni. She didn't know, but as she got ready and headed out, her mother coming in to take Tempest for the morning, she went straight to the tree.

Her little Serenity was growing strong right next to the

gazebo. She touched the leaves once and said the words she did every morning.

"Mama loves you." Somehow, speaking the words and caring for the tree herself had begun to scab the wound of her loss. Though it would never heal fully, this was hers and Dante's way of filling it up with gold.

Amara lingered, getting her mind ready for the day, before returning inside the mansion.

As she moved toward the driveway, the door to the study caught her eye. She stopped in her tracks. Dante either went to his studio or to work out in the mornings first. Since Alpha was there, her bets were on the two men fighting like boys. His study only opened when he came down after taking his shower. So the fact that the door was slightly ajar sent an alarm going through her.

On quiet feet, which was slightly absurd with her heels, she padded over to the door and peeked inside, looking to see if anyone was there.

It was empty. Pushing the door open wider, she entered the room that had once intimidated her, now looking like a daycare office, and ran her eyes through everything. Nothing looked out of place. Had Dante forgotten to lock it? She doubted that, but nothing else explained it. Satisfied that nothing was amiss, she turned to leave when something on the desk caught her eye. Tilting her head to the side, she walked over to it, picking up what looked like a polaroid.

The moment the image registered, the photo fell from her hand.

Shaking, she bent down and picked it up, staring at it again. Xavier—her biological father and perpetrator—lay dead on a table in a pool of his own blood. It was a gory picture, one she couldn't imagine Dante just leaving out in the open for anyone to find. No. Someone had broken it and left it there for them. A threat? Information? She didn't know, but she turned on her heels and power-walked to the outside building where the men trained with each other.

Seeing her walk out like that, with a mission and heels on the grass, some of the men outside called for Dante.

Her husband ran out immediately, skin glistening with sweat and brows lowered with concern.

"What happened?" he asked, jogging over to where she was, meeting her halfway.

Amara thrust the photograph at him. "I found this on the desk. Someone broke in, Dante."

His jaw tightened as he called for one of the main security guys. "I want every fucking surveillance camera from last night. Now!"

The men scattered, running to complete the task. A break-in was a big breach in security, something none of them took lightly.

Alpha came up behind her husband, taking the photograph. Dante explained who it was, and she saw his single eye train on her. It wasn't that she was sad. She had zero affection for the asshole. But she was concerned, both for their security and for her old friend, Vin, since Xavier had been the one to take him and place him undercover.

"What do you think has happened to him?" Amara mused out loud as they stood there.

Dante's face was grim. "I think we should prepare for the worst, Amara."

A shaky breath left her, and her eyes shuddered close. She didn't want to imagine the worst. She wanted to believe that her Vinnie was doing intense work undercover and not underground somewhere without any of them knowing. He had always been such a good friend to her. She needed him to come back safely.

Dante wrapped his arm around her, tugging her close to his side as she wondered when they would finally find some answers.

ALPHA

CHAPTER 30

ALPHA, TENEBRAE CITY

T HE IDEA OF BEING a father was insane but incredible.
While he did think about being a family and starting
a conversation with Zephyr, her announcement had shocked
him. Not unwelcome, of course, but just shocking.

Alpha sat in the fucking study, just waiting to go back home.
He was so done with being in Tenebrae. As much as he liked
the place, it was too much for him. He liked the solitude of
his jungle, the lush green that surrounded his compound, and
the dogs that were his family. Leah was taking care of them,
but now more than ever, he wanted to return because his wife
was expecting their first child together. Though nothing in her
body had changed yet, Zephyr was absolutely glowing, and he
was happy to see her happy.

Amara had told him to keep an eye on his wife, just in case
her need to pee increased in frequency, and to get it checked.
He'd already scheduled an appointment with her gyno when
they returned the day after.

She had confided in him the night before about her fears, not just for the baby but for her own mind. She didn't know when the next bout of depression would suddenly hit her, and she was terrified that her hormones would harm their child. Alpha had just held her close and told her not to worry, that they would get through shit together, but the fact was, he had his own set of fears. Being a father was a responsibility, bringing a child into their world and trusting the world with them. It was too much to think about at times.

"It's been confirmed," Victor told him on the phone. He'd stepped up big time to the mantle while Alpha and Zephyr had been away, proving his merit and his trustworthiness, though Alpha was still a little skeptical. Maybe he would always be.

"It was Hector?"

"Yeah," Victor reconfirmed. "The autopsy reports came back. This has the Shadow Man written all over it."

Well. Good riddance. Between Hector and Xavier being dead, both suspected courtesy of the Shadow Man, Alpha wondered what the hell was up with him for the hundredth time. It was their second last day in Tenebrae, and they were all sitting in the study, having a final meeting before they all went their way.

Dante and Amara were sitting on one couch, Tristan and Morana on another, he and Zephyr on the third, and Luna alone on an armchair. The meeting had been convened because all of them had different information, and it was time to consolidate it all.

Alpha put the phone down and looked around the room at people he had begun to consider family. "It was Hector. We can't say for sure but you can guess the main suspect."

Dante still had disbelief and anger on his face. "I have scanned the entire property, and all I found was a shadow near the lawn. Nothing. Who the fuck is this guy? And how the fuck did he get inside my house?"

Amara placed a hand on his arm, trying to placate him, her face marred with a concerned frown. She had been out of sorts since the morning when she discovered the photograph, more worried about her friend than her biological father. Victor had begun tracking Vin through his sources, too, now that Hector was dead and he was freer, but frankly, Alpha didn't have a good feeling about it.

Alpha understood Dante's frustration, though. He would be fucking pissed too, if someone broke into his home where his family lived and left behind a bloody souvenir. He looked at the photograph on the table that Amara had found. Her biological father, his throat cut clean through with a wire wrapped around it, his body slumped on a messy desk, blood all over the papers. It was a gruesome scene, one that would shake anyone who wasn't used to seeing that kind of violence.

Tristan picked up the photo, examining it for any clues while Morana typed away on a tablet. "There was no breach in any of the systems," she informed everyone. "All doors and windows were closed."

Dante gaped at her. "Then how the fuck did he get in, Morana? Because he did, and he left that for a reason."

"Have you found the party guestlist?" Tristan asked suddenly, throwing the photo back on the table in the middle.

Morana shook her head. "There wasn't one available. It must have been on paper, and it was long ago. A lot of the useless junk from Lorenzo's time was thrown when Dante cleaned house."

"What about the number patterns?" Dante spoke again. He'd shared the pattern Xander had found, thanks to the last message Vin had sent, with the numbers adding up to seventeen.

Morana shook her head. "It doesn't look like a code to me. From what Vin told you, it was most possibly numbers for The Syndicate girls. The Shadow Man told me last week to get my old codes ready. For whatever reason, he wants it to be working. I'd stopped looking at it a while ago but they're almost ready now. I'm thinking of entering the numbers into it to see if their combination leads to any result."

Zephyr opened her mouth next to him, hesitating. Alpha wrapped an arm around her, encouraging her to speak. "When Hector was holding Zen and me, he called her 5057. Said she had left her friend behind."

Left a friend behind.
5057.

Left a friend behind.

Two men.

Dark night.

Metal fence.

'Don't concern yourself, I'm keeping an eye on her.'

'More than keeping an eye, I'd say. You've got her under your thumb.Who's she?'

'5057.'

'Shit, the one who left the friend behind?'

'Yeah. Daughter of someone important. I have my orders, and you have yours. Make sure no one finds a thing. The Syndicate would kill us.'

'And we never met.'

'No.'

Something flashed in his head, a shadow of a memory teasing his brain for a microsecond before it was gone.

A headache split his head open, making him groan as he held it.

"What's wrong?" Zephyr's voice drummed into his skull from the side.

"I think I got a flash," he rasped out, clenching his eye shut as the ghost pain behind his missing eye intensified. It felt like someone was cleaving it out with a spoon, the dull edge making the pain sharper. He began to pant.

"Alpha?"

'What did you hear, Alpha?'
'What's this syndicate thing, Hector?'
'Tell me what you heard!'
'What did you get into?'
'What's this 5057? Is it someone? Who was that man?'
'Fuck, why did you have to listen?!'

The throbbing in his temples made his teeth grit, an animal noise leaving him as he held his head in both hands, breathing heavily.

"Baby?" Zephyr's hand was on his back, her voice scared.

Alpha kept a hold of his head, letting his heart calm down and his brain work whatever the fuck was happening to it. Everyone thankfully stayed silent as he breathed roughly, his body shaking as his wife rubbed his back over and over. He didn't know how long it took, but after what felt like hours, the throbbing finally subsided to a dull ache.

He exhaled, looking up to see everyone staring at him with varying looks of concern. Dante was almost up and off his seat.

"I'm okay," he told them all, his voice still rough.

"What happened?" Zephyr asked him, and he let out another breath.

"You got triggered," Amara deduced from her place, her face grim.

He gave a nod. "No idea why. Just got a flash of memory. The night I was attacked."

Zephyr gasped at his side, her hand flying to her mouth. He turned to look at her, his eye taking in the heartbreak on her face. He wished he could have told her he remembered her or anything about their time together. Maybe someday, he would get another flash that would let him share that good news with her. For now, it was just this.

"Hector attacked me," he told them, something they all already knew. "But there was another man there. I don't re-member his face clearly, but I've heard his voice somewhere. He was older. They'd been talking about The Syndicate, about 5057, and how she was someone important's daughter and how she left a friend behind."

"Well, hell," Dante muttered, leaning back on the couch again. "This is wild."

"I think that's why I was attacked," Alpha deduced. "I heard something I shouldn't have. Maybe there was more which I can't fucking remember."

Everyone stayed silent, processing.

"So it is a number for the victims." Morana broke the heavy silence, coming back on track. "Or something else?"

"Did you look into Xander's phone?"

Morana's face fell. "Yeah. He has some calls from an un-known number once a month. They don't last for more than a minute so it's difficult to get data, but from the scrambling pattern, it seems like the Shadow Man."

"He led us to him," Amara added, reminding them.

"He's involved in everything." Dante ran a hand through his hair. "I don't understand why everything leads to him and The Syndicate."

"You think he's involved in it?" Zephyr asked quietly.

Alpha didn't think so, his instinct telling him it was the opposite, given the way he was working and leaving a trail of bodies of people rumored to be in the organization.

"A few months ago," Alpha began, remembering what he'd heard on the ground. "One of my girls on the ground told me about a bunch of bodies suddenly dropping. High-profile people were killed in their homes. The rumors said it was him, but it was more activity than there ever had been before."

"What happened a few months ago?" Morana mused out loud, looking up as if trying to recall information.

Dante sighed. Amara rubbed his arm. "We need to find him."

"Can we… maybe bait him?" Morana suggested, her eyes flickering for a split second to the only person in the room who had stayed silent throughout the discussion, not a sound from her.

Luna Caine.

Who was studiously staring at her hands, folded together in her lap, her knuckles white with how hard she was gripping herself.

Alpha felt his eye hone in on her keenly.

The Syndicate taking *her*, the Shadow Man showing up and sending *her* file, leading them to *her*, now breaking in here that *she* was there. She was the only commonality between them.

His focus on her made Zephyr look at her too, followed by Dante and Amara, who followed their gaze, Morana already looking at the girl. The last one to look up was Tristan, seeing everyone staring at his sister.

"What the fuck is going on?" he demanded, his voice dangerous, protective.

Alpha understood, but apparently, everyone else came to the same conclusion he had. The logic made sense to everyone else.

Morana took the brunt of it, the only person in the room immune from his wrath. "The Shadow Man knows your sister."

Tristan's gaze swerved to his sister, who sat with her jaw trembling. Alpha felt a sliver of sympathy for her. Sitting there like that under such scrutiny couldn't be easy.

"So?" Tristan persisted, refusing to accept what was right in front of his face. "He knows all of us."

Morana took a deep breath in. "I think she knows him too. None of us do."

At those words, Tristan's eyes sharpened on his sister. He joined the rest of them as they looked at her, waiting for her to speak. It would be ideal if she denied it, but it would be better if she admitted it, better because they would finally have some fucking answers.

Luna sat in the armchair, not fidgeting, not squirming, just utterly still and pale, keeping her eyes lowered and her hands together in that tight grip, breathing in and out and in and out again.

"Is this fucking true?" Tristan demanded, his voice hard, harsh for the first time with his sister.

None of them said a word, not as she flinched at the tone of his voice. Alpha bit his tongue to tell Tristan to mind his tone, that little flinch affecting him. But he stopped himself. This was too important, too big.

They all waited as she took her time, finally inhaling deeply. She finally looked up, her green eyes shimmering, and looked around at them.

Then, she opened her mouth.

"I do know him."

The words came out in a halting, shaky voice. Words that fell like bullets on their ears, causing all of them to tense and sit up automatically at her confession. The magnitude of it hit him in the chest. The Shadow Man, the most fearsome myth in the darkest part of the underworld, the one man even the biggest monsters feared meeting on a dark night, the one ghost who had confounded all of them, was known by this tiny petite woman with a sad soul.

And then, while they were processing the words, she dropped another bomb on them, this one even more lethal, even more impactful, with even more consequences.

Quietly, the previous tremor from her voice gone, replaced by the strength he hadn't known she had possessed, she looked up. Her eyes stared each and every one of them in the eye with defiance he hadn't thought her capable of, sitting up straighter than she had before, more powerful in her stance, and said three words that hit them all like a tsunami.

"I love him."

TRISTAN

Chapter 31

Tristan, Tenebrae City

"*I* LOVE HIM."

His sister, his beloved beautiful sister, whom he hadn't known long enough but never would have suspected of even knowing about the fucker, just sat there and told them all she loved *him*.

The fucker who had led them to her. Tristan didn't know whether to kill or thank him. He was leaning more toward the murder right then.

He felt Morana's hand slip into his, holding him back from doing or saying something stupid that could damage his very new relationship with his sister. She had always been smarter, more emotionally astute between the two of them. Sometimes, he wished she wasn't. He wished she would let him rage and ask what the fuck his sister was doing with the asshole pulling the strings and leading them around on a merry chase like it was a game. What the fuck was she doing with someone who lived in a world so filthy it made Tristan feel sick? It wasn't a fucking game. Fuck, he was *pissed.*

His jaw clenched tight, he realized he was glaring at his sister, who, for the first time in their entire time, looked him straight in the eyes. The docile, damaged girl transformed right before him into a darker, defiant one, one with confidence rather than confusion in her eyes. He loved the confidence but hated who it was for, who had inspired it. How could she feel confident just thinking of a fucker who wasn't even there? Tristan would have suspected some kind of drug if he hadn't been with her the whole time.

"So, you do know who he is?" Morana asked from his side, her voice even.

His sister let his gaze go and looked to his side, right at the woman who had started the whole conversation. "Yes."

"Who is he?" Dante chimed in, leaning forward in his seat.

Luna turned to him. "He is... mine."

"You have to be specific, Luna," Amara encouraged her, more gentle than any of them, more gentle than Tristan was capable of feeling at the moment.

His sister took another deep breath, her hand going to the gold choker necklace she always wore. Tristan had wondered about it, about who had given it to her, why she wore it all the time, and when he'd asked, all she'd told him was it had been a gift. But she'd seemed happy about it, so he'd not prodded anymore.

Now, watching her touch the necklace, it became crystal clear to him. The fucker had sent her to them marked with his possession.

"He is my lover. My... husband."

Stunned silence, completely *stunned*, before gasps escaped some lips.

Tristan was on his feet before he knew what he was doing, striding toward her and almost at her before turning in the last minute, angrily pacing away, returning back to her. He leaned down, fucking *furious* with her for keeping this from him when they'd been opening up to each other every day, keeping the fact that she not only knew the fucker but she was *fucking married* to him. Married, when he'd not married for years because he'd wanted to find her? *What the actual fuck?*

His thoughts spiraled in a flurry of pure fury, but only one word came out.

"Explain."

The word grit out of him, harsh. He could feel the shock around him, but his body was buzzing with adrenaline, as though prepping to fight an enemy he couldn't see.

"Tristan," he heard Morana warn from somewhere near his back but ignored her tone, looking his sister straight into her beautiful eyes. Had she been lying to them the whole time? Had Dante's suspicion been correct, she'd become a pawn for the Shadow Man? She'd been playing them with her innocence?

He knew he was showing her a side of himself that she hadn't seen before, that maybe she'd not been exposed to before, but he couldn't control it.

"I said," he gnashed out again, staring her down. "Ex-fuck-ing-plain."

Her body flinched slightly before she straightened her spine, tilting her chin higher, staring *him* down even though she was a head shorter.

"What do you want me to explain, brother?" Luna didn't flinch this time, even though her jaw trembled.

"Ex-fucking-plain." The same word came out stunted through his grit teeth.

Her teeth gnashed too, her eyes sparking with fire he hadn't seen in her before.

She tilted her head to the side, her spine rigid. "What do you want me to explain? How I was a slave for The Syndicate all my life? How I was used and abused? How I had no one and no memories and absolutely nothing? How I wanted to *die* rather than live in that hell every single day? Do you know what that does to you? You might have felt pain and anguish, but you had a light and you had something worth living for. Let me assure you, you don't know what it feels like to be completely alone in the utter dark and feel your soul break, day after day, night after night, until it's gone and you're left an empty husk, just praying for it to just *end*."

There was complete silence, tense silence as she caught her breath, and everyone just processed her talking. She'd never said so much. His jaw went slack at her words, at the emotions and the pain in her voice, hitting their mark as pain shuddered through him.

She suddenly moved, her hands fisting at her sides. "You want me to explain how *he* found me, in that dark as an empty husk and breathed life back into me? You want me to explain how me protected me for years? How he saved me from others and from myself for *years?* How he searched for each shard of my shattered soul with patience, piece after piece, until I felt healed? How he led you to me?"

Her words fell on Tristan like bullets, knocking him back physically as he slumped on the couch; Morana's hand came on his arm, and his eyes remained on his sister, standing in the center like a vengeful goddess owning her truth.

Luna looked around at all of them slowly, seeing all eyes on her, and turned to face him again. "Or do you want me to explain how I saw you all at a club one night? How I served you drinks and not *one* of you even saw me, except maybe Amara? Or why I remember that vividly because I was so envious of what you all had? It was right before I went to my room and tried to kill myself. I almost succeeded too."

Amara gasped, her hands flying to her mouth as the memory apparently hit her. The only club he'd been to in years had been the one in Gladestone, and he hadn't even looked around at anything. And she'd been there, *right there,* right before she wanted to kill herself.

His eyes began to burn as tears streaked freely down her

face.

She lost some of her fire, her body deflating as she saw the emotions in his eyes.

"I was broken, brother," she told him softly. "Too broken to even breathe. *He* resuscitated me. *He* saved me that night, so many nights I've lost count at this point. *He* gave me a home, such a beautiful home I would love to see you all visit. *He* gave me his name and everything he had, and *he* gave me all of you. I'm not lying when I tell you the only reason you're even looking at me breathing is because *he* made me, even forced me to keep breathing against my will when all I wanted was to *die*. *He* wouldn't let me. You found me because *he* wanted you to."

Morana inhaled sharply at his side, and Luna nodded. "Yes, Morana. *He* found *you* because *he* was looking for *my* past. He doesn't give a shit about anything else, no offense. Everything he has done for *years* has been *for me*." She pointed at herself. "And if he'd wanted, you never would have found me. I would have lived without knowing my past, and so would you."

There was silence for a long moment after her tirade, silence so heavy it felt suffocating to him. His lungs felt rigid, like they couldn't draw oxygen, as his brain processed everything he had heard. He would have taken ten years of torture if it would've spared her. He still would.

"Then why did he tell us? Tell you?" Morana asked from his side as he sat there stumped, emotions mixing inside him so intensely he couldn't tell which was which.

A soft, breathtaking smile came over her face. "Because he loves me."

The Shadow Man loved his sister. His brain couldn't compute.

"Because I told him that love was selfless and giving me *you* is the most selfless thing he could have done to show me that."

"So, he's a good guy?" Dante voiced.

His sister chuckled, the sound dry. "Oh no. He couldn't be who he is if he was. He's the monster monsters fear, the devil of his own kingdom. But he's *my* devil. And only good to me, now to you, because I asked him to be."

His sister truly loved the guy. He could see it in the way she talked about him, in the way she became confident when he was mentioned. The idea of what her life had been and how he had saved her made gratitude fill his heart, but there was fury there too, fury that the fucker had known but never led them to her sooner. He could have found her sooner, saved her sooner, helped her sooner.

"He was hunting Hector for you." Alpha's quiet rumble from the side made Luna turn to him. Tristan suddenly remembered what Alpha had told them, that Hector had broken something of the Shadow Man's.

His eyes flew to his sister. Had it been her? Had Hector broken her and driven her to the point she'd wanted to die?

His heart cracked open.

"Yes," she confirmed. "And *he* served Hector to me on a platter. He hunted him and strung him up and gave me power for the first time in my life."

She gave a look around, took a breath, and admitted. "I killed Hector. I burned him alive. And. *It. Felt. Good.*"

The emphasis on each word was hard. This petite girl who was all things soft and gentle, his sister he had somehow idolized in his head? A killer? A vengeful murderer?

Zephyr gasped, her eyes red from crying throughout. "He murdered my sister."

"I know," Luna swallowed. "I'm the friend she left behind. I helped her escape and got punished for it." She turned to the others, who watched her in the same stunned silence. "Hector broke me, and... he, *Shadow Man,* broke Hector for me. When I got to him, he was hanging to his life. And it felt good to take that from him."

His fists were shaking, Morana's hands trying to keep them steady. Nothing could keep him steady now. His insides had been carved open, pulled out, and left scattered. He didn't know how he was going to assimilate, to put it all back in and hold himself together again. It wasn't just the pain and the fury for everything she had suffered and kept from them; it was also a sense of loss for the girl he had hoped she would be, the girl he had unknowingly made up in his mind for years.

"So he knew who you were, who we were, and he never told you before?" Dante questioned, his tone telling Tristan he was shaken to the core as well. "Why?"

Luna turned to Dante, speaking plainly. "Because I didn't want to live. And he knew that. He could have told me, but looking back, I don't think I would have survived, even with all of you. Even now, when I'm in a much better place, I feel isolated in the group, like I don't belong, and it takes me time to tell myself it's all in my head. I never knew love, never believed in it, never felt I was worthy of it. It took me so much time to understand that I do deserve it, and more time to accept it. If I'd come to you the way I'd been, I think I would have killed myself. And *he* knew that because he knows me better than anyone."

His sister suddenly crouched down before him, her hands coming to his knees, her gaze liquid and turned up to him.

"You are the best brother I could have dreamed of," she stated, breaking and fusing pieces of his heart together even more. "There were days I wished for nothing but an older brother somewhere, one who would love and protect me, even knowing I might never have it. That was the first thing I thought about when I found out about you. My silly little dreams as a child. It was like my wish had been granted."

She took a hold of his hands, and it struck him how their position—her on her knees holding his hand and looking up at him— was the reverse of their position when he'd found her. They had been crying then too.

"You are my wish granted, Tristan," she kept on. "Through

430

you, I feel like I have a family now, friends, people who would care if I lived or died. I can accept your love now because I can accept my own."

Tears fell down his face as did hers.

"I love you, brother," her voice shook. "I love you for never giving up on me, for accepting me as I am and not who you wanted me to be, for healing a part of me that had been bleeding since my first memory, for giving me another piece of my soul back."

His lips trembled at hearing the words, words he had lived his entire life to hear, words he had only heard once and never from his family, words that healed the part of him that had been bleeding for years too.

And, for the first time in his adult life, the words left his lips in a croaked, hoarse, broken whisper.

"I love you too."

His sister jumped up and crashed into his arms, crushing and holding onto him.

Morana began to sob by his side, and he turned to look at her, to see the most beautiful smile on her face, her eyes beaming with pride at him, her hand on his back, anchoring him in place.

And with one woman he loved beside him, having found the other who had been lost, Tristan finally felt whole.

MORANA

CHAPTER 32

MORANA, TENEBRAE CITY

T O SAY THINGS HAD been emotional would be putting it mildly.

She couldn't remember the last time she had cried or seen Tristan cry so much, not even the fateful night he had broken down in his arms. And it hadn't just been them. Zephyr and Amara had been sobbing along with them, and though Dante and Alpha hadn't cried, they had been suspiciously misty-eyed. Anyone with a beating heart would have been after heating Luna's talk. She had always been quiet, spending more time listening than talking in people's company, but last night, she had gone off, and Morana felt proud of her, not just for surviving but for standing strong.

As much as she loved and understood Tristan, he had been trying to intimidate her into talking, and she had stood her ground and tackled him head-on. Their stubbornness seemed to be a sibling trait, one she was delighted about. Tristan was scary enough for other people; the women in his life didn't need to fall into that category at all.

It had been one hell of an intense night, and everyone seemed to be sleeping it off.

But Morana couldn't. Her brain was working overtime with the information overload she'd had, and she felt like she was so close to an answer, like it was almost in her grasp, and it kept slipping.

Tristan was in an exhausted slumber by her side, snoring in the way he did when he was extra tired. Yes, he had different snores, and yes, Morana already knew them.

Pressing a soft kiss to the corner of his mouth, she slipped out of the bed and powered on her tablet, checking in on her codes.

They were done, a digital weapon ready to find data from every corner of the dark web and deface anyone.

She put a USB stick in a lipstick bullet, transferred the codes, and freshened up while they did. Getting dressed casually, shrugging on a jacket to ward off the chill in the early morning air, she checked everything. *All done.* She left a note for Tristan, so he didn't worry if she got a bit late, munched on a banana as she pulled her tote bag over her right shoulder, carrying all her essentials, and walked outside the cottage, fog low to the ground in the little dawn light as she made her way to the parked vehicles. They were heading back home in the evening, but there was something she needed to check before, something she had to see.

A guard nodded to her as she chose an automatic so she

didn't have to worry too much about manual gear and got in. Plopping down, she rotated her shoulders, knowing she really needed to see a specialist for her left side and couldn't ignore it any longer. Powering on her tablet, she logged into her Dark Web account and went in.

With everything that had happened, especially knowing how the Shadow Man was now connected to Luna, information was blasting in her brain, tidbits that had been mentioned previously all combining together.

She opened the image the Shadow Man had sent her of Luna from a few weeks ago, looking carefully at the wall and a sliver of the view on the side.

One time, Zephyr had asked around to share the best place they had ever visited, and Luna had said a name, with a soft whisper and a whimsical smile.

On a hunch, Morana typed in:

Bayford.

'Did you mean Bayfjord instead?'

She clicked on it.

Images splattered across her screen, and she almost gasped at how fucking gorgeous it was. Tall gray mountains and vast gray seas with dark beaches. It wasn't a city, more like a small town, and the only way Luna could have talked about it so wistfully was if she'd lived there with good memories.

That meant the home she'd mentioned was in Bayfjord, the home the Shadow Man had given her. Morana looked up real estate listings in the region, her eyebrows going up at the prices. It was expensive, which meant the Shadow Man had money. So what did she know about him—1. He loved Luna. 2. He was rich. 3. He was in his thirties, most likely. 4. He had property in Bayfjord.

She narrowed down her search and filtered through the directory of properties registered in the last ten years, then remembering Luna's current estimated age of twenty-four, narrowed it down to six for as long as she'd been a legal adult.

'He gave me his name, everything he had.'

Words from last night, so passionately said, came back to Morana. She scrolled through the listings, and then, following a hunch, added another filter.

'Bayfjord + last six years + current properties registered in woman's name'.

Only three results came out.
One was a seventy-year-old grandmother of five children.
Another was a thirty-seven-year-old single model.
And the last one was a twenty-four-year-old married woman.

Lyla Blackthorne.

The name rang a bell in Morana's head but she couldn't remember where she'd heard it. At the party maybe? She tried to remember but she'd been so horny for Tristan that night, everything else was a giant blob of blur.

Shaking her head at herself, she opened another browser and pasted the name in, looking up public records. Only a few hits came back and one of them made her breath catch.

Lyla Blackthorne, COO, Blackthorne Group.

Blackthorne Group.

Mr. Blackthorne.

The face suddenly came to her, a tall, intense man with heterochromatic eyes dressed in a black suit.

Dante introducing him as an associate. Amara mentioning she had met him before. Tristan greeting him curtly.

And his mismatched eyes, trained right on Luna, or Lyla, as he kissed her hand, took a seat by her side.

Her husband.

The Shadow Man.

And they'd all met him before. He'd been right in plain sight, right in front of them, literally consuming Luna, or Lyla, right in front of them.

Damn.

Morana was *impressed*.

She had already been impressed by him before, but she was even more impressed now, especially after learning everything he'd done for her. Even without Luna telling them all, it was right in her face. The luxury one-of-a-kind property in her name, the position at the company giving her power to control all his assets, the gold necklace that was an emotional talisman, and so much more they didn't even know about.

Out of more curiosity, she looked up the company to see what they did and couldn't find much except vague summaries and financial records. Her eyebrows hit her hairline.

Damn, the man was *loaded.* And the fact that he'd given all of it to Luna... *damn.*

Deciding it was time to get all the cards on the table, she looked up property in Tenebrae under his name. Nothing came up. She checked with the company name. Nada. She was pretty sure he had some, but maybe through shell companies, which would take longer to hack and find.

Or maybe he didn't and just preferred to stay in a hotel during business trips? She hacked into the top five hotels in the city and looked for a reservation under his name. Struck gold in the third hit, coincidentally the same hotel she and Tristan had stayed at once.

She dialed the hotel line, and the receptionist picked up.

"Hi," Morana said sweetly. Could you please connect me to penthouse suite 1403? My friend Mr. Blackthorne is staying there, but I can't reach his number."

"One moment, please, ma'am." The front desk lady must have checked the records. "Whom should I say is calling?"

Morana thought for a quick second, a name he would recognize. "Miss Reaper."

"Of course."

The line went on hold, generic music playing in her ear as he put her thumb in her mouth out of anxiety, almost biting her nail before stopping herself. She just hoped he answered.

And then, the music stopped, and a deep voice came on.

"I was wondering how long it would take you to figure out who I was after last night, Miss Vitalio."

Holy shit, he knew. He knew what had happened. Of course, he did. How?

"Whose phone did you hack?" she asked, so she would unhack and protect it for her friends.

He chuckled, and Morana was happy for Luna. Because while she loved her whiskey and sin voice, she could admit with pure feminine appreciation that this man had a hot voice too.

"I'll let you figure that out."

Morana took a deep breath in. "Can we meet?" It was the same question she'd texted him but never got a reply to.

"I think it's time," he agreed. "Meet me at the same place we met here."

The public pier. "When?"

"An hour."

"Should I come alone?"

"If you want us to work together, yes."

Morana hesitated.

"Don't worry, Miss Vitalio. You'll be safe. You're my *almost* sister-in-law after all."

With that, the dial tone came. Morana stared at her phone, wondering what she should do. She could go alone, but that would be stupid, especially after being shot. But she couldn't take security because he'd told her to come alone. She took a deep breath because he'd told her she would be safe, and she was going to take his word for it. For a smart person, she was highly stupid sometimes.

She sent out a text in the girl's group chat, knowing they were going to rally and get shit done in case they didn't hear from her within the next hour.

And with that, she pulled out of the compound.

It was deja-vu standing on the pier with a coffee in her hand. Though last time, it had been the middle of the afternoon and crowded, this time, it was early morning and pretty abandoned, with shops closed except for one tiny cafe and only local workers cleaning up the area. Morana sat on a bench facing the river, taking a breather and enjoying the balanced weather.

Awareness of being watched prickled the hair on her neck. She kept her right hand on the gun in her pocket, not knowing how much of a shot she would be with one hand and her left pretty useless for balancing, but it would be better than nothing, just in case.

A body sat on the bench next to her, leaving some space in between.

For the first time, he didn't tell her not to look, so she did, and for the first time, she saw him.

Damn, Luna.

He was *hot,* in a very dark, very intense type of way, his stare direct and focused, his eyes almost hypnotic. He didn't do anything to her, though, but she could appreciate his form like she appreciated Dante's extraordinary looks or Alpha's massive size—with feminine appreciation and a cheer for her girls for bagging such hotties. If she had to associate one word with them, if Tristan was *intense* and Dante was *handsome* and Alpha was *huge,* this man was *dark.*

"Good to finally see you, Mr. Blackthorne." She greeted him. "Or should I say the Shadow Man?"

His lips turned up in a way that didn't reach his eyes. "Have you told anyone else yet?"

She shook her head. "I will. We don't keep secrets."

He chuckled. "Everyone keeps some secrets, but very well."

"They already know you," she pointed out. "Dante and Tristan from before. Tristan will come after you." She remembered how pissed he'd been.

Ducks quacked on the waves in the river. The sun got a bit warmer. More people went into the cafe behind them.

The man looked out at the river, his body language relaxed. But she knew a hunter when she saw one, and knowing who he was, it was evident he was the most dangerous kind.

"He can," the Shadow Man permitted. "I might even let him get a hit in so he can get it out of his system and make my wife happy."

He called her *his wife*.

"But if he ever tries to intimidate her again—" something hard entered his voice "—brother or not, I will end him." He turned to spear her with a look, the closest thing to death she had seen on a face, and it hit her that this man had killed more terrible, powerful people than she could count. He actually meant what he said.

Morana felt her heart begin to pound with a little fear, realizing that this wasn't a man she had any control over, who could actually threaten her and her family.

"You wouldn't do that to Luna," she told him, her voice coming out shakier than she'd wanted.

The dark look on his face was wiped clean. "Let's hope it never comes to that."

Morana swallowed, finding her guts that had gotten her in

trouble more times than she could count. "You know threats don't work in a family."

A smile slashed his face, again, not reaching his eyes. It was such a stark difference to her—Tristan, who didn't emote with anything but his eyes, and this man, who didn't emote with his eyes at all.

"I don't make threats, Miss Vitalio."

"Call me Morana. You're sort of *almost* my brother-in-law."

He didn't respond to that, changing the topic smoothly. "Are your codes complete?"

Morana gave a swift nod. "Yes, but why do you need them?"

"I answer your questions, you give me the codes. Do we have a deal?"

Morana hesitated. The codes could be very dangerous in his hands without knowing his motives. "Answer my questions first," she negotiated.

He paused for a brief second before unzipping his jacket and taking out a file, handing it to her. Morana took it, seeing the snakes logo she'd seen a few times and a title on top.

"What's Project Ouroboros?" she questioned, flipping the file open.

"It was a rumor until a few days ago," he explained as her eyes scanned the words. "I found out about it during an interrogation and eventually discovered this."

The more Morana read, the sicker she got to her stomach. Electrocutions. Drugs. Mutilations. Perversions.

"They were experimenting on babies." Her words came out in a horrified whisper.

"In the fifties." His tone was direct, nonempathic. "Some very legal organizations wanted to conduct some illegal experimentations on young babies. The Syndicate stepped up to meet the demand."

Morana felt the acid from her stomach retch up to her throat, and she swallowed it back down, closing the file, unable to read another word. The fact that horrors like this existed in their world, that there were people who went through the things she was reading in black and white, sickened her. No one deserved this. *No one. Especially not babies!*

She turned to look at the man at her side who looked unfazed, and wondered what kind of horrors he had seen to remain so unmoved and neutral as he talked about it.

Finding some courage, she opened the file again and skimmed, only trying to focus on the data. "It says the project was shut down after ten years?"

"Maybe for the record," the Shadow Man remarked. "I believe it was restarted with the Alliance between your fathers, real and adoptive, and Lorenzo Maroni. The Reaper thought it was about sex trafficking but it wasn't, or at least not just that. For sex trafficking, they always abducted girls and boys not younger than six and placed them in homes. The toddlers? They were for experimentation. The Syndicate was involved in it, and the Alliance was as well."

The horror kept on unfolding after the other. "No," her denial was jittery. Her insides were jittery. If what he said was true, that meant she'd been kidnapped to become the subject of experimentation. If what he said was true, that meant Luna and Zenith and all the other girls were subjects of *experiments?*

The shock in her face and silence must have been too loud because he shook his head. "You weren't experimented on."

"How do you even know this?"

He pointed at the file. "It's all there. I just connected the dots. The girls for the experiments were always numbered. I actually found that out, thanks to Vin. Combinations of five, five, and seven."

"What's the significance of seventeen?" she asked, the question bothering her since she found out about it.

"Nothing," he told her, waiting for a beat. "The significance is of one and seven." He closed the file, tracing the symbol on top. "One and seven make—"

"Eight," she completed, a chill going down her spine. They had not only numbered the babies but also numbered them to announce their appalling project. The snakes, making an eight-figure, stared up at her.

"So, Zenith was an experiment subject?" she recalled, remembering the number.

"I believe so. Though I cannot say for certain," he mused. "I haven't heard of many kids with numbers working under The Syndicate, which makes me believe that only the ones who failed at experiments were sent out into the sex trafficking."

Morana let that sink in, absolutely nauseated at what she had learned. She stared down at the file in her hand as though the snakes on top were slithering across her skin, repelling her.

And then the biggest question she'd had for two years came to her mind. She looked up at the man who was sitting with his eyes closed, basking casually in the sun to any onlooker.

"Why was I returned?"

He didn't move, but he took his time, as if figuring the answer out, putting together a puzzle only he knew all the pieces of, keeping her on the edge. Then, he opened his eyes and tilted his head toward the file in her hand. "Because of that."

She put the file down on the bench between them. "Please explain." It was a request. She would have begged if need be, her desperation for this one answer stronger than her pride.

"Lorenzo Maroni was a puppet for The Syndicate," he started, pushing his gloved hands into his pockets. "Maybe he wanted to get out, maybe he didn't. We won't ever know. But he was the main power-hungry party in the Alliance, and hence the one who restarted the experiments by supplying the kids to The Syndicate."

"Okay," she nodded, following so far. "So, what does that have to do with me?"

"So," he drawled out, almost lazily in his deep voice. "Lorenzo Maroni took Gabriel's daughter, Zenith, and the Reaper's daughter, you, as collateral to keep them quiet. Except your father, the Reaper, made a deal with him. He had this file on the project and in exchange for your safe return, he would hand it over to Lorenzo. And Lorenzo, bastard that he was, brought you back but used you as a tool to keep Vitalio in line."

"How do you know this?"

"Because my interrogation told me your father had the file, and I found it in Maroni's office the other night."

Morana sat in stunned disbelief, her heart hurting all over again for a father she'd never met but for a brief moment, but who had loved her and protected her for as long as he lived. A sob caught in her throat, her emotions all over the place as she stared at the file, the same file her father had touched and exchanged to bring her back from a fate so horrible it made her shudder.

And something occurred to her. "Do you know his real name? My birth name?"

The Shadow Man gave her a look. "Yes."

She stared him in the eyes before looking away, not forget-ting that he wasn't a man she wanted to piss off. She opened her mouth to ask, closed it, opened it again, and closed it again.

"If someday you're ready to know, just ask," he said quietly.

"And you'll just share it?"

He shrugged. "Keeping it doesn't mean a thing to me, but it

does to you. You've been helpful in my quest so yes, for that alone, I will."

Morana nodded. She wasn't ready, not for an identity crisis, not now when there was already so much to deal with. Maybe she never would be. She had always been Morana, grew up owning the name, fitting into it like a tailored dress. It was the name her lover, her friends, her almost son called her. She didn't need anything else, her birth name a part of her past she had to let go of and move forward without.

They sat in silence for a few minutes, Morana mulling everything she'd learned over, and him thinking whatever he was. The silence, though heavy, wasn't uncomfortable.

Her phone buzzed in her pocket, a call from Amara, checking in since her hour was up. She picked up. "I'm okay."

"Where are you?" Amara asked, her voice low, letting Morana know that Dante was sleeping.

Morana looked at her side, at the man who was considering her. "Meeting the Shadow Man."

"Morana!" Amara exclaimed in a hushed voice. "Alone? Are you out of your mind?"

"He won't hurt me." She hoped. The man just smiled, the threat he'd leveled out earlier still in her mind. He would hurt her only if she hurt Luna. His track record said the same.

"I'll come get you," Amara was already moving.

"No," Morana rushed. She still had some questions. "I'll be back in an hour. If I'm not, let others know."

Amara hesitated. "Are you sure?"

"Yes."

"Okay. I have my phone with me."

Morana nodded and hung up, the call making her think of another question. "Why did you lead us to Xander? You told him about us, why? And you still call him sometimes. Why?"

His one light eye darkened at the question, the dark one already deep. He looked back out over the river.

"You said you don't keep secrets from your family," he leveled her words back at her. "Are you sure you want to know? Because this secret isn't yours to tell and it isn't yours to keep. You will be left conflicted."

"And you're not?" Morana wondered how his brain worked. He might have seemed cold and aloof to others, but there was more there: a deeply intelligent mind and a heart exclusive to one woman.

"No."

Morana considered his profile for a long minute. "Who is Xander?"

His lip twitched in a smile. "He's the reason his mother didn't give up on her life for many years. He's the leverage I've used for years to keep her alive. He's the one answer she's been waiting for."

Morana's jaw dropped, shock infiltrating her system, and everything suddenly clicked into place.

"He's Luna's son?" Her voice was a strangled whisper. Memories flitted through her mind—Luna watching Xander from afar, her looks at baby Tempest, her face at Zephyr's pregnancy announcement. Morana stared at the man beside her, rendered speechless, as other memories came in. Xander making her a sandwich, Xander learning tech from her, Xander pushing up his glasses, Xander letting him hug her. A kaleidoscope of memories she had with him, that Tristan had with him, never knowing he was his biological uncle. But he felt like a father. She felt like a mother to him. They had almost adopted him. They were going to get a dog for him next month, foregoing the cat she'd wanted for their first pet because Xander had responded better to dogs than cats. Did they have to let him go now? Could they? When he'd become such an important part of their immediate family?

"Are you his...?" she stopped. If he was, then why would he lead Xander to them?

"His guardian," he corrected her assumption. "I've raised him since he was a baby with the help of a lovely nanny. The plan was always to lead him back to his maternal family if and when I found them."

"And you led Tristan to him."

"Yes," he affirmed. "With his help and a friend of his who used to live in the same neighborhood."

"Lex," Morana guessed.

"Yes. After his family passed, both Xander and the nanny made a good case for him. He stayed with us for a year before

I sent them your way."

Everything was making crystal clear sense. "How old is Xander?"

"Six."

Another shock. They had all believed he had advanced intelligence and was around eight years old. This was more like *gifted.*

The Shadow Man extended a gloved palm. "The codes."

Morana swallowed, taking the lipstick tube out of her bag and haltingly placing it in his upturned hand. "What are you going to do with them?"

"What do you think?"

"End The Syndicate?" she threw out a guess.

"The Syndicate can never end," he stated plainly. "It needs to exist to dissuade any chaos in the vacuum."

He was right, but chaos had and would still exist. Could there be something worse than The Syndicate?

"Then what will you do?"

The Shadow Man smiled. "I'm going to reboot it."

And with that, he was up and gone.

zephyr

CHAPTER 33

ZEPHYR, TENEBRAE CITY

LAST NIGHT HAD BEEN intense. Zephyr couldn't stop crying the entire time Luna had been speaking, her horrors pouring out of her lips as the timid girl who had always felt out of place took a stand and stood facing them all. It had hurt her heart deeply, not only listening to the pain dripping from her being but imagining what tragedies had awaited her own sister, happened to her own sister, that she'd never known about. It bothered her that Zen had never confided in her and that was something she'd have to live with for the rest of her life.

Zephyr didn't know if the intensity of the previous night was the reason she was completely off-kilter, but there was a knot of stress balled up in her stomach that she couldn't explain. She'd been lying awake for a good part of the morning, seeing the dark of the night be chased by the dawn, her husband's arms around her, and yet, she felt adrift, anxious... as if waiting for something bad to happen.

Something was not right.

Zephyr got up with the heaviness in her chest, her heart beating too fast, unable to stay put any longer. She couldn't explain what it was. It was a gut feeling, a feeling she didn't get often, but when she did, she knew not to ignore it. The last time that she had, her sister had died and Morana had been shot, and she'd promised herself to never ignore it again.

Quickly slipping out of bed, her movements waking her husband by her side, she picked up her phone from the floor of the room where it had fallen the night before and unlocked it.

3 missed calls.

Her mother had called her three times.

Her mother, whom she hadn't spoken to in days, had called her three times.

Something wasn't right.

Zephyr immediately called back, her heart in her throat, pacing the room. Her movements must have alerted him even more to the gravity of the situation because her husband turned on the bed, fully awake when he saw her like that, one side of his face creasing with concern.

"What's going on?" he grumbled out.

The phone line wasn't picked up, so she rang again. "My mother called—three times. Something is wrong."

No one picked up this time, either. She dialed her father's

number. Same.

Her heart began to thunder, and the first vestiges of panic crept into her body. Unable to explain what was happening to her as she stood, she knew, just knew in her heart, that something bad had happened.

Alpha immediately picked up his phone from the bedside table. She saw him press Victor's icon at the top of his call list and put him on speaker.

"Alpha," Victor said on the line after two rings.

"Vic, go to Zephyr's parent's place," Alpha instructed. "They're not answering. Something is wrong."

"On it," Victor said immediately. "I'll update you when I get there."

That would take about twenty minutes from Victor's place to her parents. Twenty minutes too long. Zephyr didn't know how she would hold onto her emotional distress for twenty minutes until she knew.

Alpha came around the side of the bed to her, grabbing a hold of her shoulders and rubbing them in a soothing motion, trying to ease the tension she could feel gathering there.

"Let's go down," he suggested after a few minutes of Zephyr just frowning at his chest. "We can be in company. It'll distract you while we wait."

Alpha didn't like any company but knew she did, so for him to suggest it, he had to be worried, too. She nodded. It was the best thing she could do. Keep her mind occupied and keep herself from panicking. It could all be for nothing, and she just had to wait. For all she knew, both their phones broke at the same time for some reason. There would be an explanation for it.

They quickly dressed as he did and went down to the gazebo where Dante and Amara sat, discussing something. Their faces looked the same grim as the other, and Zephyr didn't know what was going on. She didn't want there to be some bad news here as well.

"What happened?" Alpha asked, seeing their looks.

"Morana went to meet the Shadow Man alone," Amara informed them, her tone severe. "She told me to let others know if she didn't respond in an hour. I didn't wait. It's going to be an hour in a few minutes."

"Have you told Tristan yet?" Zephyr asked, adding another concern on top of her own. Morana was smart, but what the hell had she been thinking about going out alone to meet the man, especially after the bullet she'd taken not that long ago? Especially after the night before. Luna might call him hers, and Zephyr had been safe with him, but still. They knew nothing about the man.

Amara shook her head. "Not yet. If she answers, she can tell him herself. He's had a rough night."

Yeah. Rough was an understatement for the night they'd all had, listening to a girl who never spoke more than a few words go on a rampage, admitting her past, that she was not only the

Shadow Man's lover but his wife, and most of all admitting to killing Hector brutally and enjoying it. Zephyr didn't fault her for that. In fact, she was grateful to the girl because if she had had the chance, Zephyr would have done it, too. But it had been particularly rough for Tristan, and it had broken her heart to see the usually stoic man so emotional in the face of a girl half his size.

Amara looked at her phone as her timer rang, looked around at them, and called Morana.

The phone was out of reach.

They all exchanged heavy looks, knowing this did not bode well for any of them. And it all happened just as Tristan and Luna walked from the lake, his arm around her and hers around him, somehow having brought them closer last night. It was good to see that they'd both still bonded and were a good evolution of their relationship.

They looked up at the group, their matching small smiles falling off their faces as they approached them. Tristan's eyes immediately scanned the space. "Where's Morana?"

Amara swallowed. "She went to meet the Shadow Man."

Tristan's whole body stilled, his eyes blazing. "Alone?"

Amara nodded. "And she's not available on her phone now. She told me to call and check on her, and I'm... worried, Tristan."

It was fascinating to see the way he changed from a quieter intensity to a loud one. She had seen a similar side of him when

Morana had been in the hospital recovering. The man moved swiftly, pacing as he took his own phone out and dialed his girl. It went unreachable for him too. He gripped his phone so hard it almost splintered in his hand.

Luna glanced at him, her look contemplative, before leveling Amara with a look, her stance slightly protective. "When did you speak to her?"

"An hour ago."

Luna nodded, looking around at them all, hesitating for a second before reaching into her jacket pocket and taking out a small phone. Quietly, she pressed a button and then waited.

Zephyr watched as, within a minute, her phone rang. She looked around at all of them before picking up the call.

"Hi," she said softly into the phone, and it hit Zephyr. She'd just called the Shadow Man. *Holy shit.*

"Can I put you on speaker?" she asked, and Zephyr glanced and saw everyone's faces wear different expressions of shock, same as hers, as Luna pressed a button and suddenly, static filled the space.

No one said a word. Dante stood up from his stone seat. Amara put a hand to her mouth. Alpha stiffened. Tristan glared at the phone but waited for his sister to do whatever she was doing.

Luna bit her lip, and spoke. "Is Morana with you?"

And then, for the first time, they all heard his natural voice. A *very* hot voice, Zephyr noted. Nothing much. Just one word.

"No."

The Shadow Man was real. A real man with a real voice. *Wow.*

"When did she leave?" Luna asked him, her voice different, darker, more tender as she spoke to him. It was such a subtle difference watching her, but she stood straighter, her shoulders back, her neck angled as she spoke to him, her entire posture not of the quiet girl they had come to know but someone else, the girl who had evidently killed a terrible man and enjoyed it. Zephyr could not have imagined Luna doing something so dark but watching her hold the phone, her stance different, her voice different, the look in her eyes different, she could see this girl do it.

"About fifteen minutes ago," the hot voice said. "What's going on?" That was a funny question coming from the man who seemed to know everything. It was a question all of them had been asking *him* to no avail.

"She's unreachable, asshole." Tristan stepped to the phone and gritted out.

Silence was on the line for a long minute, before words came. "Then I'm your only hope of finding her in time, Predator."

It was then, hearing him speak to Tristan, that Zephyr realized how different his tone had been with Luna. It had been softer for her, more intimate even as he knew he was on speaker, almost like he didn't care who heard him but talking to his girl as he wanted. His words to Tristan were delivered in a tone that sent a shiver down her spine, reminding her of the fact that this was the same man no one wanted to meet face to face for the reputation he had made for himself. It was a sobering reminder that he could be dangerous to everyone she loved.

Tristan's jaw clenched. "Fuck off."

Luna admonished him. "Tristan. He's not your enemy. We talked about this five minutes ago!"

Tristan didn't say anything; he just fisted his hands and stood there. Luna sighed. No one moved for a few seconds as the static stayed online. Finally, Dante stepped up, taking over when Tristan didn't make a move at all.

"Dante speaking," he said on the phone, giving Tristan a look. "I should have known it would be you, Blackthorne. It couldn't be anyone else."

Zephyr gasped, remembering the hot, intense guy from the party who had flirted and focused only on Luna. She'd even told her husband about the man, telling him she hoped Luna would find him hot, much to her husband's exasperation at her hopeless romanticism. Holy shit, *that guy* was the Shadow Man? Meaning he'd come there while he was already with Luna? Damn.

Before things could spin out of control, Luna refocused the conversation. "Please find her for me."

There was silence for a beat. "For you, anything, *flamma*."

Swoon.

Zephyr saw as Luna blushed at the words, her eyes flitting around to everyone and how they had all witnessed him talk to her. Zephyr was happy for the girl. She deserved love and care—especially after hearing her heavy past—and clearly, he was giving it to her.

He was still on the speaker when Alpha's phone rang, Victor's name flashing on it, making her heart drop as the reminder for what had been bothering her came back.

Alpha put his phone on speaker as well. "What's happening, Victor?"

Victor was silent for a beat. "Her mother... killed him."

It took her a few seconds to process the words.

Her mother... killed him? Him? Her *father*?

That wasn't possible. They loved each other. They had been together for so long. Her father loved her mother and vice versa. Zephyr had never doubted that, in fact, it had been seeing them together that had made her such a romantic. Victor had to be wrong. Or she was getting it wrong. There was no way.

"Him who?" Zephyr asked, because this was just a misunderstanding and it would be some robber or intruder that her mother had killed. Maybe the intruder stole her father's phone and that's why she was calling Zephyr so many times. That had to be it.

Victor hesitated. "Your father."

Zephyr felt a wave of dizziness come over her, her knees trembling. Suddenly, Amara steadied her, wrapping her arm around her shoulder. Her husband looked at her with so much turmoil in his only eye, his mouth turned down at the corners.

No.

Not her papa.

Not so soon after Zen.

Memories flashed across her eyes as her body shook, her hands gripping Amara for life.

Everyone heard the words, letting them sink in before Alpha cleared his throat. "Tell me."

Victor's voice was low. "She found a file in his old stuff. It's bad, Alpha."

"How bad?"

"Bad enough that he adopted Zenith because The Syndicate asked him to keep an eye on her after she escaped."

The words fell like bullets to her heart. No. No. It couldn't be true. Not her gentle, sweet, kind papa. Not him. Not her sister.

She heard a noise and realized it was coming from her mouth, hiccups in her throat and so much shivering she couldn't stop. This had to be wrong. Her father had loved them. Zephyr had never ever questioned his love for them both. More memories went over her mind—him picking them up from school because her mother had been working, him taking them out for ice cream on Sundays because it was just their father-daughter time, him fighting their mother and taking a stand with the girls when they wanted to move to the city farther away from them, him telling her and Zen that they were beautiful and they could do anything they wanted with their lives, and so on, and so on, and so on. So many memories, of nothing but love, for her, for her sister, for her mama. How could Victor be talking about the same man?

"Are we sure about this?" Alpha asked, his troubled eye on her form as she grappled with this.

"I wish I could say no," Victor cursed. "But fuck. I saw the file. There's a letter in there. Zen had gone to the cops and there was a ruckus at the time, so to let it die down, they instructed him to foster her for a while. It then became instructions to adopt her and just wait for further instructions. The last letter had been six years ago. Maybe there's more but this is all I can find right now."

Zephyr felt her mouth open, a wounded animal noise leaving her at each word hitting her newly healing heart, opening the scabs that had formed recently and bleeding it out all over again. Her husband grabbed her close, pulling her into his wide chest, his large hand cupping the back of her head as she shook into his body. His scarred body, scars he got because he was attacked. She remembered what he'd said about his attack, the man keeping the girl, the man he had heard before talking to Hector. It had been her father. Her father who had attacked the boy she'd loved and made him lose his memories, made her feel lost for a decade before she found him. The fact that she'd had her father over so many times for dinner and he'd just sat there, knowing what he had done to her husband. He'd sat there knowing what he'd done to them. Hell, he'd lived his life knowing what had been done to *her sister.*

Zephyr broke down.

It was everything, all at once, too soon.

How many times did the gray come before she was gone? How many times could she take this? Betrayal after betrayal, pain after pain, hurt after hurt.

Alpha rubbed her back, his face in her hair, kissing her over and over on the head to soothe her. She didn't feel soothed. She felt distraught, disgusted, disillusioned. She could feel a chasm in her heart as the world she knew went upside down again.

"What about my...?" she couldn't get the words out between her hiccups.

Her mother. Her mother, whom she'd been in a standoff with, her mother who had loved her daughters too, even though she was stubborn, her mother who had killed the man she'd loved because of what he'd done to her babies. Her mother who must be realizing that her own husband had been the danger and not her daughter's. A cry left her at the thought of her mother doing what she'd done out of love, even though she'd not talked to her for days.

"She's been arrested," Victor said. "I'm trying to get things ironed out here. She'll be out, and I'll take care of things here, don't worry. I'm so fucking sorry, Zee."

Zephyr listened to the words, going numb as everything settled around her; her past turned to dust, the only solid thing the arms that held her silently locked in.

Zephyr let herself break again.

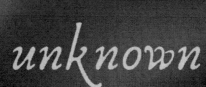

CHAPTER 34

UNKNOWN

E VERYONE HAD TO DIE one day.

Some died of disease, some of disaster, some of devastation. Some died in their sleep, some by the hands of others. But some way or another, everyone died. That was the one solution no amount of experiments had been able to find. There had been research and reconnaissance into the matter for millennia, talks of immortality in fables and longevity in alchemy, but nothing concrete. That was why he knew he was going to die.

But he had lived as a god—creating and controlling the world. And gods did not die by disease or disaster or devastation. Gods died at the hands of others like them, and so it would be with him.

"We're ready," his loyalist of many decades said. She wanted to play a little game, a drama, for the sake of her own ego, and who was he to deny her? It was a good gift to give to someone who had served him in every way possible for many years, including being a killer for him. Her last kill had been none other than Maroni's little henchman, who had tried to infiltrate his organization and had gotten in surprisingly deeper than expected, but then one thing had destroyed him, as it destroyed everyone—love. The stupid boy had fallen for a little slave girl and tried to run with her, and his loyalist had killed them both. He wasn't sure if Maroni even knew yet.

He looked at her. "Good. How do you want this to go?"

"I want the choice."

He smiled. The good old choice, one that created a ripple. One little child could create a ripple—all because of a parent's love. That had been the thing he had never accounted for. In their world, parents didn't love their children; they traded them. The love for a child was a myth. It was all business, so the fact that one single parent could have caused so many waves was unheard of but something he'd had to witness.

"I'll be watching, but this is your show," he told her. "You can do anything you want."

She gave him a soft smile. It was a smile that turned men into fools and women into friends. The smile had been a weapon he had honed, making her into one of his best soldiers. She had handled the acquisition department, so to speak, for so many years because of that smile, getting close to people, meeting them, understanding their lives, giving the team details, and taking their children. Not just her, there was a whole team of women she had trained for the same job. And after the job was done, they vanished without a trace. Somehow, the world didn't look twice at a crying woman, ignoring her on the sidelines as she blended into the crowd and moved on to the next.

And he might be gone, but his legacy, his creations, would always remain. It would never end, not with him, when he had a following of those who just lay waiting in the grass and would for years before striking.

The woman looked out the window of the location they were in—the location a little minion called Hector had leased in the name of Alessandro Villanova without his knowledge, a place where so many initiations had happened for the new members. He looked affectionately at the center where the initiates always sated themselves with the welcoming gift.

It was empty now. The whole top level was, only the desk and chair he was sitting on and a camera mounted in his front with a large screen to watch the show.

The sound of incoming vehicles made them look at each other with one last smile.

"The Syndicater," she bent her neck in supplication. "Master."

He stroked her neck affectionately. "Go have your day."

She left, and he watched the screen as the girl was dragged into the basement by her arms, her body slumped in unconsciousness. He would never have been at the same location, but had to be there this time.

It was time.

AMARA

CHAPTER 35

AMARA, TENEBRAE CITY

I T WAS HEARTBREAKING SEEING her friend break down so much.

Amara kept her hand on her back as she sobbed in Alpha's arms, both of them exchanging a look of helplessness, not understanding how to make this any better. How could anyone? Her father had betrayed her in the worst way possible; she and her mother and her dead sister, all women betrayed by a man they had loved and, from the account of things, had loved them back.

"We need to head back," Alpha told them, picking up his wife in his arms. Zephyr curled into his chest, hiding from the world and into his warmth in a move that sent a pang through her heart.

"I'll have your jet waiting for you," Dante reassured them, giving a nod to Alpha. "We're here if you need anything."

Alpha tilted his head in a silent thanks and headed inside, getting ready to leave. Amara sat back on the stone seat in the gazebo, her body slumping, her heart hurting.

"Are there no good fathers?" she mused, her voice raspy and heavy. Tristan stayed silent as he did, and Dante came next to her, holding her close to his side. There were no good fathers, and it hurt her to think of all the pain in the world just caused by that one thing. She looked at Dante. "I swear I will kill you too, if you do anything to endanger our daughter."

Dante pressed his forehead to hers. "I won't stop you."

"As sad as this is," a voice said from the speaker phone, a voice she'd completely forgotten had been on the line for the entire thing, listening to everything. "It makes a lot of sense."

"What do you mean?" Dante asked from her side. Amara watched Luna as she leaned against one of the pillars of the gazebo, the vines touching her as they went up.

"Why The Syndicate wanted to keep an eye on Zenith," the Shadow Man explained. "She was one of their secret project assets that escaped and caused noise. Usually, the organization would have eliminated her but the threat of the secret project coming out, since it involved government organizations, must have forced them to keep her alive. But they couldn't just let her be so they had one of their operatives adopt her to keep her right under his nose."

It did make sense when he put it like that.

And since she had the Shadow Man on the line, which in itself was the wildest thing to wrap her head around, she asked him the one thing she'd been wanting to for a long time.

"Do you have any news about Vin? He was my friend, and

he's not checked in with us for weeks."

There was silence on the line for a long minute.

Amara's heart began to beat too hard, her fingers clutching Dante's thigh with a grip that was hurting her knuckles, wondering if he wasn't saying something because he didn't know and was looking up information or because he knew and didn't know how to tell her.

"I'm sorry."

That's all he said.

I'm sorry, what? I'm sorry, I don't know? I'm sorry, I can't tell you? Or I'm sorry he's...

Amara looked at Luna, only to see the girl looking at her with a look that clarified it. She knew what his words meant, and she was looking at Amara with a heartbreaking look.

Amara's lips trembled. Not her Vinnie. Not her friend who'd told her he'd never be too dark for her, who had stayed with her when she'd lost herself, who had just been her best friend since she was a baby. She needed him to come back so he could meet her daughter. He'd not even seen Tempest. Tempest didn't know anything about her Uncle Vinnie.

No.

"When?" Dante asked from her side, his voice heavy. She looked at him and realized he was feeling the loss, possibly even guilty about letting Vin go.

"It's difficult to tell," the voice said, his tone plain. "The bodies were found in the river three days ago. Just got identified a while ago."

Amara swallowed, her eyes welling up. And then the words sank in. "What bodies?"

There was another beat of silence. "Vin and a girl."

What the hell? "What girl?" Dante asked, as confused as she was.

"*Flamma*," he said, and Luna looked at the phone. His voice turned much softer, with more inflection as he spoke, "it was Malini. Your friend."

Luna's eyelids fluttered shut as she took a deep breath in. She stood trembling for a long minute before letting out the breath she took. "How did he get to her?" she asked.

"I'd directed him to her," he admitted without any tone in his voice. "He was getting too close to you, and I had to redirect him, so I sent her to your friend so he would get her out for you."

Amara was surprised at the fact that he was confessing everything to Luna without hesitation. She would've thought he would be a lot more secretive and closed about his plans and his work. The fact the he wasn't was a mild shock to the system.

"So, he found her," Luna continued. "And they did run away."

"Yes," he confirmed. "I killed her master, and soon after, they escaped. But The Syndicate found them."

"Did you know this?" Luna asked him, and Tristan finally

moved, going to her and holding her shoulder while glaring at the phone.

"No."

Luna nodded, and Amara didn't know whether to believe him or not. She looked like she did but Amara was skeptical. She took a deep breath in. They didn't have the time to break down, not with everything going to shit around them. "Where are the bodies?"

The voice told them an address in the city. Amara stood up and Dante followed. "We'll need to arrange for the funeral." She looked at Luna, placing a hand on her shoulder. "We'll have one for your friend too."

"Thank you," the girl's voice shook. Tristan's arm tightened around her and there was just breathing on the phone.

Amara looked down at the phone. She might not know him but he had given her an answer and closure she'd been looking for. "Thank you," she spoke into the phone. "I appreciate you answering my question."

"You once answered mine, Dr. Maroni," the voice said. "Many years ago. I'm just returning the favor."

Amara tried to scrounge her brain, remembering the feeling of familiarity she'd felt when she'd met him at the party, and suddenly it came to her—intense man, dark voice, hypnotic eyes. The man who had come to her after one of her first conferences and talked to her methodically about helping his wife cope with child loss and about raising children.

His wife.

His wife.

Her eyes clashed with Luna's green. It all fell together in her head. The pregnancy question, the way she looked at Tempest, the behavior. She'd been pregnant once and she'd lost the child. Her eyes flitted to Tristan, wondering if he knew. Looking at the man, she concluded he didn't because he would have told her if he did. If there was one thing Tristan ever talked to her about, it was helping the people he loved cope and heal with shit that he didn't know about.

Dante called her from the back and had her turn around, putting away her deductions for later. It brought the priorities out again. Her breakdown and epiphanies could wait. Everything else could wait.

Right now, she had to go to Vin and bring him back, even if it hadn't been how she'd wanted him to return. With that thought, Amara left to bring her best friend back home.

MORANA

CHAPTER 36
MORANA, NEAR TENEBRAE CITY

SOMETHING WAS AWFULLY, TERRIBLY wrong.

Morana was driving back to the compound when suddenly, the numbness that had been perpetual in her left arm began to spread to her right. She tried to move her limbs and steer the wheel to the side of the road but her muscles were slowly going lax, the numbness spreading from her fingers to her wrists to her elbows to her shoulders and up her neck to her face. Her feet didn't move to push the brakes she already had them on, her mouth didn't move to even breathe.

The sensation reminded her of the time she'd been drugged in the club back when she'd first met Tristan.

Somehow, someway, she'd been drugged again.

The Shadow Man couldn't have done it. He'd been at a distance, his hands in his pockets, giving her the file. She had touched the file but he'd been wearing gloves. Could it have been laced with some neurotoxin that was absorbed through the skin? But she didn't believe he'd done that. Unless, he'd just wanted the codes and wanted to eliminate her.

The car sped down the road, heading to a curve as the hill began, and Morana braced herself. Thankfully, her speed wasn't too fast and she was still in the plain valley so she might get injured, again, but the possibility of a fatal crash was minimal. And thankfully, she was wearing a seatbelt.

As the car went off road and straight into a tree, Morana closed her eyes and tried to lessen the impact. The seatbelt jerked against her already injured shoulder, making her scream with the pain that broke through the numbness, the force of the impact snapping her neck forward harshly. Her bag and gadgets fell on the floor. Steam blew out of the crushed front. She sent up a silent prayer that she hadn't been driving faster, thanks to her injury, or she would have been dead around the car.

Processing the last few seconds, glad that her mind was still a bit alert somehow, she tried to move, just as her door was pulled out, her seatbelt cut off, and her body yanked out so brutally she screamed again. Masked men put her in the back of another car, her vision blurring because of the smudge on her glasses.

Whoever they were, they drove off quickly and sped away from the hill, back toward the city. Morana lay immobile, conscious until they crossed the city and sped to the other side, heading west out of the borders. By the time they hit the long stretch on a flyover, the drug took her under completely.

It was the pain in her left shoulder that brought her out of unconsciousness.

Morana looked around, trying to gather her wits about her, slowly coming out of the fog in her mind.

Her arms hurt. She realized she was hanging from the ceiling, chained around her wrists, her feet barely touching the ground. In that one second of self-analysis, she knew whatever hope she'd had for the left side of her arm was gone. The pain she felt was coming from the right side. The left was completely desensitized, the nerve damage too intense possibly to withstand any more trauma. Unless a miracle happened and she managed to escape, she'd never use her left hand again.

The thought made her want to cry but she shook it off, focusing on trying to get out, though she had no idea how.

She looked around the place, a basement, maybe dungeon of some kind, with gray concrete walls and barren interior. There was nothing except one chair, and another set of chains hanging ominously from the ceiling to her right.

"Ah, you're awake."

A woman's voice came from the darkness before the sound of heels clicking on tiled stairs. Yes, a basement like some kind of b-grade horror movie. Could they have been a little more original?

The woman slowly stepped into the light. She was an older woman, maybe in her late fifties, with grays in her darker red hair styled in a chic bob and wrinkles around her face, dressed in polished red suit pants. Not at all a woman Morana would have put in a basement with chains if she'd seen her out on the streets. The woman looked more social clubs and luncheons than underworld crime. But looks could be deceptive.

Morana stayed silent, observing her. She didn't have her glasses on her face anymore, but thankfully, her vision was perfect for far objects and the woman stayed in the line of sight. There was something familiar about her, like she'd seen her before, but she couldn't put her finger on it.

"Don't you want to know why you're here?" the woman asked, her smile looking almost maternal, but she was oozing manipulative.

"I don't think it's for a kitty party," Morana quipped, keeping her cool as she watched the older lady's smile fall off her face.

"I told you she was vile," another female voice spoke, and Morana shuddered as Chiara came to stand next to the older woman, the resemblance between them uncanny. They were mother and daughter. That was the resemblance? What the fuck? Did Chiara rope her mother into kidnapping her? Was it because Chiara was actually a crazy bitch and after Morana's life for being with Tristan? Could she really be that insane?

"I should've known it would be Tristan's lizard ex," Morana drawled out with more humor than she was feeling, like she wasn't strung up and feeling an ache the size of a continent in her shoulder.

"Shut up, bitch," Chiara hissed. "That boy is the least of the reasons you're here."

"Then what?"

The older woman looked at her phone as if waiting for something while Chiara sneered at her, but both stayed silent. A text came through.

"Now the kitty party starts." The woman gave a smile, and the door to the basement opened.

Morana watched in horror as Luna walked down the stairs and into the room, held at gunpoint by a fat man in a mask, similar to the one who had kidnapped her. *What the hell was she doing there?*

Luna looked up at where she was hanging out—*literally*—and her eyes filled up.

Horrified, Morana watched as the fat man brought the girl right next to her, under the chains on the other side. The man raised her arms and tied her to the chains hanging, her cry of pain loud as her feet didn't even touch the ground properly because of her shorter height. A surge of fury filled her veins. This was Tristan's *sister. How dare he?*

"Who are you?" Morana turned to the woman, finally breaking her silence on questions, sobering the fuck out because there was no way she was playing with Tristan's sister in danger. She'd never forgive herself if something happened to the girl. She had to protect her—for Tristan, for herself, and now that she'd met the Shadow Man, for all of them because the man would kill them if something happened to her. She'd felt his *crazy.*

"I'm glad you asked." The old lady walked around in those power heels impressively smoothly, almost like an older model doing a catwalk. She had a very odd vibe. "I'm the one who's been assigned to eliminate you."

"By who?"

"The Syndicate, of course," she tutted. "You've disrupted our plans since the moment you were taken. First, your father bargained with Maroni, then Maroni gave you to Vitalio, and then you ended up with Caine, digging your nose in places it doesn't belong. So many places and plans gone bad all because of you."

Morana would have felt proud any other time. "Is this about *Project Ouroboros?*" Morana ventured.

The older woman turned suddenly, her eyes widening as she walked closer to her. "What do you know about it?"

She said not a word, just gave the woman the most smug look she could manage.

"What do you know, stupid girl?" the woman demanded.

Morana *was* offended by the word' stupid,' but she let it go because traveling alone had been stupid. She stayed silent, and the woman backhanded her. A burst of pain flared across her cheek, making her eyes water.

"Stop it!" Luna screamed from her side, her voice shaking with the same anger Morana was feeling, projecting that same protectiveness that was coursing through her body. Morana turned her neck and locked eyes with the girl, both of them sharing a glance of understanding and companionship in that fucked up moment.

A phone rang, breaking their gaze. The woman picked up the call, and a man's voice came through the speakers. "Is everything ready?"

A whimper left Luna at the voice, and Morana turned to see her paling. Whoever this was, the girl clearly knew the voice and didn't have good association with it.

"Who is he?" Morana asked Luna, and the man chuckled, the sound so evil it sent a shiver down her spine.

"Yes, pretty girl," he goaded. "Tell her who I am. Tell her how you *blossomed* for me."

Vile nausea climbed up Morana's throat as she realized this was one of the monsters from his beautiful girl's horrid past. Her mind reeled as she realized the kind of trauma this must be inflicting on the poor girl. She couldn't even imagine it, but she could stand by her side and not let her suffer alone.

"Hey asshole," Morana goaded him back. "If you're such a hotshot, why don't you unchain me and stand here, huh? Or are you too much of a coward?"

The silence was so thick it could be cut with a knife. Morana gritted her teeth, her right shoulder pinching, waiting for retaliation. Whatever, she wasn't going to let this dick take her friend to ugly places.

"Begin," the man finally spoke the command.

"Yes, sir," the woman informed the man who was her master. Morana saw nothing but an icon in place of his face, but she assumed the phone camera pointed at the two hanging girls and showed them to him clearly. The older women went back in the dark.

And then, to her absolute shock, Chiara pressed a button, and a man walked in with Tristan. *Her* Tristan and not some random Tristan off the street. *What the fuck?*

Tristan clocked them both immediately, his nostrils flaring as he saw the two women he loved hanging there, his hands tied behind his back. She knew he could get out of a simple hold, but what scared her was the knife in his side, dug deep and held in place in a way that the more he pulled his muscles to try and disarm himself, the deeper it would dig.

"What are you doing?" she whispered to him, her eyes tearing up as they sat him down in the chair.

"Oh, I called him here," Chiara supplied gleefully, running a finger over his shoulder in a familiar way that made Morana want to cut the bitch. That was *her* shoulder on *her* man's body, and the bitch better hope she was nowhere near her when Morana got free because that finger was *going*. "Sent a little photo of you here. Told them to come alone or you die."

Morana was going to break the bitch.

Tristan stared at her, his blue eyes flared with pain but his gaze steady, reassuring her. He had been through worse before, and he needed her to stay strong as they got through this. She gave him a little nod. His eyes moved to his sister, such deep agony flaring in them. Morana could feel the despair he felt at his inability to protect her again, feel the failure he felt seeing her strung up like that.

"Now that we're all here." The man's face came on the screen finally, the phone becoming a projector and his image becoming large. Salt-and-pepper hair and a well-groomed beard, dark eyes, olive skin, and a thick neck that looked more muscular than fat. He wasn't anyone Morana had seen before, but he looked sophisticated. Not a man she would have put in the basement either, more in corporate dinners. His background was a simple dark wall that could be practically anywhere.

Luna began to panic at her side, her eyes losing focus, her whole body shaking so hard it was rattling the chains.

"Look at me," Tristan's calm, composed voice, the same tone he'd used with her whenever she'd panicked, made his sister turn to him. He breathed in deeply, wincing as the knife went a little deeper into him but doing the motion he wanted her to imitate. Thankfully, Luna kept her eyes on him, taking a deep breath in, calming herself down, fighting whatever demons were calling in her head.

The older woman, who had disappeared, showed up again. Tristan whipped his neck so fast that Morana was surprised.

Shock and pain crossed his face, so visible he had forgotten to mask it.

"Mom?" the one word, so innocent, broke her.

This was his mother? The older woman was his mother. Luna's mother. Chiara's mother? Had Chiara seduced her own blood brother? *What the actual fuck?*

"Not your mom, sweetheart," she stated, running a hand through his short hair almost with maternal affection, a gesture that made Tristan shudder.

"I was given to David to keep when you were a baby. Your mother died in childbirth."

Tristan sat, stunned in silence. He didn't utter a word, just took in what she said, and Morana could feel his heartbreak across the basement. She could also feel her own relief at the fact that he hadn't slept with his blood sister unknowingly. That would've messed up with his head really, really badly. She focused on the words the woman had said, knowing her lover was in no mental position to lead an interrogation at the moment as he tried to come to terms and process. Fuck, last night and then this, it had to be overwhelming him so much with emotional overload. And to a man who didn't know how to process emotions properly, she could understand how rough this must be for him.

"What do you mean *to keep*?" Morana asked the woman, distracting her from Tristan.

"The Syndicate gave me to David."

Holy shit. His father had been in The Syndicate, too? Morana remembered he had been Lorenzo's bodyguard; it made sense that he would be, given Lorenzo's proclivities.

"And me?" Luna asked from the side, her voice quiet as she learned the news too. Morana couldn't imagine what a fuck up must be in her head at the moment with everything. She hoped the girl she'd glimpsed at last night, the one with quiet strength, could get through all this.

The woman turned to Luna. "You're mine."

It hit Morana.

The siblings weren't related by blood. The sister Tristan had loved and looked for all his life had never biologically been his. Morana felt her eyes tear up as she looked at the anguish on his face, the realization hurting him more than the knife in his side. Her eyes began to burn, watching him come to terms with the fact that the sister he had spent his whole life making his anchor wasn't even his own by blood. He looked down at the floor for a few minutes, breathing in steadily, until his face cleared and the mask locked back in place tight.

"You took her, didn't you?" he asked the woman, a woman he had thought had been his mother, his voice void of all emotion. "There was no other way."

The older woman nodded. "I gave you a sleeping pill. Took

her out and gave her to Lorenzo."

"Why?"

"Because *he* loved her," she pushed out through clenched teeth. "Your father. Raped her into my body when I didn't even want it and loved her like she'd been a gift."

"So you sent her to hell?" Morana asked, aghast. Did their world have no good mothers? No good fathers? No good parents at all? What was this poisonous cycle their parents had begun? This couldn't go on. This vicious cycle had to stop and they had to break it, for their kids and their kids and all the kids after that so they didn't suffer the trauma her generation had.

The woman shrugged. "David lost his mind and went after Vitalio. We hadn't thought you'd kill him, though." She turned to Tristan, clapping. "Bravo."

Morana looked at Luna to see how she was receiving the news her brother had killed their father. There was no flinch on her expressive face. Either she already knew or she didn't care. Morana didn't know which. Maybe the Shadow Man had already told her. And suddenly, it hit her. Morana focused on Luna, her brain whirring.

"Do you have your phone?" she asked softly so as not to be heard.

Luna gave her a look, a look she took as affirmative. Good. There was no way a man like him would let her go without tracking her, and if she still had it on her, that meant they just had to buy time. With that goal in mind, hoping she wasn't wrong about him, she engaged the woman in conversation again.

"So, how did you end up doing his bidding?" She nodded at the screen where the sophisticated monster watched the scene unfold silently.

The woman looked at her master almost adoringly. It was sickening. "He found me. Gave me purpose. Serving The Syndicate has been my honor."

Ew. "And the lives you destroyed?"

"It was just business."

A business of lives. *Fuck them.*

"So, why the family reunion?" Tristan asked, his voice almost robotic. Morana tried to see if there was anything on his face, but it was his stone-cold mask, the mask of the predator they called him.

The woman grinned in an almost girlish way. "Things have to come full circle, you know? That's our motto. It ends where it begins."

Morana felt her gut tighten as she heard the words. A bad, bad feeling settled in. This wasn't good, whatever shit these psychos had planned. They needed to get out of there, but *how?*

The woman walked around Tristan's chair behind him, leaning forward so her mouth was close to his ear. "All of this started with a choice," she began. "It will end in one, too. You had to choose between your family and this girl. Twenty years, and the same choice."

Morana felt her body go numb at the words. Tristan's face betrayed nothing, but his eyes did—eyes she knew to read because of all the time she had spent learning their language.

He was scared.

Her big, beautiful man was scared back into a small, simple boy.

Tears fell over her eyelids as they looked at each other. He looked at his sister, a sister he had known just for a few days but loved so deeply, then back at her, a woman he had hated but loved so intensely.

"Whoever you choose will go home with you, safe," the woman continued, and god, Morana had never hated anymore more than she hated her. Fuck her for traumatizing him, for retraumatizing him, and for everything she did to her own flesh and blood daughter. Her eyes went to Chiara, watching the scene with a little smile. Chiara saw her looking and smiled wider.

"I won't choose," he stated, bringing her eyes back to him. "Not this time."

The woman laughed like she'd expected that answer from him. "I'd thought you might say that. In that case, dear boy." Her hand hovered over the hilt of the knife. "You will die, and they will both be put into the trade. So, what's it going to be?"

Morana looked at the man on screen in desperation. "Don't do this," she bargained. "I will help you if you let us go."

She wouldn't. She would hunt them down and murder them bloody. But she needed to get free, and Tristan needed to get free so he could break bones. "Please."

The man considered her. "I would have taken your offer, girl, but I gave my word to my loyalist, and I'm a man of my word," the man told her without a shred of remorse. How could people be so apathetic? So evil? How could humans have devolved into this?

"Why?" The question slipped from her in the atrocity.

The man smiled, and it was frightening. "Because some people just like to watch the world burn."

It was a chilling statement because it was true. Some people didn't have motives or reasons; they had chaos inside them that they unleashed on the innocent. Some people, like this man evidently, just wanted to watch the world dance to their strings.

Silence descended for a few moments. Her heart drummed in her ears.

Tristan looked at her, kept looking at her, until a tinny voice said from her right. "Make the same choice, brother."

Both his and Morana's eyes went to Luna, who was looking at him with the same fire in her eyes she'd had the night before.

"Lun—" Tristan started but she shook her head.

"No. Not Luna," she told him, and Morana blinked at her disuse of the name. "I'm both the lost innocent girl and the broken healed woman. I'm not the girl you lost or the one monsters broke. I'm done being the consequence of my circumstances. I am a phoenix who rose from her own ashes, and I will claim my own name, not a name given to me by a bitch of a mother or a bastard of a man."

Her biological mother slowly clapped. "Well done. Great speech."

Luna looked at the woman with disgust. "You're shameful. A disgusting disgrace in the name of motherhood. So what if you were raped? You brought an innocent child into the world and gave it to monsters. A mother loves. A mother protects. A mother sacrifices. You're not a mother, you're a monster. I have seen good mothers, and for a moment in time, I have been a good mother."

Tristan gaped at his sister, the revelation of her words hitting him hard. Luna looked at him in the same headspace she had been in last night, dropping truth after truth with a searing honesty.

"I gave birth to Xander."

Tristan started to struggle. Morana could see all the emotions overwhelming him as the epiphany, the connection that had shocked her a few hours ago, sank into him. It still rattled her and sent a chill down her spine when she thought about how the Shadow Man had found them and led them straight to Xander, a boy she loved and had become a mother to, who was Luna's actual son that she had protected somehow.

After the tirade, the older woman stared hard at her daughter before turning to Tristan. "Make your choice."

"Choose her," Luna urged him. "Get out of here. For Xander. He needs you both."

"We won't leave you alone," Morana struggled inside, not knowing how they would get out of this.

She turned to her. "I won't be alone. He'll come for me."

"Who?" Chiara asked, speaking for the first time in a while, straightening.

And then, a voice came from the screen, a voice she'd heard just hours ago, deadly and dangerous, and hope surged in her heart.

"Me."

LYLA

CHAPTER 37

LYLA, NEAR TENEBRAE CITY

S HE WAS GOING TO call herself Lyna if she made it out alive.

Malini had told her once that Lyna meant light while Lyla meant night. She had always felt like the night, and most of the time, she still did. But she also felt like the moon now, alight but with light it borrowed and stole from the ball of fire near it. A combination of both her names, it also felt like a good thing to do in honor of her friend's memory, the only friend she'd had in that hell. It still hurt imagining the girl who had helped her through so much dying just as she'd almost escaped after finding love. There was so much injustice in it. She wished she could've seen her on the other side, met her and her man Vin, who had been Amara's best friend, so they could have been a part of the group she had begun to think of as family.

She had been thinking a lot about who she felt like lately. Lyla was the broken girl who had somehow survived, and Luna had been the innocent girl her brother had mourned. After the last few days, spending time with a family she fell in love with and a man who had shown her what the word meant, she realized she was both the girls and she would always be. And so, she claimed her power, became something new, even if it was the end.

She would rather die with her fire than end with the ashes.

"We will become ashes before we are apart."

His words came back to her, along with the memory. The memory of being in his arms, feeling the safest she had felt, so whole she never questioned where she was hollow.

She watched the man on the screen, the monster of her nightmares, come to life before her eyes again and grit her teeth. He wouldn't break her again, not this time. She had been a child alone when he'd gotten his claws into her. She was a woman who belonged now.

She looked at Morana, so feisty and protective, willing to take the brunt of their wrath on herself to save her. She looked at her brother, bleeding but not broken, forced to make a choice that had traumatized him and made his life hell twenty-plus years ago, yet still willing to die instead of choosing.

But she needed him to. She needed him to live, needed Morana to live, so they could be happy together. So they could get married and adopt a dog and take care of Xander for the rest of their lives. Her son needed them and their love more than he needed her. She would never be able to give him the stability, the love he deserved, not with the demons she battled every day. She would love to be a part of his life though, and she didn't think Tristan and Morana would ever refuse that. But though she had been a mother to him, she didn't think she could be a mom. Not like Amara was with Tempest or Zephyr was with her unborn child. Not like Morana already was with him.

She remembered getting that photo of Morana, all strung up in chains, unconscious, and the message that came with it. *Take her place—alone—or die.*

Alpha and Zephyr had gone back to Los Fortis after the shocking news, and then Dante and Amara had gone to get the bodies. Vin and Malini, once lovers and now just random bodies washed up on the river in Tenebrae. They'd both gone to take care of things and make arrangements, all of them gone before she could have told any of them. All but her brother by her side and her lover on the phone.

Lyla—Lyna, she promised herself, if she made it—hadn't even thought. She had told Dainn and told her brother, showed him the message, and saw how her brother was when he *lost it.*

Dainn, *her* Dainn, had simply said three words to her.

"Trust me still?"

She would trust him till the end of her time, trust herself to make that choice.

"Yes."
"Then go."

She hadn't even questioned it. With him at her back—her mind reminding her of that time he'd stood behind her in the mirror and told her he was always behind her—she would walk into the depths of hell, knowing she wouldn't be burned.

Tristan had not thought the same. He'd told her husband to 'fuck off' and accompanied her.

And though she didn't have a number to contact *him*, she had tucked her phone under her left foot, between her sock and her shoe. She knew it was a matter of time—she hoped—before he found her.

And he would find her, because he always had.

Whether she would be dead or alive was a matter for debate at the pace at which things were devolving.

But hanging there from her chains, she surprisingly felt at peace. She had lived a good life in the last few months, the best she could have dreamed of, with her husband and her brother and her son, a trifecta of men completing her soul. And if this was the way she had to go, she was going to at least make sure it meant something.

"Choose her," she begged her brother again. Her brother, who wasn't her biological brother, but she couldn't have cared less. He was the brother of her heart and that heart loved him so deeply in just a few days, she was grateful for him. She hoped knowing she wasn't his blood sister didn't change anything on his end. "Get out of here. For Xander. He needs you both."

She could see the toll it was taking on him, chipping away at pieces of his soul as he looked between the both of them, a knife stuck to his side. She didn't even think he was feeling it.

Morana saw it too, probably better than her, and told her, "We won't leave you alone."

They were both so incredible. She was lucky to have had them. But they had to get out and she was going to lie if need be. "I won't be alone. He'll come for me."

When was the question.

"Who?" the other bitch—a sister she didn't want if that's what she was like—asked, speaking for the first time in a while.

And then, the voice of death spoke from the screen. "Me."

Lyla swiveled her head and started, at the silhouette that moved behind the monster. A *bigger* devil. *Her devil.*

"You came," the words escaped her lips, unbidden, a memory of all the times the words had come from her wracking her entire frame.

And he said the words he'd always said to her. "I'll always come for you." The power of those words, backed by the evidence of *years*, made her melt. Her heart beat a staccato, resending new life into her veins.

The monster on the screen smiled, unfazed. "Shadow Man, at last." That felt odd. Why was he not scared?

Dainn stayed behind him, nothing but a silhouette. "The Syndicater. Or should I say, sperm donor?"

That was his father? Lyla—Lyna, she reminded herself—gaped.

"I always knew you were going to be smart," the monster, his father, said almost pridefully. "I was waiting for this day."

"So I could kill you?" Dainn asked, his voice almost lazy, as if he wasn't perturbed by the situation at all. Knowing him, he probably wasn't.

"So you could become my best creation." That was an odd phrasing. What did he mean?

Dainn stayed silent for long moments, letting the tension build. She realized both Morana and her brother were watching the telecast, along with the two ladies and one fat guard in the room. Her brother was slowly, steadily moving his hands, using the distraction to try and get free.

"I was the restart of your project. After it was shut down. You restarted Project Ouroboros with me."

She had no idea what he meant or what the project was, but Morana did because a gasp left her as she gaped at the screen.

Whatever the context, the monster laughed. "Yes. A worthy adversary. An enemy worth having. Built from scratch."

Morana looked slightly green in the face, as if she was in pain or knew what they were talking about. It could be both.

"Are there any others left?" Dainn asked, with a finality in his tone. "Like me?"

"That's for you to find out." The monster just grinned. "Is her pussy still as tight?"

Before Lyla could retch, Dainn stepped out of the shadows, his face visible to everyone, and looked straight into the camera.

"For you, *flamma*."

And with those words, he vindicated her again. He flicked a lighter open, throwing it on the table. Lyla watched, in awe to the sound of stunned gasps, as her monster sat in a circle of flames, fire all around him as he stayed inside, not fighting, not moving, looking almost proud in a way that made her sick. Dainn stood behind him like the devil she'd thought of him as the fire illuminated his frame, the hues of orange burnishing into his dark skin, being absorbed by the darkness like a black hole.

The fire roared, almost covering half the screen.

He exited the frame then, leaving the monster to burn and rot as the flames engulfed him, the sight of it making her eyes moist. Memories of the monster, the way he had touched her, the way he had done things to her, the way he had *forced* her—all of them burned with him, vengeance, vindication, validation speaking the truth into her new existence. It felt like a cleansing. Her monsters, the last of them, were gone. Killed by the devil who belonged to her, just like every single one of them had been.

A sudden commotion drew her eye to see her brother flip the chair, his hands totally free, one hand pulling the knife out of his side. Blood began pouring out of the wound immediately as it opened, but he didn't care, plunging the knife into the guard's neck before bending and taking out a gun from his boot. The younger redhead woman ran up the stairs, disappearing from view before there was a loud scream that suddenly stopped.

The older woman, her biological mother, watched with widened eyes at the barrel of the gun in her face.

"Tristan..." she began.

Her brother flipped some kind of a button and lowered his gun slightly. "This is for my sister." A loud bang and her chest recoiled, blood pouring out and mixing into the red of her suit, making the fabric darker but the same color.

The woman held her chest, reeling, and looked in shock.

"And this," her brother raised his gun again, "is for me."

He shot her between the eyebrows, just as she knew he'd shot their father. A fitting end to both the monsters.

Lyla stared as her mother's eyes stared up, her body crumpling to the ground, another demon in the guise of her mother dead.

The door to the basement opened, and Dainn appeared at

the top. He jogged down and her entire frame relaxed. Evidently, the monster had been stupid—or suicidal; she remembered his stillness and lack of fight—enough to be in the same place as them.

Dainn headed straight toward her, but before he could get to her, he was suddenly stopped by her brother.

Tristan, completely enraged, punched him in the face. Dainn's head swiveled to the side, and he straightened, cracking his jaw, his eyes the way they always were—without emotional reaction.

Tristan pulled his hand back again, and this time, Dainn raised one gloved finger. "One. That's all you get."

Tristan's fist hovered in the air and Dainn stood tall, unfazed, with one finger up. Both men stared each other down and it was such a weird thing for her to witness. Before they could actually do something, she made a deliberate noise, and just as she'd hoped, Dainn broke the silence.

"Now, do you want to take off their chains or have a standoff with me?"

Lyla saw her brother's jaw tighten, his entire body shaking with rage. "Fucker."

Dainn ignored him—angering her brother even more in his extra emotional state—and came straight to her.

He raised his arms, loosening her chains and unshackling her. Her arms felt numb as she fell into his body, and he pulled her into his arms, breathing in her scent. She did the same, inhaling his dark, musky scent that immediately soothed her.

A loud cry of pain from the side had them both stiffening and immediately turning as Morana's arms came down, her eyes red with agony. Her brother immediately held her, holding her by the neck and staring into her eyes, looking so deep, like he would examine her pain through sheer eye contact. "Where?"

"Left arm," Morana gritted out, clenching her teeth.

Tristan picked her up in his arms, not behaving like he had a stab wound of his own, and headed to the stairs. Dainn turned to her, doing the same. "You okay?"

Lyla nodded. She was okay. She would be okay.

And for the first time, they stepped out into the light.

Lyla didn't know hospital rooms could be like this, so spacious and warm and well-furnished. The kinds she'd seen in the movies had always been so clinical and cold.

She lay in bed, just being kept overnight for a checkup. Thankfully, the scratches on her face would heal, and so was the pain in her shoulders. Not for Morana, though. She'd already had nerve damage from her shooting, bad enough that she should have immediately had it checked, but it was too late now. Her left shoulder, the entirety of her left arm, was disabled. She still had it since the damage was localized to it, but aside from some very minor movements for just a few minutes, she had no sensations in her arm.

Morana had broken down when the doctors had told her, sobbing so hard it had drawn Lyla from the next room to go check on her. She'd halted at the door, looking at the woman she was bonded to for life and it had broken her heart. Morana had been clutching onto her shirtless, scarred, bandaged brother and blubbering something about a tie, which didn't make sense to Lyla, but it was something because his brother immediately kissed the side of her head *so tenderly* it made Lyla tear up watching.

Lyla had stood outside, watching her brother kiss her softly on the head, on her cheek, on her lips, over and over, making sure she lay down and calmed down as he sat by her side.

And then, wordlessly, he had picked up her left hand, the one she couldn't feel anything in, and slid a ring onto her finger, pressing a kiss onto it, keeping his eyes on her.

Lyla had cried standing outside, never having seen such a beautiful declaration of love, such a profound proposal of a partnership, in sickness and in health, for life.

It was such a deep, heartwrenching proposal, and so *them*. She left them alone then, giving them privacy as she went back to her room.

From the updates she got, Alpha and Zephyr landed in Los

Fortis and got her mother out on bail. Zephyr had to be rushed to the hospital because of the stress, causing her to have early contractions. Thankfully, their baby was safe, but they hadn't heard any more news about her father's involvement yet, and if she wanted to have a healthy baby, she couldn't take any more stress.

Dante and Amara had been the rocks for everyone through the whole ordeal, taking care of everything, making sure everyone was looked after, and coordinating the crisis and death that had fallen upon them.

Lyla lay staring at her ceiling, so bone tired, so homesick. She missed the open glass ceiling of her bedroom, sleeping under the stars. She was tired of looking at ceilings that closed her in, no matter how pretty they were, reminding her of the times she wanted to move forward from.

Suddenly, she felt a presence at the door and swiveled her eyes, her breath catching as it set on the young boy standing there, right in front of the man she loved.

Xander.

Her baby boy.

So close to her for the first time.

Her throat clogged up as she watched him enter, his eyes taking her in curiously before setting on the machines around her. "Hi."

He had such a beautiful voice. She had heard it before, but it was the first time she had heard it directed at herself.

She swallowed, nervous, her gaze going to Dainn before returning to Xander. "Hi."

He looked at her briefly before his eyes skittered away again. "D told me about you."

D.

Dainn.

She knew he'd had a relationship with Xander, but she had no idea what. He'd never talked to her about it, but clearly, they knew each other better than she'd expected.

"What did he tell you?" she asked, curiosity evident in her tone.

"That you ran to save me when I was a baby," he dropped on her so casually, without realizing how her heart thundered. "That you got lost your way, and he was going to find you."

Her eyes tinged with moisture, locking with the man she'd met that fateful night that started it all. "That's right," she murmured to him, her lips trembling, her gaze returning to her son.

"Are you still lost?"

She shook her head. She wasn't.

"I want to live with Tristan and Morana." His words made her heart full. "I love them. But I'd like to get to know you."

She stared at him, at the articulate way he spoke to her, which reminded her so much of Dainn's articulations. Maybe that's where he'd learned.

"Okay," she whispered before clearing her throat. "I'd like

that too."

He looked at her again, for a second, before giving her a little piece of paper and walking out the door, where Dainn stood, his hands in his pockets, watching her silently. Xander told him he was going to see Morana and left them alone.

Lyla unfolded the paper, wondering if he'd picked up writing notes from Dainn too, and read the two words written in a childish scrawl, her nose tingling as tears ran down her cheeks. She pressed it to her chest, heaving in deep, long breaths, tattooing the two words onto her heart, her eyes locking with mismatched ones, six years of *something* passing between them.

Two little words with the biggest meaning in the world.

Welcome home.

Lyla was finally home.

DAINN

Chapter 38

Dainn, Tenebrae City

Dainn walked into the hospital waiting room, still in the suit he'd been wearing when his *flamma* had called him.

She was resting, her body exhausted, and her mind even more drained in the last twenty-four hours. He had been sitting in his hotel room, listening to her stand up to her brother and everyone else for him. Dainn didn't feel emotions as normal people did but there had been something happening when he'd listened to her—his soft, scared *flamma*—take a stand for *him*. It was a novel experience, one he'd never experienced before. No one had defended him or stood up for him in his life and the fact that this girl who'd been too broken to even live a few months ago had come to this point just made something happen in his chest. He didn't know what it was and he didn't care. All he knew was that if she'd had his unending loyalty before, now there was no force in this entire universe that could keep him from her. He was now a devotee and she his religion.

The waiting room was cozy, the more expensive area of the private hospital the girls had been brought into. He crossed the room and went to a door that was closed.

Quietly, he opened it and looked inside.

Morana was sleeping in her bed. A sliver of pity went through him seeing her like that, again, just in the span of a few weeks. But the girl was strong and she would be alright.

He'd read her reports and saw what the doctors said. And while he respected their professional expertise, he also knew he could bring the best scientists and specialists in the world and have them heal her nerve damage, at least enough that she would be able to work with limited mobility if not full.

"You still here?" the small voice asked from a darkened corner of the room. Dainn turned his neck to see Xander looking at a tablet, the lights dim, keeping watch over Morana.

He shut the door behind him and went to the couch, taking a seat next to the boy. "Yeah. Your mother is healing. I'll be here till she's alright."

The boy kept staring into the tablet, a screen with some kind of word game on it. "You think she really wants to know me?"

Dainn put a hand on the boy's shoulder. "I know. She gave up everything to keep you safe. That kind of love is rare. She already loves you."

Xander's cheeks flushed a little. "I liked her too. She's very pretty."

A little twitch pulled up his mouth. Calling his *flamma* pretty was like saying the night was dark. There were depths to the darkness, layers and layers of beauty, nuances to know. But since the boy was so young, Dainn just hummed in agreement.

"What about Morana?" Xander asked after a while. "You think she'll be okay?"

Dainn looked at the ring on her finger, a beautiful sapphire and diamond piece that glimmered like the depths of the ocean. If he could get the specialists he had in mind to see her, she would hopefully make a recovery. "She'll be okay."

The boy nodded, taking him for his word. He'd always done that. Dainn had initially planned to leave the boy with a private nanny to be raised until he could locate his family, his interest solely on the mother. But he had known that if he took care of the child under his supervision, it might endear his emotional flamma to him even more. And he'd been right. Though she had been the motivation in the beginning, Dainn had to admit the boy had grown on him. He was smart and non-judgemental and surprisingly observant. All things that he'd enjoyed watching grow in him.

"You doing good?" he asked as he always did in their monthly calls.

"Mmhmm," the boy mumbled, his fingers flying over some crossword type of game. "Just thinking about her. Do I call her mother or Luna?"

"You'll have to ask her that." If he knew Lyla, she wouldn't be comfortable being called mother because she didn't feel like one, at least not yet. He hoped their relationship got to a space where he'd call her something that would make her eyes shine and lips smile.

"Are you going to have a baby with her?" Xander asked and Dainn felt a little laugh huff inside him. He wasn't built to be a father and he didn't want to pass down his genes to any poor child, because if they were born normal and not like him, they would be tormented throughout their life. More importantly, if he ever even wanted to, there was only one woman he would have procreated with and she couldn't have more children. And he was completely okay with that as long as she was. If she ever felt the need to have more, they would just adopt. But it all up to her and her decision. He just knew she wasn't ready and wouldn't be for a while as she healed.

Dainn just shrugged, not knowing how to explain all this to a young boy. He had always been honest with the kid most of the time.

Xander yawned loudly and Dainn took that as his cue to leave. "Good night, X."

"Good night, D." This had been a routine once. Ever since he'd let Xander and Lex go to the orphanage for discovery, where Lex had helped him with the timing, this was something he admitted to have missed slightly.

He ruffled the boy's hair that he was growing out and walked to Morana, looking at her sleeping for a second, silently ac-knowledging that she was pivotal to his plans and wanting her to get better. The major reason for him feeling that way was the way she'd stood up for his *flamma* while still in chains, how she had tried to protect her, and for that alone, she had his resources.

He walked out into the waiting room, only to find it not empty anymore.

Tristan Caine sat on a chair, elbows on his knees, hands on his face, head bent like the weight of the world was on his shoulders.

Dainn tilted his head and leaned back against the wall, pushing his hand into his pockets and waiting. It was better to have this confrontation out in the open now than later, so they could get it out of the way and Lyla could focus on healing and not trying to break them apart like she had in that basement.

The man's head came up, years of instincts honed and telling him about someone in the vicinity. And his eyes hardened.

"Blackthorne," he gnashed out.

"Caine," Dainn acknowledged.

"Get the fuck out."

Dainn waited a beat, keeping his posture the same relaxed way it was. "Why? I have as much right, if not more, to be here that you do."

Tristan was up from his seat and heading toward him, his hands fisted by his sides. "Because you're a motherfucking bottomfeeder who's not good enough for my sister."

Dainn mulled the words over, his lack of reaction riling

the other man up slightly. It wasn't something that would be visible to anyone not used to watching for the spectrum of human emotions.

"I'm the only one for your sister," Dainn stated. "Good or bad, doesn't matter."

That irked the man. Dainn got curious.

"You don't like me because I kept her from you?" he asked Tristan. "Or is it because she took a stand for me?"

Tristan stayed still, and Dainn was impressed by his ability to quickly control his emotions. "It's because she deserves someone who feels for her, not a psychotic serial killer like you."

A sliver of amusement went through him. "I could say Morana deserves someone who didn't spend the majority of his life wanting to kill her," he pointed out.

There was silence as Tristan processed his words, his jaw clenched, his eyes furious. "Maybe. But I am different from you."

Dainn nodded. "Yes, you wanted to kill your lover while I wanted to save mine. We are very different."

His words seemed to hit Tristan, a reminder of what his sister had told him the previous night, about the things he had done to protect her. She was generous, his *flamma*, because she never mentioned the time he hadn't. She could have but she kept that between the two of them.

Tristan suddenly looked weary. He rubbed a hand over his

face and looked at him, still hostile but less angry. "Thank you for that."

The words were a surprise but seemed to be dragged out of him. Dainn didn't gloat. He took the words and discarded them in his head because his thanks meant nothing. Him liking Dainn meant nothing. As long as it didn't hurt Lyla, Tristan could try to kill him for all he cared.

"I have some specialists," he began, changing the topic. "Nerve specialists. If you wish, I can send them Morana's report."

Tristan walked back to the chair and slumped down. Dainn moved to a chair adjacent and sat. He waited patiently while Tristan thought the words through. After a long time, he finally spoke again.

"You think the damage can be undone?"

Dainn tilted his head to the side. "Maybe not entirely, but I'm certain it can be lessened and give her more mobility, even if for a bit."

Tristan heaved a breath in, as if the words were giving him a second life. He could understand. Morana's hands were her best tools after her brain.

"Alright," the man agreed reluctantly, as though taking a favor from him was a weight. "But keep it to yourself. Unless we know for sure, I don't want to get her hopes up."

Dainn nodded. "Understood."

They sat in silence after that. Maybe awkward, maybe not.

He knew as much as Tristan didn't like him and probably never would, he could not deny his connection to his sister. Doing that would hurt her and that was possibly the only point of commonality between them, because that was the only reason he was tolerating Tristan his their lives too, why he was tolerating a sudden influx of people that had once just been a bubble of them both.

Without a word, Tristan left the room, heading to Morana's.

Dainn sat for a few more minutes, making some calls to the relevant specialists and forwarding emails. Then, he stood up and headed to the room Lyla was in.

He opened the door and slipped inside, closing it behind him, and walked to the comfortable hospital bed she was softly snoring in. There were some shoulder injuries and some shallow cuts on her beautiful face that Chiara had put there with her nails. Dainn had enjoyed breaking them and cutting her arm off before snapping her neck. He had zero compunction about killing a woman. Women could be just as, if not more, monstrous than men and he knew that from experience.

He pushed his suit jacket off just as she turned in her sleep and blinked her eyes open lazily.

A smile came over her face, like a ray of light coming through the clouds, and Dainn watched it, almost in a trance.

"Come to bed," she mumbled out, probably forgetting that she was in a hospital or anything that had happened. Dainn wasn't going to remind her.

He pushed off his shoes and slipped into bed next to her, the space tight with his size and the bed too small for both of them. She didn't care, turning into his chest and snuggling into him like a cold creature seeking warm comfort, and Dainn felt like he was taking his first full breath in days. He wrapped his arms around her, listening to her starting that soft snore again, her lips parted and breaths falling on his chest, warming the one place that had always been glacial.

He pressed a soft kiss to her head, closing his eyes and embracing the darkness that enveloped him.

Darkness was a house he lived in, but *she* was home. He was home.

PART IV:

FOREVER

"What makes night within us
may leave stars."

— VICTOR HUGO

EPILOGUE 1

TRISTAN AND MORANA, 6 MONTHS LATER

ON A BRIGHT MORNING, right on the land where the sea met the shore in Shadow Port, Morana walked down the aisle to the man she loved, ready to become a Caine.

The day she had lost the use of her left arm had been the day Tristan had proposed to her, completely in a way only Tristan could. He had bought a ring the moment he'd found his sister, waiting for the right time and the right proposal, and to both their surprise, it had come in a hospital bed when she'd been breaking down and he'd been stabbed. He had simply sit next to her after she was told her left hand was useless, disabling her for life, and without a word, he had slid the ring on her finger, on the left hand.

The symbolism of it hadn't escaped her, and she had cried even more.

Life had been... different since then. Between dealing with the trauma dump on him and the physical adjustments for her, they'd found a new normal.

A new normal where she'd learned skills all over again with

just her right hand. So what if she could only type with one hand? She used voice commands better now. So what if it took her longer to knot his tie? He stood patiently, watching her with the love she knew he felt in his heart. He'd never said the words to her, and she didn't think she ever would, but it didn't matter to her because he showed her every second of every day.

It felt right, taking vows next to the sea they had connected over, watching the constant flow of the water, a symbol of the ebb and flow of life, doing it on land that once held their traumas and leaving it behind in the past, walking to a better, brighter future together.

Morana walked down the aisle, holding Dante's steady arm. The fact that he had been outside her dressing room, ready to walk her down, had touched her so deeply that she had almost broken down crying, much to the shrieking of Zephyr, who had just finished her hair and makeup and told her it wasn't waterproof. She had been dealing with trauma of her own, but as heavily pregnant as she was, she'd still managed to be excited for the wedding.

Dante took small steps to accommodate her gait in heels and the fact that she was burdened by the heaviest fucking gown on the planet, almost twice her weight. It really hadn't been Morana's first choice, but then Amara had said, "You'll only get married once," and Morana had said fuck it and gone for the most extravagant gown. Amara had been right.

She wouldn't get married again, not in this lifetime. Her last breath, her death, was going to belong to him.

She looked at the guests, just a family she had made for herself—Alpha and a very pregnant Zephyr. Amara, also pregnant, with a cute Tempest by her side, along with Zia. Xander, standing next to Tristan in a smart-looking suit, was finally a legal part of their core family, their little puppy in his arms. And Lyna—as she'd legally changed her name to—with Shadow Man, aka Blackthorne—whose real name she still didn't know. He had taken over The Syndicate in the last six months, and Morana still didn't know if it was a good thing or a bad one. It was too soon to tell.

And at the end of the aisle, Tristan waited for her, looking at her with those magnificent blue eyes that never lost their intensity. He still looked at her the same, like she was everything he never knew he needed, but with a violent edge that set her heart racing. She walked to him, and he took her hand. Dante kissed her on the cheek before joining Amara.

Tristan gazed at her as the officiant began speaking, saying no words but everything until he said the words that made her bawl:

"When it comes to death, you're mine."

It was a simple, small ceremony. It was *perfect.*

And then, he kissed her, savoring her, devouring her, claiming her for the world to see. He didn't take a ring since his tattoo was his, and after she was pronounced Morana Caine—a name she had chosen for herself too—he handed her a box.

"Your wedding gift."

Morana opened it, yelping in joy as a tiny little kitten with rounded ears and yellow eyes gazed up at her.

Her family cheered. She smiled up at him, wondering how she got lucky enough to fall in love with her enemy, how he had fallen in love with the only girl he'd hated. But that was their story, wasn't it?

Tristan and Morana, inseparable existence and all.

EPILOGUE 2

DANTE AND AMARA, 12 MONTHS LATER

O N A CLOUDY AFTERNOON, Amara Maroni became a mother twice over, giving birth to twin baby boys.

Both of them made it.

She cried, gazing at their scrunched faces, unable to believe they were hers, that they were together, so beautiful.

Dante Maroni looked, his heart full and relieved at seeing his sons.

Tempest Maroni stood on her little toes, holding Lulu, looking into the bassinet, her eyes wide. "My bwodas!"

Yes, she was speaking, as much a yapper as she'd been as a baby, just as spoiled too.

This time around, though, her mother wasn't there. In the last year, Amara had gotten pregnant again with twins—lord knew what super sperm her husband had—and lost her best friend and her mother.

Vin had died working for them undercover, trying to save a slave girl he had fallen in love with, going out doing a good thing. His death had hit her hard.

Her mother had passed in her sleep one night of natural causes, looking peaceful, and her death almost broke Amara. It had only been the responsibility of her own daughter and unborn twins that she had pieced herself back together and not let the hit break her completely. She missed her mother every day and wished her twins could have known their grandmother like Tempest had for a little time. Her mother, or Zia as everyone called her, had been so loved.

Amara had buried two bodies and birthed two others.

The realization was deep.

Dante walked over to her, kissing her on the forehead; her first crush, her best friend, her husband, her king.

"You're the beat to my heart." He gave her a quick kiss, which was interrupted by their daughter's loud, *"Ew."*

They grinned, knowing life would be full of ups and downs, calm and chaos, but they would play it together with the same beats and the same hearts.

EPILOGUE 3

ALPHA AND ZEPHYR, 18 MONTHS LATER

ON A HUMID EVENING, Kyra Villanova decided to have a tea party with her massive beast of a father.

Zephyr watched with a grin on her face as her huge, scarred, badass husband transformed himself into a total girl dad by sitting on a chair in her room that was too small for him and picking up a cup smaller than his fingers just by the tips, following his daughter's instruction.

The best, though, were the pink, glittery stars sticking on his eye patch.

Bear sat next to her, Bandit in the corner, and Baron right next to her daughter. Somehow, Baron, the dog who hated everyone, loved Kyra and no one else.

Her mother walked into the room, standing beside her, laughing at the scene. After everything she'd done, in a rage for her daughters, she had been living with them in the compound for months, and it had been a lifesaver with her stressful pregnancy. Her hormones and the stress had made it difficult for her to carry full-term. Kyra had come out a little premature and was smaller than usual but thankfully, otherwise healthy. And during that time, her mother had reconnected with her. They were deeply bonded now.

Zephyr watched her husband play with their daughter, wondering if he would ever remember anything else. He got some snippets here and there but never much about something specific and never something about her so far. But she lived in hope.

She looked and wondered what his mother would think looking at him now. She hoped she had fulfilled her promise to his mother.

"Rainbow?" he called her, even though her hair was back to blonde, the same color she had met him with but he didn't remember.

"Mama!" her child called, turning to find her with a wide smile. Zephyr rushed to them and took a seat on an empty, smaller chair.

"How's the gray?" he asked her quietly, knowing her struggles better than anyone. She looked at the love, the family they'd made for themselves, and locked eyes with him.

"Gone."

It would return some days, but there was one truth she had learned.

The grays never lasted forever.

EPILOGUE 4

DAINN AND LYNA, 24 MONTHS LATER

ON A DARK NIGHT, Lyna looked around her full house, her heart full.

Her family were all in her home in Bayfjord for a dinner night. They came once every three months, leaving Tristan and her to cook and prepare the meals. That was one of her favorite parts about bonding with her brother and son, both men loving being in the kitchen as much as he did, cooking the best meals for them all. That was her moment with Tristan and Xander and she wouldn't change it for the world.

Lyna—now used to her new name, one she'd made for herself—looked at the adults, Dante and Amara, Alpha and Zephyr, Tristan and Morana, all sitting around the table with the kids in between—one Maroni daughter and two Maroni sons, one Villanova daughter, and Lex, who Dante and Amara had adopted, and Xander. Xander, who lived with Tristan and Morana and was legally their child, but who spent a weekend every month with her and was biologically hers. He somehow balanced both, and so did she and her brother. They all loved

Xander and wanted the best for him, and this was the best.

She felt arms come around her waist and turned her face up to see the man who was a myth to so many and a monster to so many, standing behind her as always.

"Your family keeps getting bigger, *flamma*," he complained, referring to the pregnancy Morana had announced. It had come as a beautiful surprise and Tristan was the happiest she'd seen him since she'd known him. It was a new beginning for them.

She smiled at the words of her husband. She knew he wasn't put out by the number of people who kept getting added to his list of people to protect. He had been heading The Syndicate for almost two years now, replacing the man who had been his sperm donor, creating him in a lab of experimentation rather than human. Maybe that was why he was so different, so extraordinary. It didn't matter. He had shut down all projects and trades related to children and was flushing the market out so that a vacuum couldn't be created, eradicating the potential suppliers before they could reach the peak with money, manipulation and murder. He sat at the top of the pyramid with a council of Tristan, Dante, Alpha, and Morana assisting him. She would've thought they would have protested his takeover and his total control over the organization—especially her brother, who still barely tolerated Dainn's existence in her life.

But they all knew, even her brother, that Dainn was the right person for this role. What made people sick and disturbed left him completely neutral and still focused on his mission. That was power in this context, and none of them had what he did—the stomach to do whatever was necessary to ensure the power remained with him.

She'd learned of her own power, her own role, in the last two years too. She was his moral compass, the only one in the world who could keep him in check as he did what was needed. He didn't listen to or heed to anyone. A train could be speeding at him and he wouldn't budge but a word from her would make him move. He'd told her once that he was a weapon she could point anywhere, and she now knew that was her power.

She looked around the full house. The four cats—two her own, one Morana's and one Amara's—ran around the only dog—Xander's boy—making him spin in circles. She looked at all the people and cats and dogs, and it felt surreal to think this was her life.

"You'll keep them safe, won't you? All of them?"

His eyes locked with hers. "For you, anything."

Her eyes lingered on the born and unborn children who had good parents. "And they will never go through what we did?" she asked him.

"It ended where it began," he stated. "This is a new era."

The end of one era. The beginning of another. And this one was all of *theirs.*

Bonus Scenes

All's well that ends well. —William Shakespeare

This is the end of the *Dark Verse* series.
If you've come this far, thank you. I hope you enjoyed this journey. Please take a second to rate/review the book.
I will publish a bonus scenes novella soon. It will include deleted and bonus scenes from the series and a lot of plotless fluff and smut for all couples during the series timeline and also in the future so we know how they're doing. Turn the page for a peek at some exclusive unedited bonus scenes for each couple.

EXCLUSIVE

BONUS SCENES

BONUS: ALPHA & ZEPHYR

FIRST MEETING FLASHBACK

Z EPHYR COULDN'T BELIEVE SAM would dump her alone in this part of the town for her boyfriend, of all people. Not that she could blame her friend too much. They were both classmates and incidental friends because of their shared love for boys who were into the whole fighting thing. Sam's boyfriend was one of the fighters, scrapping once a month for extra money to put himself through college. Zephyr's interest was also a fighter, most probably fighting for money too, but not for college.

No. Zephyr didn't know what Alessandro Villanova fought for, but she knew he was there in the dingy basement of the industrial complex warehouse every other night, fighting, one of the youngest, fiercest boys.

She knew because for years she had tried to keep tabs on him on and off, just because she'd promised a dying woman that she would look out for her son. To be precise, she had promised that he wouldn't be alone, but in all the years of visiting Sam and hanging around the periphery of places that he did, she had never once brought up the courage to approach him.

She didn't know how she could.

She was all of eighteen, a short girl with too many curves that no one in her family or classes had, something her relatives liked to remind her of every time they saw her, everyone except Zen, her loving, beautiful sister.

Zephyr was confident in herself but when it came to the opposite sex, she was a little awkward. Boys in school either stared at her boobs too long or made fun of her. She didn't have any male friends to understand how to break the ice.

And Alessandro? He was the *boyest* boy she'd ever seen—tall and broad and muscular—on the cusp of becoming a fully grown manly man. She would still have elicited the courage to say hi to him had it not been for the scowl on his face, one that he always wore like he was perpetually pissed off at the whole world. She would rather stay on his periphery and keep an eye on him than risk having him turn the full force of scowl on her and reject her. In her head, she had been in love with him for years and just the idea of him finding out and rejecting her while laughing at how pathetic she was? Yeah, no, earth could swallow her whole first.

"C'mon Alpha!" A busty redhead screamed while jumping up and down, her boobs defying the gravity and the physics of her clothing by staying locked in place. Zephyr felt her stomach turn, hating her on sight. Last time she'd been there with Sam, they had walked into an alley while the redhead had been against the wall, screaming her head off for anyone to hear as Alpha had drilled into her.

Zephyr remembered the way her heart had felt shattered, which was stupid because he didn't even know of her existence. She remembered crying that night, and Zen telling her she had to at least try to talk to him or get over it.

She would get over it, as soon as she could find a ride home because her friend had ditched her and it was getting late. And this part of the town? Not a good area for a girl to be stuck alone at night. Though Zephyr didn't judge people and places, some monsters just came out at night and ate up lonesome girls.

She huddled into herself, the cold wind caressing her exposed arms and making her shiver, and looked around the almost empty parking lot. She needed to get home soon or her mother was going to have her head, not literally of course. But her parents worried and she did what she could to not give them any reason to.

"I hope you're getting good kisses out of ditching me, Sam," Zephyr muttered under her breath, talking to herself to keep from feeling scared. Metal creaked somewhere and she could feel her overactive imagination begin to get the better of her.

Maybe she should walk home. It was just a few miles. It was better than standing there waiting for something to happen.

"What are you doing in a shithole like this, sunshine?"

The deep, masculine voice coming from the side startled her. Zephyr turned with a yelp that got cut off in a split second, watching the boy of her dreams, almost a man now, standing a few feet away from her.

The ugly yellow from the street lamp fell on his massive frame, blocking out most of the light and casting gargantuan shadows on the concrete. His hands in the pocket of his leather jacket, his jaw clean-shaven and his hair a little messy, the dark slashes of his brows giving his beautiful face that severe look that made him seem older than his twenty-two.

And those eyes, those light brown, almost gold, eyes, focused intently on her.

It was the first time she saw him so close.

And she was speechless.

She was never speechless.

"I... Um—" Her brain was short-circuiting. She had to be hallucinating. There was no way he was there, right there, talking to her.

His words penetrated.

Sunshine.

He called her sunshine.

Warmth filled her veins as her hand touched her open blonde tresses.

His eyes roved over her face, and she felt herself flushing in response. Shit. She wished she was like the cool, confident girls she'd seen him hang out with. They didn't look like they would be flushing just because a guy looked their way. Although, he was a lot more than just any guy and he didn't even know it.

Not to be a total lost cause, she inhaled deeply and spoke. "I came to see you fight."

His eyebrows went up in visible surprise. Did he think she was lost or something? She looked down at her frilly green dress and realized he might. The dress belonged more in a social luncheon than in a fighting arena. But she loved dresses, fabrics that swished around her thighs and made her feel all girly and happy.

"You came alone?" he asked, still surprised. He had such a sexy voice. It was the first time she heard him talk so clearly and it made her insides all gooey. All of him was sexy, inspiring all kinds of thoughts in her head.

She shook her head, both to clear it and in response to his question. "My friend left with her boyfriend."

There was a slight furrow in his brows at her reply. "What about your boyfriend? If he left you here alone, sorry to say but he's a piece of shit, sunshine. You could do better."

Zephyr felt a laugh burst out of her, both as a nervous response and at his words.

He watched her for a beat, his own lips turning up at the corners, losing the scowl she'd always seen on his face. "What's so funny?"

Zephyr glanced at his lips, wondering what it felt like to

kiss a boy, what it would feel like to kiss him. "I don't have a boyfriend."

His shoulders relaxed slightly. It was amazing how much his body and face were telling her. "You have a ride?" he asked.

She shook her head, rubbing her arms to warm them in the sudden chill.

Before she could process it, he was moving towards her, pulling his hands out of his pockets and shrugging his jacket off. Zephyr watched, in awe and in shock, as he flicked it around her, and a heavy weight settled over her shoulders, enveloping her in warmth, flooding her senses with the scent of the leather and his aftershave, something clean and musky, but also something underneath it, almost woody.

It felt surreal.

She tilted her neck back, watching as he stood in a thin gray t-shirt that molded to his sculpted physique, the lines of his torso visible to the naked eye as he wrapped her in the leather. He was so much bigger up close, the top of her head barely reaching his neck, the size of his jacket drowning her completely, covering her dress almost completely. For the first time in her life, Zephyr felt small, almost dainty, and so safe despite the smallness.

"What's your name?" he asked her, keeping a hold of the collar of his jacket for a second too long, before taking a polite step back to not crowd her maybe. She liked him even more for it.

"Zephyr."

"I'm Al... Alpha."

He was going to say Alessandro, but Zephyr let it pass for now. "I know. I've heard your name being screamed a bit."

He looked almost bashful when she said that, almost uncomfortable, and it was endearing.

"Where do you live?"

She named the area and he nodded. "You good to walk a few miles?"

Cheesy as it sounded, as one of her favorite songs went, Zephyr would have walked five hundred miles and five hundred more just to spend time with him.

"As many as it takes," she said.

A small grin slashed his mouth, making her heart stop at the charm of it. "It might take us a while to get there."

She wrapped herself completely in his jacket as he shoved his hands in his sweatpants pockets, and they began to slowly walk together.

And in her hopelessly romantic heart, Zephyr imagined this was the beginning of their beautiful love story together, their steps taking them closer to their own happy ever after.

BONUS: TRISTAN & MORANA

MORANA'S GRADUATION

S HE WAS A NERD. Nothing else explained how she fin- ished her degree in two years instead of four unless she'd sucked off the Dean's cock, and he knew that hadn't hap- pened.

Tristan stood at the back of the open ground where the grad- uation ceremony was being held, unable to explain to himself why he was there except *she* was there. In her glasses, standing a head shorter than the old guy handing the certificates, with a fucking ridiculous smile on her face, *she* was there, alive to experience it because of him. Not that he'd ever tell her.

Fuck no.

He'd never talk to her, not even when he put his bullet in her brain as he had with his father. Or maybe he'd use the knife. Nah, too messy. Maybe he'd sneak into her room like he had last year, and simply smother her with the pillow. No, no, that wouldn't do. He wanted to see her eyes as the life drained out of them, those damning eyes that had pushed him into hell. Eyes that were hidden behind glasses so big they looked

543

idiotic. He'd seen women prettier than she was, women who could make his cock hard, women who fucked with their eyes. She did *nothing* for him. No, she wasn't beautiful. She didn't make him hard, and she sure as hell would never get to fuck him. *Never.*

She'd never see him in the first place, not until the moment she breathed her last. He would take what he was owed, and maybe then he'd find some peace. Maybe then, his chest wouldn't feel so tight every fucking second of every single day. Every single day she lived, every single day he survived, every single day his sister wasn't—

No.

"Morana Vitalio," the old guy on the stage called out, and Tristan felt his hand fist in his jacket pocket. She walked to the old guy with an infuriating pep in her step, her black attire billowing behind her like a villain's. The villain of his life.

His phone vibrated against his fist, breaking his train of thought. Loosening his grip, he took it out and put it against his ear.

"What?"

"I missed you too," Dante's annoyingly goading tone made Tristan sigh. He had been around the man long enough to not let it irritate him anymore, which also served the purpose of riling Dante since he lived to get a reaction from Tristan. "Did you finish at the warehouse?"

Never taking his eyes off the stage, Tristan answered. "Yes."

"So, you must be playing stalker now."

Asshole.

He heard the fucker exhale loudly. "I know she's graduating, and I know you're there. Just don't do something stupid."

"Like what?" He didn't like that Dante knew about her graduation, or that he was so predictable when it came to her. As harmless as he pretended to be, the predator in Tristan identified the one in Dante as one of the most cunning, patient, and consequently dangerous ones. And though Dante had his hands full with Amara, Tristan didn't like that he was keeping tabs on this girl. She was *his* to keep tabs on.

The fucker chuckled. "Whatever your weird definition of courting is."

"I'm not courting her," Tristan grit out, cursing himself for rising to the bait. Dante didn't understand how her life was forfeited, even though he knew their history. She was going to die by his hands, the most beautiful death he would give to anyone. He'd been thinking about it for so long. It would be a sight to behold.

"Whatever you say, bestie."

Tristan took a deep breath and called for patience. Sometimes he didn't know if he wanted to murder the other man or laugh at his ridiculousness. Though, the fucker was probably the only human on the planet who could get away with calling him 'bestie'. *Fucking ridiculous.*

Without another word, Tristan hung up and continued his

perusal of the ceremony.

The girl took her certificate, her smile too big on her face, shook the old guy's hand, and walked down the other end of the stage.

Minuted passed.

Her smile slowly dimmed.

Tristan looked at her as she continued standing near the corner, observing that smile trembling. Her damning smile. He hated to admit but watching her face over the years had become a study. She wasn't overtly expressive, but the little nuances as she emoted were fascinating. She was fascinating, even though she would be dead soon.

A few more names were called out before the ceremony ended and the crowd dispersed in excited chatter, finding loved ones, taking pictures, screaming in group hugs.

Tristan watched the girl.

She stood to the side alone, watching everyone, looking a little lost. Tristan watched as she kept the smile glued to her face, a slight tremor in it now that hadn't been there before. He watched her blink rapidly as she saw all the other students getting hugged by family and friends. He watched her fingers grip the certificate in her hand so tightly her knuckles swelled.

She was hurting on a happy occasion. Vulnerable. Alone. Probably the only other person on the ground alone beside him.

He watched her struggling to keep smiling even as no one

looked at her, and his chest tightened. *He* was looking at her, and she didn't even know. In some ways, she was so incredibly stupid. He didn't want her vulnerable, didn't want to witness her trying to stand strong, didn't want anything except who she had been in his head for years.

He could easily go to her in her weak moment, give her the companionship she craved, make her sing to his tune before he put her out of her misery. He could take advantage of this moment, and she would let him, completely unaware. But he hated preying on the vulnerable.

He kept watching though and saw the way she looked at a man clicking photos of a group of giggling girls. Probably a father with his daughters and their friends. Given what he knew about her shitty parent, he wasn't surprised the bastard hadn't shown. She needed to harden herself and not look like a kicked puppy just because her father disappointed her. Life was a masterpiece painted with disappointments.

Fuck her for being soft. And fuck him for letting it get to him.

Quietly, without even understanding why, Tristan opened his camera and took a photo of her. Not that she would ever see it, but her desperation to be included just made something ache in his gut, and he fucking hated feeling that. He hated her, everything that she was, every way that she had destroyed him, and fuck her for wanting to soften him. Like a lamb's wails ever made the lion spare it.

Before he could put his camera away, the hair on the back of his neck prickled, his body sensing the presence of another near it with skills that had been honed in fire. Acting casual, he clocked the man who limped to his side with a cane, a man shorter and slighter than he was, dressed in a loose suit.

"Are you with her?" the man asked, and Tristan pocketed his phone, turning to see the man. He wore glasses too, but that wasn't a surprise given most people in the crowd had them.

"Who are you?"

"Oh, forgive me," the man laughed self-deprecatingly, extending his hand. "I'm Dr. Rip. I'm Morana's... professor."

There was something off about the man, although Tristan couldn't exactly pinpoint it. Shaking his hand, Tristan tried to put his finger on what was bothering him, but just couldn't. "I'm a family friend," he smoothly injected.

The man appraised him, his hazel eyes sharp contrary to his appearance. "Nice to meet you. She's a special one."

Tristan stayed silent, pulling his hands away and sliding them into his jacket pockets.

"Very special," the professor continued with a soft smile. "Bright and inquisitive, but very lonely. She needs a friend."

Tristan's hand fisted in the pocket. He didn't want to know if she was lonely. He didn't fucking *care.*

"Since you're a *family friend,*" the man smiled in a way that told Tristan he knew more than he was letting on. "Keep her safe."

Before he could say anything, the man limped away. Tristan shook his head and turned back to see her, slightly surprised because she was not alone anymore. A boy stood too close as he gave her the company she'd so desperately needed. Someone had taken advantage of her weak moment. *Little fucker.*

The lanky guy touched a lock of her hair, trailing his fingers to her mouth, and she soaked up the affection.

Oh, hell no.

Tristan felt his jaw clench.

The boy needed to go. Obviously, because now he was a roadblock to his murderous intentions. No other reason. None at all. But he wasn't going to stand there and watch the little bastard paw her. He had better things to do.

Leaving her to enjoy the fucking company while she could, he left the ground, even though he was tempted to take out his gun and shoot the boy. Preferably between the legs.

Walking out alone into the dusk, his hands in his pockets, he thought about the different ways he would eventually eradicate the boy, the weight on his chest ever-present.

He had waited seventeen years for her death. He could wait some more.

BONUS: DANTE & AMARA

ONE MONTH AFTER TEMPEST

CONTENT WARNING: MENTIONS OF miscarriage, grief after loss of child, mentions of pregnancy, breastfeeding.

*

*

Serenity.

They would have named their lost daughter Serenity. Although Amara had no way of knowing what her temperament would have been like, but call it mother's intuition, call it anything, she knew in her heart that her lost daughter would've been the peace to Tempest's storm, and hence, would have lived up to her name.

Tempest was her brave, fiery baby who made it through the storm, now gurgling happily against her breast as she got fed.

It was the month after they got back from the hospital. Things had been chaotic, to say the least, but when were they not? Amara just sat in the back garden in the gazebo, stealing a moment of quiet in the chaos, just her and her baby girl.

"You're already so brave," she cooed to her daughter, holding her little weight carefully in her arms, in a way that felt so natural to her, like she'd been born to be her mother. "So strong. Mama loves you so much. Dada loves you so much. Everyone loves you so much."

A toothless, milky grin greeted her as Tempest freed her nipple, a little white mustache on her lips. Amara smiled, wiping her mouth with the cloth she had over her shoulder, pulling her little body against her shoulder, and burping her exactly the way she needed. It had taken them a while to figure out how to get her to burp quickly, and Amara felt a small sense of achievement that she'd been the one to find the trick.

Her tiny booty fitting in her palm, Amara stood up and swayed with her, humming softly to get her to fall asleep, suddenly aware of eyes on herself.

She turned on the spot, her heart skipping a beat at seeing her husband, the gorgeous hunk of a man, leaning against the pillar at the entrance to the gazebo, dressed in his crisp dark slacks and shirt, sleeves rolled over his forearms in a way that made her think about how they'd made a baby.

It had been four weeks since he'd touched her sexually, and she knew it was because the doctor had ordered her to refrain while she healed and rested. And as hot as his self-control was, the wait was getting to her. They had gone weeks without touching each other before but that had been different. She hadn't been able to see him, smell him, snuggle him back then. It was torture to be subjected to his hotness, scent his pheromones, and stick close to him without anything beyond a few kisses.

She wanted to ask him what he thought of her new body, how he saw the additional scars around her lower abdomen and breasts, how he felt making love to her again. She knew there was nothing for her to be insecure about, not after everything they'd been through, but maybe it was her hormones being whack that made her feel so vulnerable.

"How's my little princess?" he asked, coming forward and pressing a soft kiss to a drooling Tempest, lost in her dreamland.

"Fed and burped," Amara supplied and watched the grin slash his lips, filling her stomach with the same butterflies she'd felt when he'd turned it her way decades ago.

His brown eyes settled on her, his arms coming around her and pulling her closer. "And how's my queen?"

It would never get old, the way he called her, the way he looked at her, the way he held her.

"A little horny."

He chuckled, enjoying her torment, and Amara rubbed herself against him like a cat in heat, keeping Tempest stable against her body. Dante growled slightly, making her still, his arms firming around her. "Don't make this harder than it is."

"It's not hard yet," she told him. He wasn't hard, not fully.

Dante pressed a hard kiss to her lips. "You need to rest. Stop tempting me."

Amara felt herself groan in frustration as Dante plucked their daughter from her arms.

Dante Maroni had always been a good lover but as a husband, he was somehow better. And as a father, despite having one of the shittiest examples in existence, Dante was exceptional. It had only been a month, but he had taken to it like a duck to water. Amara knew he felt the same way about fatherhood as she did motherhood, that they were born to be parents together. She could not have asked for a better father for her child, and knowing their daughter would have him, even if something were to happen to her, made her feel truly content.

She rubbed at her chest, fixing her dress that gave her easy access for nursing, and fell in love all over again as she watched him dance with their daughter.

It was moments like this that made her arms feel empty, made the presence of their lost child a hollow in her heart. There had been a conference she'd spoken at a few years ago, about ways to heal and cope with the loss of a child for parents, especially the mothers. She remembered her paper now, her research into the topic, and how an intense man had approached her afterward, wanting to understand how to help his wife cope with the loss of her son. She had helped him with an idea.

She knew she needed to help herself, help her husband, and

eventually, when their baby was grown up, help her heal too.

"Dante?"

"Hmm?" he hummed, their daughter seeming even tinier next to his larger frame.

"I want to plant a tree."

Her husband turned to her, his eyebrows raised in slight confusion. "Is this one of your post-partum cravings?"

She huffed a little laugh. She couldn't really blame him, not when she'd spent the last month acting out of sorts, sobbing in the middle of the night and cracking up at the lamest things. She knew she was going through something, and she knew she had to let herself feel it to heal.

"I want the tree to be for Serenity," she told him and saw the sadness on his face. He was hurting too. Every time he held their princess, he was mourning for the one they'd lost, and that wasn't okay. Tempest deserved better from them. She deserved parents who would look at her and only feel love, not grief. And before she grew up enough to understand, Amara would make sure they were both healed and healthy and had dealt with their pain.

She walked up to him, holding the side of his jaw that he'd shaved clean again to not chafe their daughter's soft skin. Amara saw the years-old scars on her wrist and steadied her hand.

"We need to mourn her, Dante," she asserted quietly, her voice low but not one she hated much anymore. "We need to memorialize her and move forward. I want to plant a tree for her, so we can nurture it together, watch it blossom, and have something to always remember her by. So that Tempest can grow with the tree in place of the sister she doesn't have."

Dante blinked a few times to clear the sheen from his eyes, turning his head and pressing a kiss to her palm. "You're fucking perfect, you know that?"

Amara smiled, knowing she had to research now about the kind of plant they wanted, and changed the mood. "And you still won't fuck me."

Dante groaned loudly, waking up the precious bundle nestled in his arms.

She started screaming in the sheer offense of being woken up, the lungs on her so active and the conviction in her cries so crazy it made Amara wonder how the hell she was going to be when she grew older.

They were going to have their hands full.

Hopefully, they were going to have their lives full too.

Bonus: Dainn & Lyla

Day After Greenhouse Incident

H E GREW THE ROSES for her.

Lyla stood in the greenhouse after a grueling yet cathartic session with Dr. Manson. The older man had left her pondering with thoughts and reeling with realizations, not all of them comfortable for her, and so to distract herself for a bit, she had ventured deeper into the greenhouse. It looked incredible during the day, with the tall glass walls almost frosted with dew and moisture, sunlight pouring in and turning the colors crystalline. There was something soothing about the space to her, as though all the plants that listened to her trauma every day stayed with her in solidarity, alive and thriving and growing with a little external care. Being surrounded by them healed something in her, made her believe that maybe she could thrive and grow too with the care she was slowly letting herself accept and see.

A mark of that care, one she had received for six years but never realized, lay nestled in a bed at the very end of the long stretch of greens.

"No, Mrs. Blackthorne," Roy, Bessie's husband and the main caretaker of the gardens and greenhouse, told her while re-potting a plant. The 'Mrs. Blackthorne' still surprised her and she had to remind herself to respond to it whenever she heard it. Roy continued. "Mr. Blackthorne gave clear instructions to not touch the roses. Since I've been here, I've seen him take care of them himself."

Lyla took slow steps to reach the bed, the soil freshly turned, the plants small, with only one sprouting flowers, the others with tiny buds. She reached out to touch the petal, but stopped herself, remembering the instruction. But by memory alone, she knew how soft the petals felt, how velvety, how luxurious. It had been the softest thing she had ever touched in her life until recently, and he had been growing them and gifting them to her for six years.

Something lodged in her throat as she stared at the dark red petals, different from the almost black he used to give her. The ones on her bed every morning now were this dark blackish red. She knew it was because he wanted to differentiate her memory of destroying her older roses.

"Do they grow black?" she asked Roy.

The older man shook his head. "No. Mr. Blackthorne dyed and processed it with a preservative so it wouldn't wilt."

The sheer extent of thought, of time, of care that he put into growing the roses, giving them to her, preserving them for her so she could keep them as gifts she'd never had, made her throat burn. He had done it for six years and was still doing it. And knowing that alone made her feel something she'd never even dreamed to feel in her lifetime—precious. He made her believe that she mattered, that she was special, that she was precious. But hadn't he always done that? His actions were laid out for her in retrospect.

"Mr. Blackthorne." Roy suddenly straightened and Lyla turned around, surprised at how lost in thought she'd been to not notice him standing at the entrance to the greenhouse. Dressed in a sharp black and gray suit, in his alter ego as the businessman, Lyla felt her breathing accelerate as his mismatched, mesmerizing gaze locked with hers and he stepped inside.

"Leave us, Roy," he told the gardener in a tone that brooked no argument, and immediately, the older man complied, leaving through the side door, enclosing just the two of them in the space.

Dainn moved to her, in that lithe way of a panther, his eyes locking her in place until she had to tilt her head back to keep him in view. He stopped right in front of her, his musky, masculine scent reaching her. One of his gloved hands came to her jaw, holding it firmly, as he scrutinized her soul.

"Did you talk to Dr. Manson about last night?" he asked, his voice low, soft, almost lulling her in that hypnotic way he did.

Lyla nodded.

"How do you feel?"

That was his favorite question to ask her and something new for her. Her feelings being important was a novelty, but not one she minded at all. It felt good, great even, to have them matter.

"Much better," she told him honestly. "My reaction was more extreme, more intense than even I'd expected. It surprised me."

"Because you got jealous."

A bird chirped somewhere in the distance. Lyla focused on keeping her breaths steady, remembering the way she'd found Nikki and everything that had ensued afterward—her running, him chasing, her breakdown, him telling her the truth about her son, and most importantly, him clarifying that nothing had happened. To say last night had been intense would be an understatement. "Yes," she admitted.

She could tell he was pleased with her honesty.

"Nikki is gone," he shared, his grip tightening on her jaw in that familiar way.

Lyla blinked in surprise. "What?"

He shrugged. "I didn't like how she made you feel. I'm a married man who is loyal to his wife, and she came onto me despite knowing that. While I don't understand morals and I admit I enjoy your occasional jealousy, nothing is worth putting your mental peace at risk. So, you won't have to see her again."

Lyla tried to wrap her brain around everything he was saying. He was married to *her*, loyal to *her*, and once again, he was showing up by his actions for *her*.

She swallowed that lump in her throat that had been there since she'd seen the damn roses, and blinked at him to clear her eyes. "You didn't have to do that," she whispered.

"This is *nothing, flamma*," he stated quietly. "*Nothing* compared to the lengths I would go to for you."

The lump won, a tear escaping her right eye, and she watched his eyes track it down her cheek. She didn't know what to say, so she put her hands on the lapels of his suit jacket, and pressed down the creases, soothing him or herself, she didn't know. The muscles underneath the fabric were solid, built over years of concentrated activity, honed by mastery over every tendon, strengthened by the will of his bones. She remembered waking up one morning early and going to the kitchen, only to look out the window at the deck on the side, where he had been shirtless in sweats, holding himself upside down on his arms, every muscle on his back and arms delineated with definition and bulging with strength. He had done some kind of routine she had never seen before, and the way her jaw had dropped watching his beautiful mastery over his body still made something happen to her insides. It made her sizzle on the inside. Since then, she had tried to wake up early and sneakily ogle him from the kitchen, watching him work out slowly becoming one of her favorite things.

Pressing over those muscles now, she remembered and some

deep-rooted feminine appreciation made her melt inside.

And then another question barrelled into her mind.

"Who's going to cook now if Nikki is gone?"

His hand moved to the side of her jaw to cup her face, and he just looked at her, silently letting her process the answer. Panic began to well inside her as it dawned.

She felt her eyes widen. "I can't cook!" she exclaimed, her voice coming out higher pitched as her hands gripped his lapels. "You can't expect me to take over!"

He remained infuriatingly calm. "You cooked very well last night. In fact, I would've asked you to cook some more regardless."

The compliment felt nice, but the fear won. "I don't know how to cook."

"Maybe, but you're fantastic at it," he praised, and something within her preened at his words. "If you don't want to, I can have someone by the end of the day. But you seem to be enjoying cooking, so why not give it a try?"

"What if I'm bad at it?" she voiced her fears as Dr. Manson had suggested, being open with him. "What if you hate it?"

"I'd take poison if that's what you made with your affection." He rubbed his thumb over her cheek, his eyes intense, and it made her suddenly wonder if and when he'd ever had a home-cooked meal from someone he wasn't paying to cook for him, from someone with affection for him, as he said.

"But, I would suggest not trying to poison me."

An unbidden huff of laughter escaped her at the unfazed way he said it, surprising her again and from the flare of his eyes, the sound of it doing something to him like it had the last time. The little laughter eased up some of her worries, as did the fact that this man had witnessed her worst and was still there, standing pressed against her, holding her, believing in her. A bad dish wasn't going to put a dent in the grand scheme of things.

Taking a deep breath in, she nodded. "Fine. I'll try. But if it doesn't work out in one week..."

His lips twitched, his eyes almost warming in a way that made her feel good about being brave.

With a little press of his thumb on her lips, he stepped back and let her go, telling her he had a meeting to attend to, that he would be back in time for dinner and was looking forward to whatever she made, leaving her surrounded by roses he grew for her, in a greenhouse he built for her, in a fearless fortress he forged for her.

And it made her realize that maybe, just maybe, she wasn't the only one having novel experiences. Maybe, this all was a novelty for him too.

I will publish a novella with bonus/deleted scenes for this series next. It will include deleted and bonus scenes from the series and a lot of plotless fluff and smut for all couples during the series timeline and in the future, so we know how they're doing. To make sure you don't miss the announcement, subscribe to my newsletter. You can also find other free bonus scenes and important links below:

For all my links in one place, scan this QR code in your camera app:

Acknowledgements

This feels incredibly bittersweet to write.

This series took root in me back in 2015 when I got the idea for *The Predator*, and it only spiraled from there when I started writing it. After almost a decade of living with these characters in my head, it feels like saying goodbye to a friend I'll never see again, yet knowing it's time. This whole universe, their stories, and these characters have been with me through the ups and downs of my life for the last decade, and I feel lucky to have the chance to share them with you. I have so many thanks to give to so many people for the entire Dark Verse series and my publishing journey so far, a journey I started with my debut with this series. This series will always be so special to me because it changed my life.

First and foremost, thanks to you, the reader. Thank you, readers—the ones who have been with me since the beginning and the ones who have joined in later along the way, the ones who have supported me silently and the ones who have been vocal in recommending my books to friends, the ones who have cheered me from the sides and the ones who have

564

encouraged me with all the patience. Thank you for making me live my dream and for being here. Your presence made this journey a million times better.

Second, to my parents. They have shown me what unconditional love looks like throughout my life. I wouldn't be half the human I am without them. Though my mom isn't here anymore, I like to imagine she's looking down and watching over me, and if she is, I hope she's proud. And my dad, my pillar and my strength, I love you. Thank you for being the best father any daughter could dream of.

Third, to my friends. Far or near, you're my people. We could go weeks without talking and still be the same. You know who you are. Thank you for making my life so much richer just by being in it. Knowing we're there for each other through everything makes me so grateful. I love you guys.

Fourth, to my agent, Kimberly, for believing in me and my stories and for being such a badass. Thank you for always having my back through the rough times and always celebrating the good. You're a superwoman, and I'm lucky to have you by my side. Big thanks to the entire team who take care of everything so seamlessly too!

Fifth, to Nelly, my cover designer friend. You helped me out with my first cover out of nothing but the goodness of your heart and then became such a pivotal part of my journey. This series and my writing journey would be incomplete without you and your artistic clairvoyance of exactly what I wanted and making it a hundred times better. Thank you for everything!

Sixth, to the Firebirds, my little tribe of readers online who have made such a safe space on the internet for me. I appreciate you all so much for just adding so much to my life, and making this community such a beautiful place.

Seventh, to the Ravens, my personal team of ARC readers who have all connected with me through our shared love for these characters, and who have been so incredibly passionate about my stories, you infuse me with your enthusiasm. Thank you for being such an amazing group of people!

And last but not least, to Tristan and Morana, Dante and Amara, Alpha and Zephyr, and Dainn and Lyla. Thank you for coming to me all those years ago, for speaking to me and living in my head. Thank you for being with me through everything in the last ten years. I wouldn't be half the storyteller I am without you. I love you, and I will miss you forevermore.

Love,

RuNyx

ABOUT THE AUTHOR

RuNyx is a *New York Times, USA Today*, and international bestselling author of dark romance.

Best known for *Gothikana* and her *Dark Verse* series, she writes stories across subgenres, from dark contemporary to gothic to fantasy and more, and publishes both traditionally and independently. Her works are being translated into almost twenty languages and have been featured and listed in the *New York Times, USA Today, Publisher's Weekly*, and more.

Her unique pen name has a special personal meaning to her. When she's not writing, she loves to travel the world, read steamy romances, binge-watch crime shows, and procrastinate.

***

CONNECT WITH RUNYX:

All social media, reader group, website, newsletter, and other links are below. Scan the code in your camera app:

COMING NEXT FROM RUNYX

ENIGMA: A Dark Academia Romance (April 29th 2025)

ALSO BY RUNYX

GOTHIKANA: A Dark Academia Gothic Romance

Dark Verse Series